A Slice of Life

women babies cakes

by Sharanne Basham-Pyke

Acknowledgements

This book is a work of fiction, but some of the anecdotes come from the many, many women I have spoken to about their experiences of having a baby and the friendships they have formed at Parentcraft (or other similar ante or postnatal groups).

My own antenatal group was large, but a small group of friends formed from it and continues to meet long after the usefulness for baby tips. Of course, life is stranger than fiction so I have not attempted to include some of the things that really happened within my group – some good, some bad, some horribly ugly – because real life sometimes just doesn't seem believable.

In undertaking the research for the book, I found many similar stories from women across the UK. Where I have directly included an anecdote, it is with the express permission of the storyteller, so if you think I am talking specifically about you, then the chances are you are one of many.

Women tell me that their time is not their own. They have many people to please and many needs to meet, so they prefer stories in short bursts. Many also tell me that they like to communicate by chatting so the structure of the book follows their lead and many of the stories unfold through the characters chatting at their Parentcraft meetings. I hope this works for you.

I'd like to thank all the women who have told me their stories. In particular, the woman that is my inspiration for Myfanwy – she knows who she is!

I would also like to thank my advisors: Sian Howell, Becky Hemmens and Shelagh Weeks.

By the way, the recipes in the book should all work. They have been shared with me by friends over the years – give them a go! I've put them in italics so you can just skip over them if recipes are not your thing. You'll also find a complete list of the recipes at the end of the book…but be prepared to adapt them – baking is an art not an exact science.

Eat cake and be happy!

Prologue

1 Preparation Time

'Good God, Charlotte, what the hell's going on with your tits? Have you had a boob job? Doesn't that hubby of yours realise he's meant to suck not blow?'

Even in the macho corridors of power in our glass-fronted, ultramodern building this jars; and I feel myself prickle. I find myself taking a sneaky glimpse at my reflection in the window though to see if he's right – do my boobs look big? Am I beginning to show?

We are in the Head Office of QXL, it is silly o'clock, and Nigel, my boss – or thought-leader and chief rain-maker, as he would have it – guffaws at his own unfunny joke.

'You career girls,' he continues, smoothing his hair with his stubby fingers, and then adjusting his pinstripe shirt by tugging on the cufflinks. 'You've got to have it all, haven't you. Job, husband, big tits. Whatever next?'

I can't say anything. What should I say? What could I say? No one must know, pregnancy being a bit of a no-no for Talent Pool members at QXL, and so I just bite my lip and smile weakly as he charges off through the double doors.

The thing is, there really is no need to tell anyone. I'm not going to keep it. I've never wanted kids. Neither has Andy, my husband. It's just not... us. I just haven't sorted out the necessary arrangements yet to get rid. I just need some time to work out the best time in my diary, time to think straight, and time, unfortunately, is the one thing I haven't got. I've already left it far longer than I should have. I suppose I've been in denial. It's such damn inconvenient timing. Tick, tock, I'll need to act fast now. And, I suppose, I should tell Andy. I'll tell him tonight when he phones so that he knows where I am going and why it is important. It should all be sorted by the time I get home at the weekend.

SECTION ONE

2 Preheat the oven

Looking at the dirty, pebble-dashed exterior of the community centre and the flaky paint of the door-frame, I realise that the oatmeal linen dress is probably not the best choice for today. There's no one else here yet and the door is still locked – I've rattled it several times already. I really don't know what I'm trying to prove; it was locked the first time I tried, so I very much doubt the padlock has become unlocked in the meantime. I've become so damned impatient. It must be all the hormones swirling around. So, here I am, struck by how terrifyingly real this all is. I still can't quite believe that I'm going to be a mother.

From the moment it was finally agreed – or, I should say, after Andy insisted, Christ, that was a horrible night – right from then, a persistent little voice has been whispering in my ear, telling me that I can't possibly have a baby. Not me, not Charlotte Harrington. I never wanted one, everyone knows that, but this enormous bump in front of me is now bellowing loudly for all to hear that I most definitely am going to have… am… pregnant. There, I've said it. I'm hoping if I keep saying it then eventually I will get used to the idea and it will feel natural. It feels anything but natural at the moment. It feels hideous and I can't help feeling simultaneously both angry and horribly depressed about the whole sorry state. 'Enough of that, Charlotte,' I tell myself.

Waiting outside this dingy little community centre is just another necessary step on the journey. A journey, admittedly, that I didn't want to take. A journey that I still can't quite believe I am taking. How did I get here? And I know only too well that I can't change my mind, it's much too late for that.

'It's time to pack those dark thoughts away... once and for all. The time for that is long past. You didn't do it then while you had the chance so you can't do it now. Much, much, much too late,' I remind myself.

The leaflet that brings me here today was thrust into my hand by what I can only assume was a well-meaning midwife. It says: 'Parentcraft classes are held at the community centre on Thursday afternoons: *This is a six-week course that prepares you for the last stages of pregnancy and the birth of your baby, so the-mother-to-be should be at least thirty-weeks pregnant to join us.*

More importantly, it also says '*Tea and cake at 2pm'*. And so, here I am.

The midwife had suggested Parentcraft would be particularly beneficial for me as I am new to the area and so it would help to make local friends who are also going to be first time 'Mums'.

Lord, how I hate that! Being referred to as a 'Mum', or, worse still, 'Mam,' as the local parlance would have it. Anyway, she, the well-meaning but patronising midwife, said that any new friends I make would all be 'in the same boat', and so perfect for calling upon, and chatting to, when the going gets tough. Adding, and rather too pointedly for my liking, that some women, especially the career-minded such as myself, can find it very lonely being at home all day with a new baby.

At home! By myself! All day! I decided immediately to attend all of the classes. I am going to need all the help I can get. I can't even imagine a whole day at home on my own. Andy and I do everything together. We always have since we started seeing each other in my third year. Plus I've been working in a team since I joined QXL nine years ago. I have some evenings on my own, of course – either when I'm working away or when Andy is – but I'm usually so exhausted that I just get things ready for the next day in work and clamber into bed before it starts all over again. I don't think I've really been alone for any length of time since I was a child. And then it was when my mother and father would argue and both storm out. I didn't like being alone then so I very much doubt I'll like it now.

I am absolutely *enormous,* by the way. Huge! If one more person tries to tell me that I'm blooming… well, I really won't be responsible for my actions!

But perhaps even worse than the weight gain is the fact that my breasts are now mind-bogglingly huge! I mean really utterly enormous! Monstrously massive! We are talking seriously BIG!

When I turn over in bed these days, these great big bazoomas arrive quite some moments later – slap, slap! They make such a loud clapping noise I am tempted to shout, 'Encore! Encore!'

They are terribly veiny, too, the blue waterways of the world etched across these creamy-white balloons. Yes, they may have grown impressively from a 34B to a 44DD, but they have also grown from nice, shapely, firm, Andy loved them, to huge, heavy, saggy, sore and absolutely no fun at all. And, as for my nipples, well! They are now dark and stretched to the size of saucers. I had to ask Andy to stop touching them months ago.

I shift about uncomfortably. This bra doesn't seem to fit anymore so I'm trying to find the most supportive position offered by the heavy, wide straps that are more like feats of engineering with supporting struts and cantilevers than the pretty lacy bras I used to wear. I used to have such gorgeous breasts. I want them back. I wonder if they'll come back after this … this… bump has gone?

Finally, at 1.55pm, a clattering of keys on the steps behind me announces the arrival of a thin and strangely insubstantial woman with lank hair that looks in need of a good wash. She is dressed in unfashionable floor-length florals, and she squints through a large pair of spectacles that seem to cover her entire face.

Laden with carrier bags that are stuffed with paper, stationery and assorted junk – as well as a couple of tall, wonky towers of plastic cups – she looks as though she's stepped out of the 1970s and brought with her the materials for one of those Blue Peter 'makes' I was so keen on as a child. Alarmingly, she is the health visitor. She is the one in charge.

I can see she is rather taken aback as I greet her and shake her hand firmly. I can't help, having had time to collect my thoughts as I awaited her arrival, but pose a number of rapid-fire questions.

'Do we do exercises? Should I have brought something to change in to? Should my husband be here? Should I have brought cake? What time will this session finish? Do I need to pay?'

The health visitor nods weakly as she offers rather insipid replies and hurriedly struggles to squeeze past me and the enormous bump. After she has opened the padlocked door, she makes her escape, her stick-like silhouette disappearing as she slips inside the centre, switching on the fluorescent-tube lighting as she rushes away. The lights create a yellowish, flickering wake and an incessant insect-like buzz to mark her hurried path through the building.

Having not been properly invited in, I hover in the doorway as other women start to arrive in a giggling gaggle. I think it should be fairly obvious that I am one of the mothers-to-be given that I have a bump as big as the front end of a Volkswagen Beetle and, I fear, the backside to match – but, for some inexplicable reason, the new arrivals seem to think I am in charge.

'Yes,' I say, recalling what the health visitor woman has just told me. 'Husbands are welcome to come to all six meetings, but your husband or "birth partner" – I'm not sure that all of these women are married – is only really expected to come to the hospital visit, week five, and the final briefing session, week six, which is a must. Today's meeting will wrap up at about half-three, but if you need to leave earlier, that's fine. Yes, tea, coffee and light refreshments are available, but, no, you don't need to pay for them – although a contribution is, of course, most welcome. Just pop 50 pence, or whatever you can spare, into the tin in the kitchen.' I even start to sound a bit like the health visitor by the time I finish.

I am beginning to feel a bit light-headed and nauseous again as I shift my designer handbag onto my shoulder. I'm sure the health visitor had some Mr Kipling boxes along with the Blue Peter Christmas candelabra, or whatever it is she is planning to make with all her junk, and I wonder if she'd mind if I asked for one now to stop me from feeling sick.

However, I distract myself with the next conversation instead.

'Well, comfortable clothes are advisable because we are going to be trying out some simple yoga and relaxation techniques.' I continue with my spiel and am once again conscious that the oatmeal linen is not a good choice. 'No, there'll be no breathing exercises – that's viewed as a little old-fashioned these days. It is 1993, after all.'

Some of these women don't look as if they know where they are, let alone which decade we are living in. I hope I didn't sound too patronising when I said that though.

After two or three conversations like this, I begin to wonder whether my strong handshake has perhaps frightened the health visitor into fleeing through an alternative exit, and if I've been left to take charge of the whole session. Certainly, that's what the others seem to think as they await my next instruction.

'Everyone inside, please,' I say authoritatively and wave a hurrying arm. 'The meeting will start shortly.'

By the time the health visitor finally reappears from whatever she was doing, I have arranged the group in a semi-circle and placed a chair for her at the front.

'Goodness, you're a well-organised group, aren't you?' she says with a slightly accusing tone, glancing at me, as if, somehow, it's my fault. Which, I suppose, it is. I did put the chair there and ask everyone to take a seat. She starts mumbling in her insipid manner and offers a nervous laugh. 'I can see this afternoon is going to be quite... demanding,' she adds, looking directly at me with huge eyes exaggerated by the thickness of the lenses in her glasses, which she pushes back up her nose with her forefinger.

We start by introducing ourselves – offering our names and the length of pregnancy. As usual, it surprises me how difficult people find speaking in public, even for a few, brief moments.

'Hello... I'm Debbie Davies... and I'm thirty-one weeks... no, wait... thirty-two weeks gone... not gone! Pregnant, I mean! Sorry... you know what I mean... Sorry.'

''iya... I'm Chelsea... and this one's due next month,' says a frighteningly young girl pointing at the enormous lump in front of her and wearing what appears to be the obligatory cheap leggings, garish t-shirt, denim jacket and large hoop gold earrings.

In comparison to some of the nervous squeaks on offer, my voice comes across as probably a little too self-assured. 'Charlotte Harrington, thirty-two weeks to the day – hello everyone!' I give my best cheery wave as my glance checks the semi-circle can both see and hear me clearly.

When the brief introductions are done, the health visitor eventually asks the group to break into pairs to start to get to know each other, and asks us to discuss this first lesson's topic: any concerns we may have about the birth.

I turn to my left to introduce myself.

'Hello, I'm Charlotte,' I say, offering my usual firm handshake, adding promptly, 'I'm the Team Leader in the Research and Development team at QXL Research – we specialise in forensic accountancy and IT, and our mission is to eradicate international money laundering.'

The woman looks at our shaking hands, then at me, then at our shaking hands again, and appears confused.

'Right, luv, whatever you do say, like,' the woman says in the strongest Newport accent imaginable – not the lyrical Welsh tones that I had been expecting to hear when Andy first brought me here, but the abrasive and unloved urban accent that makes Newportonians the Brummies of Wales. 'Me, I'm Myfanwy, like – I'm a cleaner, see, 'n' what you did just say, like, well... it's gone clean over me 'ead. Whoosh!'

The woman looks... what's the word... *rough*.

'Mind you, I s'pose I do specialise in *laundering* 'n' all,' she continues, '*eradicating* skid marks from 'is keks. Proper 'ard getting them out, I tells you, but 'e do pay the bills, don't 'e, like. Anyway, what the 'ell is a 'Cuexel' when it's at 'ome?'

I take a deep breath, straighten my back and try my best not to sound too patronising.

'Well, Q – X – L is a major IT and financial research business headquartered in London, but we have offices across the UK and operate in more than twenty countries globally, and we've recently opened a satellite facility in the Business Park on the outskirts of Bristol – you may have seen the press release in the news?'

'Nah, not me, luv,' she says, and then says something like, 'I don't looks at no newspapers except the *Argus* and then not that much like – only the ads, like, if I do wants to grab a bargain or somethin' now 'n' agen. Finds some crackin' deals you doos – if you ain't fussy, like. I likes that, I doos.'

I can't help but look at this woman incredulously. Is that accent for real? Is she faking it as some sort of perverse joke? Surely, no one in Britain speaks like that anymore – as if they've just stepped out of some 1950s vox pop documentary filmed at the gates of some god-forsaken factory!

'So, concerns about the birth,' I say, deciding we'd better get on with the task in hand. 'Well, let me think, my main concerns are probably pretty standard – I mean, from what I've read I'd rather have a natural birth than a caesarean, which, to my mind, is rather unsatisfactory as it puts you out of action for about eight days, apparently, and that would be very inconvenient. Pain relief and pain management during the birth is also a big concern for me, and I do hope the midwife will adhere to what's in my birth plan. You see, I plan on using meditation techniques to avoid taking any drugs.'

'Avoid the drugs?' The awful woman says, scratching as she does under breasts that are almost as enormous as mine. 'Whassthemaddawivyou? Why the 'ell do you want to avoid the drugs, luv? That's the bit I'm most looking forward to – I luvs drugs, I do,' she says with a broad smirk across her face.

Andy was so right when he said this place would be full of scum, and he should know – being a local. In fact, he really didn't want me to sign up to these classes at all: he said they'd be a waste of time, so he'll be delighted, well smug actually, to be proved right. God only knows why he wanted to come back to Newport. It's not as if he is close to his family. He doesn't speak to most of them, not even his mother. I guess he's here to be near to his friends, although, to be perfectly honest, they are a mixed bunch and I can't honestly say that I like any of them very much.

I continue to smile politely, although I'm not sure if my face is actually displaying a smile amidst my shock at the common woman sitting in front of me whilst I look around to see if I can make my escape and talk to someone else. But all appear to be engrossed in their conversations, so there is no immediate prospect of a way out.

'So, luv,' she says. 'Whass yer problem with suckin' up all them lovely drugs then – you knows they do gives you 'em to you for *free* 'n' all on the NHS?'

Oh, my! I'll have to answer the woman. I can't just sit here in silence.

'Well, I don't want to take any drugs that may pass through my system to…' – I look down at the bump and try to find the right word – 'the bump… because drugs can make the... the… it... rather woozy after the birth apparently, and sometimes that can make it hard for the... to latch on to the nipple and suckle straight away, particularly if you want *it* to benefit from early enriching colostrum, and feeding early is really important for a good flow of breast milk in the long term. Do you understand?'

'I ain't read none of 'em leaflets nor nuffin,' the rough-woman says, scratching again under her breasts. I do so hope she doesn't have fleas. 'But you do sound like you've swallowed the 'hool bloody lot – swallowed all that bloody fem'nist stuff 'n' all, I do bet. I ain't titty-feedin'. Don't likes the idea of it, me, see, luv. Don't seem right, some'ow, sticking me titties in the little nipper's mouth – no, I'll be keeping 'em tidy for me 'usband, like.'

She pats her breasts as she says this.

'Oh, but you must,' I say. 'Breastfeeding is good for... *it*... and for you too – all the scientific research points in that direction.'

'Ah, but luv,' she says, 'titty-feedin' is for them in the olden days – much more easier and soph-is-ti-cated now to pop a bottle of proper shop-bought with added vit'mins in the microwave. All the celebs do do it. I'm not from up the valleys, you know. I don't wanna to end up like me grandmother with saggy old tits down to me knees.'

I have to concentrate really hard to grasp what she is saying.

''Sides, some of us do 'ave to work for a livin', like. We can't all be sitting on our fat arses with tits at the ready 24/7.'

'Fat arse?' I say with genuine horror. The size of my backside is definitely a sensitive subject. 'And, for your information, I *do* have to work. And I didn't want to live in Newport and I don't want to have children… so this absolutely isn't the future I had planned. What's more, my pregnancy has been awful – I mean truly, truly awful! I've spent the better part of most mornings with my head in the lavatory bowl and the afternoons with my head in a biscuit tin... and, yes, I admit it, my bottom is fat… and my breasts are even bigger, in case you hadn't noticed. Oh, and I hate them too, by the way. So, I'm not a posh bint that doesn't need to work – thank you very much. I'm a regular, working, business professional – and a pissed-off one at that!'

Well, I really hadn't planned to share all of that information with a complete stranger. I don't know what came over me. It just all came out... Oh, God! I've just unburdened myself to just about the most unsuitable person imaginable.

'So,' I say, trying to regain my composure, and hopefully a little of my dignity. 'What are your concerns about the birth? Muh? Muv? I'm so sorry, what did you say your name is?'

The awful woman seems unbothered by my outburst. She smiles and flutters her eyelashes as she says her name, 'Myfanwy – Muh-VAN-oi. Some people round yer do say Muh-fan-wee. But it's Muh-VAN-oi. Don't worry, luv, everyone do struggle with it. I'm called after me great-grandmother see. It's Welsh, like. You cun call me Muff, if you do want. Everyone does, like.'

I say her name, Muh-VAN-oi, very carefully. I can't call her Muff. I wonder if she even knows that it's rude? She's so thick she probably doesn't realise.

'Myfanwy,' I say again, pronouncing her name carefully and slowly. 'How has your pregnancy been? Anything with which you've had a particular issue?'

Myfanwy adopts a serious and pained expression as if she's just been asked to perform some tricky long-division.

'Well, I 'as this obsession, see,' she says. 'Every time I do go to the shops, I 'as to, just 'as to, you see, buy baby lotion – and now me bloody cupboard is full of the stuff. Fifty-four bottles I got, mind. Me friends do think I should join up to Johnsons' Baby Lotion Anonymous.'

'Is there such an organisation?' I ask – not really thinking.

Myfanwy snorts as a smirk expands across her face.

'No, luv, it's a *joke*. Like me saying about wanting drugs. A piss-take, like. We're like that in Newport. Don't take everything we do say as gospel, Lottie, me luv.'

I want to correct her. My name is Charlotte and only my grandmother ever called me Lottie – but I realise it's not worth it. I doubt very much I will ever see her again as it is highly unlikely that I will make the effort to come to this meeting next week. These are really not my sort of people. Besides, I'm not looking for long-term ties because Andy and I won't be staying in Newport for any longer than is necessary. That's what Andy said when I agreed to move here. Just long enough to save some cash so we can get established and then move back to England. It shouldn't take long. I have a really good job and Andy finally seems to have settled with his current employer. Newport is the last place I'd want a child to have as their home. It's a miracle that Andy turned into the man he is given where he has come from.

'Course, as well, I do 'ave a proper worry about the birth,' Myfanwy says. 'Caused me a few sleepless nights and a few nightmarish dreams it 'as – I've 'ad to wake me 'usband up for chats in the early 'ours as I'd been in a right bleedin' state, I 'ave.'

I lean forward with an expression that I hope feigns both interest and concern.

'Truth is,' she says, almost right into my face as she also leans forward, 'I'm scared that when I do squeeze the baby out, like, I'll follow through – and a proper bit of shit is going to come out 'n' all. And, well, my 'usband, might see it 'n' 'e's squeamish as 'ell.'

Good grief! I am horrified and really I don't want to talk about something like that. Plus, she has touched another nerve for me – there will be nothing polite or glamorous about giving birth and I know it, but I don't want to talk about it with… someone from Newport!

I look around desperately. I need to get away as soon as possible.

'Oh,' I say as calmly as I can. 'I don't think we want to go there, do we? All that yucky stuff is best kept to ourselves, don't you think?'

'Yucky stuff?' Myfanwy says, snorting again and offering me an incredulous look. 'Shit, you do mean? Don't a posho like you shit then? It's only sunshine that comes out of yer arse, is it?'

At that moment, the health visitor claps her hippy hands in a way that makes her look as though she is about to start psychedelic dancing, but thankfully only asks us to switch partners. I am beyond grateful to be saved.

Soon, Myfanwy is with her own kind – chatting to a woman in a garish tracksuit – and I hear her say unnecessarily loudly ''onest! Proper scared I am that I will follow through and squeeze out a nugget!' And it is greeted with much hysterical laughter. There is obviously a completely different humour in Newport, one of which I know nothing. And have no desire to know.

I am so relieved that I am no longer part of that conversation that, whilst talking to a woman called Saahi who is a pharmacist, in rapid succession I eat three of the plastic-like cakes offered by the HV. What is the matter with me? I'm like a bee, I can't seem to say no to anything with sugar! After finishing the cakes I pop a couple of Tums into my mouth to try and pre-empt the inevitable indigestion and heartburn.

Finally, the horror that is a Parentcraft class is over and I cannot get out quickly enough. Multiple waddling women with bumps in one narrow corridor does not make for a quick departure, but I do my best.

I unlock my blue convertible and put down the electric soft top – somehow it makes squeezing behind the steering wheel feel a little easier. As I yank the seatbelt across the enormity of my bump, I hear a familiar tone say, 'You're too big to be behind that steering wheel. It's too close to the baby, like, luv. You do want to walk 'ome. The exercise'll do you good 'n' all, Lottie, luv. By the amount of cakes you put away in there it looks to me that it's not just that nipper that's causing your big, fat arse.' I smile as sweetly as possible in the circumstances, thank Myfanwy for her counsel, and drive off as quickly as I can, cursing under my breath.

Then I say over and over again, 'I'll be fine. I'll be fine. I'll be fine…'.

3 A slice of Victoria sponge

The last few weeks have seen the bump grow even larger and Andy is manoeuvring around me in our kitchen.

'Well, just tell her she'll have to go with someone else,' Andy says as he puts the milk back into the fridge and thwacks the door shut. 'She sounds utterly ghastly. I don't want either of us to waste our time with her. She's going to end up being just another one of those lame dogs. You know what you're like for attracting them, Charlotte. Remember that collective of saddos you had around you at Uni when we met? She'll latch on to you like they did. It took ages to get shot of them, remember? Some of them were really persistent!'

Andy kisses the side of my head as he hands me a sugary coffee, and then stirs sugar into the coffee he has made for himself. He didn't use to have sugar in his coffee – but then, neither did I.

'Why on earth did you invite her? Anyway, it's bad enough that I have to go at all – I'm not the one having a baby, er, physically, I mean. And I don't understand why you're still going to the stupid classes with such awful people. They're not our sort. Plus it's really inconvenient, Charlotte. I'm busy at work with the new financial year and I really can't afford the time. Do I *have* to come?

'Come on Andy,' I say. 'We've been through this already. You said you'd come. Everyone else - well everyone else who is married, anyway - will have their husbands with them. I need you there for moral support. It's not until this afternoon, so you can get at least a good half day at the office.' He looks at me with raised eyebrows, awaiting an answer to his earlier question as he pours himself a bowl of cereal at the breakfast bar. I can tell he is getting cross. He never uses the breakfast bar at breakfast time; it is an ongoing bone of contention as I didn't want one when we had the kitchen designed and he insisted. So now he is using it to make a point.

'I didn't invite her,' I say. 'I can't remember how she ended up in our group. She just sort of invited herself. I can't uninvite her. We'll just have to put up with her and her foul mouth. It's only for a short time. The visit's only about an hour in total – ninety minutes tops. And we can have a good laugh about it when we come home.

Plus we'll get to meet the husband! He sounds just as common. And he's called Dai. Can you believe that? As in the name! Dai! I didn't think anyone was actually really called Dai. I thought it was just a joke name like Taffy. But seriously, that's his name. We're bound to have a right old giggle at them.'

I don't tell Andy all the details, but my midwife has been insistent about me continuing to attend Parentcraft classes, emphasising that it will be good to see the hospital and ask questions of the health professionals. She starts most of these conversations with: 'I can only advise you…' But I get the impression she's still dubious about my conviction to seeing this thing through. But what choice do I have now, really, though? Under normal circumstances I would just say no to a hospital tour. But she saw me at my lowest ebb, when I was still deciding what to do about the mess. Andy had persuaded me to keep it, we'd moved here to Newport, and everything just seemed to be running ahead of me. I remember the conversation…

'Hello, are you Charlotte Harrington? My 9.30? Lovely house. Lived here long?'

'No.'

She laughs. 'No to which of my questions?'

'No, I've not lived here long. Would you like to come in?'

'Yes, please. I'm Alison. Is your husband here with you today?'

'No, he's at work.'

'Oh, how lovely, a day to yourself at home. I always love those days, don't you? You can get so much done with no husband or kids under your feet, can't you?'

'I really have no idea,' I say as I show her into the front room. 'I'm going in to the office as soon as this is over.'

'Is everything okay, lovely?' She asks, her bright and effusive tone dropping from her face and her voice.

'As right as it will ever be now we have this to deal with.' I really can't help my curt and obtuse answers. Today is not a day for niceties. 'It didn't work so I'm stuck with it.'

'Sorry, lovely, I'm not completely following you. Why don't we have a cup of tea and you can tell me all about it... properly.'

'I... can't. I mean, I don't want to. I just...' I hear the wobble in my own voice and, to my horror, I burst into tears and plonk myself on our sofa, which sighs heavily under my weight. 'I tried to get rid of it. Andy doesn't know. I just thought I might be able to do it myself and then tell him I'd had a miscarriage. I've been so sick. Sick as a dog. He thinks I have a stomach bug. You won't tell him, will you? You don't have to tell him by law or anything, do you? I am so angry. Angry at myself. What an idiot.'

She stayed with me more than my allotted time. Then popped back in later that day, having advised me not to go into work in her special way that meant she told me exactly what she expected me to do, so I agreed to work from home. And then she was back again in the evening, before Andy came home. I know now that it must have been in her own time. She has checked on me regularly ever since, even when I felt much better and came to terms with the situation. So you see, she, this midwife, Alison, has an insight that no one else has and so I feel that I should, occasionally at least, listen to her advice.

When I arrive at the hospital I easily find my small Parentcraft group for the tour. It's not hard to spot a group of excited, pregnant women. We are asked to sit in one of the waiting areas in a demountable alongside the maternity unit, where the walls seem to wobble every time someone comes in or goes out, and I watch the door nervously. Andy is late.

They are lovely staff but I despair as I listen to their conversations as to how they are going to organise things today. Everyone seems to be over-committed, and so they appear to be quite grateful that I've asked if we can wait a while. Thankfully the crisply-attired midwife, I think she said her name was Elaine – I've met so many midwives over the past few weeks, eight at least, that I am losing track – yes, Elaine, this one is definitely Elaine, said we could wait as long as the rest of the group don't mind. They don't and I am really appreciative as I am sure they must be like me and would really like to get out of here as soon as possible. Not just because I don't like hospitals – who does – but because I know some new research, looking at the new types of digital crime that I, and my team, are really excited about, is going to reach its embargo time later this afternoon and I'd really like to get on top of it before our competitors. This is my last week in work – their choice, not mine. The HR Director said it worked better if I finish at the Easter break. So even though I don't feel it is best for me, I just couldn't find the words to say no – not without crying anyway, damn these hormones. I daren't be seen as weak or that will definitely scupper my career. I'm renowned for my clear decision-making. I've built my career on it. And I want to make sure that I leave everything in perfect shape, so there is less chance of my interim replacement totally messing things up, or worse, doing a much better job than pregnant me. What if they end up wanting to keep him instead of me?

I am trying to distract myself from worrying by chatting to the other women and their husbands in our group. I am also starting to feel a bit nauseous again. Morning sickness! That's a laugh – it has been any time of the day or night. And all that nonsense that *it will stop at 12 weeks... 16 weeks... the end of the second trimester* – complete rubbish! It's not helping that bobbing my head up and down looking for Andy is making me seasick. I am tossed, these days, on strange oceans. Where is he? Finally, I see Andy's face at the porthole door window looking perturbed/angry/flustered all at the same time. The door swings open and poor Andy is delivered into the corridor, hooked by the chunky forearm of Myfanwy, waddling and shunting her way into the corridor like an oversized American. She is accompanied by a concertinaed man. Dai, her husband, I presume. He is a good three inches, if not more, shorter than Myfanwy, round head squashed into a squat body – in fact there doesn't appear to be any sort of neck at all. Years of inbreeding and natural selection for mining and rugby I suppose.

'So, you're me Lottie's 'ubby then. Fuckin' marvellous, mun,' Myfanwy says, smirking at Andy, then Dai, and then broadly at me.

But I am not 'her Lottie' at all. She has such a cheek to assume she can call me whatever she likes. I've asked her to call me Charlotte so many times over these past few weeks but she just ignores me. Purposefully, I'm sure. Typical of her, this loud, brash woman, who seems to latch on to me wherever I go. Andy's right, again. I keep thinking I'm rid of her, but no, week after week she turns up, like a bad penny, and she just invites herself into our group. Still, only one more week of Parentcraft and no reason why our paths will cross again.

'So, when is yer nipper due?' Dai asks me as they join our group.

'I have only four weeks before my EDC, estimated date of confinement,' I reply. Confinement! For goodness' sake, this is the 20th century!

Myfanwy shrieks, far more loudly than is necessary. 'Me too 'n' all,' she says. 'We're the exact same me 'n' Lottie, like. Tidy.'

Dai nudges Andy and says, 'We'll be in bloody confinement too 'n' all, I reckon.' And Andy laughs and slaps him on the back good-humouredly. They seem to be getting along, which is more than a bit of a surprise.

Touring the hospital wards, nodding knowingly, Andy and I ask intelligent questions of the health professionals we meet, some of whom seem quite decent and not what I expected from an NHS hospital in Newport. In fact, I had expected to see the sick and dying lying on trolleys in the corridors, so I am surprised that it seems clean and well-run. Reassuring… but perhaps they are having a quiet day. My objective on my due date will be to get in and, more importantly, out, as quickly as possible.

Dai pipes up suddenly, 'Where should I stand, like?'

'Sorry, lovely,' says yet another midwife, I'm not sure if I even know this one's name, who is showing us the birthing suites. 'What did you say?'

'For the birth, like? Where will I stand for the birth?'

'Where were you thinking of standing?' asks the midwife, a little confused.

'Well, I was 'opin' to stand back yer,' he says, signalling behind the bed. 'So I don't get none of the gunk on me clothes. And I don't wanna see too much of the blood 'n' gore, if I can 'elp it.'

I find myself starting to laugh and have to suppress it with a mock cough.

'Well, you can stand out in the corridor if you want, cariad,' says the bemused midwife. 'But I don't think your wife will be too happy, if you do.'

Myfanwy punches him on the shoulder – in what I can only assume is meant to be an affectionate way.

'When should we come to the 'ospital then, luv?' Dai also asks.

'Ah, now that's a good question,' says the midwife, addressing her answer to the whole group, not just Dai. 'There is no absolute definitive answer here, because everyone is different. Some women have a very quick childbirth and for others it can take a lot longer, but, as a general rule, I would say if your contractions are about ten minutes apart, you should call your midwife and have a chat to her about when to come into the ward. If they are only three or four minutes apart then just come straight in and we can contact your midwife for you.'

'So, what's the quickest way to the 'ospital from our 'ouse, then, luv?' Dai continues.

'Well, I'd need to know where you live to be able to answer that question, lovely,' says the midwife, looking again a little confused by Dai's question. 'But I'm sure you know Newport well enough to know the most direct route. You sound like a Newportonian to me.'

'We do live over the other side of town' he says, waving in a vague direction, 'just over the top of the 'ill, like,' says Dai, oblivious to the hilarity he is causing. 'Do you reckon it is quicker to come down Victoria Avenue? Them lights can be a bugger at the bottom of the 'ill. Proper slow they are.'

'My recommendation is that you drive the route you know best. It is very unlikely that waiting at the traffic lights is going to make a big difference. Very few babies are born with the speed you see in TV dramas. Life isn't like Casualty, you know. You will have plenty of time to get to the hospital driving at a normal speed and taking your normal route. I understand your concern about wanting to get your wife here as quickly as possible, but I can assure you most babies take their time in making their appearance in the world.'

'No, it's not that,' continues the diminutive Dai relentlessly. 'The thing is, see, I've just 'ad new car seat covers and I don't want 'er ' – he makes an indicative nod towards Myfanwy – 'to mess 'em up, like.'

Two of our group, with bellies as big and round as my own, start sniggering as a nervous hysteria seems to have broken out. I hope he stops soon or he may bring on labour for all of us. 'No, I'm serious like,' he adds, looking round at the group. 'Them seat covers are smart-looking. And I loves that car, I doos.'

'See what I do mean, girls, my Dai is a right dope,' Myfanwy says, joining in our laughter. 'God, I loves 'im, I doos. I can always rely on my Dai to make a right tit of 'imself.'

'Or a left tit,' says Dai, as he and Myfanwy laugh, as if it is the funniest thing they have ever heard.

Throwing a large silk scarf over her shoulder, obscuring her bump as she does so one of the laughing ladies from our group asks everyone, 'How about cup of tea and a slice of cake in the hospital café, when we've finished the tour?'

My desire to get out of the hospital as quickly as possible falters at the mention of cake. But I know Andy will be keen to get home.

'What about you, Charlotte?' she asks me quietly. 'Will you and your husband join us?'

I am weighing up the options when, to my great surprise, Andy says yes over my head and then gives me a big smile, wrapping a protective arm around my shoulder.

As we start to walk down the hospital corridor, I say to her, 'I really like your navy suede pumps, they look like the impossible; both comfortable and pretty.'

'They are,' she says. 'Years of helping out in my mother's hairdressing salon has taught me the value of having comfortable shoes. Although, being small, I am missing my heels, Charlotte.'

Although I've seen her several times at the weekly Parentcraft meeting I have to say, 'Apologies, but I don't think I know your name.'

'John Head.'

'I'm sorry. I didn't catch that.' She must have misheard me and thought I'd asked about her husband. 'What's your name?'

'John Head.'

'Gosh, that's unusual,' I reply.

'Yes, it's Welsh. I'm named after my grandmother.'

'Was she called John Head too?'

John Head laughs.

'Not John Head. Sioned. It's the Welsh form of Janet. John Head! No wonder you looked so surprised!' She hooks my arm and we walk down a corridor with a yellow stripe on the floor that shows the way to the café. 'Follow the yellow brick road, follow the yellow brick road,' she says. 'I should be wearing ruby slippers, not navy flatties.' I laugh. I like her. She's made me feel relaxed.

The café is large and serves NHS staff alongside visitors, and there are a couple of patients in the queue in their pyjamas, dressing gowns and slippers. Some areas are sectioned off for staff, separated by trellised panels that makes it look like a garden centre. There are several large serving areas offering full cooked meals, but my eyes are immediately drawn to the cake stand.

'Let's get the puddings to sit down and we'll do the queuing,' shouts one of the fathers-to-be. So I waddle with the other women in our group across the café and, eventually, we uncomfortably take a seat at a large table. The seats are fixed in a row so it makes it tricky to manoeuvre in. After a quick discussion, we decide to enter based on size of bump. It means I am on an aisle seat. The seat of shame! The group chats enthusiastically about this afternoon's tour. Shortly afterwards, someone taps on Sioned's shoulder and a large slice of carrot cake is placed in front her.

'This is Steve, my husband,' Sioned tells me. 'Steve, this is Charlotte.'

Steve, who is intelligent-looking and handsome, reaches out his hand to shake mine, which involves me twisting in my seat – not easy.

Sioned then turns to him and says, 'I can't face the cake, Steve. Sorry darling, but I am feeling really nauseous. Just a glass of water, please.'

'Don't worry. I'll eat it. Honestly,' he says to Sioned. Then he says to the rest of us, as his good-natured smile breaks into laughter, 'My belly is going to be bigger than Sioned's at this rate. She's been so sick at times and she has all these allergies, has she told you? So I've been polishing off her food as well as my own.' He pats his belly as he walks away to find a glass of water and says, over his shoulder, 'Great to meet you, Charlotte. I expect we'll be seeing a lot more of each other once the babies are finally here. Can't wait to find out if I've got a son or a daughter.' He beams at Sioned and she grins back. I'm a little surprised, no, taken aback, at his enthusiasm. Although it was Andy's choice to continue the pregnancy, he doesn't have the same level of interest as Steve. Steve and Sioned seem to be in it together.

Annie, another of the women at our table, two bumps down, is joined by her husband, Gareth. Gareth is handsome, tall and muscular, with dark, wavy hair. He's wearing jeans and boots with a white shirt.

'I'm terrified,' he says, as he climbs over the seat to sit down. 'I was hoping the hospital visit would help put my mind at rest, but I think I'm worse now. I keep thinking about all the things that can go wrong. I'm worried that Annie will die.'

I take a sharp intake of breath. Die! But Annie's reaction suggests they have had this conversation many times. Annie places her slender hand on top of his across the table. 'Stop worrying. It's perfectly natural,' she says. 'I'm going to have a baby like thousands of women do every day across the world.'

'But women die across the world,' Gareth says. 'Things can go wrong. There can be complications, even in this country. What will I do if you die?'

Annie rubs her hand across his and looks at him full-face as she whispers, 'I am not going to die. It really is going to be fine.'

'Promise you won't die,' he says.

'I promise.' Annie looks out of the windows at the ambulances arriving, the old men and women with their walking sticks and zimmer frames. I wonder if she's thinking what I'm thinking, that it's a strange place to bring new life into the world. 'Now, shh, now. You'll be scaring the others,' she says in a hushed voice.

At this, Gareth seems instantly happy again, leans awkwardly over the table and plonks a noisy kiss on her forehead. She smiles at him, gives his hand another friendly rub and kisses him back.

I am wondering what to make of the whole interaction when Andy reappears, a huge mug of tea in one hand and an enormous slice of Victoria sponge in the other.

'It was the biggest they had,' he says as he puts the plate and mug in front of me. 'They'd run out of trays so I have to go back for mine.' He says a quick hello again to everyone at the table.

'Nice big slice of cake, there, Charlotte. You've got him well-trained. He's a keeper,' says Annie. I notice that they all look at him, assessing if we are a good match. I can tell they all think he is a good catch. Andy looks so handsome. On his return from the cake counter he chats comfortably with them, charming them. I feel tears spring into my eyes – I am grateful that I am married to Andy and grateful for the large slice of cake, well half a slice now, in front of me.

'We'll have to try to meet up when the babies are born,' says Sioned.

'Yes,' I say, but I doubt very much I will. I'll be back in work before I know it. I'll be fine. I'll be fine. I'll be fine, I tell myself again.

4 A big party cake to celebrate

'What?' There is shock in my mother's voice. 'They don't have a John Lewis?' She pauses for a moment as this earth-shattering news sinks in. 'But where on earth do they buy their furniture? Do they have any sort of shops?'

'Yes, Mummy, of course they have shops,' I say. 'They just don't have a John Lewis. Not in Newport. Well, not in Wales, actually.' I decide I'd better not mention that they don't have a Debenhams either or she will be convinced that Wales is a third-world country. 'But I understand there are a few furniture shops in Newport. That's where I am going now. I'm going to check them out.' I am lying to her; I wasn't actually planning to shop for nursery furniture any time soon, but the annoyance I feel whenever I speak to Mummy means I have to lie, and I suppose I will have to go shopping too, or she's bound to catch me out.

'Perhaps you're having those nesting instincts, Charlotte,' she says. 'You must take after *him*. I never had anything like that. Well, not that I remember. But, of course, I was terribly busy when I was carrying you. Your brother needed a lot of attention.'

'If you really can't bear to use his name, can you at least refer to him as "your father"? You were married to him for over twenty years, remember. And my brother still needs a lot of attention.'

'I do remember, thank you. Twenty years of abject misery. How could I forget? But thank you for reminding me. I can always rely on you to take' – she pauses for effect – '*your father's* side.'

As always my mother manages to both annoy and upset me within minutes of speaking. She has reminded me that I have parents who hate the sight of each other. And that I always come second to my brother, especially in her affections. And finally she has reminded me that Andy and I are now living in a town that doesn't even have a John Lewis!

I take a deep breath and continue my conversation with my mother. 'It's only three weeks now to the birth, so I'm making the most of my time,' I say. 'A trip to the furniture stores in Newport first, and then I've arranged to meet Jennie in Bath this afternoon. Do you remember my friend Jennie? Andy is going out with some friends from work this evening so Jennie and I are going to meet him later for drinks. I'm doing the driving as, obviously, I can't drink.' I know I'll feel exhausted with this busy itinerary, and I really shouldn't be adding the nursery shopping to this busy day but, hey, I've said it now.

'Hmph!' says my mother.

'So, shall I call you again at the end of the week?' I ask.

'If you like. Although I am very busy,' my mother replies.

Having edged myself behind the steering wheel, I drive to the first furniture shop I have identified in the Yellow Pages. There are plenty of spaces in the out-of-town store, so I park close to the building. It is grey, like Newport, and, I am surprised to see as I park, large with at least three floors.

But three floors, I discover, of total, utter tat. On the ground floor is living room furniture. Truly horrible white leather-look sofas with diamante buttons. Small brown velour sofas that I didn't even know they made anymore. Seriously. Hideous, revolting tat. On the next floor, I even spot an avocado bathroom suite. I thought they'd stopped making those in the 1970s. And it's not that cheap either. Who buys this stuff?

With a sense of foreboding, I climb the flight of stairs to the third floor in the hope that 'Nursery' will offer something more tasteful. Carrying this huge bump makes me huff and puff on the way up. There is no one in the stairwell, so I indulge myself and rest at the landing half-way up. Although the sky is grey, it is a warm day today and I pause to take off my jacket. My cheeks are flushed candy-floss pink when I glance in one of the many trashy, glitter-edged mirrors in the stairwell. It is like a funfair Hall of Mirrors, reflecting back my large backside and larger breasts.

Once I finally reach the third floor, I start by looking at bedsteads. They are all dusty-pink velour with large buttons, about as horrible as you can get. There is a nursery section at the back of the store and I am making my way there when I have a sudden, urgent need to sit down. Some clown passes by, balancing a teetering tower of cardboard boxes in one hand, a tray of teacups in the other, and says, 'Ha ha! It looks like you're going to have that baby right there.'

I smile politely. 'No, this…' I say, waving my hand over the bump, 'isn't due for another three weeks.'

He wanders off, leaving me to sit quietly and gather my thoughts. I am feeling very hot and flustered. I should have taken the lift because carrying this bump around is like doing an aerobics class with a two-stone weight tied to your body. It's no wonder I'm tired. I get a bottle of water from my bag and take a sip.

I am sitting quietly, getting my breath back, surrounded by the awful collections of furniture grouped by function in front of me, when I feel a pain in my lower back that grips hard. The bump contracts in to a hard lump. I have been told about Braxton Hicks. Another pain starts almost immediately in my lower back and moves into the bump. I feel a superior sense of having caught out my own body in its tricks against me; I have been waiting for these Braxton Hicks. They said in Parentcraft that these preparatory contractions may start about three weeks before the birth. Here they are then, right on schedule. But they are much, much stronger than I was expecting. A third one starts, and I find myself puffing with pain and arching my back. Gosh, they are so strong, these Braxton Hicks.

'Woo 'oo! 'iya! Lottie! What you doin' yer, luv?' cries out a familiar voice. I see the enormous shape of Myfanwy cast a shadow as she moves in my direction.

'Oh, hello, Myfanwy,' I say, trying to sound bright and cheerful. But I surprise myself at how strained my voice sounds.

'What the fuck is going on with yer face, Lottie? Your cheeks do look like they are on fuckin' fire, like. Are you alright, luv?'

'I think I probably just climbed the stairs a bit too fast. I keep forgetting about' – I wave a hand over the bump – 'this.'

'Shall I take you to Asda?' Myfanwy mouths, conspiratorially.

'What? What are you talking about?' I am unable to keep the irritation from my voice. 'Asda?'

'AS-DA,' Myfanwy says very slowly as if I am some sort of simpleton.

'Why on Earth would I want to go to Asda?'

'Well, you're obviously in labour, in you luv. If I do take you now we could probably 'ave a full trolley if I do 'elp you.'

'I have no idea what you're talking about,' I say, as an even more enormous pain grips and the bump becomes harder and tighter. I can see it physically contract.

'So you cun 'ave yer shoppin' for free, like,' Myfanwy says.

'Are you suggesting we shoplift?'

'No, you daft twat. If you do have your baby in the store, or at least 'ave yer waters break, then they do give you yer shopping for free. If you do jump in my car now, like, I cun get you there in no time at all. You could buy a big party cake, to celebrate the birth, like. Tell you what, I'll stick a few bottles of whisky in the trolley, that'll be worth a bob or two. There's a right price on 'em…'

'Myfanwy, I don't want to go to Asda,' I say. 'I am not in labour. The birth isn't due for three weeks. This is Braxton Hicks…' I find myself grunting out the end of the sentence as the pain grips.

'I'm no doctor but it do look like labour to me. Better phone that 'ubby of yours. I'll ask if I cun use the phone 'ere. What's 'is number, like? Wass 'is name again?'

'Andy,' I say through gritted teeth. 'It's okay. Have mobile phone in handbag. Can call him myself.'

'Oooh! 'ark at you! Mobile phone!' she says brightly. 'But I'll 'ang on yer to make sure 'e gets yer alright, like. Or better still, I'll take you to the 'ospital 'n' 'e cun meet you there, like.'

The pains become progressively stronger. A small crowd clusters around the velour bedsteads and discusses whether, in their expert opinions, I am in labour or not. Most decide I definitely am, while the manager flaps about in case my waters break on the hideous sofa bed that I am sitting on.

When I call Andy at work he seems irritated.

'Are you sure you are in labour?' he asks. There is a pause. 'Only the guys in the office have just suggested a curry for lunch.'

'To be honest, I don't know,' I say. 'I've never had a baby before, in case you hadn't noticed. But it is starting to feel quite...' With that yet another strong pain starts in my lower back and I feel all my muscles contract as the bump becomes really hard. As the pain subsides, I wheeze out, momentarily forgetting that I have an audience. 'Hey Andy, here's an idea. Why don't you have a nice curry with your mates, and leave me here alone and in bloody excruciating pain to work out if it is really labour before I bother you?'

'Great idea, Charlotte. I could call you later. Say around 3pm? We can see how it's going then. Would that be alright?'

'No, Andy, you idiot! No, it wouldn't be alright!' I shout. 'Come to Newport right now! I'm going to the hospital. The Royal Gwent. The one we went on the tour around. The one in your home town. Remember?' I don't know why I said all this, it is not as if there is a choice of hospitals in Newport. My newly-acquired audience looks embarrassed. One of the women, porting a brown mac and a tight perm, says, 'Don't worry love. They don't all get it straight away. Some husbands take a little time to come round to the idea. He'll come round once the baby is here.'

I feel totally humiliated. This is all so unnecessarily public.

'She's in labour,' says one of the small crowd knowingly to another shopper.

'I know. I cun tell,' she replies, equally knowingly.

'I'm not. It's Braxton Hicks…' I'm irritated at them, too, but I lose the energy to correct them any further. They can have it their own way.

'I was like that on my first,' continues the first woman, who has now taken up a ringside seat on a red velvet sofa bed. 'The big red cheeks,' she says, pointing directly at my face.

'Shall I get a glass of water for you, love?' says another voice from the other side of the circus my predicament seems to have created.

'How about I get you some hot towels and water? Oh, hang on, is it hot water and towels?' says the clown who had spoken to me earlier, but who now has a glass chandelier in one hand and a bright yellow duster in the other.

The manager strides in and then stands directly in front of me, facing the crowd. 'Ladies and gentlemen, may I have your attention please,' he announces. 'Everything is under control. I am the store manager.' He turns briefly to look at me and I see beads of sweat on his forehead, moisture nestling under his nose and on top of his big black moustache. I instantly feel nauseous at the sight. 'This lady here is in labour but, do not be alarmed, because it is all in hand. My cousin-in-law' – is there even such a thing? – 'who is heavily pregnant herself, is going to drive her to the Royal Gwent Hospital.'

There is a round of delighted applause. 'Well done! Bravo!' someone shouts from the back as Myfanwy steps into the spotlight. Did I detect a small curtsey?

'Well done, love. You're a good 'un, that's for sure,' shouts someone else.

After a few protestations on my part, I find myself hoisted up by Myfanwy and the store manager. I just pray that his nose doesn't drip on me, or I will definitely throw up. The crowd starts to disperse and I hear people say, 'That was fun'; 'I love a bit of drama, me'; and the ever-hurtful, never to be forgotten, 'She's enormous, no wonder she can't get off that sofa bed by herself.'

The store manager takes me and Myfanwy down in the staff lift, perhaps because he is scared I will put off the shoppers. It's a big lift, thankfully, but then again I suppose it is designed for moving hefty pieces of furniture. For some reason, he gives me his business card, wishes me well, and pats me on my back. It all feels out of my control now, and everything seems to be happening without my consent as I waddle to Myfanwy's battered old car.

Myfanwy slips a plastic bag on the 'Dai's very proud of this car' new passenger car seat cover. I lower myself down in an ungainly fashion into her car and manoeuvre myself into a position where I can plug the seatbelt into place, tucking it under my bump at the bottom, and over the top of my bump, sliding it under my enormous breasts.

And, with that, whoosh, we're off!

I look in the vanity mirror on the passenger side to see, to my horror, that my candyfloss cheeks are now almost scarlet. No wonder people were pointing. I open the car window to let some cool air in. Inside, the car smells of the sickening car-freshener that is hanging in a Christmas tree shape from the rear view mirror. It really isn't helping my feeling of nausea. Why do they make air-fresheners that smell like that? Only a few minutes into the journey we stop at a zebra crossing, and I am shocked to find myself having to grip the seat as I cry out in pain. The pedestrian crossing the road in front of us looks at Myfanwy inquisitively. Myfanwy winds down her window and shouts, 'Get out of the way, you wanker. Two pregnant women coming through. One in labour, like.' The pedestrian, a man in his sixties, grabs the change in his pockets the way older men do when they attempt to run, and hurriedly tries to move out of the way, although not moving any discernibly faster. He shouts back, 'Sorry luv, keep yer 'air on, on yer way, like... good luck with the baby, like,' and I feel grateful, yet horrified, that I have Myfanwy with me. At least she speaks the local language.

Myfanwy seems to have become a rally driver as we accelerate into the hospital at an alarming speed, but once again I am grateful. Grateful that it is all about to stop. The car journey and the pain. The hospital will confirm that it's just my body trying out some Braxton Hicks… trying practice contractions. As soon as Andy arrives, we can go home, let everything settle down, get back on schedule. And we can have a quiet night in, just the two of us. I feel better because I have a plan.

Myfanwy finds that most elusive of all things, a carparking space in the hospital grounds. She reverses into the tiniest of spaces. I try to open the car door, but it is too close to the car next to me to get out.

'Hey, Reginald. Reginald Molehusband,' I say, trying to make light of the dark situation. 'That was nifty parking, but you are going to have to pull forward if I am ever going to get out of this car.'

'Why the fuck are you calling me Reginald? What on earth are you on about?'

'Reginald Molehusband. From the public information films on television in the 60s and 70s. You must remember it, surely?'

'You nutty old bint. I don't remember nuffin' like that,' says Myfanwy.

After pulling the car forward, the inelegant removal of myself from the car, and her reparking, we slowly make our way up to the maternity ward in the hospital. We are greeted by the midwife on duty. 'How's she doing?' she asks Myfanwy, as if I'm not capable of answering for myself.

'Totally lost it, I'm afraid, luv. She's rantin' about some bloke called Reginald Molehusband,' Myfanwy replies.

'That'll be your parking then,' says the midwife. She takes me by the elbow and leads me towards a side room. Although I am in the wrong place (Newport), with the wrong person (Myfanwy), at least this midwife remembers Reginald Molehusband. I feel such a huge sense of gratitude that I could cry.

The corridor of the maternity ward is like every other corridor in any hospital: bright artificial lights in strips along the ceiling, smells of various disinfectants fighting for supremacy. And the occasional banging of some sort of trolley against some sort of obstacle – medicine trolley against patient bed, food trolley against lift door, stretcher trolley taking someone urgently through swing doors. I don't want to think about that last one. All corridors look the same, but I notice that here, on the maternity ward, they also have noticeboards covered with thank you notes and photos of beaming new parents with wrinkled pink, or black, or Asian parcels tucked in between them. They couldn't look any happier. They really couldn't. Perhaps there is hope for me.

'Thank you for the lift, Myfanwy. I'm sure Andy will be here soon, so it's fine for you to go now,' I say.

'No, yer alright, luv. I'll stay yer till he gets yer,' she says.

'No! There really is no need, Myfanwy,' I say as forcefully as I can without sounding too rude. But then I am gripped by yet another Braxton Hicks. The moment is lost and I feel unable to insist any further.

'So, what sort of birth do you want?' says the midwife as the latest Braxton Hicks subsides.

'Pain free?' I try to joke. 'But this isn't the birth. I've got three weeks to go yet. These are Braxton Hicks.'

'Okay, lovely,' the midwife says. She smiles at me and winks at Myfanwy. 'Here's the thing, I'd say that you're already in labour. With those contractions coming that rapidly, we need to get you ready for the birth now. So, anything I should know?'

'Y-y-y-yes,' I say, shocked. 'My husband Andy is on his way, so I'd like to wait until he gets here. And then we'd like to… aaaarrrgh,' I moan, 'have a water birth.'

'And she don't want no drugs, neither. She don't believe in 'em. She do want it to be natural,' says Myfanwy.

I could kill her.

We're left in the room as the midwife, in her turquoise uniform and surgical shoes, hurriedly goes off to 'check a few things', but she doesn't explain what. The room is quite large. There is a counter with all sorts of medical supplies lined up. I see a big pile of green paper hand towels, a box of disposable gloves and a large roll of blue paper, next to a small yellow bin. Oh, I can see now that is for needle disposal. There's also a big pot of sudocream; I must remember to add that to my next shopping list. They said at Parentcraft that it was good for nappy rash. There are some electronic diagnostic tools for which I don't know the purpose, and hope I don't have to find out. And some pulp cardboard sick bowls, for which I absolutely know the purpose and may need very shortly if I can't cast aside the image of sweat on the store manager's moustache.

'Hey, Lottie, luv. This looks like it is it. You're going to 'ave your baby. Your baby is going to be Welsh, 'n' all, the lucky little bastard,' Myfanwy says.

I cannot begin to describe my despair. How and when and why did I agree to move to Newport? How did Andy ever persuade me? The room is light and airy, but I cannot help but feel a dark and heavy sense of foreboding. This isn't my plan. The midwife reappears a few minutes later and confirms the birthing pool is available and that it is being prepared. 'So, come on then you two,' she says cheerily, 'let's get you in that birthing pool.'

The pool is being filled with warm water. I feel surges of foreboding in between the surges of pain. I've got to try to hold it together… but it wasn't my idea to have a water birth: I'm doing it for Andy. Where is Andy? I thought the pregnancy was going to break our marriage. That row was awful. We never argue and that was truly… well, I've never seen Andy so angry. I feel so cross with myself for not dealing with it all earlier and getting rid of it while it was still no fuss. Why did I tell him? I could have done it without him even knowing if I'd just done it earlier. And, of course, there was the bleak time that didn't work out.

'Aaaarrrgh! Make it stop! Make it stop!' I hear a scream and a voice before I realise it is my own. The pain is so intense that I cannot think straight. I screw my eyes shut and can think only about the pain and waiting for it to pass. Then, when it has passed, all my thinking flushes back into my head and I can open my eyes again. I think about the situation and remind myself it's done now. It's decided. So, if he wants a child, then we'll have a child. And if he wants a water birth, we'll have a water birth. And if he wants to live in Newport then that's what we will do… as long as it is only for a short time. I want to make it right for him. I don't want him to leave me.

The nurse looks at me and says, 'Just behind you there is a changing room. It's en-suite with a loo and a shower. So, if we go in there I will help you get undressed, and then you can get into the pool whenever you are ready.'

I turn towards the changing room and say to Myfanwy, quickly before she assumes she is coming too, 'You don't need to come with me. We'll only be a couple of minutes.'

The midwife takes my elbow as I waddle the few steps to the changing room. She says over her shoulder to Myfanwy, 'Are you going to be okay sitting there? You look like you haven't got long to go yourself. And, well, a waterbirth can be a bit messy, and it could all happen very quickly. I wouldn't want it putting you off the inevitable.'

'Yes, luv, don't worry about me. I'm as tough as ol' boots me, like. I'll just get meself ready for the mess, like you do say. Tidy,' Myfanwy says.

The midwife carefully folds my clothes as I take them off and ties my hair back into a ponytail for me. She is gentle. She is kind. And she doesn't rush me. I have another contraction in the changing room and she gently holds my arm as I double over in pain.

Agony clutches my entire body. This can't be right. Something must be going very wrong. But she smoothes my hair back into place when the contraction finishes and wipes my face with a cool cloth. She gently strokes under my eyes, removing the streaks of mascara. We re-emerge from the changing room to see Myfanwy has taken off her denim jacket and her cream cotton jumper and is about, it appears, to strip off her stripey top. She has pulled it up to her shoulders, showing her huge white maternity bra. Her arms are crossed in front of her, and she is trying, unsuccessfully, thankfully, to yank her bra off.

'What on earth are you doing?' I ask, as the midwife, who I now know is called Judy, bursts out laughing. I continue. 'Why are you in your underwear? I know it's a pool, but this isn't Butlin's, or the Costa del Sol, you know.'

'She told me to get ready for a waterbirth. She told me it could be messy,' says a confused Myfanwy, pointing at Judy accusingly, ''n' I don't want to get me leggings and t-shirt all wet or covered in blood and gore, do I? It's not a wet t-shirt competition or whatever *your sort* do on yer 'oliday. I wants to be arf decent when I gets 'ome for me Dai.'

'You won't get wet,' says Judy, still laughing. 'Wherever did you find her?' she whispers, as Myfanwy redresses herself.

'In the furniture store, on a sofa bed,' is my honest reply, which turns into another grunt of pain.

'Classic!' the midwife exclaims, and I know this tale will circulate in midwifery circles for years to come. Perhaps I should've lied about my name so it's not connected to me. But too late for that... she knows my name already, and I doubt if she'll ever forget Myfanwy.

The birthing suite and pool, although small, is actually of a surprisingly high standard. Water births that were all the rage in the 1980s have pretty much gone out of fashion now. Rupert, my brother, and Andy decided on a water birth one drunken evening a few months back. You'd think that Rupert, of all people, would know that it's no longer in vogue. Surely they've mentioned it in one of his pretentious male magazines. The NHS has such trouble getting funding for anything that it only really catches up with demand as it goes out of fashion. I discover from Judy that the new investment is rarely used. It's only really the knit-your-own-muesli types who use it… and me. Damn Rupert and his stupid ideas. And, anyway, where the hell is Andy?

Judy goes to the cupboard and returns with a bright pink rubber ring and a small scoop. I stare at both. 'Don't worry,' says Judy. 'You may want to use the rubber ring to lean on. It'll help you be more comfortable. I'll use the scoop if there are any solids.'

'Ewww,' shrieks Myfanwy. I am reminded once again that this isn't going to be pretty, and that I really don't want her, of all people, to see.

Getting into the pool helps enormously with the pain. The contractions have become so strong that I simply don't know what to do with myself when each one comes. I can't think straight. Now, I try to think back to my research on pain relief and ask for the tens machine.

'Luv, an electrical-pulse generating tens machine and water don't really go well together, d'they? You'll be electrocuted,' points out Myfanwy. I am surprised. She's right.

'I know you said you didn't want any drugs, but would you be prepared to try the gas and air, to see if that helps with the pain?' asks Judy.

'Yes,' I scream. 'Give it to me now. Right now.'

Thankfully, the gas and air relieves the pain so much that everything seems to slow down. I hope it will give enough time for Andy to get here and find me. When Judy gives me an internal, which is complicated over the side of the pool, I haven't dilated very much, but the investigation starts off the contractions again. And the pain is unbelievable this time. Far worse. Pain like I've never felt before. Something must be going seriously wrong. If it were really this painful, there would never be a second child in any family. No one would ever elect to have sex again. I scream, I can't help it. Even the gas and air doesn't seem to be helping as much now. Myfanwy, despite her own enormous bump, hangs over the edge of the pool and rubs my shoulders. Where is Andy?

Judy smiles at us with the sort of smile that she must use for couples about to become parents, and scoops discreetly.

I don't know what is more embarrassing: my screaming, the scooping, or Myfanwy and me being treated as a couple.

'How... much... longer?' I ask.

'No one knows, lovely. You're doing really well. Just keep going. I'm here,' says the cool, calm Judy.

'And when it's here,' I ask in hushed tones, 'how long until I'm me again? When can I have me back?'

'I can't answer that one either, Charlotte. But it does happen. Eventually, you will become you again. But you'll be a mother as well as you.'

That is terrifying.

I don't know how long I've been in the pool when Judy announces, 'I'd love to stay with you, Charlotte, but I've got my husband's family coming round this evening and he will go mad if I haven't got dinner ready. If this baby makes an appearance soon then it won't be a problem, but I'll introduce you to Gail, just in case. She'll take over if I have to go before you've delivered. And there are two students who would like to observe a water birth, if that's okay with you?

To be honest, I now don't care anymore who is, or who isn't, in the room. I just want this unbearable pain to stop. You could parade a circus through here and I really wouldn't care. I just want Andy. Where is he? Didn't he leave as soon as I called?

Gail pops her head around the corner of the door with an expression that makes it quite clear she isn't a fan of any fancy idea like a birthing pool. As I really like Judy, I hope that this is quick so I don't have Gail, but at the same time I want to hang on until Andy gets here.

Judy gets the monitor. I lay on my pink rubber ring so that I can stick my enormous belly out of the water and instantly I feel an urgent need to push. More than a need. It's the most instinctive feeling I have ever had. I start to push down and grunt. Judy moves into action. She tells the two students, who seem to have just beamed in at some point during this process, I know not when, to stand close so that they can see the baby emerge.

With that, the door flings open, and Gail ushers Andy into the birthing pool room. He is flustered, red-faced, and has his camera in his hand.

'I'm so sorry, Charlotte. Cancelling my meetings, traffic, you know how it is. Then I went home to get the camera and I couldn't find it anywhere and then I'd remembered I put it on the side table in the hall so that I'd be able to grab it without delay. Sorry. Then there wasn't a single space in the car park – they're packed in like sardines. I've had to park streets away. I've run here like some sort of bloody lunatic.' He is shaking as he comes over to me.

'Watch out for that posh camera by the water, luv. It do looks expensive, like.'

Andy turns and notices Myfanwy, with her own enormous bump, sitting next to the birthing pool. At least she now has clothes on.

'What are you doing here?' he asks.

'I found yer missus 'uffin' 'n' puffin' on a sofa bed. I was all fer takin' 'er to Asda. But no, she wanted to come straight yer. So I drove 'er yer, like,' Myfanwy says.

'Asda? As in the supermarket? Anyway, that doesn't matter. Thank you for bringing her here. I really appreciate it. Here, let me give you some money for your petrol,' Andy says.

'No. Yer alright luv. I don't need yer money. Just 'appy to 'elp.'

With that the urge to push returns.

'Fucking hell!' I shout. And the room turns silent and looks at me. I hear an animalistic grunt and do not care in the slightest that it comes from me. Andy looks horrified but shakily snaps the first photo. Within a few minutes of Andy's arrival, Judy, the midwife, takes my hand and places it between my legs and I feel the head crown, just like they said in Parentcraft. I can feel the head and the hair. Another urgent need to push follows and I grunt, 'Get it out of me. Get it out!' I'm unable to suppress it despite Andy's continued look of shock.

Myfanwy starts collecting up her things to leave.

Judy says, 'Charlotte, I'm going to need you to stop pushing so that I can check whether the cord is wrapped around the baby's neck.' She calls the two student nurses forward. They stand sheepishly by the edge of the birthing pool, watching intently. It really hurts as she probes with her fingers and unloops the cord. Then she says to me, 'That's it, lovely girl, on the next one I want you to push really hard down into your bottom. As hard as you can.' She turns briefly to Myfanwy and Andy, 'Sit down!' she barks, and they do as they are told, like two well-trained circus dogs. On the next contraction I push down as hard as I can, with more strength than I knew I had, and I feel the baby's head emerge.

'Stop now, lovely, let me just sort a few things out.'

'What? Stop now?' I feel there is no way I can suppress this urge to push, but I do. I hold on. Andy clicks on the camera and catches the image of the head emerging. 'So, on the next contraction, you can give me another long, deep push,' says Judy. On the next contraction, I start to push and it hurts like hell, and then, suddenly, I feel the most incredible sensation as its shoulders and body wriggle out. The huge, enormous relief washes over me, and Andy clicks again as his child is brought into the world. What an incredible relief. Relief, relief, relief. I know I am meant to think beautiful maternal thoughts, but I can only think of the film Alien, and the image of the creature bursting out and I say, 'Thank God that is over.'

'It's a boy, Charlotte,' shrieks Andy with more emotion in his voice than I have ever heard before. 'Thank God. It's a boy. I have a boy, a son. Oh my God! I have a son. He looks like my father.'

The relief is truly overwhelming. What on earth went on there? How long was all of that? I have no idea. Minutes, hours, days? I think I was hallucinating at one point. How and when did the student nurses arrive? I'm sure I heard the Star Trek warp as they were beamed in. Oh God! I think I was swearing.

'Sorry about the swearing,' I say apologetically.

'No need to apologise, cariad. I've heard far worse. Far, far worse,' says a beaming Judy.

I can't believe it is all over and my thinking is coming back. It is warm in the pool, but I am shaking. My hearing seems to be on super alert; I can hear everything – the traffic outside, the water pipes for the radiators and the clattering of equipment being put away. And I feel amazement. It's over.

'Let's call him George after my father,' Andy says.

Andy and I haven't discussed names. I had thought to myself, briefly, that if the bump turned out to be a boy that I may call him Jeremy after my own father. But I so want Andy to bond that I agree to George immediately. A good name. Regal. Solid and dependable. And I suppose using my father's name is always going to create an issue with Mummy.

'George. George Harrington,' I agree.

The baby, with umbilical cord still attached and the placenta still inside me, is placed gently on my chest. Exhausted and overwhelmed, I don't know what I am expected to say. I decide not to mention my thoughts of Alien or Star Trek, so I say, 'Thank you, thank you, Andy.'

'No, thank you, my darling, darling wife. Look at what you made, you clever thing. You made our son. Our gorgeous boy. Our George,' Andy says.

Andy takes another photo. I smile weakly, exhausted, with a mucky George lying on my breast and sitting in a pool that now looks like watery oxtail soup. (Weeks later when we have the photos developed, we decide there were only a very few select people we would ever want to see these photos. My mother is aghast when we show her – not by the oxtail soup but, she says, 'Charlotte, you can't show these photos to anyone. You have no clothes on!')

Unfortunately, I don't have the last contraction that is meant to bring the placenta away, so I have to get out of the pool and go to a delivery room for some 'help' from a surgeon and for a few stitches to the tear that happened when the cord was unlooped. Judy passes baby George to a bewildered Andy as she wraps me in a dressing gown and, as I am a bit wobbly, we waddle off, Judy on one arm and Myfanwy on the other. Judy really has to go, she tells me. She's already late, but I really don't want her to leave me with someone else. Myfanwy has offered Judy a lift to make up some of the lost time, and so I say goodbye to both of them – goodbye to Judy with genuine gratitude for getting me through this horror and goodbye to Myfanwy with genuine relief that it is all over.

They leave me with a nurse who looks about twelve years old.

The surgeon who is to stitch me is devastatingly good looking. He is young, probably in his late-twenties, and as I slip my feet into the stirrups I look at my legs and wish I'd had chance to have them waxed. Andy had been joking with me just the other day that he could no longer tell which were his legs and which were mine.

It is more than an hour before my return to the birthing suite with an even wobblier waddle and delicate and precise stitches in my vulva and vagina, and the new nurse by my side. I don't like her. I don't know why – maybe because she is obviously only twelve years old and some sort of an imposter, a child on work experience perhaps, but really it is probably just because she's not Judy. I love Judy.

I now desperately need to pee, so we stop off at some toilets on the way back to the birthing suite. The child-nurse gives me a jug of water to pour over myself as I pee. There is lots of blood, and the breeze block sanitary towel I'm now wearing is already showing its newspaper stuffing. I discover she's a liar too as well as a child – she said it would help take the sting out of it, but it is like peeing over razor blades.

When I finally re-enter the eerily quiet birthing suite that no longer holds a host of onlookers, Andy is sitting on the little seat with baby George in exactly the same position as when I left. George has been wrapped in a blue towel and has a little muslin hat on his head. The only other thing that is different is that I can see that Andy has been crying. He looks up at me as I enter the room and says, 'Thank you, darling Charlotte, for giving me the most precious thing on Earth.' I am taken aback. The diminutive child-nurse backs out of the room to give us some time on our own. She's very perceptive – for a child.

'Charlotte, this has been the most emotional experience of my life,' says Andy. I've never seen a new life start. I've seen death. I saw death in the army and it's not nice, but you learn to control those emotions. I know how to deal with them. I saw my father die. I saw his life slip away, and I saw him take his last rasping breath. I thought that was the most emotional experience I would ever have. But this, this is the start of life. This is George. And we created him. Through our love for each other we created a beautiful little boy.'

Thank God. Thank God. Thank God. I had been so worried that he wouldn't want it when it arrived. He can be like that. And what would I have done if he decided he didn't want it? I'd be stuck with a child I had never wanted in the first place. I've even checked out how to have a child adopted – in case. I don't know what to say. He seems genuinely overwhelmed with emotions I hadn't expected from him – and emotions that I don't feel in myself. Perhaps I am too exhausted. Perhaps that emotion will come once I've had some sleep and adjusted. No need to panic.

And Andy can be really soft and sensitive at times and I love him all the more for it. I love my husband with all my heart. I really don't know whether there will be any love for anyone other than Andy. Perhaps it will come in time. Don't panic, Charlotte. I'll be fine. I'll be fine. I'll be fine, I tell myself once again. For now, I am happy that Andy is pleased with George. That's what's important.

5 Weighing the ingredients

"He's a whopper," says the nurse as she hands him to me, and I struggle to know quite how to hold him. "9lbs 1oz," I say, to at least try to sound like I know something. I've never held a baby properly before, not really. I can't believe this. This stupid NHS hospital says I can go home later today. I'm terrified. I don't know how to look after a baby. Nor does Andy. I think it is totally irresponsible of the NHS to let us take it home. I need some sort of training. A course. An assessment of my capabilities – a test to prove I can do it. None of our friends have babies. We won't know what to do with it. This is so ridiculous, and I feel such a bloody fool, but I haven't really thought about *having* the baby. Not having to look after it. I mean, I have thought about painting a room to make it into a nursery, but I haven't thought about having a baby actually living in it. I haven't even got the furniture yet, and I don't want to ever go back to that furniture shop, far too embarrassing. I'll have to find somewhere else. I have been so busy thinking about being pregnant and getting used to that idea that I just am not ready to have a baby come home with me. Not yet, anyway. I wonder if they'll let me pick him up later, when I feel a bit better prepared?

I mention this to a nurse and she laughs at what she assumes is a joke. Truth is, I am genuinely terrified. I am frightened they'll see I don't know what to do. That'll probably be for the best. They're bound to know by now, though, aren't they? And yet they keep mentioning me taking George home and having George to myself. George this and George that. Well, George is a bloody baby and I am bloody terrified. I don't want it. I don't want it to spoil my life with Andy. This is such a mess.

I've never changed a nappy. I've never bathed a baby. Thankfully, so far, I've made my excuses and I've managed to persuade the nurses to do the changing and bathing, but, at some point, they are going to expect me to do it – and then they'll know for sure. I expect they'll take George into care at that point. Andy will be upset, but I think it is probably for the best.

I try to pull myself together, at least for the time-being, so I say to myself sternly, 'Charlotte, don't be so silly. You'll be fine. No one knows exactly how to look after their first baby. You and Andy will just work out what's right as you go along. So, stop worrying.' I wish I would heed my own advice. But, of course, looking after George is not my biggest worry. What if I don't love him? What if I never love him? The truth is I don't want this. I just want it to be Andy and me. How can we go back in time?

6 Chocolate brownies

My once beautiful house is now an absolute tip. My life is adrift, and I am all at sea. Floating, rudderless and helpless. I thought things would slot into place. How can just one baby generate so much mess? How can he take up so much time? How can it be that I don't even have time to load the dishwasher? It is all so frustrating. Why is it such hard work? I have now read all the baby manuals, I've done my research. I know all the things I need to do for George. He is clean – I've learnt how to bathe him. He is fed – I know how to breastfeed him. (I find it repugnant, to be honest, but I made such a big thing about it at the early Parentcraft meetings that I can't back down just yet.) He is in a routine – I didn't need to learn that, I'm good at routines. He has lovely clothes, mostly gifts from friends at home and work colleagues who have visited. Even my team of IT researchers and analysts, not renowned for their Emotional Intelligence or sensitivity, have turned up with presents, vouchers and flowers. But nowhere, and no one, tells me how to love him. They all just assume I do. It's hard to admit it to anyone, not Andy, not even myself, but… I just don't. I love Andy. I didn't want a baby in the first place, but I was hoping that when it arrived I would have an epiphany and it would all fall in to place. But no, nothing. I don't hate him – George. I don't want to harm him. I just don't feel anything for him, really. I'm too exhausted to feel anything! Health visitor, or as I call her HV, Mrs Insipid the stick insect, is oblivious and, let's be honest, she's pretty stupid. Every question I've ever asked her, she doesn't know the answer, and she whimpers and laughs nervously saying things like, 'No one has ever asked me that before.'

I tried to broach the attachment issue with her about a week ago, but she jumped to all the wrong conclusions – asking me if I felt suicidal, in a hand-wringing, Uriah Heep, ever-so-humble way that she must have learnt on a recent training course…. Dickens for the Suicidal, perhaps! And then, when I lied and said not really, she lost all interest. If she'd probed just a little bit deeper or asked just one more question, I may have been able to tell her that I increasingly find myself wondering if Andy would be better off with a different wife who could love his son.

All of my questioning though has led the stick-insect HV to encourage me to join a few little get-togethers in cafes in Newport's town centre every couple of days or so. Begrudgingly, I have to admit she is right on this one, I'll give her that. Some of the nice ladies, Saahi, Sioned and Annie, are there. We've visited just about every café Newport has to offer. It feels like a safe haven when I go along, and it at least gets me out of the house – a bit of fresh air and a brisk walk help a bit. Plus, my insatiable desire for cake seems not to have waned, and it gives me an opportunity to eat as George seems to sleep peacefully in his pram during these meetings and saves his screaming and crying for when we are alone and I'm exhausted.

I've not said anything to the other women in these little groups when we meet, though. They wouldn't understand. Other women are just so good with their babies. They're natural. I am not. They are deliriously happy, besotted with their babies, cooing and fussing, living in a post-birth paradise. I am not. Plus, it would upset them. Plus, if I'm really, really honest, I'm ashamed of myself. How can someone like me, professional and educated, not cope with a baby? When it's natural. Women, even girls, all over the world, cope. Not only cope, but thrive. And in difficult circumstances – circumstances that I cannot even begin to contemplate, and they manage. How is it that I am so useless? It must be just a matter of time until I get it. So, I continue to hope that the bond will just happen soon without anyone noticing its absence.

Unfortunately, or perhaps fortunately, we have already exhausted the supply of cafes in Newport that were prepared to have women and prams taking up lots of space and only buying a cup of tea and a slice of cake. Plus, some of our breastfeeding has obviously put off some customers (mostly women!) who have tutted noisily and flounced out muttering things like, 'I really don't need to see that!' You'd think they'd be supportive. The men, who you'd expect to be leering over our naked bosoms, don't seem to be bothered, and to be honest, don't even seem to notice most of the time as they offer a cheery, Newport, 'Alright, luv,' as if they hadn't seen my enormous creamy breast emerging from my cashmere jumper.

Today, we're visiting a café run by volunteer Christian women with pinched faces and heartless souls. I am just tucking into a chocolate brownie when a leaflet is shoved under my nose.

'Do you believe that God, the almighty, will redeem you from sin?' asks a woman in a floral pinny.

'I, I, I don't know,' I reply, as chocolate brownie crumbs cascade down my top. It is very crumbly. Not as good though as the gooey ones I had in the last place, and tricky to eat and stay clean. 'Do I need to, to be able to eat cake here?'

'Have you begged God to forgive the sins of your child?' she continues, looking at a pink bundle in Annie's pram.

'She doesn't have any sin. She's a baby,' says Annie.

'Margaret,' shouts someone from the kitchen, and the pinnied woman scuttles back to see what they want.

Shortly, a small woman with a beak-like nose comes over to the table. 'I'm going to have to ask you to leave.'

We are astounded.

'Why, because I don't think my baby was born with sin?' asks a very angry Annie.

'No, of course not.' She glances back and frowns at Margaret. 'No, it's because our other regular customers can't get in with all these pushchairs and some of our customers, and our volunteers, are not comfortable with the way you are flaunting your … breasts. We have God's work to do here. I hope you won't make a big scene.'

I glance across the room. Margaret is standing in the doorway to the kitchen with her arms folded across her chest, looking very prim. She is obviously doing God's work.

I go to say something, but Sioned touches my hand gently. 'Don't even bother. They're not worth it. You can all come to my house on Thursday,' she says.

As we leave, Margaret stands by the exit trying to thrust leaflets at us and says, 'May God have mercy on your soul,' 'Repent and find eternal happiness', and finally, 'God loves you.'

'Funny way of showing it,' says Annie.

'Here's my address,' says Sioned, scribbling on bits of paper ripped from her notebook, as we childishly and purposefully block the entrance with our prams. ‘Let’s take as long as possible to say our goodbyes,’ says Sioned. ‘Look, I can see them fuming from here. We can meet on Thursday. 2pm. I’ll bake a cake.’

7 Chocolate cake with a hint of orange

Sioned greets me as I make my way down her path with George in his ridiculously heavy car seat, and his omnipresent nappy bag (now the size of an army kit bag) slung across my shoulder. 'Welcome, Charlotte, welcome, come on in,' she calls cheerily from her porchway. Sioned has tied her bouncy red hair into some sort of twist at the back and pinned it in place with a large clasp. Curly red wisps have fallen onto her face and at the back of her neck, achieving that enviable feat of looking both casual and glamorous. I feel a pang of jealousy as I huff and puff my way into her house and into her large living room.

One of the other mothers that I have seen at our cafe meetings waves at me, with a baby's dummy in her mouth, as she perches on the edge of the sofa to take her baby from her car seat. I lower George's car seat to the floor almost knocking myself out as the giant size holdall laughingly referred to as a 'nappy bag' whacks me in the back of the head so hard that I could cry. It's taken me hours to get ready, literally hours. I'm exhausted. One of the other women, I can't remember her name, Tracey? Sharon? Debbie? comes to help me, and I feel such deep intense gratitude for her kindness that I feel like I am going to cry again. I've got to get a grip or I am going to make a fool of myself in front of all these new mothers who could be my lifesavers.

There are lots of women here. More than at the café in Newport. They all seem to have taken to motherhood with the expected aplomb, aplomb that I just don't have. I notice glorious smells are wafting from the kitchen. Traditional cakey smells. How the hell has Sioned found time to bake, for goodness' sake? I used to bake. I was quite good at it. I entered country shows for years. I used to be able to turn out a fine lemon crunchy top and my lime drizzle has won first prize before. And it's quick. And easy. Perhaps this is one thing I will be able to do to impress them when we meet at my house – hopefully many weeks away, so that I have chance to clean. It's all just too much to think about now, so I suppress my urge to cry from the pain in my head and the kindness of others, find myself a place on the large comfy brown leather sofa, and flump into it.

I look at the women in front of me. Damn, Sioned has regained her figure. She's wearing tight-fitting jeans. Damn, damn, damn her – it just all seems so easy for her.

'My husband doesn't like it if I carry a bit too much weight so that had to come off straight away,' she says to one of the others as she taps her tight little buttocks.

'Well, how have you done it so fast? I'd like to know your secret,' says the woman in front of her. I look down at the rolls and rolls of my belly. My jeans won't go anywhere near me. Seriously, nowhere near. It's revolting. HV said, 'Nine months growing, give it nine months to go back.' Nine months! I will definitely be suicidal by then.

One of the group, I must try to learn their names, but my mind is like a colander, says to Sioned, 'So, tell me about that cake, I want to know exactly how you made it. It smells great, so it might be a nice one for me to bake for my husband.' God, they're all at it, baking for their husbands. I'd better get my act together soon or Andy will be leaving me for someone who can find time to make a cake... and at the same time lose weight!

'Do you really want to know? Well, I fancied making something traditional, so I had a look in my Grandmother's recipe book and I found a recipe that was ideal for the Aga,' Sioned begins.

An Aga! Thank the Lord! I thought I'd never find people like me in Newport, but Sioned seems to offer some hope. I glance around and I realise that Sioned's house is really quite lovely. I start to feel a bit of my dark cloud lifting, just a tiny bit, and I allow myself to start to relax, just a little, as George sleeps in his car seat. I can't believe he has slept for so long. He never sleeps for me at home. Twenty minutes at the most. Thank God he hasn't woken up yet.

Sioned is chatting away, *'It's a rich chocolate cake, but it has a hint of orange, is that okay with you all? It is in the Aga now,'* she continues, suddenly speaking like a TV chef, *'so I'll just check if it is ready to take out to cool. That's the thing with an Aga,' she smiles at an imaginary camera, 'they're great, but you do have to keep checking as nothing is guaranteed to cook in the cookbook time. For example, my Grandmother's recipe said that the 225g of plain chocolate – I converted all her measurements to metric a few years ago, it took absolutely ages, I've got scribbles all over her cookbooks.' I'm almost sure I detect her turn her head to smile to a second imaginary camera to the left of her kitchen at this point before looking back. 'Anyway, the book said it would melt in about twenty minutes in the simmering oven, but it took about thirty-five minutes in mine as we have turned it down since the weather turned so nice. It has taken me all day to make this cake, so I hope it is going to be worth it. My mother has been over since first thing this morning so that I could have a clean run at it.'*

I realise, with a little relief and some respite from beating myself up, that most of these women that seem to have everything under control have one major asset that I don't: a mother who lives nearby and does things for them and with them. No good wishing that I am nearer to my mother as I know she wouldn't do these sort of things even if I lived next door.

I move from the sofa so that I am standing at the kitchen oasis. It's real marble, not melamine. Thank God, I've found someone with half-decent taste. I thought everyone in Newport would have houses full of the gruesome tat I saw in the furniture store. Marble and an Aga! I have found an oasis and like Sioned all the more. A cup of tea is placed into my hand, as Sioned says, 'This cake has been at the back of the simmering oven for nearly an hour now, so it really should be done by now. I'll see if a skewer comes out cleanly.'

It does, and she leaves the cake to cool on the worktop. I am so hungry. My sugar craving has not stopped: I'd hoped it would stop after the birth but it hasn't. Cake! A chocolatey smell wafts under my nose and remains there to taunt me. I'm insatiable.

My own baking experience goes back a long way. My mother insisted I join the WI when I was a teenager, so that she could get all the gossip from the village and pick up news about what my father was up to! I hated going at first because it felt like I was spying on my father, although, obviously, he wasn't there, but after a while I really enjoyed being with the ladies. I was at least forty years their junior, so they all made such a fuss of me, and curiously seemed to like having me around, which is something that could never be said of my mother.

Sioned, our tiny host, continues in her TV celebrity chef voice, *'Well, I took some unsalted butter and caster sugar, beat them together, then stirred in the melted plain chocolate, mixed in a handful of ground almonds – oooh, heck, are you lot okay with nuts?* I should have thought of that before. Are any of you avoiding nuts because of breastfeeding or allergies?'

Thankfully, none of us has a nut allergy or is avoiding nuts due to breastfeeding. I honestly didn't know I was supposed to avoid nuts. Bit late now. About half of us are still breastfeeding. That's another reason why I can't give it up just yet. Mrs Insipid has told me that it is unusual to have stuck at it and many women, especially those that can least afford it, give up almost immediately. She said, 'Educated women, such as yourself, seem to stick at it,' and it does seem to be the professional women who are still feeding, so I feel honour-bound to my education to keep going.

I can see Sioned has put an enormous amount of effort into baking this cake. In the background, she is continuing with her recipe and I tune back in. *'Then add six egg yolks, fresh brown breadcrumbs, three teaspoons of cocoa powder, with the rind and juice of one orange. The Fairtrade Foundation sell a lovely cocoa powder, by the way.' Fairtrade – another connection. It feels nice to be mixing with someone who is from the same social group as me, even if they are Welsh.*

She continues, 'I then whisked the six egg whites with a pinch of salt, put about a third of it into the mixture and stirred it in gently. With the rest, I folded it in to the mixture with some milk and white chocolate. Just roughly chop the chocolate. Then you just bake on the bottom of the roasting oven for about 35 minutes, the top will have set by then, and then 50 minutes or so in the middle of the simmering oven. I've also made this ganache for the topping.' She reaches for a pan on the side of the Aga. 'It's just 150g of plain chocolate and 150ml of double cream. I stuck it on the simmering plate until it all melted and then moved it to one side to cool. When the cake has cooled a bit, I will pour the topping over the top and sides to finish it. That is where I am up to. So, come on, let's take a look at the cake now and see if it is cool enough yet.'

'Well, I must say it all sounds very accomplished for your first attempt,' I say, realising these are the first real words, apart from hello and thank you, I've uttered since I arrived, and surprised that my voice is a little shaky.

'Oh no, it's not the first time I've made it,' Sioned says. 'I've made it two or three times a day, every day since I invited you here. My mum has been over to help. Every one of my neighbours, and my mum's neighbours, and Steve's golf club, and his mountain bike club, and my choir – they've all tried it. I couldn't risk it being a failure.' This woman really is like me. Intelligent, educated and, let's be honest, more than a tad obsessive. Thank God there's someone else out there! I was beginning to think I was all alone.

With that, there is a loud knocking at the front door. Sioned leaves me at the kitchen oasis with the others as she goes to answer it, making her way past a small group of women who seem to be collectively burping their babies by bouncing up and down as they talk in the hallway. I feel safe at the oasis. Perhaps she has rescued me, saved me! She certainly seems to be like me. I hope she likes me, too. She could be my friend.

I hear Sioned say, 'Great. You made it.' And my blood runs cold as I hear the response. 'Yeah, luv. Proper 'ard to find it is, like, isn't it, luv.' Dear Lord, Myfanwy. I thought I'd seen the last of her.

'Look everyone, it's Myfanwy,' says a cheery Sioned.

'Oh, hi Myfanwy,' says an equally cheery group of women.

'Hello,' I say as brightly as I can in the circumstances.

'Oh, well, fuck me sideways, I didn't know you was going to be yer, Lottie, luv,' says a grinning Myfanwy. I grimace. 'The last time I saw you, I saw yer fanny 'n' all.'

Thankfully no one seems to have paid any attention to the abomination that is Myfanwy. 'Anyway you were telling us about making this cake for the choir, the golf club and Uncle Tom Cobbley 'n' all… isn't that a bit obsessive?' asks Annie, another one of the women who seems to have got her figure back already. 'Are you sure you haven't got OCD?'

'What's that then, luv? Ooo do 'ave OCD?' asks Myfanwy, who has plonked a baby car seat on a kitchen worksurface and is already, and uninvited, starting to tidy away some of the cooking implements and loads Sioned's dishwasher.

'Well, you may have a touch of the OCDs yourself, Myfanwy. Its Obsessive Compulsive Disorder. Do you have a bit of a fixation with tidying up?' Sioned says. 'Mind you, I could do with a bit of OCD myself for my housework. It would be nice to get my house properly tidy for once. If I could have OCD for a week and then a fortnight of anorexia afterwards and get my figure back, like Annie, that'd be just great. I'd be sorted.' Hurrah to that! Although neither Sioned or Annie need to worry about getting their figures back. Unfortunately, it seems that Myfanwy and I are in the same category on this one. She is still enormous.

'Look! You've made a bloody cake!' says Myfanwy, as if Sioned hadn't noticed. 'Is this this cooking and baking stuff you do do? Isn't this get-together meant to be about us lot, the mams like, relaxing, luv?' Myfanwy seems to be taking over everything in the kitchen, including the conversation. 'And about the babies, like?' She continues. 'That's what you did say when I did see you yesterday in town, like, Sioned. That's why I did come along, like. Isn't that right, Lottie, luv?' Myfanwy throws me a beaming smile as she says this and I do the best I can to smile back. And I'm not her Lottie, by the way!

'Of course it's about the babies. I just really wanted to get this cake right for everyone,' says Sioned. A perfectly understandable and reasonable position. Not *everything* has to be about the babies *all* the time. Thank goodness we can talk about something other than the incessant chit-chat about baby's weight, baby's growth centiles, baby's this, baby's that. I, for one, am grateful to have something different to discuss, especially as it is cake. Good for Sioned for breaking the incessant baby talk, that's what I think, as I am offered, and take, a generous slice of cake.

And gosh, can that woman ever bake a cake! The cake is very rich but absolutely delicious. She puts my lime drizzle to shame. I can see I am going to have to up my game considerably.

'Better than sex, this cake is definitely better than sex,' says one of the women, with a mouthful.

‘’ell, yes,’ says Myfanwy. ‘But that don’t take that much these days, do it, luv? I ’aven’t even done it yet since the baby, like. Far too painful for me fanny. Oh, and I used to love a good ’ard shag too ’n’ all. I’ve ’ad to do a fair bit of seeing to ’is needs over the past few weeks, like!’ Then the woman nudges me with her elbow and, as if she is purposefully trying to make me squirm, says, ‘I do mean giving ’im sucky-offie, like. Warrabout you, Lottie?’

Some of the others start to giggle, with embarrassment presumably. Myfanwy looks positively gleeful at causing so much consternation. I decide not to answer, so I take another mouthful of cake.

As we sit in Sioned’s lounge with our umpteenth cup of tea, I am drawn to Sioned as she is my sort, and we have a quiet tête-à-tête. ‘So, did you plan to get pregnant, then, Sioned?’ I ask, hoping that she is like me in this respect.

‘Gosh, yes,’ she replies. ‘We’d been trying for years. We had just started trying a different type of IVF, more… how can I put it delicately… intrusive. We were delighted. It’s cost us a small fortune, but it’s worth every penny.’ She takes another sip of tea and glances across to her sleeping baby with warmth and love. ‘What about you?’

I try to make light of my circumstances and stray a little from the truth. Quietly, I say, ‘Gosh, no, not at all. I know this sounds silly, but we’re not quite sure how it happened. We’ve worked out that it was either really romantic, on the last day of our holiday in Mauritius, a little afternoon delight before we left for the flight home and me a bit forgetful with the pill while I was away on holiday, or, less romantically, and more likely, it was at the service station on the M4.’

With that, a booming voice blasts, ‘What, *you* did do it in a service station? You dirty cow.’ It’s Myfanwy’s voice, of course. And now most of the women are looking at me.

I feel as if I should explain myself, not for Myfanwy’s benefit but for the other women who are looking at me. ‘No, not in the car. In a Travelodge, actually! Not that that is much better, really. I was working for a client in London, and I had to stay up there most days during the week and Andy, that's my husband, had a temporary contract working on a project in the South West. The work meant he was away a fair bit, too. The workload was so great on both of us that we didn't stand much chance of being at home at the same time during the week, and it was eating in to our weekends too, as we were both so shattered. So, when we could, we'd find a mid-week evening when we could both get to the services on the M4 and still make our early morning meetings wherever we needed to be the next day. We met like this just a few days after we got back from Mauritius. I think it was near Swindon. Anyway, somehow it happened. Initially, I thought I had picked up some sort of flu bug while on holiday and that's why I felt a bit off colour and tired. It never even crossed my mind that I could be pregnant. I think I must have gone into denial a bit.'

I don't why I am telling them all this. I don't need to justify myself to them, or to Myfanwy, of all people.

Everyone smiles politely. No one judges or makes any comment until a confused Myfanwy says, very loudly, 'It's bloody 'ard to follow what you do go on about, with all 'em posh words. Are you saying you're a prozzie then luv? It's alright; we're none of us judging you. Life's 'ard, like.'

Everyone laughs whilst looking confused. I am the most confused of all, and very offended. 'Why? Why would you ask that? A prostitute? I don't understand why you would ask that?'

'Cuz you did say that you do 'ave clients. That's what a prozzie do say. I saw it on a doc-u-mentary. On the TV.' She says 'TV' loudly, and slowly, as if this was the bit of her sentence that needed explaining.

This should have been my opportunity to tell Sioned about my circumstances. How I really didn't want a baby. That we had always said we didn't want children. Our life was about each other. That I'd finally booked an abortion. That when I told Andy he went berserk… not because I was pregnant, as I would have expected, but because I planned to get rid of it without consulting him. How he decided, there and then, he wanted a child after all. How he decided, at that moment, we would move from our lovely flat and buy a house in Newport – his home town. How he has made every important decision about our lives from that fateful moment. And all the rest of the sorry tale. But no, the moment is lost due to that stupid, stupid woman, Myfanwy.

And again, the bleak thoughts wash over me. Why, oh why, did we move to god-forsaken Newport in the first place? I must have been out of my mind to agree. But, then again, I wasn't really given much choice by Andy. He made that quite clear without actually saying it. And when I finally told them in work, well, Nigel's, my boss', reaction was typical Nigel. He stared at me for about ten seconds and then made a series of rapid-fire decisions that simply couldn't be unpicked. 'So, Charlotte, moving to Newport, eh? In Wales? That'll be career-limiting. I'll move you into the Bristol office. There's a difficult team down there that needs sorting. I take it you don't have any objections? Oh, and I have a project in London that I need you to sort beforehand – before your brain goes all mushy. It'll be a good opportunity to prove yourself.' And without waiting for an answer, he turned and walked out of his office, leaving me there to slowly pick up my notebook... and laptop... and the remnants of my once meteoric rise at QXL. Then he popped his head around the door with a beaming smile and said, 'Aha, that explains the tits,' and was gone again.

In truth, we didn't have to move to Newport, did we? We didn't need to move at all, although I know a one-bedroomed flat is not a long-term solution. But we could have moved somewhere nearby. Or we could have moved to Bristol to be near my new office. Or Bath. Bath is nice. I have friends from university who live there, although Andy doesn't like them very much. Or we could have moved anywhere, really. But Andy jumped at the chance to move back to Newport. I was so surprised. He'd never said he wanted to move back. He'd always mocked his home town. Couldn't wait to leave on the couple of occasions we'd briefly visited his mother before they fell out. Now he couldn't wait to get back. He had our flat on the market before I could draw breath. And, I must admit, we were able to buy a four-bedroomed house for pretty much the same price as we got for our tiny one-bedroomed flat. So, moving to Newport, organising the new team in Bristol, and leading the project in London all meant that I didn't have much time to think about what my life would be like with a baby. So, I try to forgive myself just a little. It is understandable why I find myself so unprepared for my current predicament.

The laughter in the room dies down and the chatting resumes, but I feel lost again. This afternoon would have been lovely if Myfanwy hadn't been here. It was all going so well before she turned up.

'Why on earth did you invite her, Sioned?' I ask discreetly.

'Who?' she says, whilst brushing cake crumbs from the kitchen work surfaces.

'Her,' I say, as I nod in her direction. Who else could I mean?

'Myfanwy? Oh, she's alright. Just a typical Newport girl. You'll meet lots of them.'

God, I hope not. There surely can't be anyone as awful as this woman, but Sioned seems genuinely unbothered by her presence so I let it go. Myfanwy doesn't fit in with this group so I imagine she won't join us again at our new weekly meetings.

Sioned is chatting to Annie and some of the others in the kitchen as they make yet another cup of tea, so I slump back on the squishy sofa. Then Myfanwy, her baby clutched tight to her breast, manoeuvres herself towards me, leans over and says quietly, 'You cun just pick 'im up, you know. For a cwtch, like. For you. 'e don't 'ave to be crying nor nuffin. Just cuz you wants to, like. You cun do it just for you.' I gawp at her open-mouthed. She knows! She's seen it. Where the others haven't, she, this god-damn awful woman, has seen that I haven't bonded with my child. I am in a desert and there is no one to help me. She has spoken to me quietly, and I almost thought there was sensitivity in her voice. But what's her game? Perhaps she means to blackmail me.

'What do you mean?' I ask with all the calmness I can muster.

'You don't cwtch 'im, do you, luv? You don't just 'old 'im.'

I don't want to give her any more ammunition, but I blurt out unexpectedly. 'I… I… I can't. He might start that awful crying again, and I just can't bear it.'

'It's alright, luv. It's normal. Don't force it, like. You'll be alright, Charlotte, luv,' she says in a whisper which must surely be a mocking, faked concern. I don't want her to be nice, for her to be kind. I can't cope. At least she didn't call me 'her Lottie' this time. With that Sioned, Annie and the others come back in the room, bright and bubbly, carrying a teapot and a jug of milk, and Myfanwy says very loudly, 'Fuckin' 'ell 'ow much fuckin' tea are we going to fuckin' drink yer today, like?' and the universe returns to normal. But with a new paradigm, one where Myfanwy knows my innermost concerns. I didn't see that coming! And I've been ambushed. I can't imagine how she will use this new-found information against me, but I must be on my guard. And if anyone else were to find out then they might take George from us, and then Andy would be devastated. I'll just have to keep the abominable Newportonian sweet.

I am going to have to play this very carefully now. But my brain is so addled I just can't think beyond the next feed. My breasts start tingling and then I get the let-down of milk and a few seconds later George wakes and starts to cry. Did my milk cause him to wake? Or was he starting to wake and did my breasts spring into action in response? Nature is a mystery to me. Whichever, I pick up the clean, pink George in his blue baby-gro, and position him. He latches on immediately and draws deeply on my nipple, and I feel the milk being drawn across my chest. I don't enjoy this. It still hurts when he latches on as I have developed cracked nipples.

Myfanwy rests her hand gently on my arm and says, 'I do love that feeling of me milk comin' through. Knowin' I am giving me Chardonnay the best there is in the world. You are the one that told me about breastfeeding, Lottie, luv. Thank you, luv. I feels so close to 'er and know I would do anything for 'er and to protect 'er like'. It's a great feeling isn't it, luv?'

Is she mocking me for my lack of maternal extinct? I cannot tell, but she seems sincere, seems moved. I smile, well, grimace as it is as much as my cracked nipples will allow. I will deal with

Myfanwy another time. When my brain comes back. God, I hope it comes back soon.

She then says loudly to everyone in earshot, 'I didn't realise that we were all committing to baking though, luv, when we do 'ost our get-togethers. I'd better go last so that I do 'ave time to practice mine. I am not renowned for my cooking skills, like. Oh, 'ang on, I could buy a Sara Lee from Iceland, though, that'd be nice. A posh one. Black Forest gateau. I could even buy some squirty cream 'n' all.'

Surely, they'll reject her now. Squirty cream! They'll see that she isn't right for this group. A cleverly-phrased put-down now on my part will seal her fate – and exclude her forever… but I'm too slow. My brain won't work quickly enough. 'That'll be fine, you don't have to go to any bother,' says Annie, dipping in to the conversation. But it won't be fine. Not for me. We are not Sara Lee women. Myfanwy is not one of us. I don't want her here. I certainly don't want her to come to my house… and I certainly don't want to go to hers. It's probably in a ghetto. She sticks out like a sore thumb, but the others don't seem to have noticed, or don't seem bothered. And it is impossible for me to say anything now she knows the truth about me. She has me over a barrel. I briefly consider dropping out of the group altogether. But I have been lonely like the HV said and, to be completely honest, I think I am going a bit mad.

8 Madeira cake

'So what, Charlotte, is so bloody hard about ironing a shirt? You're at home all day. I'm out at work for what, ten? Eleven? Twelve hours some days. In all that time you can't find five minutes to at least iron a shirt for me. What's happened to you? It's pathetic. I thought I knew you. The Charlotte I knew would be all over this. You're a different person, and I really don't like it. You need to get your act together and pull your socks up. If you can't manage now, with all the time in the world, how the hell do you think you're going to manage when you are back at work?'

I reach for the shirt in his hand, but he snatches it away. 'Don't bother, Charlotte. I'll do it myself... again! But this really has to change. This cannot continue. It's not good enough.'

So here I am. In Newport! With a child. And I have a profound fear; I am terrified the novelty of a baby is wearing off for Andy. He has fads on things and then loses interest. The garage is testament to that. We have motorbikes, mountain bikes, cross bows, a mini rifle range, camping gear and golf clubs. I am dreading the day when he decides he's had enough of George and wants his next new toy. I'm terrified that the next thing that goes wrong he'll be off. He's threatened he would in the past when things haven't gone his way. An un-ironed shirt could be it.

He's right. I am pathetic. Earlier this morning, Andy had a go at me about the state of the house. Now I am sitting on a kitchen stool under a spotlight, and I've just let him rant at me, again. I can't think what to say. I am letting him down. The house is a right state. He's right. I'm not on top of everything. I have let things slide. And now, now he's ironing his shirt and I just can't stop crying. I am sobbing! Sobbing? Me, Charlotte Harrington, sobbing over an un-ironed shirt and a pile of dirty dishes. I used to manage a team, trouble-shoot a project, analyse root causes, negotiate a deal, present to the Board. Now, it is all I can do to make sure George doesn't disturb him. I remind myself, through my tears, that it's another good reason to stick at the breastfeeding although it is completely exhausting. How many times did George wake last night? I can't even count anymore. I think it was four times, but it may have been more. I know I fell asleep sitting in the rocking chair with George on my boob. I woke cold, stiff and very uncomfortable and then, climbing back into bed, Andy told me how exhausted he was from disturbed sleep and to keep my cold feet away from him. If I weren't so terrified that the next thing will mean Andy packing his bags then I would put George on a bottle so that Andy can see what it is really like.

So today I can't even work out which to do first: take over ironing Andy's shirt or load the dishwasher. He's right. God knows how I'm going to manage it all when I go back to work. Like he says, if I can't manage now when I am at home all day. I am useless. Totally useless. I should kill myself and then Andy could marry someone else. Someone who could do all these things *and* fit into her jeans. I don't suppose it would take him long to remarry. And he could get some hired help in the meantime.

Hired help!

Hired help!

Why didn't I think of it before? It shows how addled my brain must be. I'll order a housekeeper, or a cleaner... or a mother's help. Oh, perfect, perfect, perfect. I hear the front door slam as Andy leaves for work. I'll go and buy a copy of *The Lady* now.

My enthusiasm is dampened by how long it takes me to get myself and then George washed and ready to go out. Over three hours. And I haven't even got any make-up on. I am standing by the front door, with George in his pram. I am alongside the note I have stuck to the wall. 'CHECK KEYS!' I must check I have my keys as I forget everything these days. And it will be the third, no, fourth time I've had to sit on the doorstep and wait for Andy to come home from work. Check keys – yes! So hey, we're ready to go when George's face goes red and he breaks into a slow smile followed by a resounding fart and a smell that means he has filled his nappy… again! I've only just changed him. I sit on the bottom step of the stairs and cry all over again.

I change George yet again, which involves another clean outfit as his babygro is splattered in yellow poo. I walk all the way to the newsagent only to discover they don't stock *The Lady* and they will have to order a copy. In the meantime, they suggest I put an ad in their window. When the woman in the shop reads my note, she says her daughter-in-law is looking for a little job, providing it is cash in hand. Two hours, twice a week to start, six pounds an hour. Twenty-four pounds a week could save my life, and my marriage. She's going to get back to me when the woman can start. Not this week, unfortunately, but soon.

But, that night, my delight is shattered. I proudly present Andy with an ironed shirt for tomorrow and tell him my good news. I'd found a solution! Or so I thought!

'Jesus, Charlotte. You are completely losing the plot,' says Andy. 'What is the matter with you? You can't afford a cleaner. Who do you think you are? Lady Bloody Muck. All your middle-class pretensions. You've just had three months off work. Your pay has halved and our costs have gone through the roof so how, *exactly*, do you think you are going to be able to afford a cleaner? What you need to do is be better organised. Then all of this wouldn't get on top of you. Of course, if you didn't spend quite so much time sitting around eating cake with all your new friends, you might find a bit more time to do the basics… and maybe lose a bit of weight too, which wouldn't go amiss. It is about time you pulled yourself together and started to think about me and George first and not yourself.'

So, I phone the newsagent and ask them to pass on the message that I am not going ahead with the cleaner. I feel absolutely lousy.

Andy comes over to me as I put the phone down and he puts his arms around me. 'Charlotte, I'm so sorry,' he says. 'I'm being a git. It's the lack of sleep. It makes me so bad-tempered. I really am sorry. Forgive me?' We make up. He makes dinner. It's his way of saying sorry. And afterwards, while I'm still sitting at the table, he pretends to be a waiter with a teacloth draped over his arm. He places a big slice of madeira cake in front of me, and a mug of tea. 'For the lady, compliments of the house,' he says, in a mock-French accent.

I laugh and he ruffles my hair affectionately as he makes his way back into the kitchen to start loading the dishwasher. It was a silly argument. We are both just tired. Not just tired, we are exhausted. It is nothing. Just silly, silly, silly.

9 Parkin

Andy will be getting up for work in just a few short hours, and I still have to iron a shirt for him. After the silly squabble, I've made a concerted effort to have a shirt ready for him every day. He's right, it's the least he can expect when he is out working all day and I am at home.

It is my turn to host Parentcraft this afternoon. I am so nervous. I couldn't dodge the bullet any longer, though. We've been to some houses twice already. So I had to volunteer last week. I prepared a little project plan straight away, not in MS Project or anything too over the top, just in XL, and I should be able to fit in a little nap later this morning, if everything goes to plan. I used to be able to clean the house *and* bake a cake, but with my brain as it is I knew I'd just have to devise another way. Then one of the old brain cells kicked in and I thought of an alternative recipe. I just hope I've remembered it properly.

I was cleaning most of the night and I am exhausted, but I had to grab the chance while Andy and George were asleep, and apart from the hoovering, cleaning is a pretty quiet business. Yellow dusters flick and rub silently. Bathroom and shower cleaner spray their fine mists inaudibly. The gentle glug of bleach into the toilet, sinks and washbasins cannot be detected by the sleeping. Newspaper rubbing white vinegar onto the windows makes scarcely a squeak. I've left the noisy hoovering for this morning, along with the last load in the dishwasher and the last load of washing in the tumble dryer – they were all too noisy for my night-time cleaning frenzy.

The bed is empty and scented candles mask the smells of bleach and disinfectant, yet Andy doesn't notice a thing when he wakes up. He has a meeting to get to, so it's not really that surprising. He takes a shower – I'll have to reclean it. He eats his breakfast and then leaves the bowl and spoon and a big milky mark next to the dishwasher – it won't take long to clear that up, though. He goes through his normal morning routine, and I follow him around and try to keep calm as I watch him undo so much of my work. He wakes George – grrr! – then slobbers all over him. He really adores that child. And now, finally, he is gone. George, unbelievably, is asleep. I can get on now.

I need this morning to dust the coving. I had hoped to bake something really impressive, something Annie and Sioned would like – they're my favourites of the group. I wish I had an AGA. But I knew I had to pick something easy instead. I have to be realistic. George will just have to wait for his feeds – I'll have to break his routine, just for today. The thought of upsetting his routine is making me feel uncomfortable; it has taken me so long to get a routine that works for all of us. I also really need a sleep now but, I realise, sadly, there is no time for that.

I am totally exhausted by the time they arrive. Where did the morning go? What happened to lunchtime? I think that was when I was rebleaching the loo – just to be sure.

It's fine, it's fine, it's fine. They like my house (or at least they say they do) and although it is not as grand as Sioned's beautiful home, they are all very complimentary about how we have decorated. They especially like the electric blue sofas and yellow walls. One of the Debbies (they all seem to be called Debbie so when I forget a name, Debbie is always a fair guess) says how clean it is. I could have kissed her. They all seem happy and relaxed as I bring in another pot of tea and place it on the wooden table we bought from Oxfam's Fair Trade catalogue as our Christmas present to each other a few years ago. The large group of women are all chatting happily. They are talking about how they met their husbands. One of the Debbie's is regaling them with her story.

'I decided he was *the one*,' this particular Debbie tells us, 'when he came into The White Hart, our local, when I was out with some friends from work. I'd never seen him before. I was already dating someone at the time, but that didn't last long anyway, just another in a long string of boyfriends. Anyway, he had a long-term girlfriend when I first met him, but I made damn sure that they split up. I knew as soon as I saw him that he would be the man I would marry. He is gorgeous in a swarthy sort of a way. And he makes me laugh so much. He is so funny. He came over to our group and said, 'Whose coat is that jacket?' I creased. I love that way of speaking. It's so Valleys. I love his Valleys accent.'

Well, I suppose someone has to.

'If anything, he played it up,' she continues. 'He was in a rugby team with some of his workmates and they started coming to the pub quiz on a Sunday night most weeks. They would sometimes call him 'Boss', and he would make a big thing of playing it down, saying they weren't on duty and all that. I love that. He is so in control. I watched him for ages, and then I started tracking him.'

As she is talking, Debbie reaches deep into her enormous nappy bag and pulls out a small hairbrush. She brushes her fringe, leaving the rest of her corkscrew perm untouched, before returning the brush to the cavernous bag, and returning to her story.

'I saw that he caught the late-night bus after the pub quiz, so I started catching the bus home myself, pretending to all my mates that my little Ford Fiesta was off the road. See how devious I am! Anyway, I was standing behind him one day at the bus stop and I popped a note in the pocket of his jacket which said, 'Would you like to go out for a drink one evening?' And then I put my home number. How brazen, how forward! I've got such a cheek. I love me sometimes, honest to God! Anyway he didn't ring, so I thought he wasn't interested. I got my car back on the road and stopped catching the bus home from the pub quiz. It had been a right pain catching the bus anyway. I had almost forgotten about the note – or tried to obliterate the whole embarrassing episode from my mind more like – when about a fortnight later he called. He said he hadn't found the note in the pocket until then as he had taken the coat into the dry cleaners the following day. The girl in the dry cleaners had given him the note back in a little sealed plastic bag, like forensic evidence. It was even more embarrassing for her. Apparently, she had thought the note was for her from him and she had rung – but she had hung up straight away when she heard a woman's voice (mine!). I don't know why she told him all this. She could have just kept quiet, and he'd have been none the wiser. Aren't people odd? He phoned me straight away when he got back from the drycleaner's, but only to tell me he had a girlfriend. It made me all the more determined that he would be mine.'

We, particularly me, are fascinated with Debbie's story and this insight into her past. It's been a long time since I've really had a girl chat about things other than babies. A very long time now I think about it. In fact, my friends and I tend to meet with our partners. And when we've met up separately for drinks, well, I don't know what we've talked about all these years, to be honest. Superficial stuff. I don't think I know intimate details about any one of them. That's strange because I already know intimate details about nearly everyone from Parentcraft… and way too much from Myfanwy. But time for our Thursday afternoon is running out, so we stop our story telling for me to serve more tea and my parkin.

'The first time I had 'parkie,' as I call it, was on a summer's day after a trip out with my grandmother,' I tell them. 'I don't know how long we had been out, but it felt like all day to me. I was only little, about three or four years old, and my feet were aching from all the walking, but I went on without complaint. I always just loved being with my grandmother. Even at that young age, I knew I just wanted to spend as much time as possible with her and would do anything to extend our time together. When we finally arrived at my grandmother's house, she put a large white enamel bowl of cold water on some newspaper on the tiled floor of her kitchen and we stood in it together, cooling our blisteringly hot feet. She dried my feet by patting them with a soft towel. Not rubbing them hard as my mother would. She always took such care with me, like I was the most precious, delicate thing in the world. And I with her. And I patted her feet with the towel in my clumsy, childlike way. Later, we sat in the lounge, by a made-up fire that was not yet burning (it was ready for later in the evening) and placed our toes on the cool tiles around the fireplace. After a good rest, my grandmother had asked me if I wanted to make parkin. I had thought it was called parkie after the man in the official peaked cap we had met as we wandered around the park that day. So, for me, it will always be called parkie. My grandmother thought this was so funny that she called it parkie too from that day forward. It was our special word, and we smiled at each other whenever we said it. She was a wonderful woman, my grandmother.' I don't add the truth, that she loved me in a way my mother never did.

Several of the women smile at my description of my grandmother, and they tell stories of similar relationships with their grandmothers too.

'I have made parkie many times since, and I am not sure whether this is exactly how my grandmother made it that day, but the taste and the smell always invokes strong memories of the amazing, strong lady that was my father's mother…' I stop myself from saying what comes into my head next: that she was more of a mother to me than mine has ever been. 'She was such a feisty lady,' I continue. 'I really adored my grandmother, and she loved me too. She taught me how to bake. She was so brilliant, and she could make really sophisticated cakes and refined delicacies, but I always liked her simpler, more artisan stuff, like parkin, best.' I smile at the memory. 'I like to make it a few days before I need it,' I tell them. I can't help but smirk. Little do they know that this was an absolute necessity. I could never have fitted in baking a cake this morning along with everything else. 'I am sure it tastes better after a being stored in an airtight tin. This was made on Tuesday morning. I hope it's okay?'

To my huge relief, and thanks to my careful planning, it is an enormous success with them all, even Sioned, with all her allergies, tries a little. Myfanwy stuffs big pieces of parkin into her mouth and talks with her mouth full, but she is very complimentary, too. Of course, I expect it is all part of her masterplan to blackmail me. That is exactly how my mother behaves. Compliments are to be treated with great caution as she will shortly seek out payment. So I keep a guarded eye on Myfanwy, especially when I have to deal with something for George.

As breastfeeding mothers we all consume innumerable cups of tea and coffee along with lots of cold drinks. After a couple of hours, my lounge looks like a bomb has hit it, and it makes me feel rather twitchy. All my hard work. I can see that I am going to have to placate Andy. And I haven't prepared dinner, so it will have to be a take away. Actually, thinking about it now, as much as I have enjoyed the afternoon, I'm beginning to look forward to them all going so that I can put George to bed and try to get things back, at least a little, into some order. Sioned and Myfanwy are absolute stars with cleaning up the mess. Neither of them can sit still for five minutes, constantly tidying, gathering up the plates and the cups and saucers, getting people more drinks, almost to the point that they are taking over my hosting role. But when Myfanwy starts cleaning out my cupboards, well, enough is enough, and I insist they all sit down and leave it to me.

I am happier tidying up in the kitchen. Truth is, I don't think I like children at all, really. They are so boring. And so demanding. They interrupt our conversations. Chardonnay, yes, she honestly called her Chardonnay, is Myfanwy's daughter. She named her after the reason she got pregnant. 'Lucky really, like. The week before 'n' she would 'ave been called Liebfraumilch,' she says. Today Chardonnay is in sickly pink. She's wearing white socks with crocheted tops that fold over and make her look like a shire horse. She has slept all the way through today's Parentcraft, as has George, mostly, thank heavens. But the others have cried, fed, pooed and vomited. Sometimes on a rota, sometimes all at the same time. Several of the babies have just breastfed all afternoon. I don't know how Annie, Sioned and Myfanwy can stand it, but they all say they enjoy it. They enjoy the milk coming through. I just don't understand how they can. I think they must be just saying it because they think that is how good mothers are meant to behave. But they do look as though they sincerely like just sitting doing nothing, waiting for the hot drinks to go cold before they will take them across the baby for fear of a hot drop splashing on their little darlings, while their babies guzzle incessantly.

I make a comment about how frustrating I find sitting doing nothing. 'But it's not doing nothing, Charlotte,' says Annie. 'It's feeding my baby. It is the most important thing I can do for her health and my own.' And I feel ashamed once again. This is almost word for word one of my speeches about the importance of breastfeeding from our prenatal days. I must take my own medicine. It is of my own making, so I have no one to blame but myself. I'm sure I see Myfanwy smiling smugly, but she busies herself in Chardonnay's nappy. That woman has a fascination with nappies. She changes Chardonnay all the time. God alone knows what she is personally doing to the environment. However, I must admit, my early attempts to use a reusable nappy service quickly gave way to buying disposable nappies from the supermarket. There just aren't enough hours in the day. I recognise that Parentcraft is my saviour. We no longer really invite each other; we sort of agree on the next location and then we all turn up on a Thursday afternoon at 2pm. I really don't think I could bear to be at home with George all the time without something to break up the day and get me away from the relentless grind. It is such hard, thankless work, looking after a baby, even though he is not difficult, he just doesn't sleep enough. So it feels completely endless. I haven't yet admitted to them that I am looking forward to going back to work, but I am. And I now also feel terrified that I won't be able to do my job. My brain is such a mush. I can't even remember *what* I did, let alone *how* I did it. How I will manage with the housework is yet to be determined, but I am just hoping that it will somehow become easier once I get into a routine.

Myfanwy tells us loudly that she has blow-dried her hair into a 'Rachel from Friends' look today. She looks quite different. She has done her make-up very lightly, and you can see the freckles on her nose. When I mention her freckles she is embarrassed and rushes off to apply more foundation. 'I think freckles look great,' I say. I'm trying not to be so harsh with her. 'And Andy loves them. Actually, he has a bit of a thing about women with freckles. It's one of his favourite things. That and skinny red-heads. God knows how he ended up with fat old me.'

Oh, damn, that didn't go the way I intended. Instead of being nice to Myfanwy, I've managed to put myself down. Why did I do that? Now I've admitted that I'm fat (although anyone can see that) and also that I really don't know how I managed to get Andy. We met at uni. He was studying engineering. I was in computer science. I had a crush on him for ages before we got together. All these years later and I still can't really believe my luck. And I really don't know how I manage to keep him.

'Hey, Charlotte,' shouts Sioned. She is in my kitchen again where she is loading the dishwasher for a second time. 'Could I have the recipe for this parkin? Could you write it down for me, do you think? It was delicious. Steve would just love it.' She had missed the description earlier in the afternoon of how I made the parkin as she had been changing Jack's nappy upstairs.

'Yes, no problem. I'll write it out and bring it with me next week,' I say, hoping that I'll remember. I'm just so forgetful these days.

'Yeah, it was bloody luvly that parkie stuff you did make. I'm surprised you cun cook, luv,' says Myfanwy. 'I wouldn't 'ave 'ad you down as the type.'

'What? In what way? Just because I am a modern woman with a career doesn't mean I can't bake a cake. That's the whole point of feminism, Myfanwy. I can be a Senior Analyst and Team Leader in Research and Development and still enjoy baking a cake. I can be a woman and stand up for my rights without being militant. I can enjoy things my mother, my grandmother, my great-grandmother enjoyed and it doesn't distract from my ability to be equal with a man. I can still enjoy traditional pastimes if I choose. Feminism is about that choice. That's the point, Myfanwy.'

That was a bit of a blast from the past – from a module on 'Women in the Workplace' that I had signed up to before I met Andy. He hated it when I told him I was doing that module. In fact, he did his best to dissuade me from going by always making me late by keeping me in bed, which I must admit, didn't take much persuading, I just couldn't get enough of him. He said it made me sound like a militant lesbian, and, after going on and on about it, it was, he said, the only thing he didn't like about me. He said it all seemed so unnecessary, and a remnant from the past, as I was already a strong woman who could hold her own with the computer science geeks. I was flattered that that is how he saw me and I eventually dropped it. He was right. It didn't fit with my career plan and I picked up an extra module on forensic interrogation of databases, which proved to be very useful at QXL.

Myfanwy looks at me dumbfounded. 'No, I was surprised you cun bake cuz you is posh, like, luv.'

'I'm not posh,' I say, feeling confused after my feminist outburst. But I suppose I am posh to someone like Myfanwy. If she met, heaven forbid, some of my posh friends, I think she would pass out. They certainly would.

'Anyway, why wouldn't someone who is posh be able to bake a cake?' Sioned asks. Good old Sioned.

'I thought they did 'ave 'people' to do that sort of thing for 'em, like,' Myfanwy says. 'A woman 'oo does, like. Cuz no one I do know 'oo is posh cun, luv. Anyway, it's me Lottie 'oo do always think you cun only be a strong woman when you do be-'ave like a man, like.'

I realise, with great surprise at her insightfulness, she has a point. I hadn't realised before this moment, but perhaps I only really rate women that do traditional male roles. Engineers, scientists, mathematicians. Do I value women who are in traditional female roles? I don't know if I do. I am distracted from my philosophising though as George starts to cry from the nursery, so I decide to park that one. Now is not the time.

George is fully awake in the nursery so I take him downstairs with me. He needs a feed so I hold him to my breast and take alternate gulps of cold water and very cool (cold really) tea. It won't be long until I will be back at work, I think. And, once again, I immediately feel guilty. My mind is full of such conflict these days. Most of the Debbies are going back to work soon. Some of the group are already back at work. Annie, Sioned and I have slightly better, but not great, maternity leave entitlements from our employers, but none of us is going back on exactly the same terms and conditions. I, foolishly, had casually mentioned some flexibility in working hours to our HR Director when she was in front of me in the queue in the canteen a few weeks before I left work, which set the wheels in motion before I knew what had hit me. All sorts of assumptions were made on my behalf, and then I felt trapped into taking what they have offered me. Three days a week, but with a sizeable impact on all my benefits and my overall package to accommodate this. They don't pay bonuses to part-time staff. They only told me all the details after I had signed a commitment to return on a set date and on these terms. I know technically I don't have to tell them until three weeks before I want to return, but they said that wasn't convenient for their planning cycle, so I had to commit to dates. The HR Director, a woman in her mid-forties, and hugely ambitious, looked so pleased with herself too as she told me how much money they would save as part-time women did just as much work as their full-time male counterparts! She then said, 'Isn't that fantastic,

Charlotte? Just think, you'll be able to do just as much work as you did before but in just three days!' And before I could muster up the words, 'But for forty percent less pay,' she continued with how she had lined up other people to take up my place in the Talent Pool because, 'Of course, you won't have the time,' and she looked at me eagerly, expecting my eternal gratitude. I just couldn't think what to say, so I said, 'Thank you,' having just waved goodbye to all my hard-earned benefits and my bonus, and having reduced my hours to something I no longer wanted. Damn the hormones. And damn my weakness.

As we have talked about returning to work today, I am beginning to fully realise the impact having a child will have on my career plan. Even those of us who are returning to reasonably well-paid jobs find there is a price to pay for being the sex that is responsible for creating the next generation of humankind. A responsibility, let's remember, that I didn't want. Turns out we have to accept a drop in grade or salary simply because we want – need – part-time work, or a guarantee of location, or some other practicality to make working possible. It's outrageous when you think of it, but it is common practice. At least, I take some comfort, we are all in the same boat. I had thought it was just me.

Sioned works for a big media company. I am terribly impressed. I thought she'd be on really good terms and conditions, but although they have a great reputation as an employer, Sioned has told me, in disjointed snippets over the last few weeks, that even they are not that great at looking after women when they return from maternity leave. That surprises me as I thought they'd be 'right on'. But she explains it still very much depends on how good your boss is at interpreting the rules. Even she, despite being quite senior within her business unit, has encountered a few surprises. As she has decided to take a short career break in addition to her maternity leave, Sioned not only has to take a drop in grade when she returns later in the year, but will also have to travel to a different location which will add about an hour to her daily commute, substantially eating into the benefits of working part-time. But her new line manager, who is based in London, is insistent that she has no jobs suitable for part-time working in Wales and that Sioned should consider herself lucky that a part-time role is being offered to her at all. This line manager went on to say that they are only offering this because at the SMT, Senior Management Team, Sioned's former line manager stood up for her. The new line manager then implied that there must have been 'something going on between them' to have earned such a privilege (ignoring completely the fact that Sioned is very good at her job). And Sioned says she felt unable to challenge the implication partly because it was only a vague reference, but mostly because it was embarrassing, degrading and untrue. So she, like me, just said, 'Thank you' instead.

'Most people go back full-time,' says Sioned. 'It is easier than trying to buck the system. Plus there is a lot of resentment of part-time workers, especially from the single parents, who still have to cover unsociable hours when part-time workers don't. Then there is always the fight over bank holidays. I know they will pile on the pressure once I am back. I've seen it happen so many times before. They'll have me working full-time before I know it if I'm not careful. Thankfully, I'm going for a stint in news. Apparently, they are more accommodating. I was offered a move into current affairs, but they are really bad. I've seen it happen to other women returning from maternity leave; their part-time hours become longer than a standard working week, but their pay remains steadfastly based on part-time hours. So, News is good news.'

We discover, through our chatting, that these sort of things happen all the time, in every sector. Decisions are made which could often be, at best, the minimum the policy allowed, or, at worst, totally at odds with the stated values of the organisation. Sometimes even illegal! However, worst of all, in our collective experiences, is the fact that the managers concerned are often young, but childless, women. We find, again through our discussions, they are much harsher and more inflexible than their male counterparts. Sadly, we realise this is because they want to show how strong they are and to prove that they don't favour women. One of the senior women at QXL actually said to me, at my farewell drinks party the evening before I went on maternity leave, 'Well, you chose to have a baby, Charlotte. You women today, you want it all. I had to sacrifice having a family to have my career.' Emotion erupted inside me!

Everyone just assumed I wanted a baby. Everyone assumed that a baby was a selfish decision – something for me. They assumed I was having a baby as a self-indulgence, or to have time off work, a sort of bonus break. No one considered for even a moment, that there was possibly another motive, that I had the baby for Andy. The truth is that I knew after the god-awful row that, for the sake of our marriage, I would have to agree to keep the baby. I should have just kept schtum, and he'd have been none the wiser. It hadn't even crossed my mind that he'd want to keep it. I knew from Andy's reaction that no matter how tough it would be for me, I had to keep it to ensure our marriage survived. He said it was my decision, but I knew from his face that he would never have forgiven me if I went ahead. What I didn't expect is that I would be punished for making this decision by my employer, by colleagues, by society as whole, and even by other women. As if I am just adding to the world's population problems. Surely I can't be the first woman ever, in the history of mankind, to have ever felt like this, or to have been in this predicament. So, how come I've never heard of anyone else… ever?

There were so many people at work who were negative, or worse, spiteful. So, I should sacrifice having this baby for Andy because you had to make sacrifices, should I, snooty colleagues? How does that represent progress for women, HR Director? Why wouldn't you strive to improve the lot of all women, or any parent, and not force people to make hard choices, Members of the Board? Let us have it all. Unfortunately, all of this was my inner voice. With my hormones still leaping wildly in my bloodstream, I kept my external voice quiet at the drinks party and opted for the blank smile that said nothing of my true feelings.

For my own part, despite all the right noises being made about the value of women in the workplace and the power of diversity in reflecting our customer base, the reality came down to decisions by my own line manager. In my case, the completely insensitive Nigel. God help me!

Of course, I know, I am being too harsh on everyone. Not everyone is against me. Some people were pleased, genuinely pleased, that I was having a baby. Men and women. Colleagues, friends and family. But I found that irritating too – as if I had found my purpose, my meaning, my raison d'être in producing the next generation. But what about this generation? What about this woman? What about me? Aren't I worthy in my own right? Am I only useful if I reproduce?

At our Parentcraft meetings, we conclude that until men start requesting part-time hours and don't have to explain why, and that we too can ask for reduced hours without having to explain why 'we are not coping full-time,' which is tantamount to admitting we've failed at being a working mother, then women will always be fighting the battle that part-time work is somehow a perk. Hmm, reduced pay, stress-inducing logistics, guilt, caring for a baby whilst working professionally, all this is a perk? Society still has some way to go to achieve equality.

I enjoy our discussion resolving society's injustices. I feel my brain whirring a little back into action. I feel grateful that the grey cells are still there. Perhaps they can be reawakened in time for work. It's been a long time since I've voiced my views. I don't even know for sure they are my views. They are from a different Charlotte, one at Uni, one that hadn't met and fallen in love with Andy. One who hadn't yet stepped willingly onto the corporate treadmill. One who hadn't yet enjoyed the corporate politics, following the movers and shakers, spotting the rising stars, positioning herself to take advantage of business relationships, and hadn't yet felt proud to be striding around in a corporate suit, busy, busy, busy. Shockingly, I realise that Charlotte was over a decade ago. She feels like a different person. Full of left-wing politics, women's rights and fair trade. I was definitely 'right on' as we used to say in the early Eighties. Bolshy, yes, but incredibly naïve. Meeting Andy changed everything. He gave me a reality check and got me started on my business career.

When I say 'we' are discussing this topic, of course, it is we professional women! Myfanwy doesn't contribute much to these conversations except the occasional, 'I thinks that men and women are different, like,' and other equally vacuous comments.

Late into the afternoon we are sitting in my lounge on the blue sofa, the 1930s leather armchair and the chairs I've picked up in antique shops. I've gone for an eclectic style and I am very proud of the look I have achieved. Women, babies and breasts seem to be everywhere. The room is also full of excited chatter and laughter as I finally tell them of the difficult time I'm having with my breasts. Not just that they are so big, but that they leak all the time. Even before I had George I had to wear breastpads. Then ever since he was born there is just so much milk. It gushes everywhere and George can't always feed properly because of the vast quantity. I'm sure that is why he seems to always be feeding. We are awash! I explain how I have to express at least a couple of times a day, and a couple of times at night, to try to keep the leaking levels down. Myfanwy leans over to me and says quietly, 'Luv, that is why you do 'ave so much milk, like, cuz all that pumpin' do stim-u-late even more milk production.' Reluctantly, I acknowledge to myself that Myfanwy have a point, again. She can be very wise on this baby stuff.

Even the breastpads aren't sufficient some days and I have to sit with towels wrapped around me. When they arrived at the house earlier that day, I had left the front door open and they caught me walking around carrying my breasts on a tray. 'They are just too heavy, this is the only way I can cope.' I was near to tears, half-laughing, half-crying tears, but the women just smiled. They didn't seem to think it was odd. It dawned on me that we were all in this together. It felt liberating. It was Myfanwy who said, 'Poor thing. They must 'urt like buggery'. Choice words! My breasts have morphed into rugby balls, hence the tray. Mrs Insipid has said the milk flow will eventually regulate itself and I will be fine. Roll on the day!

With the added confidence that they really weren't judging me, I told them another confession. 'Did I tell you about Joan's birthday present?' I say. 'Joan,' I explain, 'is my 70-year-old neighbour. I'd wrapped her present for her birthday and dropped it round on the day, but she was out with all her friends from her Bridge Club. I left it in her porch. She phoned me that evening to say thank you. I'd bought her a really nice blue glass vase. Anyway, she said that she loved it, and I shouldn't have, and all the rest of it and then she said, 'Oh, and thank you for the little coaster too.' So I apologised and said I wasn't sure what she meant. 'Oh, that little white drinks coaster that you put in the wrapping like in pass-the-parcel. What a sweet idea. I have my whisky and ginger standing on it now.' It must have been a breast pad that had fallen out while I was wrapping her present! I decided not to tell her. Well, she seemed so pleased with it!' Sioned and Annie smile at my story, but Myfanwy honks with laughter. You'd seriously think it was the funniest thing she'd ever heard.

Sioned takes up the reins. 'Did I tell you that I had been saving up all my used breastpads in a carrier bag to go for recycling? And did I tell you about their exciting journey along with a few dirty nappies? My sister, Catrin, has a friend in London who has just had a little boy and they are quite hard-up, so Catrin had asked me if I had any clothes that she could give to her. I packed a bag of some of Jack's things, things he wore up to about two weeks old – well, they grow out of them so fast, don't they? Some of them look like they have never been worn. To be honest, some of them haven't. I had so many presents from my colleagues as well as my family. So I packed them all up. When Catrin arrived, this was last week, she was being really off with me, which is unusual for Catrin. I had just started giving Jack some boobie, so I couldn't put him down. So I had to direct Catrin to the bags from my armchair. She wasn't pleased that I didn't just drop everything to see to her. But I told her which bags to take. Anyway, a couple of days ago, Catrin phoned me up and she was really cross. She had taken the bags to her friend's mother, who had passed them to her auntie, who had passed them on to her son to take to London, who had eventually taken them round to her friend. Her friend had phoned to say thank you for the clothes, but was the last bag some sort of a joke. What was the meaning of sending the stinking breastpads and dirty nappies?'

We all laugh. Really laugh.

And this is the way our Thursday afternoon rolls on. Threads of conversation. Incomplete stories, laughter and never quite enough time to finish before being interrupted by a baby.

And I enjoy it. I really do. I feel… happy, secure, I suppose, with my house full of new friends. 'I should write a book,' I say.

'About us. All of us.' I glance at Myfanwy. She'd be too rude to include in a book, but I don't tell her that.

'Oh no,' shrieks Myfanwy, 'I'll be the bloody fat one.' She looks horrified. 'There's always a thin one and a fat one in a story about women friends, like, so that 'as got to be me. I don't wanna be the fat one. And one's a slag. There's always a slag, and her friends introduce her to someone that she doesn't really like at first and then he turns out to be *the one.* And then one of the friends, and this is the big shocker, is always gay. Like no one has ever thought of that before,' she adds, with a dismissive humph!

'Well, I think I can confidently say that none of us are gay as there are lots of babies here who confirm we are definitely heterosexual,' I say. She's right though, there usually is a fat one. Myfanwy is fat, there's no denying it. I can't help myself as I meanly think, 'Hurrah, at least this time it isn't me!'

After he has a short nap, it is time for yet another feed for George, and it feels like it will never stop. I want to get back to my guests. They are leaving, shouting their goodbyes from the hallway as I am imprisoned by the feeding chair in his nursery. I can't get up without disturbing him, so I have to call my goodbyes back, quietly, as the last one, Sioned, finally leaves and I hear the front door slam shut . And once again I am left to the quiet of the house, and the mess.

10 Welsh cakes

'Welsh cakes today, my lovelies. I made them myself. Where's Sioned? Oh, there she is,' Annie says, as Sioned's petite frame tip-toes its way through the babies lying on the floor. Sioned's hair has been re-permed and highlighted at her mother's hairdressing salon. All of the hairdressing staff coo over the baby while she is pampered, apparently. Aren't people funny about babies!

Sioned is looking very sporty in her tight navy leggings and Nike trainers. She is wearing a roll-neck top that's navy blue with white spots. She looks great. I am so envious.

We are talking about the births.. again!

'Birth plan.' says Annie. 'What a load of rubbish that was! It was bloody awful. I won't be having another baby, that's for sure.' She suddenly looks at us sheepishly, and checks that the use of the word 'bloody' hasn't caused offence. After the horrors of childbirth, and hearing Myfanwy's foul mouth, I am not as shockable as I was just a few months ago, plus we all agree that a birth plan was just a tactic to keep us occupied by Mrs Insipid and the rest of the 'health visiting' profession.

'Changing the subject, let's talk cakes instead, do you all want to come to hear my recipe?' says Annie. 'I know that you all love to hear about how cakes are made. Come on in to the kitchen everyone, and you can have them hot off the bakestone.'

We follow Annie's tall frame and make our way through the open-plan house into her kitchen, which is too small for all of us. The property has been knocked through into this open-plan living space which works surprisingly well given that the house was never designed to be used in this way. It makes it sort of charming. However, there is a step down into the kitchen from the living room, so two of us, Myfanwy and me, squeeze next to the oven, tucked in the corner, whilst Sioned and the others, mostly Debbies, stand on the step. There are fewer of us each week now as more and more go back to work. There is a delicious smell of cake mix and the kitchen is very cosy, especially with the warmth coming off the bakestone on the cooker, which is already very hot.

'I make these all the time,' says Annie. 'Gareth loves them. My nan used to make them for me, and she used to let me help because they are so easy, even for little children. Charlotte, are you paying attention?' I nod obediently. 'I know you love the recipes too. *All I do is take 50g each of Welsh butter and lard, and mix it into 225g of self-raising flour. Then I add 75g of currants and a handful of sultanas, 75g of caster sugar,' she points at different jars and packets as she is saying this, 'and a good pinch each of cinnamon, nutmeg and then I add Hawarden honey.* I get it by mail order from the Conwy Honey Fair. It is fantastic.'

'Is it free-range 'oney, luv?' asks Myfanwy.

'I don't think you can have bees that aren't free-range, can you?' answers a confused Annie.

'I was joking, luv,' says Myfanwy. 'You lot! 'onestly! I may be coarse, and from the 'port, but I'm not thick, you know.'

Annie laughs and continues, 'I don't think you are thick Myfanwy, far from it. But where was I? Let me tell you about these Welsh cakes. *I add one medium beaten egg, pat out the dough until it is flat and about 1cm thick and use this teacup to cut out the dough. Then I just pop them on the bakestone until golden on both sides. Have one hot off the bakestone and just sprinkle some of that sugar and cinnamon on them.'*

'Hey, Annie, these look fantastic. I've never actually had a Welsh cake before. They're like a drop scone, aren't they?' I say, having taken a Welsh cake directly from the traditional Welsh bakestone on the top of the small modern gas cooker, holding it with a napkin as it is still very hot. 'Do I put butter on it?'

Annie, Sioned, Myfanwy and the others look at me as if I have just committed a heinous crime. Myfanwy looks at me straight in the eye and says, 'Why… why… would you want to put butter on a Welsh cake, you crazy fuckin' English bird?' Annie, Sioned and the others all snigger, but seem otherwise unbothered by her foul mouth.

Myfanwy continues, 'Mind you, I'd be a great big fat pig if I could cook, like. I am sure Chardonnay is going to love them through my titties, though.'

Sioned announces she is feeling a bit queasy as it is all getting too hot in the kitchen. I agree. 'Let's all go back into the living room then, it is much too hot in here,' I say. 'Do you want to get the rest of the babies out of their car seats now?' I don't... but I do.

Annie's house is a good-sized end of terrace, nicely decorated and in good order. 'Gareth is very good at DIY and the garden, and I am a good cook and cleaner,' she says. 'So, that's how we split the workload. I know it sounds a bit traditional, but we are working to our strengths.'

'Does he do his fair share of nappy changing, then?' asks one of the many Debbies.

'Oh gosh, no. He's useless. He approaches it like it is brain surgery, gowned up and sterilised, and then he starts gagging at the smell, so I do the nappy changing. It's not worth the fuss.' She laughs. And they all laugh at the various types of competence, or incompetence, the husbands exhibit in helping with the most basic of tasks. Andy does well in this league, and I feel proud. He is a dab hand at changing nappies and doesn't mind at all. In fact, he takes a curious pride in George's output. As George is still breastfed – yes, I'm still sticking with it – he's commented it doesn't stink like bottle-fed babies. That's probably why he is so keen that I stick at it; he says I should continue even when I go back to work, although the fact he doesn't have to wake up at night while I do all the feeding may be influencing his commitment to 'breast is best'. He says he is impressed that George's poo is the most amazing colour, bearing a striking resemblance to the colour of Marks and Spencer coronation chicken, just without the lumpy bits. I think it is odd that Andy is fascinated by it. He'd go mad if he knew I'd mentioned it to anyone.

Annie continues. 'I just laugh so much at Gareth. He has a tissue stuck up either nostril,' she says. 'Poor Ruby must be terrified seeing that coming towards her. No wonder she cries, I would cry too! Ruby really doesn't like Gareth changing her nappy at all. She only wants me to do it. She cries and cries if Gareth does it, so I do it. I don't mind. I quite like it that she needs me.'

How can a baby have decided who she wants to change her nappy? Honestly! It's nonsense. Annie is fooling herself, but I don't say anything. I like Annie but she's definitely wrong on this.

We have another good afternoon. I feel the sense of responsibility and foreboding lift when I am with them and it helps to keep me sane. The stresses of motherhood dissipate in their company. I can learn from them and monitor how George is developing. The eldest, Ruby, is often the first to do things: smile, laugh, roll over. Then Jack. George was born three days later so I can check that about three days after Jack has done something new, George can do it too. Amazing that all of that is programmed into his DNA. Thank God, he seems to be normal. I was convinced there would be something wrong with him as punishment for not really wanting him.

We spend another afternoon laughing and sharing our funny experiences, and Myfanwy guffaws occasionally. She is still awful and gross, but I have mellowed a bit towards her. I must admit, she is hysterically funny. And I now realise she is not nearly as stupid as she pretends to be. And she does seem to know a fair bit about babies, I'll give her that.

11 Apple cheesecake

We're back at Annie's again this week – a last minute change of plan as one of the Debbie's was due to host but called this morning to say two of her older children have chicken pox and she is going to be nursing them. Consensus seems to be that it is good to expose babies to these diseases as early as possible, but I am relieved we are going to Annie's instead. I really don't need George to be ill and grouchy on top of everything else. The gang tell me he won't catch it though because he's breastfed. I have no idea whether this is true or an old wives' tale. Another thing I'll have to research when I get home.

Annie is telling us about her mother today. They have a strange relationship. Her mother pops round all the time, but apparently they are not close and not like mother and daughter ought to be. I find this comforting as my mother and I have always had a strained relationship, and it is good to know that I am not alone. It dawns on me that I have never thought to ask any of my friends, from home, or Uni, or at work, about their relationships with their mothers. I just assumed everyone's mother was delightful and charming in public then cold and hostile behind closed doors. I've lived my whole life, so it seems, walking on eggshells for fear she was going to blow at any moment. Annie had a great relationship with her dad apparently, so she tells us, but her parents divorced when she was quite young. And her father died not long afterwards. In between times her mother had remarried to a man called Des. Her story is terribly complicated and I am struggling to follow the plot with my frazzled brain. Annie's mother often seems to be making trouble and Annie explains she is often the cause of arguments. 'She's so demanding. And selfish. And childish. And yet somehow she manages to manipulate me, winding me around her little finger. It drives boyo to distraction. And she is so rude to him. She treats him like a piece of muck she has scraped off the bottom of her shoe. He puts up with it for my sake, but, honestly, you have to have the patience of a saint with my bloody mother,' Annie says. She's not been as honest as this with us before. It is a moment of intimate friendship and trust but then, just as I think we are all going to open up a bit about our mothers, she says, 'You'll have to tell me what you think of this cake I've made.' And we are back on the subject of cake! 'I went to Caerphilly yesterday. Have you been there yet, Charlotte?' She continues, 'It is really quite pretty, you should go. Fabulous castle. You'll like it. I bought this amazing locally-made organic cheese there.'

'What sort of cheese is it, luv?' asks Myfanwy.

'Caerphilly,' Annie says, rather confused at the question. Then she laughs realising that Myfanwy is just joking with her. She continues. 'It is so white and crumbly and delicious. I guess you'll all want to know how I made the cake?' And we do. We've really got into the swing of presenting our recipes like celebrity chefs on TV. We've got the camera angles off pat. 'Well, I wanted to go for something I could make in advance. It was meant to be for Gareth's tea really, but with the change of arrangements today it was handy as it meant I could just pop it in the oven just before you all arrived. That way I don't need to fuss around with it. So, this is ideal. *It should be ready to take out of the oven in about ten minutes as it has been in there for about an hour now. The first thing I did was peel, core and thinly slice the apples. I used dessert apples. Then I sifted some white self-raising flour with one teaspoon of baking powder' – she shows a teaspoon to our pretend camera – 'and stirred in 75g of light muscovado sugar, 50g of raisins, 50g of sultanas, 50g of roughly chopped walnuts and the apple slices. I then beat in two eggs and a little tiny bit of sunflower oil. I put half of the mixture into the cake tin, and then crumbled on the Caerphilly cheese. I used about 225g, I reckon. Then I added the rest of the cake mixture and just left it rough on the top.'*

'Wow, that sounds just great, but none for me, thank you,' says Sioned.

'Oh, Sioned, give it a go. It may sound a bit odd with cheese, but it is just a twist on a cheesecake really,' Annie says.

'No, it's not that, it's that it is no dairy this week as part of my elimination process. I'm so sorry. But I would really like the recipe though so that I could make it for Steve.'

'It's okay. I've done a printout for you already. It's here.'

I am reminded that I haven't brought the parkin recipe for Sioned. It's around somewhere. I looked for it earlier. I remember printing it… just not where I put it. I'll find it tonight though – perhaps in the fridge. I just can't remember anything these days. It's so frustrating.

Later in the afternoon, when it has cooled, Annie serves the cake. 'Wow, that is delicious,' I say. I'm genuinely impressed. 'I thought it sounded a bit mad but actually the cheese is quite tart and that works with the sweet apples. I'll have a second slice.'

'And me, too, 'n' all, like. I do like a sweet tart, I do,' says Myfanwy, winking at me. 'I bet you do too 'n' all, Lottie. You look the sort.'

With that, poor Sioned rushes to the toilet with her hand across her mouth – just because of the smell of the cake. She hasn't even tasted it.

We will have to return to Annie's story about her mother another day. We never seem to be able to finish our conversations.

12 Black Forest gateau

The phone rings.

'Why me?'

'Cuz I cun rely on you, like. You're like me mam in that respect. I knows when you do say you will do summin then you will, 'n' cuz I'm desperate.'

Reluctantly I agree to go early. I don't even want to go at all, let alone early. But she's right, I am the sort of person who does what I say I will… even when it really inconveniences me. It drives Andy mad. He says I've got to learn to say no.

Too late now. Myfanwy opens the door. We have been meeting for weeks and weeks and Myfanwy has finally offered to host a Parentcraft at her terraced house in Newport. Annie and Sioned said yes straight away. What could I say? I've been trying to think of excuses all week. I'm sure she doesn't want to be host, and I am sure we would all prefer to meet at mine, Sioned's or Annie's. There are no others left now; Debbie, the final Debbie remaining in our group, went back to work last week. I had an excuse all lined up. I was going to call them individually mid-morning to offer my apologies, but I was caught completely off-guard by Myfanwy calling me this morning and begging me to come round before Annie and Sioned because she was 'desperate'.

Before I had chance to think I heard myself agreeing to arrive at around 1 pm. And, despite myself, I am early.

'Hello, Myfanwy, I'm sorry I'm a bit early. I always seem to be early,' I say.

'Oh, do call me Muff, luv … or Fanny, all me friends do, like,' she says as she helps me take my coat off. I am balancing George in his very heavy car seat, plus the compulsory nappy bag over my shoulder.

'Why,' and immediately I realise I may regret asking this question, 'are all your nicknames related to female genitalia?'

'Jenny 'oo? Some of me friends do call me Jenny Taylor, actually,' says Muff with a big smirk. 'It's no coincidence, luv, some of me other friends do call me Growler… and me enemies do call me twat.' I tut at her language and shake my head disapprovingly.

She laughs with delight at my disapproval. This has become a familiar pattern.

Muff is a cleaner. Or Muff is a scrubber, as she prefers to say. Her immaculate house is at odds with her filthy mind and foul mouth, but she does, sometimes, tell the most incredibly funny stories. Stories from another world. A world of which I know nothing. The story of Newport low-life. I now accept that she is part of the gang of four and there is nothing I can do or say that will move her on, so I may as well just get on with it. Well, actually, if I'm honest, I'm starting to enjoy her stories. And she is wonderfully funny most of the time. But her foul mouth can just be a bit much sometimes.

Muff welcomes George and makes a big fuss of him. Fussing and cooing. She only saw him last week for heaven's sake. And he smiles at her. He can do that now. People seem pleased with this development, especially Andy, who was convinced he was smiling at him weeks ago when it was probably just wind.

Myfanwy lives in a typical Welsh mid-terrace house, probably originally built for dock-workers. It is much smarter, and bigger, than I expected. It is also in quite a nice part of town, not in some ghetto as I'd expected. Today is full of surprises. I feel a bit ashamed of my assumptions. I'm being like my mother. The house is, as I said, immaculately clean. I pick out the scents of polish, and then bleach, and then air freshener. Not unpleasant, but rather overwhelming. The woman's obsessed. She and her husband, Dai, obviously pay attention to every detail in their house, but everything is over-fussy and elaborate. The house really, really is spotlessly clean. From her front door, I walk down a short corridor into Myfanwy's living room. Family photographs are everywhere. The walls are covered. It is like a rogues' gallery. There are photos of what appears to be nieces and nephews, then a few family weddings where a number of the guests look very dodgy indeed. I've never seen so many tattoos in a wedding photo – and not just the men. Even the bride seems to have quite few, too. One seems to be a cowboy wedding judging by the attire, but I notice a big sign in the background that says Pontypool RFC, so I'm guessing not real cowboys.

Her living room is quite large, very clean – I think I'm becoming obsessed with her cleaning skills – but completely full of photographs and ornaments. Everywhere! Every space has something on it. There are doilies under cheap tacky ornaments on every surface. It is decorated in cream and dusty pink with a very plush, dusty pink deep-pile carpet. 'Oh, this is a lovely room, Myfanwy,' I say out of politeness, and then add, 'isn't it difficult to keep this carpet clean though with a baby?'

'Oh, it's not too bad, luv,' beams Myfanwy, as I settle into her cream leather huge sofa which is far too big for the room but actually extraordinarily comfy. 'A lot of people do think I am mad having cream and pink, but actually the sofa is really good, like, cuz you can just wipe off the baby sick and baby poo quite easy.'

'So,' I ask, 'where is the disaster you urgently need help with?' referring to our earlier telephone conversation.

'In the bin. It was too 'orrible for words. I did just chuck it away,' Myfanwy says.

'So, why did you need me to be here early, then?' I ask.

'I don't, luv.'

'Why didn't you tell me so that I didn't come early?'

'Aww. Didn't think of that, like, luv.'

It'll be a long wait until Sioned and Annie arrive. I'll just have to sit it out. Myfanwy fills the time by talking non-stop. Thankfully, a lot of it is really funny, although there is a fair percentage that I don't understand at all. She places a large mug of tea in my hand, which I put onto the coaster on the small, lace-tableclothed side table. I can hear George stirring in his car seat, and my breasts spring into action. Myfanwy gets me a large glass of water while George latches on. I'll wait until my tea is cold to drink it. It's how we do things now. Myfanwy tells me about her family, pointing at different photos as she does. They are lots of them: aunts, uncles, cousins. She has an incredibly close relationship with her parents and her sister. From her stories I see a life very different to my own relationships. She and her mother and father, and her sister and her family, seem to spend huge amounts of time together. They all holiday together. They go to the pub together. Everything. They all appear to like each other and choose to be together. I can honestly say this is nothing like my family interactions. Time together is a strain and done out of obligation. Christmas is painful. The best day is the day after Boxing Day when Andy and I can leave my mother and her criticisms. I've just realised that George will give me an excuse not to have to do Christmas with my mother this year. I smile at him.

After the hour's wait, Sioned arrives first with Annie arriving about five minutes later. The room becomes full of women, babies, car seats, nappy bags and a huge crocheted blanket, which Sioned has put on the floor, and there Jack and Ruby lie next to each other as they each wake from their journeys. Chardonnay, Myfanwy's baby, is, I assume, still in her cot upstairs. George has latched onto me again and is sucking away furiously. Will this child never be satisfied? It is constant. But I won't be the first to give up breastfeeding. I just wish one of them would stop so that I can stop too.

I still find it all such hard work. I thought it would be easier by now as George is eight weeks old. Every week there is something new, every week I have questions to ask. 'Is yours doing this yet?' or 'I've noticed that George does this, does yours?' And I listen. I listen intently. I try to learn from what they say, and I gain some confidence to admit my own shortcomings on occasions. We never cover all the topics we want or get to talk to everyone at the same time. Constant nappy changing, feeding, tea and cake keep us busy all afternoon, every Thursday.

When I return from nipping to the bathroom, I find Myfanwy in full swing. She is describing her heightened obsession with cleanliness since first discovering she was pregnant, and has Sioned and Annie in fits of laughter. She is describing her cleaning frenzies. She says how much she is obsessing these days and how she found herself at 3am sterilising the light switches around her house! Her nesting has got even worse since the birth of Chardonnay apparently, and, she admits, she is even more obsessive now. She has continued hoarding too, not just baby lotion. The tins in her stuffed cupboards are 'fronted' on the shelves and in date order (like in supermarkets). And, like her CDs and LPs, they are now in alphabetical order too. Apparently alphabetti spaghetti is first.

'Don't knock that over,' she says with a broad smile, 'it could spell DISASTER.' I have to admit this is funny. I find myself laughing a lot at her stories. She is so free and relaxed about… everything.

'Well, girlies, 'spose you do want to know how I did make this little beauty,' says Myfanwy pointing at the Black Forest gateau on the coffee table. 'Well, I did go to the freezer about two hours ago and took it out and put it there, on that plate, like, to defrost….Yep, sorry, girls, it is shop-bought cake from me. Sara Lee. Take it or leave it.' Myfanwy has a huge smile on her face. We all nod that this is fine and we will opt for the 'take it' option rather than 'leave it.' At least Sioned is lucky as she can use her 'get out of jail free' allergies card to avoid it whereas I am given almost a quarter of cake, and then she covers it with sugary squirty cream, without any consultation as to whether this is what I would like. I prepare myself for the horror of tasting it. It is going to be really synthetic. I close my eyes as I take a mouthful and find, to my complete surprise, that I like it. What is going on? It must be the after-effects of having a baby. I'll check out later if there is any research on the topic of losing all refinement in your tastebuds post-birth.

At that, Sioned says, 'Charlotte that reminds me. Have you got that recipe? The recipe for parkin?'

'I can't believe it. I've forgotten it again,' I say. 'What is the matter with my memory? I am so sorry, Sioned. I have printed it out for you, but I have forgotten to bring it with me again. I put it in my handbag, but I've brought a different bag today. I am just so forgetful at the moment. I will remember when my brain has converted back from its current state of mush. Let's hope it's before we all get old and haggard!'

'Don't worry, no rush,' says Sioned. 'I'm sure you'll remember next week.'

Myfanwy says, 'Listen up girls! 'ere's a story for you. Dai 'n' me was out on the wazz last night. It was me sis's birthday, so our Mam did 'ave Chardonnay for us and we 'ad our first night on the lash on our own since Chardonnay was born. We did walk 'ome from the pub. Actually, to be 'onest what I really did was I walked, then I did puke, then I walked a bit more, then I did puke a bit more, get the picture? I thought the first three times or so I chucked up that I 'ad managed to get away with it without Dai noticing. Shows 'ow pissed I was. Of course, 'e'd noticed. He was 'oldin' me 'air out of the way while I did puke in the gutter, wasn't 'e. When we did get in, 'e bunged me straight in the shower and made me brush me teeth. Then fuck me backwards, didn't we have a fuckin' fantastic night. Now, you know it 'asn't been right since Chardonnay arrived, I'm sure they didn't stitch me up right.'

'What, you mean your fairy?' says Annie.

'What? My fairy? What do you mean, luv?' says Muff.

Annie blushes wildly. 'Your foo-foo. Your mufty. Your muff. Down there. I can't think what else to call it!' she continues.

'Oh, what, you do mean me cunt? Yes, I mean I don't think they stitched my cunt up right. I've had a good look with a mirror and it don't look at all right to me.'

We all gasp in complete shock at her use of the 'c' word. Myfanwy is delighted. She is causing so much shock and consternation once again.

'Oh, I do 'ave so much fun with you lot. You are all so shockable. You posh birds – none of my friends even flicker when I do tell 'em me stories.'

'It's funny, but please don't use the c-word with the babies around, Myfanwy. They are listening all the time, even at this early age,' says Sioned.

Myfanwy has a look of incredulity on her face. She slowly scans Jack and Ruby on the crocheted blanket. Looks too at George pressed against my breast. They are all fast asleep. She allows her eyebrows to convey her thoughts. Her expression makes it obvious that she thinks Sioned is being overly-prissy and too prudish. But she is also delighted as she recognises it makes her jokes work better if at least one of us is offended, so she carries on with her story.

'Okay. I'll leave out the *c-word* if you are all going to be so fuckin' prim. 'onestly! Let me tell you me story. Well, all it needed was a little drinkey-poo and I was away, wasn't I? Dai didn't know what 'ad 'it him, I cun tell you. Like I said, we 'aven't done it since I did 'ave Chardonnay.'

'What, at all?' Annie says.

'No, not full-on sex, like. You know, we've had a little play around, you know, like you do, luv.' She nudges Sioned with her elbow. 'But it's me. I just couldn't get into the mood for weeks, so I ended up giving 'im sucky-offies for a quiet life. Not that 'e was complaining mind, 'e did think it was all 'is birthdays come at once. Ha-ha. Cum at once. Get it? That's a good one. No, but anyway, last night, I don't know if it was because I knew Chardonnay wasn't yer, or because I'd had a fair bit to drink, but I gave 'im one 'ell of a seeing to. 'E can 'ardly walk this morning. But you do want to see the grin on 'is face, girls. I'm telling you, 'e carefully manoeuvred down them steps, given 'is delicate state, beaming from yer to yer this morning. 'e even said good morning to the postman. And 'e can't stand that postman ever since I said I liked his 'air.'

'Hang on a moment. So where is Chardonnay now, Myfanwy?' I ask. 'I assumed she was in her cot upstairs.'

'No, no, luv, she's still at our Mam's. Mam said I could leave her there a few more hours so I went back to bed to sleep off my 'angover. 'ence why I had to go for a frozen cake, girlies! I ruined the one I did try to make. I spent far too much time shagging.'

She didn't even have the baby here when she phoned me in a panic and so desperately needed my help. Then she went back to bed to sleep off her hangover while I was running around like a lunatic so that I could be here early. Why did she do that?

'So how are your boobs Myfanwy, they must be killing you, by now?' asks a concerned Annie.

'Well, I've expressed off about three and a 'arf bottles today, 'ad to throw it away of course. It'll be pure Bacardi Breezer. But I've got so much breastmilk frozen in the freezer anyway that it don't matter. By the way, 'ave you tried those Bacardi Breezers yet? They're bloody lush. My tits are killing me though. Look.' She pulls up her top and bra in one fell swoop and shows us her breasts which are, in her words, 'doing a Dolly Parton,' and she makes each one of us feel how hard and hot they are. I don't quite know how to react, so somehow I end up touching her breasts and agreeing they are, indeed, hot and hard. 'You should 'ave seen them squirting when I was lying in the bath earlier just now. Like the fountains outside City 'all in Cardiff, they were.' Sioned, Annie and I pass a glance that expresses just how glad we are that we missed that particular spectacle.

'So, when we got in last night at, ooh, it must 'ave been gone one, I was completely ratted,' Myfanwy says, continuing with her story. I thought we had finished the topic of what happened last night, but obviously not. 'Dai followed me up them stairs. So I started wiggling my arse, all sexy like, or so I thought. Poor sod, I've looked at the size of my arse in the mirror this morning, 'e must be really desperate if that do give 'im a stiffy. Anyway, we 'ad a bit of a snog on the stairs, and 'e's getting a bit, a bit, what's the word I'm looking for?'

'Amorous?'

'Loving?'

'Sexy?' we suggest.

'Like a fuckin' 'ornbucket. That's the words. Well girls, I can tell you now, 'e certainly did it for me. Twice!'

Too much information. Sioned has realised that it is going to be impossible to get Myfanwy to watch her language if she asks her, it will make her rebellious and do it all the more. We are all from very different backgrounds, and so it is silly to expect us all to behave in the same way and have identical values. Sioned adopts, as we all try to, a laissez-faire approach to Myfanwy's choice language instead. If she doesn't get a reaction perhaps she will stop.

At the end of this outrageous story-telling, and in an attempt to change the subject from Myfanwy's sex life, I pluck George from my breast to show them his new outfit - white with navy blue and red piping. A gift from my great aunt that arrived in the post this morning. To my surprise, they say things like 'Ach-y-fi!' and 'Yuk!' I then discover George has managed to do one of his amazing exploding bottom tricks. I could cry. Coronation chicken coloured poo has squirted out of the leg holes of his nappy and at the top too, all over the back of his new clothes. I had only changed him into this brand new nautical outfit about two minutes before we left the house. I doubt these stains will ever come out. I won't mention it to Aunt Matilda. She'll tell my mother and then, somehow, it will all be my fault. I'll put the outfit straight in the bin when I get home.

Exasperated, I take him off to the dining room with the nappy bag over my shoulder, ready to change his nappy and then change him into a completely new outfit – I have learned already to have at least two spare changes of baby clothes with me if I even step outside the front door.

With that, there is a knock at the door. I call to Myfanwy who tells me to go ahead and open it and see who it is. After a brief conversation I call out, 'Myfanwy, there's a workman at your front door who says he is called "Kev the Lay". He says he is your "carpet man". He says he left one of his cutters behind when he finished laying your brand new carpet a few hours ago!'

'Busted!' Myfanwy grins at the group. 'I am really 'ouse proud, like, and couldn't have let you lot see me tatty old carpet, so as soon as I knew we were going to each other's 'ouses on a Thursday afternoon I ordered a new dusty pink shag pile. I love that name, shag pile, and I did get Dai straight on the overtime. They do call him Dai the Doubler at work now because 'e 'as done so many double shifts to pay for the carpet. That's why we had to wait a few weeks for you lot to come yer, like. Ha ha! Can't believe it, busted straight away. Didn't even last a day.'

Kevin the Lay shifts awkwardly from foot to foot, looking for his cutters whilst trying to avoid looking at the busted Myfanwy and the abundance of breasts in the room.

'Oh, Myfanwy, poor Dai,' says Annie.

'Poor Dai, my fuckin' arse. 'e got his own shag pile last night, didn't 'e!'

When we all finally leave, after eating the whole cake, and drinking innumerable cups of tea, Myfanwy gently touches my elbow at the front door. 'Thanks for coming early, Lottie, luv,' she says. 'I felt really grotty this morning. Kev the Lay had taken far longer than I thought fitting the carpet, 'n' the cake was a disaster so I thought you might be able to help. 'N' I was right. I cun rely on you, like I thought. 'N' I wanted to make sure you did come along. I knows you need to get out. And I cun see how much you do like a good laugh 'n' all. You always end up laughing at Parentcraft 'n' leave with a big smile on yer face. I likes that, I doos.'

Once again, she has me sussed. She is a constant source of amazement.

13 Lemon Pots

Weeks pass, and Parentcraft regularly visits mine, Myfanwy's, Annie's and Sioned's homes again, and occasionally a Debbie or Tracey will rejoin and host. Today, however, we are back at Myfanwy's house – this'll be our last Parentcraft before I return to work. I can't believe six months have passed so quickly.

Myfanwy has had her curly dark hair cut into a mid-length style, and she is looking like she has lost a bit of weight, damn her. But she still has her absolutely foul mouth. She opens the front door to me and George and before I even have chance to say, 'Sorry I am so early,' she greets me with, 'Thank fuck you are yer. It's a fuckin' disaster in that kitchen, I'm telling you! Get in yer quick! I'm just not up to your lot's standard, luv, I could fuckin' cry.'

I follow her into the kitchen, and see the fridge door is open. Myfanwy is standing next to it, looking rather weepy over the eight lemon pots she has made this morning. The expression on her face is one of terror and foreboding doom. I feel a degree of sympathy for the woman.

Myfanwy phoned me early this morning to say, 'The cake situation ain't going well again, luv'. Why always me? I have no idea! I tried to protest, I reminded her she could always defrost a cake, as she has a couple of times before, and everyone was happy with that, asked why her mother couldn't help, or someone else, but finally agreed, under some duress, to come to her house a bit early again to help out whilst she got things prepared. She got me at, 'I knows I cun rely on you, like.'

'The recipe did say they were easy, that's why I chose it,' Myfanwy says. 'Damn that Delia Smith. 'er picture of them lemon pots looks nothing like these. Damn 'er, and 'er silly, smiley face. Damn Norwich Football Club. Damn, damn, damn! And buggery! And what do you think about these ramekins, then? I bought them from the pound shop in Maindee yesterday. Do you think they will be okay straight from the fridge to the oven, like?'

I check the ramekin – it has oven/freezer proof stamped on the bottom. So I do my best to reassure Myfanwy, but it must be said that her mixture does look really sad in the base of each ramekin.

'I'm sure when you have baked them they will be just fine, how did you make them anyway?' I ask.

I really must learn to not ask these sort of questions because Myfanwy tells me, in great detail, how she made everything, starting from three days ago. Apparently, Chardonnay is really cranky as she has had colic for the past three nights. Myfanwy tells me how she has had quite a few interrupted nights sleep and is not functioning at her best. This takes about ten minutes and is the precursor to her finding the right lemons.

To move her on, I say, 'Why don't you talk me through how you made them. Treat this as a practice run for telling Annie and Sioned your recipe. You know they both like to hear the recipes. They won't rest until you have told them every fine detail.' She looks panic-stricken and in a moment of unplanned kindness I say, 'I tell you what, why don't you tell them it's Delia Smith's recipe if they don't like it and claim it as your own if they are a huge success? I won't let on its Delia's, if you don't.'

'Good idea, luv. I bloody love that,' Myfanwy says. 'I wouldn't have put you down as a liar, tho' Lottie, luv. What a surprise. Good girl. Well, this is 'ow I did make 'em, like. *I whisked up some large eggs with caster sugar and lemon juice, and the zest of some lemons. I made sure I bought them unwaxed ones like Sioned said the other week, took bloody ages to find 'em.'*

I move her on quickly before I hear more of her lemon shopping stories.

'Then I did whisk in some single cream. That's the mixture in the ramekins now.' She says, nodding towards the pale yellow splodge at the base of each ramekin. 'Okay. Let's do it. I'll stick them in the oven now, then if they are a disaster I will just serve the Sara Lee. They'll 'ave to eat it frozen. It'll be alright though. I'll tell 'em it is icecream cake. They won't know it's not. Bung the kettle on will you, luv.'

I am taken aback. She's giving me orders now. But, politely, I say, 'What do you need hot water for?'

'Two things,' replies Myfanwy. 'One, I do need to put these ramekins into the oven in a roasting dish filled with boiling water.

Delia do say so, and two, you cun make us a cup of tea,' she smiles, cheekily.

So, I make tea!

Myfanwy bakes the lemon pots for about twenty minutes and they look fine… better than fine, they actually look quite good. 'Delia 'oo?' she says to me. 'Delia Smith?' She feigns hard-of-hearing. 'No, never fucking heard of 'er. These little beauties are all my own invention.' She smiles and nudges me. 'Sound convincing?'

She has prepared whipping cream as per the instructions and has kept back a little zest for the toppings to add when she is ready to serve. It appears she can follow instructions.

Thank goodness, Sioned and Annie arrive shortly afterwards. 'Well, girls, listen to this,' Annie says. 'You know what a dope Gareth can be at times. Honestly. Remember how he completely freaked at the little hat they popped on Ruby's head when she was first born. Remember? He thought it was because half her head was missing! Well, you're going to love this story. It was my mother who started it. She mentioned to Gareth that she thought there was something wrong with Ruby's hearing. So, that was it. Gareth went in to panic mode. The thing is, there's always something wrong with Ruby according to my mother. So, you'll never guess what Gareth asked the health visitor this week? He asked her to check out Ruby's hearing thoroughly. The health visitor asked if there was anything in particular concerning him. Had he observed something? And he said he was worried because he is deaf in one ear. So the health visitor took him really seriously, and with great compassion said, "Oh yes, I can understand your concern. Do any other members of your family have the same condition, parents, grandparents, siblings?" And he says, "No, just me. I pierced my eardrum with a wire coathanger when I was eleven".'

'You are not serious, Annie. You're making it up surely?' I say. 'He can't possibly have thought that Ruby would inherit his deafness when it was an accident? And how did he manage to get a wire coathanger in his ear anyway?'

'Don't ask. What a nutter,' Annie says. 'Seriously, though, he asked the health visitor. I was desperately trying to suppress my laughter. Even when she tried to convince him that it couldn't possibly be genetically passed on when he had had an accident. I kept a straight face when he looked at me. I didn't want to undermine him. That night, I found him with Ruby on a blanket on the sofa, waving her favourite rattly toy around to see if she looked in the right direction. Even so, he's still not convinced.'

'Aww! Bless him, Annie. He's a sweetheart isn't he,' says Sioned.

'So, how are you getting on with your cakes this time, Myfanwy? Have they worked?' asks Sioned.

'All sorted now,' says Myfanwy. 'They're me own recipe, you know. Lemon pots. I did make up the recipe, 'n' everything. All me own invention.' She gives me a big conspiratorial wink.

'Sorry, I am cutting out citrus fruit from my diet this week,' says Sioned. 'Still, I'll be fine with a black coffee today as I have already had an enormous lunch.'

I feel so sorry for Sioned. It must be so miserable going through this elimination process. She doesn't look unhealthy though, far from it. She is incredibly slim for a woman who has had a baby. I am very envious as I look down at my stubborn rolls of fat.

I'm relaxed with these women. Something about having been through childbirth has brought a strong bond that I genuinely didn't expect. We are all laughing uncontrollably at poor Gareth as we tuck in to the surprisingly good Lemon Pots (good old Delia – you can't go wrong with Delia) which are sitting on the table next to the Sara Lee 'icecream cake' that is there as Myfanwy's reserve. I imagine we'll also finish that by the end of the day. I really don't understand why I eat so much cake when I know I am trying to lose weight.

'So, Lottie, luv,' says an eager-faced Myfanwy, 'do you 'ave your childcare sorted, now, like?' It appears that no matter how many times I tell her, she is going to carry on calling me Lottie regardless. I had caused some consternation a few weeks ago when I admitted that I hadn't yet sorted childcare. In fairness to myself, I really thought it would be easy – that you'd just phone and book a place. I didn't know anything about waiting lists and nursery places.

I should have been back in work by now, but my return date has been delayed by a couple of weeks. It seems that the way it works is that I have to stick to my committed dates with QXL, but it was fine for them to write to me and extend my time by a fortnight due to 'operational requirements'. Sioned and Annie say this is not right, but I haven't got the strength to argue and I don't want to go back to a bad feeling with the already prickly HR Director. I've also discovered the promotion I was hoping for before I discovered I was pregnant has also been delayed for operational reasons. Budget reasons actually. Now it seems that the promotion won't go through this Financial Year, according to the HR Director who called me at the most inappropriate moment – she always does, I don't know how she manages it, I think George's exploding bottom and she have a hot line – and really couldn't understand why I was disappointed. So it is now going to be next April, at the earliest, before I can expect a pay rise, which extends the amount of time we will have to spend in Newport. Can I bear Newport any longer? I suppose I will just have to wait. Andy will be pleased though. He's enjoying having his mates nearby. And I'd certainly miss the Parentcraft bunch. Anyway, the decision to extend my maternity leave caused me some surprise. I wasn't looking forward to going back in the same way I was at the beginning. George and I have our routine. I am very lucky, he's such a good baby. I'm dreading stopping breastfeeding actually – it's our special time together. I've decided to keep breastfeeding when I return to work, if I can.

Anyway, all three of the remaining Parentcraft were aghast that I didn't have plans in place, and I decided I really would have to do something when Myfanwy started suggesting people she knew who would 'look after the kiddie, like'. I realised the conversation was hurtling towards her suggesting that she could do it. Perish the thought. Andy would have a fit if George ended up with a coarse Newport accent. Yet he wants to stay here. I'm not sure I really understand people from Newport at all. They bad-mouth it all the time and yet they want to stay. Why?

SECTION TWO

14 Carrot cake

Once I finally did it, returning to work wasn't anywhere near as bad as I expected. I didn't think I'd cope with working and looking after a child, but working is so much easier than looking after a baby all day. And yet people think I am marvellous to be working full-time. I can honestly say that the time in work is a doddle in comparison to the evenings and weekends, where I have to look after a baby and a husband. What's more, in work, people say thank you. I quickly got into the stride of it and colleagues at all levels seemed genuinely pleased to see me again and wanted to see photos of George. I felt very proud as I showed them the little pocket photo album I'd taken to carry around with me for just such moments. Time passed and I'm not sure when, but at some point my mood finally fully lifted to my pre-pregnancy days. I've got used to, and rather enjoy, having little George around now. He has developed his own little personality, and he's a handsome boy, like his daddy. And he is a clever little thing too. He likes sitting with me while I read to him, and I'm very proud of his ability to count. Andy and George adore each other, of course. They have rough and tumble fights on the sofa before bedtime. Sometimes it's a bit too much and it ends in tears, but Andy is great at soothing him. When Andy does some DIY, George gets out his toy hammer and toy drill and 'helps'. It is so sweet. He's like a mini version of Andy to look at, but I think he has a fair bit of my nerdy personality. I'm rather proud of that too.

I have become very skilled at managing our lives around all the conflicting needs – I've had to, really! There wasn't much choice. All of Andy's sports and socialising with his friends; George's needs, first as a baby, then as a toddler, then a little person; and lastly my needs, which mostly are not my needs but work's. My promotion finally arrived but it took so much longer to materialise than the HR Director led me to believe when I was on maternity leave. It took a couple of years, in fact. But I got there in the end, well, in title at least. The catching up on pay seems still to be taking its time but, as the HR Director stated quite forcefully, I have to be patient. I can't just expect these things to happen overnight.

My mood has definitely improved, I'm glad to say, as vouched for by my team of developers at our last team meeting. I mentioned, just in passing, that one of the secretaries in the Global Marketing team, who is heavily pregnant, and ratty as hell, was very rude to me when I asked her about the Autumn campaign. I said, quite casually, 'I'm glad I didn't have massive mood swings when I was pregnant.' The raucous laughter that followed was rather uncalled for! After they'd wiped their eyes and all settled down again, John, my Team Leader, sheepishly gave the full-horror confession… I would bite their heads off, apparently, if they said the slightest thing I didn't agree with, or roll my eyes and huff and puff. How embarrassing. I had no idea! I thought I'd kept my hormonal surges well-hidden from my team and work. I joined in their laughter, though, when they told me. I can see the funny side of it. Me, thinking I was this calm swan, and the team avoiding a wild goose. I checked out their version with Andy later and he said I was bloody awful throughout most of my pregnancy and that he'd had to put up with a lot, what with my moods and then the forgetfulness. Ironically, I can't remember the forgetfulness very much at all now. I remember complaining about it at Parentcraft, but not why it was such a big deal.

In the early days of being back at work I wasn't sure if I would be able to stay in touch with Parentcraft. But thanks to the efforts of Sioned, Annie and especially, bless her, Myfanwy, who reached out to me regularly, I was kept abreast of the goings on. And as I started to feel more like myself, the more I appreciated their friendship. I'm glad they keep in touch. I like this touchstone on reality. They still meet every week, and I get there whenever I can. I've not managed to get there quite as much this year, certainly not as much as I would like. I always intend to go but, it seems, work always needs me on a Thursday afternoon. I went back to my full-time hours as soon as I could – it's the only way to have a career at QXL. Even when I had my full-time hours back, it was still really hard to get my promotion approved and I saw my assistant – two in fact – promoted over me before I finally got mine. Nice guys, and they worked hard, good Subject Matter Experts, they deserved their promotions – in fact, I coached them for the interviews as they had become quite specialist, and needed some of my 'all-round' knowledge. I was really pleased it worked for them, but, as for me, I seemed to be in a fugue for a long time, and had lost my identity at work somehow. Being an all-rounder seemed to be my downfall. The 'me' opportunity just didn't seem to come round. Then, finally, they announced they were creating a new role that I knew would be a perfect fit for my breadth of skills. I was so excited I could hardly contain myself. I rang Andy straight away from the office. I only bother him at work if it is something really important. And this was, is, really important to me. Andy said he was pleased for me, but I'd have to consider how it would work with George. As if I hadn't thought about that. Honestly, he can be such a dope at times, bless him. But to my great disappointment, at the interview they said the new role would be based in the Bristol office, not London, or overseas, as I was expecting. Nigel, my boss, strode through the open plan office in his pinstripe suit, his usual smug look on his shiny, fat face, shouting hellos across the office and slapping the guys jovially, but rather too heavily, on their backs as he strode by. I wonder if he has any idea how much they grimace when they hear him coming. He thinks he is the best boss ever. Arriving at my desk, and standing over me, he told me with great delight, and very loudly, so that all could hear, that it was all sorted, the interview panel had approved my promotion, that he had, in fact, sorted it, and that he'd sorted it for me that the role could be based in Bristol. Sorted! I think he genuinely thought he was doing me a big favour, as he gave me a big wink, but he'd never asked me. And a mean thought flashed through my mind that this meant no relocation payment nor extra travel expenses out of his P&L. Was this the real reason for his glee? I suppressed my disappointment. He hadn't asked, no one had asked me, whether I wanted my base to be Bristol. And I never said anything as it meant admitting that it is, in truth, Andy who wants to live in Newport, not me. So, with good grace, I said thank you. My team stood up from behind their cubicles and gave thumbs up, and a small round of applause broke out. Nigel assumed it was him and gestured that it was nothing really and that he 'sorted' things all the time. I was so hoping for a good reason to move away from Nigel being my direct boss. I was hoping for a good reason to move away from Newport. I was hoping to move away, once and for all, from this stage of my life and back onto my real career trajectory. But, in truth, I'm not sure if I would have persuaded Andy to move. He seems very settled, although he is very grumpy most of the time. Men, eh!

So that brings us to now. After another busy day at work, and having collected George, I am standing in my hallway when I press 1571 on the phone. 'Oi. Missus. Isn't it about time you got yer arse in gear? It's been bloody ages since we did see you last time. Next Thursday. Sioned's. That's the one in Caerleon, in case you can't remember,' is the message. No need to guess who that is. Thank goodness I now use 1571 so at least I can just hear the message and immediately delete it. I used to have to press 'play' on my old answerphone machine and the message would blast across the hallway. It was very embarrassing at times, and I was concerned that George's first words would be something rude he'd picked up from one of Myfanwy's messages. Myfanwy has no filters.

Today is a bit of a Parentcraft reunion of sorts, as I realise it is over two months since I managed to get to the last one. I have booked the afternoon off. I think I deserve it. What's more, they all seem so pleased to see and greet me with, 'Hello, stranger'; 'Good to see you looking so well, Charlotte, and great to see George too'; and 'Fuckin' 'ell, look what the cat's dragged in'.

George, Jack, Ruby and Chardonnay play together nicely… well, most of the time. George is the peacekeeper as Jack and

Chardonnay often fight. Sometimes Sioned and Myfanwy have to pull them apart. They are both full of fighting spirit! Ruby is much more placid, like George.

'Just a quick carrot cake from me today, you lovely ladies,' says Sioned as she triumphantly presents a very large carrot cake with mascarpone topping. It looks delicious. I've been so good with my diet at work the last couple of months, but this cannot be missed. I scarcely eat a thing during the day. I'm back to my pre-pregnancy weight, although my size and shape seem to have been permanently altered. I'm not fat… but I'm certainly not skinny either. I'll just have to be careful that this cake doesn't take me back to square one… or round one in my case.

'Come on then, give us the low down. How did you make it?' Annie asks. It's the familiar routine from when we first met and they seem to have kept the tradition going - rattling off recipes, like a TV chef.

'It's not hard at all, this one' says Sioned.

'Not 'ard, is it, luv. Poor Steve. Gorra a proper floppy one as 'e?' laughs Myfanwy. They laugh. I laugh. I find it reassuring that she never changes.

Sioned continues, *'The topping is very traditional, 250g mascarpone, two tablespoons each of orange juice and icing sugar, and a little orange rind. The cake is pretty standard too – cream 225g each of unsalted butter and caster sugar. Sift in 175g of self-raising flour, one teaspoon of baking powder and ½ a teaspoon of allspice. Then add 4 eggs, the rind of one large orange, one tablespoon of fresh orange juice and 50g of ground almonds. Beat it well, then add 350g of finely grated carrot and 125g of coarsely-chopped walnuts. I put the mixture into two cake tins, then I baked them for about 35 to 40 minutes in the centre of the AGA. Then, I made some carrot spaghetti and fried it in a tiny bit of butter! I'm not sure if this is going to work, but it looks pretty on the top of the cake, especially with the icing sugar.'*

It is, as it looks, delicious! No lunch for me next week as I take a second slice.

'Luvly, luv,' says Myfanwy, as she stuffs cake into her mouth. 'Did I tell you I think I do 'ave the same thing as me Mam?'

'What's that?' I ask.

'Necrophilia, like.'

'Oh my God! What?' I say.

'I think I do 'ave got the same thing as me mam do 'ave, necrophilia,' repeats Myfanwy, slowly, as if we are all simpletons, as she munches on the carrot cake and signals a thumbs-up again to Sioned.

'What on earth do you mean?' Annie says.

'The same thing as our mam, necrophilia. She's 'ad it for yers. It's a right pain. She's a bloody martyr to it.'

'Hang on, Muff, are you sure you mean necrophilia?' Annie asks.

'Yes, yes, she's 'ad it for yers. It's a right pain,' Myfanwy repeats. 'And I'm starting to get it now 'n' all, like.'

'So what are you getting exactly?' Annie enquires, dubiously.

'You know, the tiredness like. I just can't keep me fuckin' eyes open. It's terrible, it is. I might be in the middle of talking to Dai, or sorting out something for Chardonnay when, whoosh, I'm gone.'

'That's not necrophilia, that's narcolepsy,' says Sioned.

'Is it? What's necrophilia then, luv?' asks Myfanwy.

'Technically, it is a love of the dead, but it actually means, in practice, having sex with dead people,' Sioned says.

'Ah, right you are then, no dead sex for me. It's not that necrophilia I've got, its nar-co-lepsy.'

'Thank God you haven't been to the doctor about it yet. You could have been having a very embarrassing conversation with her. And I don't think you have narcolepsy *or* necrophilia,' Sioned says. 'I think you could be pregnant, Muff!'

'Shit. Fuck me backwards,' Myfanwy says. 'Sioned, you could be fuckin' right! Come to think of it, I was like this with Chardonnay, like. Anyone got a pregnancy test kit on 'em?'

'Yes,' reply Sioned and Annie simultaneously, as they start to hunt in their handbags. It is obviously a good time for trying for a second baby, even though I'm sure I remember that all of us swore that we would never have another after the horror of the first.

Somehow, they seem to have relented. Whatever hormone it is that makes you so forgetful during pregnancy and after having the baby must also make you forget the horrors of childbirth. I suppose its nature's way of making sure women have more than one baby. Not me though. There is no way I am going back to that. I am only just beginning to feel my head and my body are coming back to me. And my career is still several steps behind where it really should be despite the promotion – I really should have had that years ago. I must let it go. I seem to be mentioning it all the time. But I should have. And I shouldn't have had to fight tooth and nail for it like I did. Nor should I have had to explain at the promotion board how I was going to 'manage'. I bet they didn't ask any of the new fathers how they were going to 'manage' with a young child. But what can you say? So, I just answered the question honestly about all the arrangements I had in place for childcare so that I could manage working full-time. The panel nodded sagely as if this were a totally familiar question and answer.

Myfanwy returns from the loo with a beaming smile on her face. 'Muff is up the duff!' she announces with great delight. 'Me mam is gunna be so pleased, she's been nagging me fr'ages to 'ave another one.'

Annie and Sioned wrap their arms around her and offer heartfelt congratulations. I join in the congratulations. I'm pleased for Myfanwy, but I thank the heavens that it is not me.

15 Bara Brith

It is only three weeks later and I am managing to squeeze in another Parentcraft. I so enjoyed the last one, it did me good, lifted my spirits even more. And Myfanwy's latest message of, 'Oi, twat features, come 'n' see us on Thursday. We're at Annie's this time. 'Er new 'ouse, mind, don't go to 'er old place like a complete wanker,' made me laugh out loud when I heard it. I hadn't realised I'd been feeling the pressure of my new role – all self-imposed, I know – but I so desperately want to show them that I was worthy of this promotion and that I could be ready for another step-up very soon. My promotion has also meant even more hours at work, and balancing everything Andy and George need was a constant battle even before this. Now I have the additional pressure of showing how well I am coping because I suspect everyone will be watching my performance, looking for cracks. So, as an investment in 'me', I've decided to take the occasional Thursday afternoon off. I admit, I then work in the evening, when I have got George to bed and Andy is watching the TV with a can of beer. I rest against his shoulder with my laptop on my lap so that I can catch up with what I have missed during the day. In my job, it's vital to be on message 24/7. The stresses of my new role do not come from managing a bigger team, although they are by no means easy – they include my old development team, who are pretty much self-sufficient these days, and a new bunch of techie prima-donnas, who are hard work but manageable. Nor do the stresses come from the bigger budget I am now managing. In fact, both of these factors were criteria for my promotion, so I am rather surprised to find they are much easier than I expected. I have some wiggle room now that I didn't have with the smaller team and the very tight budget. No, the stresses come from the incessant meetings and conference calls, where I agree to do a whole host of things, but never have the time to implement them properly before I am rushing off to the next meeting or call. And the calls are getting earlier and earlier… and later and later. I was speaking to colleagues at 6.30am one day last week, while sitting on the loo with my hair still wrapped in a towel. (I was at home you'll be pleased to hear.) And then, on the same day, my former assistant called at 9.30pm. He's a good guy, but he needs some coaching. As he's based in Hong Kong now, it was mega early for him. As a global company it just works out like this some days. It's not every day, of course, but it is increasingly like this. As a result, my work feels a bit slap-dash to me at the moment, and I hate that. I will have to create some space in my diary to do this new role properly. Because I love working. I was really good at my old job, and I really want to show that I can be even better in my new one. With that in mind, I am amazed to find that I have made this 'me time' for Parentcraft when there are so many other priorities. A bit of self-preservation must be kicking in, something we talked about at our last leadership training event.

By mid-morning today though I was feeling really cross with myself for committing to Parentcraft. It was really difficult to leave at lunchtime when I knew the morning meeting I had attended (badly chaired by guffawing Nigel) overran. They are reconvening at 2pm. But, I did it, I left the office. And I'm here now and, although feeling guilty for not being at work, I'm beginning to relax and enjoy their company again. I'm definitely looking forward to laughing. Laughter is always on the menu. And it is a special sort of laughter, perhaps because we all went through having our children at the same time. The result is an incredibly strong bond with this lot. I laugh in a different way especially at the totally outrageous, but hysterically funny, Myfanwy. And I love it.

We're at Annie's new house this time, a 1930s semi-detached. It's really very pretty. The garish, clashing 'Changing Rooms' colours of the very early 1990s have waned; out with the lime green and in with the oversized patterns. There are more subtle shades in Annie's new décor, although the wallpaper on the chimney breast in the main room is quite pronounced in a vibrant red alongside her black wood furniture.

'Go on then, how did you make it? We can't have a Parentcraft and not hear the recipe!' I say.

Annie grins broadly. *'It's Bara Brith. That's Welsh for freckled bread,' she says to me. 'It's a doddle. My grandmother used to make this with the bread leftovers from Sunday tea, so I don't know if other people make it this way, but it's the way I do it. Take any dried currants, raisins, or other dried fruit providing it is chopped up small, and soak them overnight in a cup of cold, sugary, milky tea. In the morning mix it with 450g of self-raising flour, one egg, four tablespoons of soft brown sugar, and some mixed spice. Sometimes I add some marmalade too – not today though, I didn't have any. Just bung it in a greased loaf tin and bake for about one and a half hours or so. The usual "skewer coming out cleanly" is the test. So you have a choice now, you can have it with butter, with cheese or with jam.'*

'Oh, so you can have this with butter?' I say. 'Not like Welshcakes.'

'No, luv, only a right twat, someone really thick, like… or English, would put butter on a Welshcake. That's fuckin' mental!' says Myfanwy. Her mouth is already crammed with a large slice of bara brith, as she has opted for the butter-only variety. She nudges me with her elbow – from Myfanwy this is a sign of affection.

I choose to eat mine with butter. As I am licking the crumbs from my fingers, Sioned says to me, 'Did you ever find that recipe for, what was it called, Parkie?' What a memory she has! I had forgotten all about it. It was from one of our first Parentcraft meetings. I promise to try to find it for the next time we meet up, or print out a new version. It'll be on a back-up drive somewhere in my archives.

Myfanwy and Annie are sorting the tippy-cup drinks, slices of fruit and small boxes of raisins for the four children, who are making an unbelievable amount of noise for such small beings.

Sioned and I are sitting on Annie's new leather sofa. We have got into quite a deep, but loud to overcome the noise of the children, conversation lamenting our commute to Bristol, and worse still, the queues to pay the toll on the way home. Funny how you have to pay to get into Wales, but it is free to get out, I say to her. Sioned says it is because it is worth paying to enter God's own country. The Welsh! They take every opportunity to remind me we live in Wales and how much they love it. Yet they slag off Newport *all* the time. They tell me it is a sign of affection. But if I dare to criticise Newport, well, they are on me like a ton of bricks.

I mention how much I like Sioned's hair. She blushes. Isn't she sweet. She has started to grow it and is wearing it straight, with just a simple centre parting. I really like it. I wonder if mine would work in such a simple style? Sioned always looks glamorous whatever she does, though. Perhaps it is because she is so slim. Her original intention, she tells me, had been to tie it up each day, or twist it into a fancy French pleat, but most mornings she finds herself up against the clock getting Jack ready and allowing sufficient time for the commute to Bristol, so usually she jumps in the car with her hair still wet from the shower and hopes that, with the air vents in the car on full blast, it will be dry by the time she goes into the office. Today, she is wearing a bottle-green trouser suit with a tight polo neck jumper in cream. Her figure is trim and petite – probably due to all the running around she does. She never stops. And she has joined a gym, too. How does she find the time? I wish I could get my act together like Sioned. I am in awe of her resolve.

She is telling me about her working day in the media, and I love hearing about it. My work is so important to me and I like to get a feel for how other people's working lives pan out. Sioned's air-conditioned offices of glass and chrome remind her, she says, that business is always a bit fake – living in a bubble while the world passes by outside. I don't feel like this. My work is everything to me. It keeps me sane. She works in a large open-plan office of hotdesks, so there is little opportunity to stamp your own mark. Sioned says she finds this beneficial as she cannot bear to have photos of Steve or Jack on her desk. She finds it far too distracting. Whilst in work she likes to focus and crack on with her workload, and then get out as quickly as possible, but since the arrival of her new boss she is, she says, enjoying it a bit more too. But she is racked with guilt when she is not with Jack. And then she is racked with guilt when she is not in work. Ah, just like me! I definitely don't want to be at home all day, but I still manage to feel guilty. I don't think I am making Andy a very good wife, and I am just not a natural mother to George. I know that. But we muddle by. I do my best for them both and try to appease my feelings of guilt. Then, every now and again, I phone my mother and I feel guilty about everything all over again. I don't know how she manages to do that to me every time.

I can relate to Sioned. I feel we are quite similar in many respects. She tells me that she usually selects a hot desk in the far corner of the office well away from the rest of the team, even though they are a good team and she likes her new role. There are very few people within earshot in the early morning so that is when she tries to make the majority of the calls of the day. It used to be you couldn't work effectively because of the noise in the office. Now you can't work effectively because it is too quiet. It's a good observation; it is very quiet in our office too. Sioned says she always chooses to start early if she can – it is the only chance she has of getting on top of everything. She feels guilty about leaving Jack so early, but it seems to be working out okay with the variety of childcare arrangements she has in place. Again, she is like me. Unlike me though, her mother takes Jack a couple of days a week, and her mother-in-law has him on the other two days. (She takes a Thursday off for Parentcraft and to have some time with Jack.) And they are both there, and her father and father-in-law, on call, if anything, like being stuck in traffic, goes wrong. In fact they bicker good-naturedly over who can have him the most. Definitely not like my parents. Neither of them have ever looked after him. They've never even offered. It's only a very occasional visit and then it is exhausting as I have to wait on them. I'd prefer they didn't bother. At least I don't have to put up with them at the same time. They would never be in the same room together… my wedding was a logistical nightmare.

The first crèche I used for George was lovely, and very professional, but too professional in some things as it closed at exactly 6pm. I couldn't always guarantee to be there on the dot, what with the traffic, and the toll, and the people who would want to catch me for 'just one minute' when I was trying to leave each day. There were just too many times when I pulled into the car park to find all the staff standing at the doorway with their coats on and bags over their shoulder, with little George standing with them – coat on, backpack on his back, lunchbox in his hand – just waiting for me. I caught them rolling their eyes. And then, one day, the manager spoke to me about it. Called me into her office! Told me how it was my responsibility to be there on time. The crèche closes at 6pm, she said. Everyone has their own commitments, and they can't all wait for me. I was politely, but well and truly, told off. I found a childminder the next day and did the swap at the end of the month. The childminder works from her own home, so I can drop George in the morning. She gives him breakfast and takes him to nursery. Then she picks him up and I collect him at round about 6pm – and I add in an extra £10 if I have been late during the week. The crèche was great, but I just had to move him. I couldn't cope with any more stress in my life. And trying to get out of meetings at exactly 5pm was impossible most days. I was missing so many important decisions because they were made after I left. This childminder arrangement is so much better for everyone. But my mother wasn't pleased that George was no longer in a crèche. 'Childminders are... common. You chose to have a baby. You should be at home with him. Like I was,' she said unhelpfully. So, I felt guilty again.

Sioned has broken off the conversation with me and commanded us all to listen to her. She wants to tell us a story. It's not like her to hold court. She has a big smirk on her face.

She starts with, 'I have a funny story today. I'd called the IT helpdesk the day before yesterday and it actually resulted in a visit from a real-live human being. Very unusual these days, I can tell you. I, along with some colleagues, have been asked to trial some new technology, some new social media stuff. The company, they told us, "is considering everything in readiness for the next millennium". Now that is what I call forward planning, not just a few years, but a whole millennium!' She smirks again. 'Everyone in my team has been asked to undertake some research into social media and to develop an online presence, a personal website, a sort of blog. It is to my chagrin that I am telling you this, girls, and it must go no further – my professional reputation would be destroyed.'

She then looks seriously at us, and we nod our heads in a way that convinces her of our permanent silence on the matter in hand. Myfanwy shrugs and then nods as she mimes pulling a zip shut across her mouth.

'Darren, from the IT Team, was sitting alongside my hotdesk and had taken over the controls of my laptop in its docking station,' Sioned continues. 'He's a nice lad. He's only about twenty-two or twenty-three. He was wearing a shirt and tie with smart trousers yet he still managed to look scruffy. I have never been able to work out why, just something about his mannerisms makes him look untidy. I asked him, "Why am I receiving all these perverted invites? Surely they can see we are just a normal couple. What makes them interested in us?

'Girls, how I could have made such a basic error is beyond me! It is such a fundamental mistake. "Well, the world is full of strange people, Sioned," Darren said to me. "You are bound to get some strange comments if you post stuff and allow the whole world to access it. There are some real nutters out there, you know." "Yes, I know, I know," I told him, as he reset some of the security settings. "But they all said the same sort of thing, inviting me and Steve to sex romps. Now I know a lot of people think the internet was invented for pornography, but why did they pick on me when there are so many sites they can visit for that sort of thing? I just don't get it." He said, "Well, yes there are lots of porn sites, heaven knows, I should know." At least he had the good grace to look embarrassed at this statement. Poor lad, he blushed to the shade of beetroot. But then he said, "But….hang on a minute. Have you added a photo to your personal website?"

I had. I'd added a beautiful photo of Steve and me on a cruise ship from years ago, long before I was pregnant. We had both got quite tipsy on cocktails on the deck and thought it would be a laugh to have our photo taken because it was such a tacky setting. I was posed on this flower bedecked swing and Steve was pushing me. Surprisingly though, it is a really nice photo of both of us, which is rare, and we both look so relaxed and happy. I had captioned the photo, "Sioned and Steve are willing to give anything a go, including a tacky photo". And then I added, "Interests: making new friends". Then I had tagged the keywords "swing" and "swinging" and added the extra information, "Sioned in front, Steve behind". Do you understand what I'd done, girls? Darren was laughing like a drain. Even then it took me a few moments for it to sink in. I shrieked at him. "Oh no! Delete it fast! No wonder I was getting all of these comments. They think we're swingers." God, I am so naïve sometimes. I begged him not to tell anyone. I would be a laughing stock.

'Then I said to him, "While you are at it, Darren, can you delete all my internet searches today, too, please?' He looked a bit bemused. "Why, what've you've searched for? Swings?" he asked. He was still laughing at my faux-pas. I told him that I need a new stylish fridge-freezer and I'd like to have a brightly coloured one. I'd tried to think of a good manufacturer. I wanted to see what it looked like. So I typed "SMEG colourful images". I was so shocked by what came up! "Came up" really is what happened. I begged him to delete all the images from my history before I got the sack. This made him laugh all the more. "You really are dippy of late Sioned. What's up with you? You never used to be such an airhead," he said. I swallowed hard as a second thought for the day took a moment to sink in. I left him deleting records on my laptop and made my way to the ladies toilet. And, there you have it, girls. I am dippy. Baby number two is making its presence felt already. That's my news! What do you think of that, ladies?'

Annie throws her arms around her with glee. Myfanwy whoops with delight. I offer my congratulations. She's as mad as the rest of them.

16 Dark chocolate log

I do my best to stay in contact with Parentcraft. I was a bit concerned that it'd all be about the new pregnancies, and then new babies, assuming that the talk would be about baby this and baby that all over again. And, to be honest, I was a bit concerned that it would bring all those memories back from when I was pregnant with George. All those negative feelings that I've worked so hard to get rid of. I was especially concerned that it would remind me of those bleak, dark days when I nearly terminated. I don't want to think about that. I don't want to be reminded. But they kept reaching out to me and made sure I stayed in touch. Myfanwy had left several extremely embarrassing messages. I long ago realised it is a Newport thing to insult you and swear at you as a sign of affection. Or, at least, I hope this is the case as most of Myfanwy's messages start with, 'Oi, fanny features…' or worse! Her last message on 1571 began, 'Hey! Scrotum sack…' Seriously, how does she know how to shock me every single time?

Annie phoned me last week to tell me the venue for the next Parentcraft and to persuade me to come along. I felt flattered that she'd bothered, it's normally Myfanwy who stays in touch. I found myself blocking out the slot in my new Outlook diary. It's one of the new technology changes I've implemented at a corporate level, taking us away from our old Pegasus mail. I'm feeling rather proud of myself as getting the whole organisation to move was quite a challenge. I want to tell Parentcraft about my success and it is also an attempt to divert the conversation away from babies. In a rare quiet moment, I start telling them about this project. 'So,' I say, 'I went in to the office really early as I had been preparing a business case and I was finalising the slidedeck for the C-levels...'

Myfanwy interrupts with hoots and her honking laughter.

'What's so funny?' I say, genuinely confused.

'You. Saying the 'c' word. Class, luv. I do luv it.'

'I still don't understand. What c word? I haven't said the c word. What are you going on about? Have you been drinking, Myfanwy?'

'No, I ain't been drinkin' luv. Chance'd be a fine thing. I'm laughing at you. You, you just called your bosses cunts. That's as funny as fuck. You said 'cunt' level. I fuckin' love it. 'Specially from you, like.'

'Oh no,' I say, 'You've got the wrong end of the stick. I said c-level. Its business-speak. It means Chief Exec, Chief Finance Officer, Chief Information Officer – that sort of thing. They are all c-level. We also say the c-suite.'

'I think you're the one that 'as got the wrong end of the stick, luv. And everyone in your so-called business world. It must have started as a joke somewhere, cunt level, and now everyone is calling them top bosses 'cunts.' Fuckin' marvellous, mun,' Myfanwy says.

What can I say? What's more, knowing some of the c-level people involved, she could well be right, they can be right c's… characters.

I'm feeling particularly excited as my career at QXL may finally really be starting to take off again. They appointed a new MD of European Markets a few months ago. I've not met him yet, but I've been on several conference calls with him. He sounds great. He's implementing a new strategy and has some great ideas on how to take the business forward. On a conference call yesterday he was saying how he really believes in diversity in the workforce and he was horrified by how under-represented women are at QXL. So my skills may now be both needed and noticed. It's been a long time since I've felt valued. And I feel so much better in myself for knowing I am wanted. Plus, he said, he is really okay about homeworking and being flexible. This could give my career an unexpected and much-needed boost, and hopefully my pay packet too, as my promotion never really resulted in the pay increase I was expecting. Let it go, Charlotte, I tell myself. I want to tell Parentcraft about all these new possibilities. This week we are meeting at Myfanwy's. I knew that would mean a noisy, rambunctious afternoon, but hopefully I'll be able to get a few minutes of airtime.

Now, here's a real shocker. Myfanwy has become something of an expert cake maker. She has made an amazing dark chocolate log…well, she would, wouldn't she? She hoots as she tells us repeatedly, 'It is a chocolate log. It's actually called a 'log', you knows, like a turd, like!' It's enough to turn your stomach listening to her sometimes but, in fairness, the cake is fantastic. It is amazing that from those first sad lemon pots Myfanwy has developed into what can only be described as a very good baker. Very good indeed. I am amazed. Her obsessive behaviour means she has mastered some very complex techniques, too. She practices all the time, apparently. This chocolate log has been covered in chocolate coating that is rich but not too sweet, and she has made a fantastic apricot jam with a tiny amount of chilli that gives it an extra kick and a delicious afterburn. I am very impressed. I reflect on how wrong I was about her. She never used that information, about not bonding with George, against me. I make a mental note to tell her about the Women's Institute. Not that she would really fit in with all the posh ladies, but she would definitely enjoy their baking days. She's so crude. But she's so talented. Her language is awful. But she's so funny. I am always in a state of confusion with Myfanwy. She is so contradictory.

'So, go on, tell us how you made it! Is it yours or Delia's, by the way?' I say, smiling at her.

'It's mine, you cheeky mare!' Myfanwy says. 'Do you think I'd take the credit for a Delia, Queen of Cuisine, cake? It's mine. All mine. Well, I do think so anyway. After a while, it's 'ard to remember which ones people 'ave told me about, which ones I 'ave read, and which ones I did just make up. *To make this, I got out loads of apricot jam from the cupboard. Our mam's been 'elpin' out loads, and jam, that's really easy, like. I've got a pot each for you to take home. You just makes it the same as any other jam. I gets a kilo of dried apricots. Don't buy 'em from a health food shop or supermarket, they cost a bleedin' fortune, get 'em from an Indian shop or in the market. Otherwise you'll need to remortgage the 'ouse to pay for 'em, like. Leave 'em to soak overnight in about three litres of water. In the morning you cun chop them up if you needs to, add the juice from six large lemons – you cun use waxed or unwaxed, don't matter – bring it all to the boil, and then simmer for thirty minutes or so until they are proper squidgy, like, then add three kilos of jam sugar.*

'Don't look at me like that Lottie, luv,' she continues. (I hadn't looked at her any way in particular.) 'You can't make proper jam without proper sugar. Then take a red chilli and chop it as fine

as you possibly can. DO NOT rub yer eyes nor yer fanny with chilli on yer fingers. It fuckin' kills.'

I don't even want to think about that sentence.

'Then add the chilli and boil the 'hool lot for twenty minutes. I read all about 'ow to check for the setting point of jam by looking for wrinkles and stuff like that, but then I did buy a proper sugar thermometer in Poundland for one pound, and so now I do just measure it to 105°C. There is a big line that do say "setting point" on it.

'For the chocolate log,' she laughs again, 'fancy calling a cake a log, I can't believe it, 'oo in their right minds would do that? Anyway, what you do is, right, melt 250g of butter, add at least 200g of dark chocolate, darker the better, this was that 74% stuff, take it off the 'eat, quick like and stir it slowly until it's all melted together, like. Add 450g of me chilli apricot jam, 100g caster sugar, four large eggs, then fold in 250g self-raising flour and add 50g ground almonds and some dark chocolate cocoa powder. Carefully, mind. When you are 'appy with it, put it in a shallow baking tray. I'm not sure 'ow long it took, thirty minutes, maybe more, I just kept skewering mine until it came out clean. Then pop it on a wire rack to cool enough so that you cun fill it with the dark chocolate buttercream.

'The filling is even easier. Melt 50g of the same chocolate in a bowl over simmering water. When the chocolate is cool enough, beat in 100g of butter, then gradually beat in 200g of icing sugar and a tiny drop of vanilla extract. Mine was a bit stiff so I 'ad to add a drop of milk too. Beat the butter in a bowl until soft, then gradually beat in the icing sugar. You might need to beat it again. I did. Fold in the melted chocolate until it's all mixed in. You'll know when it's right cuz it'll all be the same colour.

'Then you just spread on the buttercream and roll it up! I was thinking of making one of me shiny ganaches, but then I thought, you can't polish a turd, so I dusted it with icing sugar instead. That way you wouldn't think it was shit.'

Despite the numerous references to excrement, the cake looks exquisite and tastes divine, and very refined. It is at complete odds with Myfanwy. I am amazed at her skill. I wonder if it is all an elaborate lie and she has somehow become a personal friend of Delia Smith.

There are two new babies lying on the floor on the crocheted shawl in front of us. Sioned had a little girl, Megan, and Myfanwy also had a girl, a second daughter. She called her Silver because 'she did come second, see, ha ha,' as Myfanwy says, every time she is asked. Poor child.

Annie confides she and Gareth have been trying for a second baby but are having difficulty conceiving. They have just been referred to a specialist. She seems to take it all in her stride though and doesn't complain. She asks if I want more children and I answer no, perhaps a tad too quickly, and with perhaps a bit too much vigour, as I see Annie is literally taken aback. Again, everyone assumes all women want babies, and more babies. And I just don't. I may have mellowed as my rattiness subsided, but I know for sure one child is enough. George comes over to me crying, coughing and spluttering. I feel panic, I don't know what to do. Quick as a flash, Myfanwy turns him upside down and I quickly scoop out a handful of sweets from his mouth. Where did he get them from? Why did he put them all in his mouth at once? He finally takes an enormous gasp of air. He could have choked to death. I hug him closely until he stops crying. Definitely, one child is more than enough.

With these new babies on the floor, children running around, teacups and plates of cake everywhere, the house is bedlam. I have to give up trying to tell them about work. They are not really interested. Annie is trying to tell them a funny story, but it is hard to get their undivided attention with the crying babies and choking children interrupting the flow all the time.

'So, let me tell you this,' Annie says. 'Gareth was cleaning the house last Saturday morning on one of his top-to-bottom style spring cleans. He does this every couple of months when he gets paranoid about germs and becomes convinced we're all going to die from the plague or something, so I let him get on with it. I don't know why he always does it on a Saturday morning. Well, I do know, really – it's for two reasons. One, so that he can make the point that he has cleaned the house and we can all live healthily ever after, or at least until his next anxiety attack about dirt. And two, so that I can hear him moaning about it. He's a lovely man, but he does like things just so. And just so means his way.

'He was having his usual rant about the state of the house. Ruby and I know to keep out of his way when he is like that. We could hear Gareth muttering away upstairs. "State of this house. Don't know who makes this bloody mess. Look at this toilet. Can't you keep your own stuff tidy?" He can be quite a pain when he's in this mood. Ruby and I smirked at each other and sniggered quietly. We were sitting together in the big armchair, and I carried on reading with her. We could hear, and see, him from our main lounge, stomping down the stairs. I knew, from his mumblings, that he was angry at the state of the bathroom! He appeared to be holding a large clump of hair – probably excavated from the plughole. Ruby and I exchanged another glance. Ruby adores her daddy, but she already knows it is best to say nothing. As Gareth turned at the bottom of the stairs we heard him yelp. The next thing was we saw him scoot past the open door on one leg, waving both arms like synchronised windmills, still clutching the clump of hair, trying desperately to regain his balance. He was skating along on a wheeled wooden toy, a bright blue-painted hedgehog that was acting as a roller skate for this unexpected adventure. His journey, on one leg, continued in to the kitchen where the escapade was abruptly curtailed by Gareth head-butting the fridge door. This made the bottle of plonk on top of the fridge wobble so furiously that it fell and smashed onto the floor, splattering red wine and tiny fragments of glass in every direction.'

Annie is crying with laughter as she tells us. It makes it all the funnier. 'I just couldn't help myself and started laughing. Ruby laughed too. It was hysterical. Gareth was furious. He doesn't like it when we laugh at him, but that makes it all the funnier. And it was so funny. He is such a dope at times. Don't tell him I told you. It'd make him so cross, but it is simply too funny not to share,' she says as she wipes away tears of laughter.

Sioned, Myfanwy and I all laugh, shake our heads and our collective body language says, 'Husbands, eh!' I'm reassured to hear that it is not just me who has a grumpy husband. I'm relieved to hear it is perfectly normal. I've been worried that Andy is grumpy all the time because he doesn't love me anymore. I always worry that Andy will stop loving me one day, that he'll wake up one day and realise that he could do so much better than me. But no, look, they all have grumpy husbands in their own way. What a relief! It was worth coming just for that.

17 Tarts

Pregnancy felt like forever. Yet time seems to be speeding up every year. Time passes. Years pass, in fact. Where does the time go? Nursery and then school bring new challenges in managing everything. There are so many celebrations, assemblies and little shows that it seems like every week there is at least one, if not two, things parents are invited to. Andy does his fair share of these. He likes being one of the few dads that turn up. All the mothers and the teachers make a big fuss of him. They don't do that for me. And Andy always stays and chats at the end of each event, whereas I always seem to have to dash off. The older George gets, the easier life becomes in many ways. Significant milestones are when he can wipe his own bottom, and put on his own seatbelt in the carseat. I can't believe how much quicker we can get things done as a result of these. Now, as a seven-year-old, he dresses himself, can tie his own shoelaces and packs his bag ready for school each day. He is a good boy.

Andy, George and I fall into our stride. We make it work. Family holiday times are the best when we can all relax together. That's when we all seem to be at our happiest, so I regularly book weekend breaks, and short holidays to Spain to give us all chance to be together. The rest of the time is a bit of a logistical nightmare. Once a week, usually late on a Sunday afternoon, Andy and I have diary meetings to work out who will be where so that our household functions as it should. It is irritating that the majority seems to fall to me as Andy has 'red lines that he will not cross', like squash on a Tuesday. But I know there is no use mentioning it as Andy will go into a sulk and then he won't help with anything. At least this way he does some of the routine tasks. We manage somehow. And Andy and I are content with the arrangements.

I am so busy at work and I just seem to move from one major project to the next. I've recently been given some great opportunities and am managing to do some overseas travel as George is big enough to be left with his dad. I even went to Australia on one exhausting week-long trip, although, not for the Olympics in Sydney with the C-suite; they'd sponsored some sort of networking event there. I was supposed to be hosting an event. Then at the last moment they decided they needed me to go to a presentation in Munich instead, and someone else (Nigel) took my place. I was so jealous. I can't imagine how much fun that would have been. Myfanwy is right – they can be right Cs sometimes.

I am flattered that Parentcraft continue to contact me and encourage, sometimes insist, that I stay in touch. And I continue to enjoy their company even though our lives are taking different directions. The new millennium seems to have heightened this desire to keep the contact going. I think the arrival of the year 2000 made everyone reassess what was important and reprioritise.

Parentcraft always likes to know how George is doing, and I am glad to report that he is doing well. He's a good boy, quiet and studious. He really doesn't give me much trouble at all. I can rely on him to get on with his homework, and his reports show he is very bright, especially at maths and science. He seems to have a natural gift for computers. I am amazed how the time has flown by. But they, Parentcraft, always keep in touch, even if I let things slip due to work. Rude, foul-mouthed, hysterical messages from Myfanwy still appear on 1571 from time to time, but more often are left on my mobile now. One evening, about a month ago, Annie phoned me and chatted as if we had spoken only the day before. With a great deal of glee, she announced that she had recently been appointed Treasurer at the PTA, the Parent Teacher Association, at Ruby's school. She told me that they have organised a fundraising event which involves going to see the Rocky Horror Picture Show in Bristol.

In an excited voice she said, 'I've put your name down, and Andy. I know I can always rely on you, Charlotte. All the teachers and their partners are going, and we are all going to dress up. It'll be such fun. Claire, a woman from the PTA, has signed up ten couples already, so I am relying on you to come. We've booked two coaches, so there will be about a hundred of us altogether, all in the gear.'

I didn't want to go. I was too busy, and I thought Andy would hate it. In fact, I was worried he'd refuse to come with me. I had been doing a lot of socialising and networking events on my own because he made such a big fuss about 'being dragged along like a spare part'' Contradictorily, he also gets the hump about the amount of time I was out without him. There was no pleasing him. I explained to him that it was important for my career to be seen at events, but that seems to make him even more crotchety. But on this one, I really didn't feel I could say no to Annie. She was so excited. And sounded so pleased with herself. I couldn't let her down.

Fast forward to tonight and, embarrassingly, the arrangements are that we meet at the school gates at 5pm, on a Friday evening. All the members of the PTA – teachers, partners, everyone – are dressed up in sexy outfits. Some, I would say, are fulfilling unfulfilled fantasies, some evidencing their sexual preferences (probably best not to enquire further) and others totally and utterly embarrassed to such an extent you wonder what has made them agree to come along in the first place. We nearly cause about five accidents with drivers gawping at us. Who can blame them, especially outside a school. I feel completely self-conscious and totally exposed – which I am.

Myfanwy is here, wearing a wonderful fuchsia-pink basque.

'Gosh, Myfanwy,' I say. 'That looks amazing. And it fits you like it was made for you.'

'Well, it was made for me, you tit wank. I did make it, like,' she says. 'Dai the Doubler, 'e's has been doing lots of extra shifts down the factory, like, so I've 'ad loads of time on me own especially as Chardonnay and Silver loves staying at me Mam's, at the mo. So I did buy meself a sewing machine and found out that I am a dab 'and. I did all the boning 'n' everythin', like.'

Tit wank! Honestly!

I am impressed, though, with her basque. Immensely impressed. That is really complicated needlework. Is there nothing she can't turn her hand to? As she walks away, she says over her shoulder, 'you look like a right tart'. I hope it is meant as a compliment tonight.

Sioned looks totally stunning in an all-in-one black leather-look S&M outfit. However, I notice how skinny her arms and legs are. She is a keep-fit fanatic these days, so she's muscly, but I hadn't realised quite how very tiny she is. Now that I think of it, I realise she has been wearing big baggy training gear the last few times I've seen her. As she does so much sport and aerobics and she is always dashing off to the next thing for one of the kids, it had made sense.

But she looks quite flat-chested and her legs look a bit too skinny, in my opinion. As everyone is milling around waiting for the coaches, I take her to one side. 'Sioned, I hope you don't mind me saying, but I think you need to put on a bit of weight now,' I tell her. 'You have a lovely figure, but I would say you are a little bit too much on the thin side now.'

'I know,' says Sioned. 'It's these intolerances and the nausea. It is still causing me real problems. My throat swells on anything dairy these days and then the thought of animal fats make me feel sick, so I have had to become vegetarian, well more vegan most of the time really. But I hear what you're saying, Charlotte, and don't worry, I am keeping an eye on it.' With that she dashes off to help Annie sort out the new arrivals and check that everyone has paid in full.

Claire, the chair of the PTA, is rather a 'big girl', as Myfanwy would say, and she has, I discover, lent Gareth a basque. She had given him four to choose from in a carrier bag at the school gates a few days earlier. They were so furtive in the exchange. Annie was giving Claire cash for the tickets, Claire was giving Annie a carrier bag with a selection of basques – it looked like they were doing a drug deal. When Annie took them home, she laid them out on the sofa for Gareth to inspect when he got in from work. He said, apparently, the unforgettable, 'Whose corset is that basque?' And Annie said, 'It's yours, darling, if you want it!' Isn't it funny how women find it erotic for their men to be dressed in women's clothing? But it seems they all do. I hadn't really thought about it until this moment. I glance across at Andy. Well, maybe, I can see what they mean. Andy does look sexy tonight. And the men definitely seem to be enjoying themselves. I find it curious that a group of men who spend so much of their time being macho and alpha are relishing the opportunity to dress up in women's underwear. What's going on there? I've not seen so many men mincing about since... since… well, ever!

Much to mine and Andy's joint surprise, it looks like it's going to be quite a fun evening. Even the husbands who, like Andy, have been complaining non-stop about going, have to admit it is a great laugh. I was worried that Andy might sulk and spoil the night for me (and everyone else) but in fact the reverse is true and he becomes the life and soul of the party. Lots of people come over as we board the coach to tell me what a laugh Andy is. I feel quite proud that he is making an effort. Andy, further behind me in the queue, looks at me and gives me a wave and I feel happy. This should be a fun evening for everyone. It's a Friday night, George is sleeping over at my Joan's, my neighbour who he adores, and I don't have to drive. I relax and have a glass of wine on the coach, served in a disposable plastic cup by a very gorgeous Magenta in a perfect French maid outfit, who, it turns out, is the Deputy Head. She offers me an appropriate little jam tart. I see Andy check her out as she leans over to fill our glasses. I nudge him and he laughs. 'I'm only human, Charlotte,' he says with a big grin on his face and he squeezes my arm affectionately.

After the show, which was fun, a really good production, we tour the pubs around Bristol. Claire and her husband have brought along two sets of friends. Sally and Kevin. Clive and Michelle. Both couples are staying with Claire in Newport overnight. They seem very nice and friendly, and they join Andy and me on the pub crawl. I find myself giggling uncontrollably at the stupidest jokes. I think I may be a little bit tipsy; it's a little Dutch courage to help me walk the streets in, basically, underwear. We are all getting on famously, and I hang on to Andy's arm as I teeter around the streets in my high-heeled shoes. My feet are killing me. How did I ever manage to wear these all day? But I've noticed Andy looking at my legs admiringly, so it's worth it.

When we finally climb back on the coach, Annie does the headcount. Four people are missing. Kevin and Michelle have gone AWOL, along with Claire and her husband. And the two who ended up staggering along with us, Sally and Clive, are not a couple. Sally is Kevin's partner. Clive is with Michelle. No one in the missing party has a mobile… where would they put it? So a search party, led by my handsome Andy, sets off to the pubs and clubs to try to track them down. It is passably excusable for the two guests to get lost, but Claire and her husband are meant to be in charge. They should be here on time.

Myfanwy, Sioned, Annie and I make an amazing team as we fire into action, moving people who urgently need to get back for babysitters into Coach A and then sending it on its way. Coach B waits for the search party to return. Sally and Clive are sitting on the bus looking frantic… then furious… then sheepish in equal measure. After about thirty minutes or so, the search party returns with no success. We conclude, after some discussion, that wherever they are, they will just have to find their own way home, even if that means an expensive taxi ride. That's their lookout. We can't keep everyone waiting any longer.

I explain the situation to Sally and Clive, who say they fully appreciate our predicament, and our decision, but they are meant to be staying at Claire's house. They had dropped their cases off there earlier in the day and therefore they only have the Rocky Horror costumes they are now dressed in. Somehow I end up offering that they can stay at our house. That spoiled that plan! Andy flashes me an exasperated look but, thankfully, he still seems to be in a good mood. He enjoyed leading the search party, so he doesn't make a scene. Sally and Clive both seem like nice, decent people. Myfanwy leans over from the set in front of us and says, 'that's really nice of you to offer to let them stay, Lottie, luv. Knew we could rely on you to save the day. I would have offered, like, but I'm 'oping is goin' to shag my arse off.' What can I say?

'We are like evacuees during the war being allocated homes in Wales… well, except for the S&M clothes,' says Sally, with a snigger.

'The buggers, they'll be drunk in a nightclub somewhere and won't have realised the time. I'm going to give Michelle such a hard time when they all finally turn up,' says Clive.

Clive and Sally were easy guests. Clive in the guest bedroom and Sally in George's Power Rangers themed bedroom. She has a Pikachu Pokemon tucked up next to her when I take her a glass of water. Andy and I get the giggles as we lie in bed thinking about what we could and should have been doing. Ah well, even the best plans go awry sometimes. And we giggle all the more as we cuddle, or as I now say, cwtch, up together. It has been a fun evening and we are happy.

The following morning, Annie rings me to tell me the missing partygoers have returned. All is well. I drop off Clive and Sally. I decide to keep my distance, there is bound to be an enormous row. Best that I don't get involved.

As I arrive home, the phone in the hallway starts to ring. It's Joan. Bless her. She asks, 'May I hold on to George for a little while longer? We are having such a good time and we would like to feed the ducks at Tredegar Park, if that's ok with you and Andy?' I agree, of course. I hear George's delighted whoop in the background.

So, an unexpected child-free morning. I decide to pick up where we should have been last night. Andy is in the bathroom brushing his teeth. I take his hand and lead him back to bed.

We had such a brilliant night. Such a good laugh. One where both Andy and I were ourselves again. I lie in his arms. Happy, relaxed and I feel carefree. I really love him, despite all his grumpiness. He kisses me on top of my head. I think he must have been reading my mind. I think we are ok.

About three hours later, but still lying in bed after a totally indulgent brunch and a read of the newspaper, I receive another call from Annie. 'Oh my God, Charlotte, you'll never believe it,' she says. 'I was just looking up Claire's details on the internet. You know she runs that Care in the Community service for the council? Well, I was trying to find the details on 'alta vista', and I've found Claire, yes I found Claire right enough, on her… wait for it… dominatrix website! Get this, Claire and her husband are swingers! All of those others… the other four, what were their names? Sally, Clive, thingy and the other one, they are all swingers too! What do you think about that? They must have thought their luck was in when they saw a hundred people in sexy underwear at the school gates. We don't know exactly where the four of them disappeared to in Bristol, but I think we can all guess. No wonder Clive and Sally were both furious and yet embarrassed. They must have known they were off shagging somewhere and they were missing out.' She pauses for breath and bursts out laughing. 'Oh yeah, and Gareth is totally mortified, he says he feels defiled because he looked at the front page of her dominatrix website and he said, 'Bloody Hell! She is wearing the corset I wore last night.'

I laugh and relay the story to Andy. We both have to hold our sides as we belly laugh. We haven't laughed like that in years. It's all thanks to Parentcraft.

18 Checking the recipe

I can't believe it. I am too early, again. After the Rocky Horror Show, I don't manage to see Parentcraft for quite a while. My life must seem really boring from the outside. Life is work, work, work. I'm really busy as I have just picked up a major research project and we are at the 'storming' stage – storming, forming, norming being our current methodology – but somehow I was persuaded to meet up with Annie, Sioned and Myfanwy. Myfanwy's voicemail on my mobile began with, 'Oi, spunk bubble…' That has to be the worst to date. But when a message that is that rude makes you burst out laughing in the middle of the office, you know that it is time for a boost and a laugh that only Parentcraft can bring.

Sioned is walking towards me through the drizzly grey rain, arms laden with her children's rucksacks and other bags, and we meet at the gate to Annie's house. At least she is early too. Jack is wearing a dark blue raincoat, an electric blue school sweatshirt with a yellow polo shirt underneath, and dark grey trousers. He is a handsome little fellow, takes after his father. Megan is holding his hand and has on pink wellies with a Teletubby on the side, and a bright pink raincoat.

Sioned greets me warmly as usual, giving me a quick kiss on the cheek. As we make our way up the steps together she says, 'Where's George?'

'Oh, he's going straight to his after-school club, and then he has his piano lesson,' I say.

'I want to see George. I like George,' says Jack.

Sioned looks at me disappointedly. 'I would have liked to have seen him too, Charlotte. We haven't seen him for ages.' I feel guilty. He is a busy boy these days with all his extracurricular activities. And he is too old for all this, it's more for Megan and Silver. But it hadn't crossed my mind that Jack, Ruby and Chardonnay may want to see him. And that George would have enjoyed seeing them, too. In truth, I hadn't thought they would be here either. I'd just assumed they'd be doing their own activities.

Our meetings on Thursday afternoons were a haven for me when I was on maternity leave, mostly to get tips on looking after babies, but also I knew it did me good to meet up with other women.

It was a bit awkward when they spoke of the feeling of not just loving, but being in love with their babies. I remember just nodding during these conversations. Well, what could I say? It just didn't happen for me. I didn't wish George any harm. I looked after him. He wasn't neglected. But I didn't feel the same sort of emotions they describe. I knew I was capable of love because I was, am, madly in love with Andy. Head-over-heels sort of in love. It's different with George. I do love him now, of course I do, and we have found our way together. We love each other. I think I did love him then, just not in the besotted way Parentcraft seemed to love their babies. The way Andy and George love each other. I think I was just scared. And I am enormously proud of him. I am proud of his academic achievements. He seems to be doing very well indeed, according to his teachers. And we, George and I, have found our own space. We know what we need from each other to get by. But the fact I didn't have these overwhelming maternal feelings is still a taboo. That is my dirty secret that I cannot express. No one is allowed to say that they feel what I felt, which is a kind of neutrality, about their own child, and so I never, ever, say it out loud. Not to anyone. Only my deep inner voice, and guilt, occasionally try to surface it, and I suppress the feeling immediately. Sioned and Myfanwy have repeatedly explained to Annie and me that the same amount of love is duplicated for the next child. No need to share or split the love. Whallop, there's another dollop, they say; love enough for number two. These conversations are difficult for Annie and me, but for different reasons. I am now skilful at smiling without commitment or agreement. I couldn't manage in the business world if I weren't. I'm sure it has never crossed Annie, Myfanwy or Sioned's minds that I didn't love George the way they loved their first-borns. Myfanwy was, I thought, just biding her time to do the full exposé on me, so I was always on my guard with her in the past. But that wasn't true. She still says some ridiculous, insensitive and crude things at times but thankfully, she is always hysterically funny; that's her redeeming feature.

And before I know it, here we are, back on this topic of babies again. The conversations must be more difficult for Annie who is, she tells me, longing for another child, but she smiles and engages in the conversation graciously. Myfanwy and Sioned are discussing whether to have a third child. Why? I just don't understand. I know this is truly awful, but I fantasise occasionally about George being away at boarding school or something, so we could have our old lives back. A life where it was just Andy and me. A life when Andy wasn't grumpy with me most of the time. I'd miss him, of course, I would. Then I feel really wicked and incredibly guilty because I do love George. Just in my own way.

Looking back, I now think I was probably suffering from post-natal depression in those early days, not that I would have ever admitted it then, nor now, to anyone, but I do remember saying, 'I am totally stressed out,' and 'I don't want to go home and be on my own with it'. That was probably a sign that things weren't right really.

Sioned and Myfanwy must be mad to have gone through it all again to have baby number two. And now they are contemplating baby number three. Another baby would be just awful. I'm so glad Andy and I haven't fallen into that trap. Annie has just the one child too, of course. She and Gareth saw that specialist and tried IVF, as she had on Ruby, but she ended up having a couple of miscarriages. One was quite late in to the pregnancy too – twelve weeks, and she'd already told family and friends. In the end she just found it too heart-breaking to keep trying. Too much for her… and for Gareth. It put them under a lot of stress.

We, Parentcraft, tried a few meetings at Parent and Toddler groups over the years, but they were often run with strange rules by strange women who seemed to take charge, strangely! Far too many seemed to be linked to some God Squad or other, and it felt like an offer to convert you (or sell your soul) was on offer alongside the tea and biscuits. I skipped most of those meetings. They reminded me of that awful Christian café in Newport that we were expelled from. Thankfully, we have reverted back to meeting each other in our own homes.

Sitting in Annie's house, I am once again enjoying a good catch up when there is a huge commotion. This can only mean one thing – Myfanwy has arrived with Chardonnay and Silver. At least that means we will all be laughing soon. Myfanwy always makes us laugh.

As Chardonnay and Silver run upstairs to join Jack, Megan and Ruby who are playing in Ruby's bedroom, Myfanwy bangs open the door to Annie's living room, sees me, points and shrieks, 'Rocky Horror Swingers, cun you fuckin' believe it? Remember that? Dirty little fuckers.' And despite – or maybe because of – her vulgarity, she creases us all with laughter once again.

After a while, the children descend back into the living room and the noise level in just a few minutes is unbelievable. It's going to give me a headache. It makes me realise how quiet George is. I can take him anywhere and he will sit quietly and do some maths puzzles or play on his game boy. The noise in Annie's house sits upon us like a heavy fog interrupted occasionally by Myfanwy's foghorn voice. I try to go back to where we were in our conversation, 'So, what was that you were telling me, Annie?'

'My mother has upset me again,' Annie says, while Sioned and Myfanwy fuss over the noisy offspring. 'I don't know why I let her get to me. I really don't. Do you know what she said to me this week? She said it was probably best that I had the miscarriage as I'm not a natural mother. Honestly! That woman. She does my head in.'

I am appalled. What a cruel thing to say. But I am also intrigued as to why her mother is so horrible to Annie. This may help me understand why my mother is so horrid to me at times. I want to know more. But we are interrupted by the need for food/drink/bottom wiping! Yes, I have to wipe other people's children's bottoms now. How did that happen? You see, this is what it is like all the time.

And whenever I meet these wonderful women I am always reminded me of those early days. God, George was so demanding all the time. The constant need for changing, feeding, cleaning, wiping – the list went on and on. And I remember how I didn't have one second to think. There was no time to eat my own food. Any colour lipstick would do, certainly no time for nail polish. Clothes were selected to match the colour of baby sick or baby poo. Patting my breasts to check for wet patches whilst talking to people. Choosing my clothes for ease of access to my chest – unlike the time I took the advice of that stupid Mrs Insipid and wore a button-through dress on a trip to Cardiff and ended up looking like I was naked whenever I breastfed. That was embarrassing! I don't know how I stuck at breastfeeding for so long. It must be my stubbornness – I get that from my mother. I laugh when Myfanwy tells us about eating a chocolate biscuit behind a cupboard door so that she didn't have to share it with Chardonnay and Silver. I used to prepare food parcels and toss them into the cot with George so I could sit down and eat my lunch in peace. I didn't tell the others that, though. You're meant to sacrifice everything for your baby. Including your lunch.

I am astounded to hear myself agreeing to take George on a trip with them next week, half-term, to a leisure centre somewhere in the Valleys. They're going on a coach but, they say, as it's full I can just join them there. 'I'd love to! George will really enjoy that,' I hear my voice say. Really! I mean, really. What is the matter with me? I know I've got a big week at work next week. This'll put huge amounts of pressure on me. But something deep inside must be reminding me that I need their company.

19 Cheesecake

Swimming! I'm not sure whether George's progress will suffer from missing his piano and Chinese lessons that are scheduled on a Wednesday. It takes a lot of planning to ensure they can manage without me at work too, and, from a personal perspective, it takes a lot of planning as a trip to a leisure centre involves shaving my legs and underarms. In fact, for me, it is more like an exercise in deforestation than shaving. I don't bother shaving in the winter if I can help it. The recent fashion for business trouser suits has meant I haven't had to bother for quite a while. I discover I have cultivated Ernie Wise's short, fat, hairy legs. I opt for a new shorts-style bathing costume so that at least I can avoid the bikini wax – I really couldn't face it.

George and I manage to arrive early at the leisure centre, despite the ridiculous amount of time it takes to travel less than twelve miles from home, but it's not long before the group joins us in the communal changing room. Some of the women, evidently, have opted for waxing. Myfanwy takes great delight in showing Sioned and Annie, and particularly me, her 'go faster' stripe. I really didn't want to see that. I'll be scarred for life. I don't like my own, but I certainly don't want to see hers. She honks at the look on my face and says, 'It's like a beautiful flower, innit luv, with unfolding petals, like. They did say so on Good Morning Britain.' I can assure you, it is not. With that, Myfanwy slips her go faster stripe into a slinky black swimming costume and makes a loud 'thwang' as she stretches the straps over her hefty shoulders.

The pool, to my surprise, is actually very good and it has a shallow area for babies and under-fives. Sioned gets in with Megan, and she takes Silver with her. There is a water slide too in the big pool that the other children are big enough to go on. George, Ruby, Jack and Chardonnay rush on to it in excitement, measuring themselves against the cut-off height figure every time. I can only assume that they think they may have shrunk in the water from the last time they measured just a few minutes previously. With so many of us there, plus the people from the school, Valley Folk, as Andy would call them, we are able to share the workload of taking the children into the pool and letting them splash around plus getting the occasional five minutes to go for a swim ourselves. Pure bliss – visits to the swimming baths so rarely include any form of swimming since having George. Thankfully he has already learnt to swim, so he needs less supervision than he did.

Myfanwy is what Andy and Myfanwy (it must be a Newport thing) would call a big girl. In the water, although a good, strong swimmer, I notice she has an unusual technique. Somehow her bottom seems to be higher than the rest of her body. And she does have a very large bottom, much bigger now than mine, I'm pleased to say, now I am back in shape. I laugh heartily when Jack swims past me and says, 'Aunty Myfanwy is being chased by the Loch Ness monster.'

'Yeah, I'll never drown, me, like, luv,' she shrieks as she swims past us too, looking positively gleeful. 'I've got all this extra buoyancy in me bum, see.'

The next time I spot Myfanwy, she is at the top of the waterslide with lots of little children around her. I've noticed that the heavier you are, the faster you come down the slide, so I wait near the bottom of the slide to observe Myfanwy's descent. This will definitely be a laugh.

I hear a loud shriek, a whoop, a bump, and a very foul curse, so I know she is on her way down the slide. Moments later Myfanwy shoots forth, throwing Silver into the air from her lap. A startled, wide-eyed Silver flies through the air and then, plop, disappears under the water as Myfanwy bounces along the surface of the pool like a bouncing bomb. People all around rush and grapple to rescue Silver and bring her coughing and spluttering but, thankfully, laughing to the surface.

'Where's Muff?' asks Sioned, who is now standing nearby with Megan holding her hand, and we turn to look at the end of the pool. Emerging from the water are two very large black lycra buttocks floating on the surface. Is she dead? But eventually Myfanwy finds the floor of the pool with her feet and is able to stand again. 'See', she says to the small crowd that has gathered, as she coughs, splutters and staggers to the side of the pool, 'I'll never drown, me. Bum buoyancy. Bloody marvellous, mun.' Sioned and I have to hold each other up we are laughing so much. I'm having such a good day, and I have the added advantage that I know Myfanwy has a funny story to tell later – I know, because I am part of it. I'm tingling with the anticipation of making them all laugh.

It is fun, but the little ones get cold so quickly and then it takes forever to get them all out of the pool. They all want to stay longer, but several of them are shivering and looking quite blue so we take them out and all crowd into the shower. The water is blissfully warm in comparison to standing around in the pool, but it takes a long time to have George's turn, the blue children take priority. In the changing room, I rub George quickly with a large yellow towel as he sits on my lap. I dry his hair as best I can with the weakest hairdryer ever invented – those attached to a wall in a leisure centre. Finally, I get to shower, in public (who designed this set-up?) still in my swimming costume obviously, and then dry myself. My hair is a disaster and my skin still smells of chlorine, but it'll have to do as they are all eager to move on. After all the fun of the pool, we move on to the next horror. We make our way to 'all the fun of the fair' that is alongside the leisure centre. It has definitely seen better days. Rubbish and dust is swirling everywhere.

A one-legged man, struggling with a crutch and a sweeping brush, is pathetically clearing up some rubbish alongside one of the not-so-attractive attractions. 'Aw. That poor man,' says Sioned. 'Did you see the sad expression on his face?' She shakes her head compassionately. 'It is the sort of expression that says, "I know I've only got one leg". Bless him.' That makes me laugh, and then I feel guilty for laughing at his misfortune.

The whole funfair is pretty filthy. 'The dust bunnies could make a bloody warren in yer,' says Myfanwy, wiping the seats of one of the rides with a wet wipe.

We've decided to go on one of the more sedate-looking rides. Myfanwy buys the tickets for the day. There seems to be reams of them as every ride costs three, five or ten tickets; what sort of a system is that? The man selling them is another disenfranchised-looking employee, a young one this time. His accent is like Wallace from 'Wallace and Gromit', and Myfanwy's habit of, what I can only assume is subconscious and unintentional, accent mimicry gets the better of her as, at the end of the conversation, she loudly says,

'Grand, lad' in a Northern accent and gives him the thumbs up. It's all terribly embarrassing, but ridiculously funny. My tummy is aching from all the laughter today.

Next, we pay for a few more dozen tickets for a trip on the ghost train. It is truly pathetic. 'Hey, the scariest thing about this ghost train is the man that sold us the ticket,' Sioned giggles.

'The scariest thing in the world is Philadelphia, innit, luv?' says Myfanwy.

'What? You're scared of Philadelphia? The city? Or the cream cheese?' says Sioned.

'No, 'ang on, I don't mean Philadelphia, do I? What's it called? Kiddyphilia? Kiddiefiddling?' says Myfanwy.

'Do you mean paedophilia?' says Sioned.

'Yeah, that's it. I 'ate that. Proper scary… so what's that Philadelphia, then?' enquires Myfanwy.

'You know what Philadelphia is, Myfanwy. It's cream cheese. You put it on bagels. You make cheesecakes with it all the time,' I say.

'Ah, that's right. I knew I'd yerd of Philadelphia somewhere before, like. No, I'm not scared of Philadelphia. It's paedophilia I'm scared of, Lottie, luv, not Philadelphia,' she says, in a tone that appears to be accusing me of having said she is scared of Philadelphia. Then she nods wisely. Sioned, Annie and I crease with laughter.

Myfanwy then says, in the middle of the fair, with people all around us, 'What do you reckon to this then, Lottie, luv? Perhaps if I do dress up in stockings and suspender belt, do you think it might do it for Dai? What d'you reckon? I've tried everything, like, well, 'e just don't respond, if you do know what I do mean. Limp. Floppy. Nothin', like. God, I needs a shag. I needs to be loved. I tell 'im I'm going up to bed, but 'e just stays downstairs watching telly and in the end I do give up and go to sleep, or sort meself out, if you do know what I do mean. But you do get bored of wankin', don't you, luv? I say to meself that maybe tomorrow will be different, but it 'as been months and months and months now. 'e is just not interested in me no more.

'So I asked 'im if anythin' I did was puttin' 'im off, like, turnin' him off. 'e said there is one thing. When we did first meet we 'ad this joke about a tummy banana. I did call his willy a tummy banana, see. Well, Dai says 'e wished 'e'd told me right back in the beginning. 'e says 'e finds it sickenin'. I always thought it was our silly little joke. I feels like a right fuckin' prat now. See, yers ago, whenever we were doing 'it', we would put on the TV really loudly, for the sake of the neighbours, so we could 'ave a really loud shag. Anyways, Captain Banana was on when I 'ad my first ever orgasm one Saturday morning. I was really noisy. 'e says 'e can't remember that at all and all a tummy banana makes 'im think about is a turd on 'is belly, like. 'e says to me ''ow am I meant to keep my erection when I have that image in me 'ead?' What do you think of that then, Lottie? Anyways, I've 'ad to do somethin' about it. I'll tell you all about that later, though cuz, obviously, I wouldn't want anyone to yer and embarrass you, like.'

I cringe with intense embarrassment. We're in a public place! Of course people can hear. Even if we weren't, what are you meant to say to a confession like that? Sioned and Annie take it all in their stride. I'd assumed, with her hard-working husband, two children who just seem totally unbothered by everything, and a mother who drops by all the time to help, that everything in Myfanwy's life was just perfect. The others seem to be not only unperplexed by this confession, but they start offering tips. It is all too much for me, so I make my excuses (which are true, I do have to pick up some ready meals from M&S) and George and I leave to make our way to Sioned's, who is hosting this afternoon.

As we are driving towards Newport, George says, 'Thank you Mummy, that was the best day of my life. Thank you for taking me.' Wonders will never cease. With all the skiing, sailing and other extracurricular activities I'm paying for, why would he like a leisure centre and a tacky funfair best? I really have no comprehension of what makes him tick, he can be such a strange child at times.

At Sioned's house, Myfanwy says, with delight in her voice, 'So, come on then, girls. I'm goin' to need your sex advice. But there's a bit more to this story and it's really funny. Lottie, luv, get ready so you cun tell ’em your bit.’ I feel myself tingle with the anticipation, a bit like stage-fright.

‘So, anyway, you knows now cuz I told you ’e aint interested no more ’n’ I ’ad to do somethin’ about it, now wait till you do yer this. I’ve ’ad a right wild time out with me mates last Saturday. Well, ’e aint interested in nuffin, so me ’n’ the girls we did go out on a Nerd night. ’ave you yerd of ’em? We ’ad on those round, black-rimmed, thick glasses, the geeky clothes and we ’ad all bought big, ugly false teeth, like. Ha ha ha! We looked fuckin’ great. Well, we looked bloody awful really but great, if you do know what I do mean.

‘We got completely wasted in town. Absolutely wazzed. I mean ratted, like. It were amazing, like, ’ow many men took a real liking to the teeth though. I am going to use ’em again. Great pulling tool. Janet Street-Porter must get shagged all the time. Anyway, this is really funny. Tell ’em, Lottie, luv.’ She looks gleefully at me, signalling for me to tell the rest of the story. I am glad of the opportunity to share this strange occurrence with Sioned and Annie. It was so funny, but weird, what happened last Saturday night. I still don’t really know what to make of it all, so it’ll be good to tell them.

‘Poor Dai, Myfanwy!’ I say. ‘It’s all those double shifts you’ve got him working, it’s no wonder he’s so tired all the time. But, back to this story. Saturday night, well it was about 3 am on Sunday morning actually, and our home phone rang. Both Andy and I sat bolt upright in bed. You don’t get phone calls at 3 am unless it’s very bad news, do you? So Andy rushed to answer it. I could hear he was very confused and was saying, ‘What? What?’ Then I heard him say, ‘Okay Dai, calm down. I’ll get Charlotte to come round now and sort out whatever has happened.

‘Andy then rushed back into the bedroom and said, “Get round to Myfanwy’s right now. She’s been shot in the head”.’

Sioned and Annie gasp in astonishment. I’m quite enjoying this story-telling role. ‘I jumped out of bed, dragged on some clothes and dashed out to the car,’ I say. ‘I drove over to Myfanwy’s house and ran up the steps, not knowing what I was going to find. Myfanwy was in her living room with congealed blood all over her face. I gasped with shock.

'I rushed to the bathroom and grabbed a towel, soaked it under the cold water tap, and then squeezed it out. I brought the towel back in the room where Dai was pacing around, wringing his hands. Honestly, he was no use to anyone. He was pacing around like an expectant father. I started mopping up the blood, but I couldn't find the wound. "Have you been fighting?" I asked Myfanwy. She was very drunk indeed, so it was hard to get a coherent answer.' Myfanwy looked very proud at this part of the story.

'She slurred something about a great night, plastic bag, nice boy, hotdog. I mopped her up a bit more, but still couldn't find the injury. "Have you been fighting?" I asked again. "No, not fighting, luv, 'andbag," Myfanwy slurred at me. I opened her handbag and there was a half-eaten hotdog. Slowly, I pieced together the events of the night. She'd bought herself a hotdog from a van for the taxi ride home. She'd paid the taxi driver in the cab and then, as she stepped out of the taxi, she had stepped one flip-flop onto the other flip-flop, causing her to fall headlong into the garden wall, thrusting her hotdog into her face and squeezing tomato sauce up her nose and across her face. Combined with the graze from headbutting the wall, she looked like she had been in a fight, especially as she still had the goofy teeth in which made her face look disfigured. Poor Dai. He must have been so worried. Fancy thinking she'd been shot!

'Myfanwy then took the hotdog from me and started to eat it. "It's been on the pavement and in your handbag, for God's sake, Myfanwy. You can't eat it," Dai said as he took the hotdog and threw it in the wastepaper basket in the corner of the room. As Dai bundled Myfanwy up the stairs to bed, I let myself out to the sounds of Muff slurring, "But I loves a bit of sausage, I do".'

I thoroughly enjoy telling this crazy, nonsensical story. I can rely on Myfanwy's tales to make us all laugh.

'Why did Dai phone Charlotte though, Myfanwy? Why not your Mam?' asks Sioned, laughing.

'Cuz I've told 'im you cun rely on Lottie whenever there is an emergency, that's why. Anyways, that's not the 'arf of it,' says Myfanwy gleefully. 'Wait till you yer this bit. Even Lottie don't know this bit yet.' She grins at me and takes up the reins again of the storytelling.

'I met this lovely bloke called Neil. Really beef. Smart-looking… well, in a geeky sort of a way of smart-looking. 'e 'ad the glasses and braces on. We was getting really pissed together. Then 'e did take me back to his flat.'

We all gasp in astonishment and horror. Me most loudly. I wasn't aware of this part of the story.

'Yes, and 'e was saying 'ow great I did look, which is a laff, cuz I was dressed as a nerd. And I said, "You'd think I look good in anything." His suit was 'angin' on the back of the door in a dry-cleaning bag and I said, like, "I'd bet you'd think I'd look good in that bag." And 'e said, "Hell, yes", so I stripped off and put it on.

'Well, girlies, he fucked me from one side of his flat to the other. That bag really did somethin' for 'im, I cun tell you. It was a bit 'ot 'n' sweaty in the bag for me, like, but I liked the fuckin', I did.'

We gasp again in surprise… and shock… and horror… at her actions and her language. She loves it. She really enjoys shocking all of us – but she especially enjoys shocking me. I can just tell by the way she is looking at me that she is taking great delight in telling me this horrific new development in her life.

'Myfanwy, it's not my place to approve or disapprove of your behaviour. It's not that what you are telling us is shocking. It's the fact you decide to tell us all so openly that I find surprising. You need to be careful what you say, Myfanwy, and also who you say it to. Don't go blabbing this story to everyone or news is bound to get back to Dai,' I say.

'Yes, Ma'am,' she says, and salutes me.

'I'm thinking of you, Myfanwy. And Dai. Just think about what you're saying. And think about what you are doing.'

'Dai's not gunna to find out, Lottie, luv,' Myfanwy says. 'This lad was only about twenty. They're not gunna go to the same places, are they? Unless this Neil bloke decides to 'ave a party in our front room, or in the factory canteen, then 'e is never going to bump into Dai. Dai never goes anywhere. 'e never wants to do nuffin'. 'e always says 'e is knackered, but 'e is just boring. Boring and middle-aged well before 'is time, that's Dai. But you all know that already. And you do know 'e never turns up when I arranges to meet 'im with me friends. 'e's a boring old fart. BORING…OLD…FART! 'e don't want me. And I'm sick of it. I don't think 'e'd mind two 'oots that I shagged someone else. One less thing for 'im to do.'

20 All that sugar… it'll rot your teeth

Although I was horrified by this new development, I must admit that I was also fascinated by Myfanwy's double life. And her sex life! It is so different from my boring, mundane life and non-existent sex life. I vowed to make an even more concerted effort to attend the next Parentcraft, this time because I really wanted to hear Myfanwy's stories.

'Did I ever tell you about 'ow it 'appened? You know, 'ow I did come to take redundancy from Evans Wire last Christmas?' Myfanwy is in full swing as I enter the room, and wants to ensure she has our full attention before giving us the story of her most recent escapade. 'Lottie, luv, 'urry up 'n' sit down, will you? I wants you to yer this 'n' all. So, I 'ad gone back to work after my maternity leave with Silver even though I really didn't want to, remember, but I 'ad to or you do 'ave to pay the maternity leave payments back 'n' Dai said we couldn't afford that. Anyway, they 'ad been reducing my 'ours over the years and yet giving me more and more to do, like – not just me mind, all the cleaners, like. Anyways, we were all getting ready for the staff Christmas party and they asked about two 'undred of us to go into this meeting room in the factory. The room is 'uge, they do use it for conferences for the rest of the Evans Wire Group, but even so, with two 'undred people in there it was a bit of a tight squeeze. We 'ad 'ad to queue in the rain to get in and then found ourselves like sardines, especially those of us at the back. Someone behind me said, "Can you smell gas?" So, it started us all laffin' nervously, like. So when the management, or thieving bastards as we do like to call 'em, said we 'ad been identified as at risk of redundancy, we burst out laffin'. "Slightly better than being gassed," said the man next to me, "but not much, and on the day of the Christmas party too, you would 'ave thought they could 'ave waited until after Christmas, wouldn't you?" When the nervous laughter subsided, well, we all went to the flattest Christmas party I've ever been to 'n' I got totally pissed.

'The redundancy money did come in very 'andy though, a few weeks money was good, like. So I became a proper 'ousewife. I 'ad always wanted Dai to be my provider, my protector. I chose him because 'e is a real man, like. But once 'e was all of those things, the real man, the provider, the protector, then what was there for me to do except keep Chardonnay and Silver 'appy and fill my time with 'ousework? The thing is, you see, lovelies, and don't laff, but I'm very clever.'

We laugh.

Myfanwy continues, 'It is just that I am not the slightest bit ambitious, like. It drove me teachers fuckin' mental. They was furious when I did leave school at sixteen – they all wanted me to go to university, 'n' all. Ha, that's a bloody laff. No one in me family 'as been to university. I didn't wanna be the odd one out. But the teachers wanted me to, see, I was one of the brightest in the class.'

Well, no surprise there. I imagine the bar is pretty low in a school in Newport. But university? Really? Myfanwy? I don't think so.

Myfanwy continues in full swing, 'Well, that's not true, I was the brightest. I didn't 'ave to work 'ard neither. I could just do it all and it drove 'em mad that I just wouldn't apply myself to studying.'

Dear Lord, can you imagine what that class must have been like if Myfanwy was the best? It doesn't bear thinking about.

'I passed all me exams.'

She must be lying.

'I never used my qualifications to get a job,' she says. 'In fact, I ended up lying most of the time saying I 'ad none because I 'ad been turned down for loads of interviews cuz I was young and over-qualified. I 'aven't even told you lot cuz you'd think I was a right nob or that I was making it all up… but it's true. The fact that I do talk with a Newport accent makes people think I am thick. I 'aven't even told Dai about all them GCEs.'

This must all be a pack of lies! There is no way Myfanwy has even one CSE let alone GCEs. It must be complete rubbish. I tut.

'Anyways, Dai was delighted, if truth be known, that I was made redundant. As much as 'e is the man of the family, so 'e wants me to be the perfect wife. 'e do want me to stay at 'ome and look after the kiddies. All 'e ever wants to do is stay at 'ome. 'e is happy to be the provider and support me. 'e's very traditional and 'onourable like that. Now, like I said, I've never been ambitious nor career-minded nor fem'nist nor nuffin like that, but I've always known what I do want in life, 'n' then, suddenly I finds I do 'ave everything I 'ad planned. 'ubby! Kiddies! 'ouse! The lot! Anyways, I am unemployed now. And I am sick of it.'

This is a new degree of honesty from Myfanwy and Sioned, Annie and I look at each other and then back at Myfanwy.

Myfanwy has never managed to shift all the weight she put on during her pregnancies, probably not helped by all the baking she does now, and the amount of sugar she uses. Having never done any baking before, she has certainly become quite a master with even really difficult techniques. For a big woman she has a surprisingly light touch and a real knack for creating recipes. Today she is presenting us with a Victoria sponge. She switches seamlessly from telling us about her working life, or lack of it, and sex life with Dai, or lack of it, to her cake in her TV chef voice.

'No sex with Dai but at least there's cake, eh girls? This is a classic. And so fuckin' easy too 'n' all. I thinks this one were in an ol' Mary Berry cookbook my Mam did 'ave on the shelf. 'ave you ever yerd of 'er? I loves 'er, I doos. I loves 'er photo on the cover of the cookbook. She's like me Mam 'n' me Nan 'n' every nice old lady that ever lived all rolled into one with none of the barkin' old hags in the mix, neither.

'So, you wants the oven on ready, like. *Gas mark 4. You do need two cake tins for this. Spread some butter on 'em to grease 'em up, nice and proper. Four eggs, big uns, free-range if you do want, Sioned, into yer mixing bowl with 8oz of caster sugar, cuz it is fine like, you don't want it gritty, 8oz of self-raising flour, 2 teaspoons of baking powder 'n' 8oz of lovely Welsh butter. Don't buy any of that other stuff, it ain't as good. And don't even think about margarine, not in a Victoria sponge. It's alright in some stuff, but it is crap in this. Mix it all up. Stick 'arf in one tin 'n' 'arf in the other. Bung it in the oven – I'd say 25 minutes max, but keep an eye on 'em. Check they're baked – touch 'em 'n' they should feel springy then bung 'em on the cooling rack. Let 'em cool. Don't rush it, that's what I do say. When you're ready, spread one side with strawberry jam, mine was lovely this yer. Put whipped cream on the other side and stick 'em together. That's why some people do call it a Victoria sandwich.'*

She nods knowingly. 'To make it look pretty sprinkle over some caster sugar. So easy, mun, but fuckin' gorgeous.'

It is really good! She does have a knack for these things, even this simple recipe has an ultra-light and fluffy sponge, and the intensity of the strawberry jam is incredible. She has become really crafty too, I mean at craft making. I already knew about her basque-making skills, but now we seem to have all her skills around us – homemade candles, homemade doilies, homemade tablecloths, homemade everything! I don't know where she finds the time. But then again she doesn't work and her mother is always having the girls for her.

Myfanwy grabs our attention again and flips to another new topic. 'Girls, girls, listen up!' she shrieks. ''ave you been to that new dentist yet in town? Well, if you 'aven't got an NHS dentist, go and register there because they are taking on new patients and that won't last for long, will it? I just 'ave. I've 'ad to leave our one cuz of the new dentist there. 'ere's why.

'Anyway, our Debbie, well not our Debbie, another Debbie, works at the dentist I do go to. She told me that a new dentist 'ad started 'n' she told me 'e's a real looker. Well, you knows me girls, I likes to 'ave a laff. You know Debbie, don't you? I've told you about 'er before. She used to work with me at Evans Wire. She's a right laff.'

Yet another Debbie! However will I keep track?

'So we did set it all up. Debbie went in to the dentist and said that 'is new patient was in the waiting room (that's me, like) and she was warning 'im that I am a friend from school - with the worst teeth she 'ad ever seen. He thanked 'er for the 'eads-up but told 'er not to worry, 'e was used to seeing awful teeth.

'Well, I walks into 'is surgery, dolled up to the nines, with real 'igh-'eeled sexy shoes on, a very tight skirt and even tighter blouse, with the button undone to expose me cleavage with me gorgeous big titties in me uplift bra so 'igh up they are nearly under me chin. 'e couldn't take 'is eyes off me chest and I kept me big gob shut.

‘’e asked me to sit in ’is dentist chair and then ’e says, somethin’ like, “Okay, there’s nothing to worry about,” in ’is professional patter, like. “I’m just going to tip you back in the chair and take a look at your tits…teeth, I mean teeth.” Debbie sniggered into her sleeve. I’m sure she snotted on ’er sleeve too ’n’ all and I stares straight ahead, like, so as not to laff. ’e starts to blush wildly. I likes that, I doos.

‘’e asks me to open my mouth and as I do ’e bursts out laffin’. “You rotters,” ’e says as Debbie and I crease up laffin’. I am wearing my ’ideous nerdy teeth. “Oh, and you’d got me all in a fluster, too. You swines!” Debbie and me were pissin’ ourselves. It was fuckin’ ’ysterical!

‘Shame really. I suspect ’e’s a damn good dentist, given ’ow good ’e was with ’is ’ands, but I won’t be able to go back there now, like. That dentist chair saw a whole lot of action after the surgery was closed that day, I cun tell you. Everyone ’ad gone ’ome except ’im. I ’ad to come back for a ‘special’ appointment, if you do know what I do mean. One not in the appointment book, like. I ’ope ’e wiped down the seat later, before ’e do ’ave patients in in the morning. Still, I’ll ’ave to change. ’e said it was best if we didn’t see each other again as ’e do ’ave a girlfriend. That’s why I do ’ave to register with another NHS dentist in Newport. ’opefully one that won’t be quite as sexy, like, ugly would be better, really as I’d actually like to ’ave a check-up rather than a touch-up this time.’

She is shocking! But fascinating. All of this she keeps secret from Dai, of course. As I said, Myfanwy has become quite crafty in all sorts of ways.

21 Cheese and wine

I continue to attend Parentcraft meet ups whenever I can. After the financially successful, but morally questionable, trip to the Rocky Horror Picture Show, I find myself making my way to another of Annie's fundraising events for the school PTA. It is a cheese and wine party this time. I like Annie. She said she knew she could rely on me, so I don't want to let her down, even though this week is proving to be especially difficult logistically. Andy has some new friends at work, so there are more trips to the pub and office pub quizzes every Friday for him, as a result. Anyway, he agreed to babysit for me tonight, a Friday, although I fail to see why it is 'for me'. I don't say I'm babysitting for him when he goes out.

Easy enough, a cheese and wine party, or so you'd think. But Annie has managed to pick the most incredibly cold night of the year. It is absolutely freezing as I make my way to her house. I drive carefully along the icy roads. She has persuaded me to 'sleep over' too, saying excitedly we will have a giggle and we can try on each other's clothes, as if we were some Barbie-obsessed six-year-olds about to swap a pink fluffy outfit for an even more lurid shade of pink. But the more I think about it, the more excited I feel about the whole thing, including the sleepover and trying on each others' clothes. I really must get a life.

The night should be commercially successful for her PTA though. Having sold over a hundred tickets (she is a damn good sales person, it must be said, I wish I had her in my team) I feel honour-bound to help her with the logistics of the event, even though this will mean trudging through the snow at some point. There is no point in taking the car to a cheese and wine party because we can't drink and drive. And I fear it is going to be far too treacherous to be on the road later even in my 4x4. When I finally, slowly, arrive at Annie's new house, a flurry of big soft snowflakes start to tumble from the curiously coloured skies. Everything is glistening under the orangey street lamp glow – the ground is definitely cold enough for it to settle and it hasn't rained for days.

Annie nudges open the door and ushers me quickly inside. I wave to Gareth who is helping Ruby with her homework in their front room. Ruby runs over and flings her arms around my waist and then inspects the snowflakes while they are still unmelted on my overcoat. She is a lovely girl. She is very tall for seven-and-a-half, much taller than George is. Annie calls me through to HQ – the kitchen.

Annie tells me she has received lots of calls during the day from people calling off due to the terrible weather – and asking for their money back! It's a school fundraiser, not a commercial enterprise, for goodness sake, but Annie has said she will see what she can do. The wine and most of the food was delivered directly to the church hall this morning, and so it only remains for us to carry the few final bags of bread and cheese up the hill from her house to the hall.

Sioned and Myfanwy arrive and we stand in the hallway among the wonderful collection of plastic bags, enormous coats, alpine headwear and assorted skiwear – fetching combinations of recent Christmas presents.

Myfanwy appears to be wearing some sort of Peruvian hat – they're all the rage, she tells us - the sort with the ear flaps and long knitted pieces that look like plaits. She looks as though she has come from an episode of Pippi Longstocking. She is wearing the most enormous black ski gloves. Annie has insisted we swap and change our clothes combinations before we go out, in an attempt to make sure we are all equally well-covered, which means that we all look equally distasteful too. As we are swapping garments there are lots of comments from Myfanwy, ''oose coat is that jacket?' ''oose shoe is that boot?' and the particularly hilarious, ''oose hood is that snood?'

'I'm going now, love,' Annie calls to Gareth from the front door. 'I may be some time.'

We all giggle. I actually feel a bit tipsy already, that hot toddy that Annie insisted we all have in the kitchen was very warming but quite strong. While we were getting ready, a layer of ice formed on top of the settled snow, and it is like trying to walk on a skating rink, a skating rink on a hill! It is hilarious and despite the bitterly cold wind I find myself laughing uncontrollably as we all slip down the slope.

When we finally reach the hall there is no one else there, but Annie has the keys. We help Annie to lay out the food, letting the cheese and red wine have sufficient time to breathe before the hordes arrive.

An hour after the start time we have to admit that we are unlikely to get to more than the twenty people or so that have already made it through the snow. Wine for a hundred and only twenty people in the room – we should have known there would be trouble.

One of the men who has made it through the snow is quite a wine buff and offers to give a short lecture on wine-tasting. We agree this is a great idea. So, we start working our way around the different bottles, trying them with different cheeses and noticing how the taste changes. He emphasises that there is no hard-and-fast rule about red wine with red meat and white wine with fish or chicken – it is all a question of taste. Your own taste. 'But 'ow will I know?' asks Myfanwy. 'I'm tasteless. Totally tasteless.' Well, ain't that the truth!

At about 9 pm, a veritable blizzard picks up outside, so we stand at the window watching the swirls of snow and debate whether we should all just head for home now before it becomes too bad. There's a genuine risk we could be snowed in if we hang about much longer. Someone tries a taxi company who say they are not picking up any more fares this evening. Somehow, and I think this may have been the wine talking, we collectively make the decision to take another couple of bottles of wine out of the returns crate while we wait for it to pass over. Armed with our new-found expert knowledge, we put our tasting skills to the test.

Well, I am ashamed to say that things get a little out of hand. There is a toy cupboard for the playgroup at the end of the room. Someone decides it would be fun to get the toys out and have a go on them. Rhys, the wine-tasting aficionado, is standing at the cupboard door, surveying the shelves when Myfanwy bends down in front of him and, when level with his trouser fly, embarrassingly says, in a slurred voice, 'Oh, you've got a lovely Thomas down there,' whilst taking a Thomas the Tank Engine truck and trying to squeeze herself onto the seat. Rhys looks very proud.

Sioned is sporting a very trendy alpine ski outfit with an incredible knitted cardigan – she bought it on a city break to Tallinn, apparently. Her hair is cropped quite short, but it has a bit of a wave in it – it looks sort of 1930s. She looked very sophisticated on arrival at Annie's earlier in the evening. Not anymore! She is now looking rather dishevelled. Her hair has stuck to her head making her look like a newborn, and she has a red wine smile, and keeps hiccoughing.

'How do you do this?' asks a very drunk Sioned in a very slurred voice, looking very perplexed at a toboggan.

'Just shove it between yer legs, lie back and enjoy the ride,' shouts Myfanwy. Rhys raises his eyebrows again, smiles and then nods approvingly. He appears to be learning a lot.

They get out all the little bikes and trikes and start riding around on them. I am so ashamed of myself as I don't take much persuading to join in. The only way to move on such a little bike is to not sit on the seat but have your bottom sticking right up in the air.

'We ought to be careful. That's really dangerous,' Rhys says.

'Only if there is a low-flying rapist,' replies Myfanwy. And everyone in earshot giggles uncontrollably. We are behaving like schoolchildren. Or drunks. No, worse, we are behaving like drunk schoolchildren. And I willingly join in. What is the matter with me!

Finally, after playing with the toys for a while, laughing and making a right racket, we realise it is nearly 10 pm… and we really should have locked up and gone home ages ago. I glance around the room. The place is wrecked. There are bottles and cheese everywhere, and a number of squashed toys – oh dear, I think we may have been too heavy for a couple of them!

'Leave it, leave it,' slurs Annie. 'I can come back really early tomorrow and tidy up. It's not too bad, they probably won't even notice. Let's just go home.' We all know this can't be true. Annie won't be here early in the morning. And they definitely will notice.

But we can't find the door! Now I know this sounds ridiculous, twenty adults in one church hall and not one of us can find the door. But we are all very drunk and we have all put on our coats, hats, scarves and gloves, so we are very restricted in our movements anyway. Well, I say all. Myfanwy can't find her huge black ski gloves anywhere. We all start hunting for them, checking our pockets. We even go into the church to see if they are on the altar. (Don't ask me why!) We have the giggles by this stage too, and we are all so drunk that everything seems incredibly funny, especially Sioned's hiccoughs and the fact that Myfanwy keeps walking into doorways and knocking her hat off. She decides she must have grown while we've been shut inside the church. 'I'm Alice. One of those bottles tonight must 'ave 'ad 'drink me' on it,' she says. This seems like a reasonable explanation.

To resolve the three problems of:

1) several people being unable to stand upright

2) Myfanwy repeatedly knocking her hat off her head, and

3) the fact we have lost the exit

we decide it would be a good idea to get on our hands and knees and follow the person in front around the room until we find the door. We look like the survivors in a post-apocalyptic sci-fi movie. The sort of film where the whole of humanity has been struck blind. Or in our case, struck blind drunk. We are in this position, on our hands and knees and in a large circle, when a very, very irate vicar bursts through the red curtain. Aha! That's where the door is hiding.

After a bit of a telling-off and us looking suitably ashamed (gigglers were pushed to the back of the group) we finally say our slurred apologies to the vicar, promise to pay for any damage, wonder if God will forgive us, and set off through the red curtain and out of the enormous oak door, staggering on our way home through the snow to Annie's house. Gareth is not amused to have very noisy drunk women arrive. He bundles us in to the kitchen, where he starts making pots of coffee. He is not impressed when we ask him if he made a cake while we were out – which we all seem to find incredibly funny.

Gareth hands a cup of steaming black coffee to Myfanwy. 'What the heck is going on with your head, Myfanwy?' he says, taking the Peruvian hat from her wobbly head. There, inside her hat, are her enormous ski gloves. No wonder she kept knocking her hat off, it must have made her at least ten inches taller and not one of us had noticed. We laugh uncontrollably, and noisily, and wake up Ruby. Gareth is very cross with all of us, especially Annie. But for me, the laughter of the evening lifts my spirits. Things have been tough at work – well tough both at work and at home for some time. I laugh with these women in a way I don't, I can't, with any of my other friends. My friends from home, and work, take things far more seriously, and I have a professional reputation to maintain. Plus, I'm known as the sensible one. I feel I have to live up to this reputation. These women, Parentcraft, and I must admit especially Myfanwy, give me something I just don't seem to get anywhere else – they make me laugh, a deep belly laugh that makes my tummy ache, and it's liberating. It's wonderful. And that, I assume, is why I keep coming back for more.

22 Mix the ingredients thoroughly

When we, Parentcraft, first met, our lives had converged into that single point. There is no way we would have become friends if we had not met at Parentcraft. We did not mix in the same circles. We did not have the same interests, well, except cake. We were brought together by HV, Mrs Insipid's, lack of organisational skills. God bless her!

But the contrasts are stark. The directions from motherhood have made us, if anything, all the more different. My life is packed full. I've been working so hard, but I just can't seem to get that next promotion. Life can be quite tough at times. And Andy is very moody. He's always nit-picking. I just can't seem to do anything right for him these days. At least George is a good boy for me. He is quiet, studious and he is very clever. I'm proud of that. And although George and Andy are inseparable and adore each other, we often have our own little chortle at our GUM jokes – George and Mum.

Today I have a major report to complete and I am deeply engrossed in the analysis when my mobile vibrates on my desk.

'Cun you babysit the kids this afternoon, me Lottie, luv?' Myfanwy's voice asks.

'Why me? And I am not your Lottie!' I do try, every now and again, to ask her not to call me Lottie but I don't know why I bother. She takes great pleasure in doing so to wind me up. She finds it amusing.

'I've run out of people to ask, like. And I know that you do work from 'ome so that's not like real work, issit, 'n' you could 'ave 'em for me for the afternoon, like.'

'Well, it depends what you're planning on doing, Myfanwy,' I say, trying not to sound too prim. 'And I am working.' I try to explain working from home is real work but give up. 'I don't have time to look after children as well as work.' Myfanwy goes on to explain she has met someone at the pub and she wants to go to meet him this afternoon as Dai is working a double shift.

'Well, no then, in that case, I can't. I'm sorry Myfanwy, what you do is your own business but I won't be part of a deceit.'

'Fair play, luv. I'll ask someone else, like,' she replies cheerily, as if this is a perfectly natural and normal conversation, which it is not. 'I'll let you know all the details though when we meet up next Thursday.'

She doesn't even seem to notice the disapproval in my voice, which is masking my intrigue. I'm looking forward to hearing all about it at Parentcraft already, and I block the time out in my online calendar.

23 Almond, orange and polenta cake

Thursday arrives and I hurry to get everything ready for Parentcraft. I suspect, with some self-disgust, that I am more than just a little intrigued as to what Myfanwy has been up to, even though I do not approve. I am fascinated. I suppose it is also about time that I am just a bit more honest with myself and admit that I enjoy hearing about her sexual liaisons. This is all part of my new honesty. Richard, the MD of European Markets, has recently launched a mentoring programme. So the decision to attend has been with the encouragement of my mentor who advised that I need to make some 'me' time. Like on an aeroplane, he said, you need to put on your own oxygen mask first to be able to help others. So, here I am – having some of the aforementioned 'me' time, breathing in my oxygen. Of all the things I could choose to do, some sport - netball perhaps; or education – my French is definitely very rusty; a massage – some time to just relax; yet I have chosen Parentcraft once again. I still feel as though I owe them something for helping me through the black times. I can admit it more fully now – I lost it there for a while. I think I may have been suicidal some days. It's hard to remember exactly how I felt. I was definitely a bit mad, that's for sure. The constant tiredness, my desperate attempts to make sure that George was the perfect baby so that Andy would be happy and wouldn't leave me, the pressure I put on myself to do everything right – and I had the added pressure of my dirty secret. My secret that I didn't have the bond you're supposed to have. And that is so appalling that I'm not allowed to discuss, or even mention it, ever, to anyone. There were some dark days. Sad days, which is sad in its own right because I was meant to be so happy if I were to believe everything people told me about motherhood. Thankfully, I never got to the point where I wanted to harm George. I just found I did everything in a perfunctory way so to the outside world there was no reason for criticism. No-one could suggest neglect. He was clean. He was fed. He was adored, by Andy. And I looked after him as best I could from the strange bubble I had created around my lack of feelings. This is why I feel grateful to Parentcraft for getting me through that time. And they managed to make me laugh. And I did have fun. Lots! It wasn't all bleak.

I'm hosting this time. At least George will help me tidy up when he gets in from school, bless him, if Andy sees all the plates and cups, he'll moan about the mess and shoot off to the pub. It's a regular pattern these days… even when there isn't a mess.

Annie starts with her update and it obvious she is very agitated about something.

'Well, the truth is I've always had a difficult relationship with my mother, as you know. She is very controlling. Very manipulative. The fact that I have to call her Mother. It's so very English, isn't it, but we are Welsh. Honestly… my mother!'

Her words strike a chord. It has been a bone of contention with my mother for some years that she insists I call her Mummy. It is so pretentious!

'It is so pretentious!' continues Annie. 'But once she had decided she was going to be called Mother, well that was that – I called her Mam once when I was quite little, about seven or eight, and she slapped me so hard across my face that I had a red handprint on my cheek for ages afterwards. I was with my little friend Jane. And Jane never really bothered with me again after that. I think her mum must have told her to stay away… birds of a feather and all that. Mother never said sorry. She never says sorry for anything.

She has never liked Gareth. She's jealous, you see, that I have a wonderful man like Gareth in my life and that he loves me for who I am. I probably just haven't admitted it fully until recently that she really doesn't like me very much at all. She is such a snob that it is difficult for her to accept my relationship with him because he is,' Annie pauses for dramatic effect, making air quotes '"only an electrician". She thinks he is beneath me. Not that she worries about me, only that this could reflect badly on her. She has been truly vile to me over the years. But what I really struggle with is that she has been horrible to Ruby on occasions. I can't ever forgive that.'

Myfanwy puts her arm around Annie's shoulder but Annie doesn't cry, or even well up, she just smiles gently, a distant, accepting smile that says 'this is just the way it is'.

'You know, there are so many things over the years that I could have fallen out with her about. Seriously, if I hadn't learned to just bite my tongue, we would have fallen out hundreds of times. For example, she always made it perfectly clear that she prefers my brother and sister to me… and now my brother's and my sister's children to Ruby. Her preference is not even subtle. When I once felt brave enough to ask her about it she acted as though I was neurotic, insisting that my brother and sister need more help and said things like, 'Well, you and Gareth are all sorted, aren't you? You don't need my help. Are you after money?' I don't need her help, that is true, because I have had to sort it myself. Making it sound as though I was after her bloody money. Although in truth, we could have done with some financial help at times, certainly in the early days. My job pays reasonably well, admittedly, but Gareth is self-employed and there have been times when he has had no work at all. We could have done with some help then.

Poor Simon, my brother, he gets really embarrassed and when we have a quiet moment together said, "Sorry sis, I didn't know she was going to do that. I really don't understand why she does this to you all the time." At least he acknowledges it. Sometimes I think I must be bonkers and making it all up. But it's not Simon's fault. Or Susan's. It's hers.

She had me running around one day last month finding investment options for her. She drives me mad. Then, lo and behold, about three weeks later she mentioned, during one of her frenzied telephone conversations, that she'd given the money to some investment company in town. She said it wasn't as good a return as the ones I had identified but the bloke needed the business!

We sympathise with Annie. Her mother does sound like a nightmare. I've only met her a few times at the chldren's parties, and she seemed quite aloof. Sioned and Myfanwy are so lucky to have their mothers. As we pass around my almond, orange and polenta cake and cups of tea. They ask for the recipe, I hope it is not out of politeness. *'It's really very easy. Grease a 23cm round cake tin. Beat 200g of unsalted butter together with 200g of golden caster sugar until they are pale and fluffy; then add the juice and rind of a small orange, plus three beaten eggs and 200g of ground almonds. Then sift in 200g of polenta, I can't get this cake to taste exactly the same as the one Andy, George and I had on holiday in Italy last summer, it might be because I use instant polenta, but that does make it such an easy cake to prepare. Sift in a teaspoon of baking powder. Beat again until smooth. Spread the mixture into the cake tin, and smooth with a palette knife. Bake at gas mark 4 for about 35 to 40 minutes, until it is golden brown. Cool on a wire rack. I made two, so there is plenty for seconds if anyone wants more.'* I say, as they nod their approval. We turn our attention back to Annie.

'My mother is not a loving person and she is not an easy person to love either,' Annie continues. 'She manages to fall out with everyone. She always has. She managed to fall out with our old neighbour, Mrs Price, who we've known for donkey's years. My mother decided she was going to contact the council to have her evicted for her 'aggressive' behaviour. Honestly, Mrs Price wouldn't say boo to a goose. She's not even five feet tall and I doubt if she weighs more than seven stone… and she must be ninety, if she's a day! How she managed to fall out with her I will never know!

I remember she said she couldn't come to Ruby's second birthday party as there was a programme she wanted to watch on TV. She goes through these phases when she becomes obsessed with something on TV. Her own granddaughter's birthday party and a TV programme is more important. She could have recorded it – but no, she wanted to see it there and then. She can never wait.'

'But she and Ruby get on, don't they? Ruby gets on with everyone, doesn't she? She's such a lovely girl,' says Sioned.

'Ah, no, not really. Not anymore. Ruby doesn't bother with her very much these days, and I must admit I am rather relieved. She used to phone her all the time, but she can see now how much Mother upsets me. And it makes Gareth angry that she has me running around at her beck and call. Everything has to be done immediately for my mother and for some reason, I don't know why, I just can't say no.'

I wish I could take this opportunity to talk about my mother too, I know that Annie, at least, would understand but, instead, I sit and listen. I can't. Annie hasn't yet finished.

'When my father died, it also came out, at the funeral would you believe it, that my mother had had an affair for years and years with my uncle. I remember that we were all very close when I was very small. We even used to go on holiday with their family, for goodness sake. As you can imagine there was a big family stink about the whole thing. Susan was terribly upset and stopped talking to my mother for a while, so did Simon, and a number of my cousins and other family members. I tried not to be judgmental, though, I work on the basis that shit just happens sometimes.

I'm not saying she was never good to me, she was, but that was worse because I would never know which Mother I would get – the nice one or the nasty one.

Guess what she had her last big falling out with me about, a couple of months ago?'

Annie looks around our group. We shrug our shoulders.

'It was when Ruby won that prize for gymnastics. She went berserk that I hadn't told her and my sister about it before I told you lot. Now let me explain, this did not mean Susan got to hear about it from some stranger. Not at all. I told her myself. It was just that during the conversation I mentioned to Susan some of the things you'd all said. Susan mentioned this to Mother in passing. Mother went crazy. She phoned me, she was shouting and screaming at me! It was all very, very odd indeed, so I just left her to it, left her to cool down. I phoned Susan and she was absolutely fine and didn't have a problem at all. Mother then phoned me again the next day to tell me how cruel and selfish I was not to include Susan in Ruby's news and that I should have told Susan before I told anyone else, if I were a true sister. About a gymnastics prize! She is mental! Seriously, I'm talking about a school gymnastics prize here! It doesn't make any sense. That's the thing with Mother - she can be very peculiar at times. And I just have to cope with her madness.'

We all sit in silence, nodding awkwardly and trying to think of something appropriate to say.

Myfanwy breaks the awkward silence by saying, 'She's fuckin' mental, mun. 'as no-one got any 'appy news today? Pass me another slice of that fuckin' polenta cake before I slit me throat, what's with you miserable bloody lot?'

And we laugh, with relief!

24 Grease the tin

New wallpaper, another new carpet, the woman decorates more often than I think about it let alone do it. This must be the third complete change of décor, at least, since we met.

'Girls, girls, listen up, cum in yer,' Myfanwy calls us into the kitchen. 'Don't let the kids yer this one, we don't want 'em dropping it in to the conversations with their Dads nor at school nor nuffin.'

Although none of us, I'm sure, approve of Myfanwy's infidelities, her tales of debauchery are fascinating and intriguing nonetheless and we cannot resist listening to the next instalment. I, personally, am both horrified and fascinated in equal measure. How can she do it? How does she do it? Why does she do it? How does she have the time? Myfanwy doesn't need any encouragement to give us every, and I mean every, detail. I wonder what the others make of it but they seem to be so accepting. 'She's just a typical Newport girl,' says Sioned 'that's what they're like. She doesn't mean any harm by it.'

'Well, I goes over to the pub, like, we 'ad arranged to meet at. I did meet 'im last week when I was out on the wazz with our Sharon. You knows I don't get out much.' We all exchange glances – she goes out all the time! Well, at least once a week, which feels like all the time to those of us too exhausted by work and everything else to really put the effort in to socialising. I couldn't think of anything worse than a night in the pub, when I could be sleeping.

'Well, I didn't know lawyers could be so dirty. I'm sure some of this muss be illegal. Annie, you'd know. Is anal illegal?'

'Muff, our office negotiates contract law. I am the office manager. I oversee the negotiation of the deal, I authorise the documents, I write up the contracts, I conduct research and file the reports. Anal sex doesn't come up that often!' replies a startled Annie.

'Myfanwy, please, you really aren't going to share those details with us, are you? That is too gross. I'll have to leave now if you are. I really, really do not want to hear that sort of filth,' I say.

'What do you take me for, luv? Of course I'm not going to share the details of my botty story. 'onestly, you lot, do you think I do 'ave no decency?' She is quite indignant.

'Okay. Just tell us what happened. But leave out the disgusting bits. And watch your language,' I say.

'Well, if I do leave out the disgusting bits and watch me language then there won't be no bloody story, you twat,' she continues happily. ''e, this lawyer bloke, 'ad a case that finished in the morning, much earlier than was expected, like. Copper 'adn't turned up for the yering. 'e says it do 'appen all the time. 'e phoned me at 'ome, like, so we did meet up at mid-day. I'd arranged to meet 'im in the pub where we did meet one evening last week. Well, this time the pub was empty and just felt totally abandoned. It weren't sexy at all, like. And 'e'd forgotten his wallet, so 'e says to me 'Do you want to see me beast?'

'ey up! I thought. But it turns out 'is beast is a motorbike. 'e 'ad his motorbike outside round the back of the pub. Said we could go back to 'is 'ouse to pick up his wallet, like. Imagine that!' She shakes her head in disbelief. 'A lawyer on a motorbike!

'is bike, the beast, was big, and black, and throbbing. I bloody loved it. 'e did put on shades like a New York cop. 'e's not good looking nor nuffin but 'e looked really quite sexy in all the gear, despite his pinstripe suit – that spoilt it a bit. I jumped on behind 'im. I wasn't wearing any knickers so I pulled myself really close to his back. It was bloody lovely.'

We all are aghast and shocked once again but, in truth, we are all fascinated at Myfanwy's double life. And now I know she went out without wearing her panties! How could she?

'We got back to his 'ouse, which is a real bachelor pad. Everything was black or chrome. The flat was nice and clean like, but sorta sterile, like. It didn't look lived in, nor nuffin, like. 'e explained 'e is 42, not married, no kids, no baggage – and I thought, 'ang on, 'ow do you get to be 42 with no baggage but it turns out 'e is a Gemini.'

'What has his horoscope sign got to do with it?' We exchange confused glances but then shrug and decide not to interrupt the flow of the story. 'Carry on,' Annie says, waving at her like traffic.

'Anyway, what was the point of going out again, like? I was in the mood and I could see 'e was, if you do know what I do mean! So I says to 'im, 'What shall we do?'

Well, 'e's inventive... and flexible, I'll give 'im that. Not a 'uge cock, like, but nice. Well 'e gave me a lovely seeing to. And then, he turned me over and, well, you know that bit. 'e says 'e do love a big arse. And I 'ave got a lovely big arse. I won't tell you any more bum stuff, like, because my decency won't allow it.' She smirks broadly at us, delighted at our shocked faces. 'Hmm. It was a lovely afternoon but I'm a bit sore now. I can't sit comfortably. So I've arranged to see him again the next time 'e's available and Dai's working a doubler.' And then she says, 'Do you want to yer my recipe now?' And, for once, we don't.

We are astounded at her story, and shocked once again. Poor Dai. But what can we do? It is like Annie says, no-one is going to stop Myfanwy from being Muff.

25 Prune cake

I've managed to get some 'me' time a few weeks in a row. When my mentor asked when I made time to invest in myself, to liaise with other women to discuss their issues and the solutions they proposed – I couldn't think of anything. So I said that I occasionally met with a group of women that I had known for a number of years, when I could make the time. He was delighted that I am working with a women's network! Imagine his horror if he knew the topic of our conversations. Myfanwy is giving us the next instalment. The lawyer had been back in touch with Myfanwy, we discover at our next Parentcraft (women's network) meeting. 'Is Dai a doubler today?' he had asked. 'Great. My house, midday. Dress as a school girl. Big white cotton knickers. I've got a big surprise for you.'

Myfanwy is in full swing telling us another of her outrageous tales of depravity –I can't help but be fascinated. It is so different from my mundane life. She is a good storyteller too, I'll give her that, she has us all waiting for her next revelation as she slowly takes a sip of her tea. I always feel excited when she tells me her tales but I always feel so sorry for Dai, the cuckold. But what can I do? I suppose I could tell Dai? But it is none of my business. And what will that achieve? Absolutely nothing. So, I sit and listen with embarrassed fascination.

We have met at Sioned's house and today's offering is a prune cake. Sioned gives us a rapid recipe.

'I based it on one of Delia's.'

We all nod our approval. We all like Delia.

'But I adapted it a bit along the way. *I put loads of prunes to boil and then simmered them for about seven or eight minutes. Then I drained them and mashed them but left some bits quite chunky. Then I added 200g of butter, about 200ml of water and 300g of condensed milk and brought it all to the boil, stirring all the time to stop it sticking. Then I let it cool.*

I sifted 220g of flour, half wholemeal and half plain, a pinch of salt and half a teaspoon of bicarb. When the prunes were cool, I stirred in the flour then added a tablespoon of marmalade, I used the blood orange marmalade that Myfanwy made for me.

I cooked mine in the Aga on a low shelf for about two hours – I had to put some baking paper over the top of it because it had started to go a bit dark. Once it was cool, I drizzled over some melted marmalade to which I added some of the water I boiled the prunes in.'

'I wonder why prunes get such a bad press when they are so delicious?' I ask.

'Cuz they do make you shit!' says Myfanwy, always able to bring any situation back to its basest level. Once she has our attention, she takes the opportunity and continues with her story from earlier. 'So, I dresses up as a school girl. I still 'ad my old uniform at me Mam's although I had to rifle through her wardrobe and then I snuck it out. I was dropping Chardonnay and Silver off with 'er so it was easy to distract 'er. 'ey, girls, it all still fitted me. What d'you think about that then, eh? Well, it was a bit tight in places but I still got it on. Mind you, I was fuckin' 'uge in school, mind. I did put on a black uplift bra, a white school blouse, my old school tie, navy pleated skirt, long white socks - they are actually Dai's old five-a-side football socks, I couldn't find any school ones and didn't want to ask if they had any size 8 girls socks in stock in Shaw's – they do know me in there!

I tied me 'air up in bunches and even pencilled on some freckles across my nose – then I drove to 'is 'ouse, like. Well, that felt really strange. School uniform and driving! Weird, mun!

When I got there, I parked round the back and waited till there was no-one about so I could make a dash for the backdoor. 'ang on, that was me story last time, wasn't it! Ha ha! I knocked on 'is door loudly - 'oping he wouldn't keep me waiting long and I wouldn't be spotted by one of 'is neighbours. After a few seconds, 'e opened the door dressed as a Headmaster. I burst out laffin'. He had the hool outfit including the mortar board 'n' cape - 'e was taking it very fuckin' seriously.

'e led me into his living room where there was a blackboard and a small chair in front of it. On the blackboard there was a list of: 'Ten things that result in punishment'. I was laffing and giggling when 'e pointed to item number seven: No giggling. With that, 'e got a cane from behind the back of the blackboard. "Bend over," he said. So I did. WHACK! He whacked me on the arse. It bloody 'urt. I mean it really bloody 'urt. It wasn't pretend smacking. Tears sprang into my eyes. 'e looked really pleased. A broad grin stretched across his face. "Good girl" 'e said. "Good girl. Now sit on that chair for your lesson. Sit still, mind" and 'e pointed 'is cane at number six on the blackboard list: 'No wriggling on your seat.' I cun tell you now, I 'ad no intention of wriggling – my arse was smartin', like.

I was sat on the little chair in front of the blackboard. He knelt down in front of me and pulled two scarves from under the seat. 'e tied my ankles to the legs of the chair. "Now you sit still for me," 'e said. I was still trying to suppress my laffter despite the painful throbbing from the whack on my arse, which was not sexy at all. Just bloody painful, I cun tell you. 'oo gets off on that? Mental people, that's 'oo.

It was all so silly I 'ad to bite the back of me 'and to stop meself from pissin' meself laffing. That's what I used to do in school to stop meself laffing 'n' all.'

'Seriously, Myfanwy,' I say. 'Where is this story going? I don't want to hear any more about some sicko. And the whole schoolgirl thing is revolting. It's abhorrent. That's just paedophilia really. Plus I have been permanently scarred by some of your tales.'

Myfanwy is delighted by the horrified expressions around her in Sioned's kitchen so she takes no notice and just continues her tale.

'It's not like Philadelphia, Lottie, luv, it's like St Trinian's. It's just a laff!' Myfanwy looks confused, unable to understand why this tale isn't okay, and then she continues cheerily. 'When 'e is all aroused I do think to meself well, 'is flat might be nuffin much to write 'ome about but at least 'is cock 'as got good taste. Then do you know what the dirty bugger wanted me to do? 'e was so aroused by this point that he wanted to fuck me with my tits pressed against the window pane so that passers-by would see. I'd 'ave loved that, mind. But, well, anyone could 'ave seen me - including them lot finishing afternoon shifts at Dai's factory.

Well, I wasn't 'aving that, was I. So, I insisted on a shag and got out of there as quick as poss. Needs must,' she says, looking very proud of herself, her face streaked with a broad grin. 'So, 'oo else

’as got any news this week?’ she says in a tone of voice that suggests she had been discussing the price of postage stamps.

We are aghast and, unsurprisingly, no-one is prepared to follow that. So we take our prune cake and head for the lounge, desperately trying to think of new topics of conversation.

26 Nutty loaf

Gareth has given the front room a lick of paint over the weekend and Annie is telling us how difficult they find it to fit in all the household chores when what they really enjoy doing is sitting and watching TV together. She seems to be managing just fine to me – a decorated room, clean and tidy house and time to bake an incredible chocolate and hazelnut loaf. 'Great cake, by the way. What's the recipe?' I ask.

'I've got a copy of the recipe typed out for you all up in the bedroom but I'll tell you now anyway,' says Annie. *'Melt 110g of unsalted butter, stir in 85g of plain chocolate, add 125g of caster sugar. Then add in 125g of plain flour, ¼ teaspoon each of baking powder and bicarb. Add around 120ml of soured cream and beat in two eggs then stir in a teaspoon of vanilla extract. Finally, fold in 70g of ground hazelnuts. Pop the mixture into a greased loaf tin and bake at 170 degrees for about 45 minutes. Easy!*

But, enough of my recipe let me tell you about Mother, she's gone a bit odd' as she hands Silver and Megan a bowl with raisins and cut up pieces of grape to each of them.

Each time we've met of late, Annie has been opening up about her relationship with her mother and her childhood experiences. I find it fascinating, it's one of our connections.

'What do you mean, she's gone a bit odd. She's always been odd,' I say, popping more cake into my mouth. It really is delicious. It'll have to be another week of cutting back the calories at work.

'She's always been mean and cruel, as you know, but this is really odd. I first noticed it a couple of months ago when the phone rang, I picked it up to my mother's voice saying, "Oh very devious, Annie. Yes, I've got to hand it to you that was very clever sending around your spy dressed as a postman. What exactly are you up to? I know you are after my money. But you don't fool me, my girl. I spotted it straight away. Do you think I wouldn't spot a different postman? Do you really think I'm that stupid?"

So I said, "Mother, what on earth are you talking about? You told me last month that Ted, the postman, was retiring. You told me you gave £10 towards a retirement gift for him even though you think he is lazy. You told me last week that a new postman had started and that you didn't like him as he didn't look very clean to you. Don't you remember?"

To which she replied, "Don't try and twist this all back on me. I know what you are up to!"

She hung up. I let it go though and didn't mention it when I phoned her later in the week. She seemed alright, well her usual snide self, but okay. Then, a couple of weeks later, she phoned me and said, "Where is it? I know you've sent that bloody awful man here to hide it from me. Well you can just tell him that he can come and put it back."

I said, "What on earth are you talking about, Mother? What's gone?"

"That thing, you know, what's it called. Voices come out of it. Don't pretend you don't know what I'm talking about, Annie. Don't patronise me. You know exactly what I mean."

It took me a few more moments to work out she meant the radio. She was honestly accusing Gareth of driving to her house to steal her radio. She's definitely not right in the head.'

Although this is all desperately draining for Annie, I also feel quietly relieved to know that there are people other than me that struggle with their relationship with their mothers. I know from all I've read in the papers and seen on television that lots of childhoods aren't great, but from what Annie tells us it seems she was very poorly treated by her mother probably right from the day she was born, perhaps even before she was born. And it resonates deeply with me. She was sometimes physically abused, but it was the emotional side that hurt Annie as she always seemed to have been short-changed in the affections of her mother. For Annie though, and the thing she will always struggle with, like me, was that she was treated inconsistently – treated reasonably well some days and then really poorly at other times. She never knew if she was coming or going. So, poor thing, she never had any idea which version of her mother she'd get. She had spent most of her childhood confused by her emotions. Just like me. Perhaps that's why I've found it so hard to bond with George? I find I like him much better the older he gets. I find it easier to relate to him. And then, of course, whenever I think like this I am struck by the guilt again. I am not a good mother. I'm not a natural. Damn all these complex emotions.

And of course, for Annie, like me, it all had to be hidden too. Annie was not allowed to say to anyone she had a problem with her mother. How does a child say that anyway? 'My problem is that I don't think my mother loves me.' That's too hard for any child to articulate. Hell, that's too hard for anyone to articulate, let alone a child. So she didn't tell anyone, not even her grandparents.

'I had such a great relationship with my grandmother. Mother was always jealous of that – Nanny and Mother had never found their common ground and the air was always a little strained whenever they were in the same room together,' says Annie. 'My Nanny gave me things Mother never could, like genuine, undemanding love and friendship.' This is another connection I have with Annie.

Annie tells us that in her early years her mother had often been very angry with her when she came home from nursery or school or from staying with her grandparents. Annie had adored her father who, by all accounts, appears to have been a loving man. But she had been unable to rationalise or understand her mother's erratic behaviour. Her father was probably unaware of the effect that the break-up of his marriage to Annie's mother was having on his eldest daughter as he was too wrapped up in the irrational behaviour of his wife.

With hindsight, Annie tells us in her cool, detached way, her mother was probably suffering from a combination of three things: post-natal depression, the beginnings of her problems with alcohol and pure exhaustion from having three children under the age of five.

Her mother was volatile. An outburst, or explosion, was both unexpected and expected at the same time - it certainly went alongside every big event in Annie's life. She anticipated the crescendo from her mother every time there was a birthday, or when it was Christmas, or a family party. Waiting for the outburst was agony and then when it was over and her mother had calmed down again, they could get on with life.

With the benefit of maturity and a few more life experiences Annie now talks coolly, and, if anything, probably a little too rationally, about her issues with her mother.

'I think that she was jealous that I had taken my father's attention away from her, and that I had not been the boy she had longed for.'

Over the years, Annie's mother was either horrible to Annie or pretty much ignored her and was openly jealous of any attention Annie got from her dad, even in later years when her parents had divorced.

'I suppose I had thought that because my father made Mother angry, that when they got divorced, well I thought she would be happy with me. But actually, she just diverted her venom towards me all the more. It was just as well I had to go to school each day or she may have killed me. She nearly did most weekends. Her drinking was worse at weekends and everything I did seemed to just irritate her more and more. Not that she was always violent towards me, well no more than I deserved, I suppose, but the bitterness made her tongue the most painful weapon and I was often on the receiving end of that. Of course, I don't remember all that much about it, just that I was very sad to be at home and very glad to be at school.'

Yet another connection, I understand completely and it brings back how much I loved my own school. It was so much nicer than being at home. School was stable, rules were kept, it was consistent, there was routine, it was manageable. Yes, I loved it. I'm glad Annie is like me.

Annie continues, 'My mother remarried very shortly after the divorce from my father. She was nice to me for a little while. But that good relationship didn't last long. By the end of the school summer holiday she was back to her nasty, vindictive self. My new step-dad, Des, was an odd sort of a chap. He would lavish me with attention some days, and then, without warning, almost completely ignore me. I was already a crazy mixed-up person even back then, I just hide it much better now.'

I notice how Annie's body language changes as she reveals this to us. She still sounds calm and remote but as she pauses, I notice that she has curled up onto the sofa, with her arms crossed across her chest. It is more difficult for her to voice the history with Des than she would have us believe. I feel honoured that she trusts us enough to open up.

'All my childhood memories have become very hazy,' she continues. 'I don't know if any of the things I have told you are the complete truth. It is just how I remember it. That and the guilt. It wasn't long before my stepfather's attention became more overt. I've never told anyone this – not even Gareth. Whenever my mother was out, my stepdad was much nicer to me. When she was around he would be very cool towards me and then really tell me off for any small misdemeanour, much to my mother's glee and she would say things like, "Thank you, Des. That's what that girl needs. A bit of discipline. Her father mollycoddled her. It's ridiculous. No wonder she is so cheeky and unruly. He's done so much untold damage, that man. Thank goodness you can sort her out."

I remember one summer when I was lying sunbathing in the garden,' Annie continues, 'when Des, my stepfather, turned the hose on me. He said it was to cool me down in the sunshine. He did it without any warning. He was laughing his head off. I was trying to cover myself up. My little bikini had gone clingy and see-through when it became wet and I was really embarrassed. He brought over a big fluffy towel and made me strip off in the garden. He rubbed me down with the towel. But here's the thing. I felt so guilty because I liked it. And although I was also hugely self-conscious I liked him fussing over me and all the attention. And I liked him touching me. Of course, I realise now that he was getting off on it, but as a child you don't know these things so I just felt guilty for feeling that way. Thankfully, it never went as far as actual abuse.'

It all sounds very abusive to me. I had no idea that she had endured the unwanted attention of her stepfather. How awful. Poor thing. I want to say this but I don't want to interrupt her while she feels comfortable with talking to us.

She continues, scarcely taking breath. 'I don't think Mother knew. I did try to tell her a couple of times but she wouldn't listen to me. Come to think of it, she was probably already drinking quite heavily by then so she probably didn't know what was happening most of the time.

Although we were by no means well-off back then we weren't hard up either yet my mother was very mean. She would deny me any sort of luxury, in fact she would often ration the basics. She had locks on the cupboards and the fridge. I was hungry for quite a large proportion of my childhood. My mother quite often took Simon and Susan out for the day and would leave me at home with a list of chores to do. I was like a modern day Cinderella. You probably think I'm making it up now, don't you? But it's true.'

Annie tells us she suspected her mother was purposefully leaving her alone with her stepfather sometimes. I can't believe that. Why? Why would her mother do that to her? It doesn't make sense to me. Annie goes on to say that she isn't sure, but it was such a crazy, mixed-up relationship so who can say what her mother intended. Annie tried to tell her mother that something wasn't quite right with the way Des was touching her but her mother refused to believe her. And Des started calling her new names, 'my special girl,' 'my darling Angharad,' and then later, 'my secret-keeper,' and then later again, when she had avoided being alone with him, names she didn't like, 'slut' and 'tart'. Annie insists that it never became sexual abuse. But I suspect she may be lying about how far it went. It doesn't add up, and if it wasn't actual sexual abuse then it was almost certainly grooming. But those were much more innocent times. She didn't know about stuff like that back then. Annie says she never actually, specifically, told her mother all these things as such so she feels she can't blame her mother for not acting on it. And reminds us Des and her mother divorced, which is what probably saved her from his approaches. It's sad. Poor Annie.

Annie tells us all this without any emotion in her voice. There is always a distance to Annie. She looks into her tea cup but still has an inscrutable smile on her face.

'Of course, I blame myself. I should have stopped him touching me right from the beginning.'

'Annie,' Sioned exclaims. 'It is never the child's fault. NEVER!'

'Thanks, girls,' she says with a cheery smile. No difference in the tone of her voice to when we've complimented her on a recipe or passed her a cup of tea.

27 Another layer

'Girls, girls, listen up. I've got another one for you,' shrieks a delighted Myfanwy.

'Okay, okay,' says Sioned. 'But keep your voice down this time. We are in a public place after all.' Sioned rolls her eyes disapprovingly, warning Myfanwy that she means it. We're trying a pub with a play area today, even though Silver and Megan are a bit bored of it, and are sitting at a table with drinks and snacks and painting each other's nails. The older children are all at various after school clubs. They all have busy lives. The smell of chip fat is heavy in the air. Staff have to wear whacky hats – they don't look happy about it.

'Well, this one was such a pervert.' Myfanwy is gleeful.

'Before you go on, Myfanwy, who is he, where did you meet him, how did you meet him?' Annie asks.

'Well, we've got that internet-thingy that you've all been going on about at 'ome now. It's great. I cun do me shopping 'n' everything. But me friend, Sharon, told me about these great sites where you can 'ave a right laff chatting to blokes, like. You don't 'ave to meet them if you don't want to, nor nuffin. It started off as a dogging site but it's not just that anymore.'

'Hold on, hold on, you'll have to enlighten me. Dogging site? I can tell by the expression on your face it has nothing to do with dogs,' I say.

'Well, that's where you're wrong, smartarse. It did originally start off with dogs actually. It is for people who like to watch other couples 'aving sex. So, you do take a dog with you in case you are stopped by the police and you can say like, "I'm just taking the dog for a walk." It's just become known as dogging.'

'So, hang on, how do you know you are going to see these people having sex? I don't get it.' says Sioned.

'Well, that's the beauty of that internet-thingy, couples who do want to be watched cun give the details of where and when, and those who do want to watch cun come and 'ave a look. It's what the internet was designed for according to Sharon. She says it used to take ages to organise and then you ran the risk of a wasted journey if it all got called off – no way of letting people know, see. Now with this internet-thingy you cun post, 'ark at me with all the jargon, you cun post all the details and then update it if there is a change of plan.'

'Oh my God, Muff, that is so seedy... and so dangerous. You need to be careful about what you are getting in to. Dai may find out for a start,' Annie says.

'Don't worry, Annie. I'm careful, like. So anyway, this guy, Justin, 'e and me got chatting on the site, and I really liked 'im so we arranged to meet. Just go out for a drink, like.'

'Sorry, sorry, hang on,' interrupts Annie. 'I will let you complete the story soon but I just want to clarify, so you didn't go 'dogging' with him. And this Justin isn't the lawyer? So what happened to him?'

'Oh 'im! He was a skank and a liar as well as a lawyer. Seriously, there was always some reason why 'e couldn't pay. 'e'd forgotten 'is wallet, the cash machine ate 'is cashcard. Always bloody something. I don't mind if they wine, dine and sixty-nine me but I don't like being taken for granted. They need to treat me like a princess. 'e would just phone me when 'is balls were full - so I dumped him. Now 'as anyone got any other questions about the lawyer or anyone else?' She scans our faces. 'Good. So let me tell you about Justin. First thing you should know is 'e is a teacher.'

'Are you just working your way through all the professions? Lawyer, teacher, wasn't there a postman too? And a sailor a while back? Are you aiming for tinker, tailor, soldier, spy?' I ask.

'Stop interrupting you lot! I'll never get through this story unless you stop interrupting. So, Justin is the teacher, and I met 'im on the dogging site. All clear? We goes for a drink in Caerleon, right. I don't know why they always choose bloody Caerleon. All Dai's mates drink in Caerleon. I could get caught out one of these days, but it won't be my fault. It'll be the vodka's.

Justin and me went for lunch in the pub. 'e paid. No lost wallet! I liked that. We 'ad sausage and mash. I loves sausage, I do. Then 'e said that 'e was really into 'istory, 'e's a 'istory teacher and we should look round the Roman remains. I thought it would be pretty dull. I went there on a school trip and I was bored shitless. But actually it was really interesting and 'e seemed interested in it 'n' all. 'e's from Somerset and 'e said 'e'd never been to Caerleon before.

Cun you believe that? Never been to Caerleon when you are interested in ’istory. Seems mad to me. ’e said ’is real interest was mediaeval ’istory. So I guess that explains it.

After ’e ’ad looked at the remains for bloody ages it started to drizzle with rain and ’e said we could go back to his place. I was relieved cuz time was getting on but I thought ’ang on a minute I’m not going to Somerset this afternoon. I got kiddies to pick up later. But ’e said that ’e is a teacher in Cardiff now. So I said so, “’ow come you’re not in work now then?” ’n’ ’e said ’e was chucking a sickie so ’e ’ad to be careful not to be seen so it made more sense to go to ’is place as ’e wouldn’t bump into any of the other teachers out there. Well, that suited me like. So, I phoned our Mam and asked ’er whether she could pick up Chardonnay and Silver from school and ’ave them for a few hours for me. She’s ever so good like that, me mam.

Justin’s car was lush and we ’ad a good ol’ snog down by the amphitheatre.’

‘Is that a euphemism?’ I ask.

‘What d’you mean, luv?’ asks Myfanwy. I explain what I mean.

‘No, you complete twat,’ she continues. ‘We really had a snog by the amphitheatre. Are you ever going to let me tell this fuckin’ story? So, we had a snog by the amphitheatre, get it, before we set off so it must have taken us about an hour to get over to ’is place, all in all. ’is ’ouse is quite remote. No close neighbours.

’e took me in the ’ouse and asked if I was in to role play. Given my experience with the lawyer, I was a bit concerned about role play in case of the giggles ’n’ smacked arses ’n’ all, but I said I’d give it a go in any case, like.

Well, ’e brought me this blue dress and a white linen wimple thing. ’e went on ’n’ on about it, said it was authentic in style from 13th century Wales, said women in Wales would ’ave worn pretty much the same as women in England and most of Northern Europe, said the fabric may have been different and possibly heavier in colder countries. ’e seemed to be into details like that. It was like being on a school trip to St Fagan’s. Mind you, come to think of it, ’e could have told me that about a sack cloth though, I wouldn’t have known the difference. All I can say is that it was damn itchy, a bit like a sack cloth. Women back then must 'ave 'ad skin like leather with all the chafing. Plus no knickers! I likes that bit, mind. 'e says there are quite a few paintings from that time which show village scenes and women are warming themselves by the fire and are clearly not wearing knickers. Is that right, do you reckon? 'e even had these little leather shoe things for me to put on. I was a bit curious 'ow 'e 'appened to 'ave the right size but I decided not to enquire further. Some things are best not to know.

Well, guess what he did then?'

'I assume it is something terribly vulgar,' Sioned says.

'No, it surprised me though,' says Myfanwy.

'Goodness me, if it surprised Myfanwy goodness only knows what he must have done.'

''e changed into an outfit like the pied piper and started playing me a tune on this little flute thing. Seriously! I was trying really 'ard not to laff, like, because 'e was taking it terribly seriously. I couldn't help it, though, I just burst out laffing.

'e was very cross and took me firmly by the arm and said, 'You have mocked your Lord and Master, you must be punished,' and I thought, 'uh-oh, 'ere we go again. Sounds like there is more arse smackin' on the cards,' but I was determined there would be no smacking or slapping this time. It's just not sexy, is it! 'e took me, nicely mind, into the back of the cottage and guess what he did 'ave there?'

'Seriously, I don't think I can guess. Was it a donkey?' I say.

'Oh, you disgusting thing. You've shocked me. You of all people, Lottie, me luv,' Myfanwy says in both mock horror and delight. 'No, it was a stocks. Wooden stocks that they used to put people in in them olden days. 'e said it was based on an original design. So I 'ad to sit on a little wooden stool and put my ankles in, which he then locked and then put my wrists in and then locked that.'

'Oh my goodness, Myfanwy. That is so dangerous. What on earth were you thinking? Why didn't you just get out of there? It is so scary – you were putting yourself into such danger,' I tell her.

'Nah. It weren't dangerous, luv. 'e did climb underneath and lick me out.'

We all shriek our collective dismay whilst Myfanwy looks very pleased with the shock and disapproval she has created once again.

'Not much of a punishment though, is it, like? It wouldn't stop me from doing it again. More likely to make me do it all the more,' she says, and snorts with glee.

'But that's when it did get a bit scary. 'e took me out of the stocks and offered to bathe me and wash my back for me, 'n' all soppy stuff like that. Then 'e started saying really weird stuff like 'e would love to be able to run a bath for me every day so that I could step in when I'd 'ad a 'ard day, 'e would love to be able to wait on me 'and and foot. That freaked me out. Well, I don't want 'im running a fuckin' bath for me. What would Dai say? I don't want 'im in my 'ouse, doing things for me, messin' with me 'ousework. So I says somethin' like 'we'll 'ave to see' and then 'e says 'e do really like me and would I consider moving to Somerset with him when he moves in the summer? And I says, "No, luv, I'm Welsh, see." Cheeky bastard. Moving to Somerset indeed.

So I were trying to make it clear that I meant no and I didn't have no time for no more silly chit-chat because I needed to get 'ome soon for the kids. Then 'e started all the kissing. Big slobbering kisses. Yuk! I've got a bit of thing about tongues in me mouth. Not nice. I'm alright with cocks, but not tongues. So I gave him a quick sucky-offie. Well, girls, it was tiny. Poor sod, and with a name like Justin too.

So, 'e drove me 'ome and dropped me off at the end of the road. I decided there and then I wouldn't be seeing 'im again. Plus any man who specifies the meat content of a sausage for a pub lunch on a date isn't worth bothering with, are they, like?'

I don't know what to say. Her stories aren't sexy and yet I find myself on the drive home hoping that Andy is in a good mood this evening. It's been a long time for us… weeks! No, longer… months. In fact, I can't even distinctly remember the last time. Although I disapprove of her behaviour, and I feel really sorry for Dai, I can understand that she has needs – sexual needs – that simply aren't being met in her marriage. But women aren't meant to say this, are they? Good girls don't complain. That is very sad for her. And, I've just realised, for me too.

28 Double layer cake

'Wait until you see what I've got on my mobile phone.' Muff is beaming from ear-to-ear.

'What do you mean, what you've got on your mobile phone?' asks Annie.

'Get with the times, luv, you cun 'ave cameras 'n' videos 'n' everythin' on yer phone these days.'

'Why would you want that? If you want to take a photo you can use your camera, if you want a video, you use a camcorder. Why would you want it on your phone? Surely the quality can't be very good?'

We've met at what has now become one of their regular haunts, a pub in Caerleon. I'm not sure why they've chosen it actually, it's only redeeming feature seems to be that it is mutually inconvenient for everyone. We all have to drive to get there so our choices are either a dry night or an expensive taxi. This has also meant another dry spell for our cake consumption.

Myfanwy hands the phone over to us, and we gather round to see what's she's done this time.

'Oh my God, Muff,' shrieks Sioned. 'You can't show us stuff like that without warning. Jesus! We're in the middle of the pub. Anyone could have been walking past and looked over and seen that. Dai could have walked by, or one of his mates, or your dad, or a neighbour. God, Muff, you just don't care, do you?' After taking a big gulp of her drink Sioned adds, 'What's more, I'm scarred for life... again!'

Muff is beaming with delight at the shock she has created.

'Why, why, why on earth would you think I would want to see you doing that?' I say. 'And how on earth did you come to be in that position anyway?'

'I've 'ad one of the best fuckin' nights of my life,' says Muff. 'And when I do say fuckin' nights, I do mean fuckin' nights. Girls, if you've never 'ad a doubler, and I'm not talking Dai the Doubler 'ere, I mean a genuine doubler, then you 'aven't lived.

It was only last Saturday, and I was out with our Tracey, you know, my sister-in-law, well my ex sister-in-law I suppose she is now like because she did divorce my brother. Anyway, it was 'er 'en party cuz she is marrying some twat. And you know, she's a helluva girl, so I knew it was going to be a wild night. Dai was working a double night shift at the factory so I got our Mam to baby-sit and said that rather than disturb them by getting back late at night I would stay at our Tracey's for the night. Well, that was it, wasn't it. I knew I 'ad a free pass so I went for it. Big time. I loves them new alcopops. They are great for me cuz, as you know, I don't really like the taste of alcohol.' We exchange glances – first we've heard of it. 'So we 'ad four or five of those at our Tracey's while we were getting ready to go out. I've done really well at Weightwatchers so I was feeling all slim and sexy and I'd bought this great dress from Primark and was wearing really high strappy sandals, you know the ones that I bought for Debbie's wedding that I didn't wear in the end, they're lush. I 'ad a new thong that is so tiny it goes right up my arse. We did the 'cun you see my thong' test and…'

'Hold on, hold on, what's the 'can you see my thong' test?'

'Well you do put your thong on, bend over and say 'can you see my thong?' and if the answer is, 'what thong?' then you know you've got a small enough thong on!'

We now exchange confused thong glances.

'Anyway, back to me story. So, we did meet up with the girls in town. We went to the Murrenger, and then the Queens, or whatever it's called now, and there were thirteen of us altogether. God, we 'ad such a good laff and I was really good because I just stuck to the alcopops all night whereas some of the girls were doing chasers, the lot. They're right slags some of them, mind. Real dogs when they've 'ad a drink and they were fuckin' wrecked. Three of them 'ad to be put in taxis and sent home before closing time. On the way to the Stowaway, or whatever it's called now, we went to McDonald's and Debbie was sick in there.'

'Hold on, hold on again, I thought you were on a diet. Why did you go to McDonald's?'

'I just had the salad in the bun in Macky D's cuz of me diet. It was great – they didn't even charge me. I did eat meat later that night, mind, but then you did see that in the video clip.' She honks at her own joke. 'And then, for some reason, we were thrown out of

McDonald's by this little lad. I can't remember exactly what it was over, I think it was when I asked him, 'can you see my thong?'

Bits of the night then go a bit 'azy but I do remember queuing to get into Tiffany's, or whatever it's called now, and they wouldn't let us in. Debbie, not our Debbie, another Debbie, went off with one of the bouncers round the back of the carpark too. And they still wouldn't let us in. Just as well really because one of the other bouncers there is moonlighting from the factory where Dai do work, and it would 'ave been round that place like wildfire and Dai would 'ave found out exactly what I got up to. They're like that in factories.

So we went on to the Stowaway, or whatever it's called now, and the fresh air did us no good as two more of our group decided to go home, just because they do 'ave babies who would get them up early. I told them to phone their Mams and get 'em to babysit overnight so they could stay out longer. That's what Mams are for. But no, they wouldn't 'ave it. Said they didn't like to ask. Wimps. So I think at that stage there were about eight of us left, but I could be wrong. We was trying to get served at the bar but it was 'eaving in there and there was this big bunch of lads blocking our way. Fit lads, mind, nice firm bodies, so I did a quick hip grind on a few of them, and yes, very yum bums, nice. So we all got talking, like.

I started chatting to this one guy, Scott, gorgeous, absolutely bloody gorgeous and 'e was all over me like a rash straight away. I mean 'e was seriously good looking but so cocky. So I asked 'im 'ow they all knew each other, and 'e said they worked together, so I asked whether they were out on a stag night, and 'e said they worked together. It was very noisy in the club, so I asked 'im again, because I thought 'e must have mis-yerd me, and said I knew they all worked together but were they on a stag night. So I thought 'e must be a bit thick, like, or perhaps English, so I asked 'im again, but slowly. 'e burst out laffing, and explained 'e 'adn't understood a word I'd said and was just guessing answers. I thought that was really funny. 'ow cun you not understand me, like? I speaks as plain as day. Turns out they were on a stag do, 'n' are English. So no wonder 'e couldn't understand me, like. 'n' fair play, it is noisy so 'ard to yer in the Stowaway, or whatever it's called now.

As the night wore on, more and more of the girls dropped out and went 'ome. Debbie, the other Debbie, not the first Debbie, went off with some great ugly git. 'onestly, 'e was snogging 'er all over her mouth and I thought, 'you wouldn't be kissing her like that if you knew what else had been in 'er mouth tonight. Macky Ds and cock. At about 2am, it was only me and our Tracey left. Well, I wasn't going to waste my night by going home too early so we said let's go to Maindee for a curry. I knows all of 'em, down there. I used to go in a lot with Dai, and now the kids do love a curry 'n' all. They don't mind me in there, I pop down in my nightie and slippers sometimes to pick up a take-away, and they never mind. Mind you, all the waiters stand as far away from me as possible whenever I do go in. Worried what I might do, see. They like it really, mind. It's a laff.

As it was really late, I banged on the window of the curry house, flashed my tits, and then pressed them against the window pane.'

'Muff, enough of this, you didn't really flash your breasts and press them against the window, did you?' asks Sioned, in disbelief.

'They were lucky to only get my titties. I sometimes do flash the chocolate starfish,' says Muff.

'Where on earth do you get your terms of reference? I have never heard of a chocolate starfish. I can imagine what you mean though so please don't explain any further. Honestly, I just keep learning new obscenities from you all the time, Muff,' says a dismayed Sioned, tutting furiously.

Delighted, Myfanwy continues her story of her outrageous night. 'Anyway, I shout from the doorway, 'Hello, Mr Curry Man, are we too late? Cun you still serve us? It's four of us like. Me 'n' Tracey, the one in the veil, 'n' these two beef lads all the way from England.'

'For you, Muff, anything!' and he speaks to a couple of the young waiters in Punjabi who reluctantly get a tablecloth out of the drawer and re-lay a table. 'For my very favourite customer, anything at all.'

'Oh good, show me your willy then.'

'Oh Muff, you are so funny, are you back on your usual or are you still on your diet? And what about your gentlemen friends here and this beautiful young bride? Madam? Sirs?'

I goes to the toilet and I do chase a few of the waiters around, 'aving a laff like. A couple of the chefs come out to see what all the commotion is, and wave and shout, 'Hello Muff, we thought it must be you,' and, 'you're late Myfanwy, lovely. And you've not got your slippers on?'

'Yes, boys, I've got a free pass. I cun stay out all night, if I wants, like.' I flash a wink at Scott and 'is mate, Joe.

On my way back from the toilet I do forward-rolls down the length of the restaurant to a round of applause from the staff and the few remaining diners, who all seem to be very drunk, several are asleep, one actually with 'is cheek in 'is tandoori chicken. Just as well I'd done the thong test and been thoroughly waxed to within an inch of me life... and an inch of me fanny, it's like Hitler's moustache down there at the moment, if the truth be known. When I reach our table I did do the splits, to rapturous applause from Scott, Joe and Tracey. For a big girl, I'm quite supple, you know.

Tracey orders the usual, chicken tikka masala and a chick pea curry for me as I'm on a diet, you know, both with arf 'n' arf. Scott and Joe think this is hysterical. 'Chips with a curry, delicious,' they say 'but half chips and half rice is pure genius. Why don't all curry houses do this?'

''oose chapatti is that naan?' I ask. The boys do think it is the funniest thing they have ever yerd, better even than arf 'n' arf. They do say it like half and half. It's pronounced arf 'n' arf round yer, I do tell them. They will know yer English if you do keep saying half and half.'

We eventually finish the meal and the boys pay the bill and I could tell by the way Mr Curry Man beamed, they must 'ave left a massive tip. Remember to split it 'arf n arf' they say, laffing.

Scott and Joe invited me and Tracey back to their hotel and we decided to go for it. Tracey, she was 'ammered at this point, but she still 'ad 'er veil on and 'er 'just married' sign pinned to 'er bum. 'Last night of freedom,' she said with a smile, 'why not carry on drinking at the hotel? Do it in style!'

I think we must 'ave got a taxi from Maindee to their hotel but I can't remember that bit at all. Next thing I knows we were trying to get someone to open the bar because it was locked up – I thought big posh 'otels like that do keep the bar open twenty-four/seven but apparently not, and they wouldn't reopen it just for us, they said. But I do think it was because they could see we was already ratted and we was being very loud. So the guys suggested we go 'n' raid their mini-bar. They were sharing a room, they said. They are not from round yer, see. I can't remember where they did say, it was in England somewhere, though.

We raided the bar and got everything out of the fridge on to the bed. We ate the chocolate and the peanuts, and started mixing cocktails. Then we decided it was not enough and we wanted chips and pints of beer. So we ordered chips and beer from room service. It was so funny because the chips arrived on a big silver platter. They were alright like but not as good as our local chippy, like. Bit posh. The waiter even brought one of those fold-out tables to put them on and then little pots with tomato sauce and, wait for it, mayonnaise! I was nearly sick at the thought of it. 'oo would put mayonnaise on chips? Later I discovered there are lots more places you cun put mayonnaise, oh, but you saw that too on me phone, didn't you.

So Tracey, goes off to the loo, when she comes out she says she is going 'ome. I pulls her back in to the en-suite bathroom to ask her what was wrong and she said she had thrown up, and was feeling bloody awful, and wanted to go 'ome. For someone who is a right slapper like Tracey, she 'as some funny ideas. I told her I didn't think Joe would mind that she'd chucked, I really don't think 'e would 'ave, but she went 'ome anyway, leaving me snogging Scott on the one single bed and Joe sat forlornly on the other.

Scott picked up the little pot of mayonnaise and started dipping his finger into the mayo and dotting it around my neck line. 'Yum', he groaned, in a very deep husky voice, 'a pearl necklace. Do you like pearl necklaces Muff?' I said that I do, very much.

We exchange a confused look in our Parentcraft group. 'What's a pearl necklace then? It's obviously not a necklace made of pearls, is it!' asks Sioned.

‘God, you lot!’ replies an astonished Myfanwy. ‘Just ’ow closeted ’ave your lives been? Are you really living in the 21st century or ’ave you just slipped through a black ’ole and are actually Victorian virgins. Fuck me. Thank goodness you ’ave me to enlighten you.’ She explains, in graphic detail, a pearl necklace, to our collective enlightenment.

‘Anyway,’ says Muff, ‘let me continue – you’re gunna to love this story. After a while, Joe says ‘Do you mind if I join in?’ and I said, ‘Oh no, I’ve never done anything like that… oh, go on then.’ So he started stroking my leg while Scott was kissing me. ‘Perhaps you’d like a double string on that pearl necklace?’ said Joe, with a wink.

Next thing I know, Scott’s got my tits out and is giving them a good sucking and Joe moves round the bed, unzips his trousers and drops his cock into my mouth. He didn’t even ask if he could!’

‘Would it have made any difference? Did you want him to ask?’ Annie says.

‘Yes, I wanted ’im to ask. Now, I’ve never been particularly fond of giving sucky-offies, as you know, but I had a good old gobble on his dick. That’s when he picked up my mobile phone and started filming. Do you want to see it again?’

No, was the conclusive answer!

‘And that’s when I had my roasting.’

‘What? Do you mean a telling off? From whom?’ asks Sioned.

‘Good God, you are so naïve, aren’t you, my lovely, lovely friend. I do love you to bits. It’s like talking to a child. You know nuffin, do you? Don’t worry, I’ll tell you all about it. Well, like I said I started giving him sucky-offie, Joe that is. And from that well, I never looked back – well it’s hard to look back when you are on all fours giving sucky-offie to one, with the other giving you a good ’ard shafting from behind. That’s why it is called a roasting you see it’s like a hog roast, one at either end. I can tell you now, it was fantastic. I love it from behind. It’s my favourite. Well you saw ’ow much I was enjoying it. We kept going at it until the morning. Then I booked a taxi and I was out of there and back at our Tracey’s before 6:30am.

She didn't even ask me what 'ad 'appened so I didn't show her the mobile footage.'

No, probably wise, we agree.

'Strange thing is, as fab as it was, I 'ave no particular urge to do it again. It's one off me bucket list – a doubler. So girls, what do you think about that?'

I simply don't know what to say. The differences between us and Myfanwy were obvious from our first meeting but they are even more stark now. Over the years, although I still find her embarrassing, I have to admit she is hysterically funny as well as kind and generous. She would give you the shirt off her back but unfortunately it looks like it is not the only thing she is prepared to give away. It's a totally different world. How can she do it? Poor Dai.

29 Baked Lemon and Blueberry cheesecake

Another few months pass before I manage to make my next Parentcraft. Annie, Sioned and Myfanwy have organised their lives around a Thursday afternoon, but I have to put work first. There always seems to be some crisis at work that I'm needed for. But, I'm here this week, so I'm feeling quite proud of myself although I'm keeping an eye on my Blackberry for urgent messages.

We are sitting in the dining room tucking in to hefty slices of her Baked Lemon and Blueberry cheesecake, which Sioned has drizzled with warmed blueberries (they become lovely and unctuous when heated with a dash of maple syrup, she tells us.)

'Hey Muff,' Sioned shouts across the table to her. 'Don't be scared. It is made with Philadelphia not Kiddiefeelia!' Myfanwy flashes her upright middle finger. We've all learnt our own ways of dealing with Myfanwy. I can laugh at her and with her now. She's not so bad.

'Go on then. Do it. Tell us the recipe, Sioned,' Myfanwy says.

'Use an 18cm round cake tin with a spring release, line the base with baking paper. Pop 150g of digestive biscuits in the food processor with 25g of melted Welsh butter and about 50g of stem ginger in syrup. Blend until it is in evenly crumbed. Press this mixture onto the base of the cake tin. I baked just the base in the roasting oven of the Aga for about fifteen minutes, then removed it and let it cool before I gave it another fifteen minutes but in the baking oven this time. I find this is the best way to get a really crumbly base that doesn't go soggy when you add the cheesecake mixture. I left it to start to cool whilst I made the filling, which I made using 400g of Philadelphia, juice and rind of two small, unwaxed lemons, 125g of caster sugar, four tablespoons of crème fraiche and one egg, all blended together. Spoon and then spread the mixture onto the warm (not hot) base. Then push a small number of blueberries around the edge, about one inch from the edge of the cake tin. Bake in the roasting oven of the Aga for twenty-five minutes, then into the simmering oven for fifteen minutes. I'm sure it'd be easier in a conventional oven – you wouldn't have all this faffing about to do, but moving it about is definitely the best way in an aga.

Then finally about forty minutes in the baking oven. Leave it to cool for about thirty minutes then release the tin and use a palette knife to carefully remove it completely and transfer to a serving plate. You can eat it warm, but I let mine cool and then warmed some blueberries with a dash of maple syrup until they started to ooze – just drizzle this over each individual slice.'

As we 'ooh' and 'aah', I decide to tell them my story, although I realise that I am feeling a bit nervous about 'sharing', as they put it. Quickly, before I lose my nerve, I say, 'Well, I have a story for you that I think you will all enjoy.'

'What the fuck? You? You do 'ave a story? You never 'ave a story. You do only ever talk about work… or Andy… or George and his schoolwork. You never tells us anthin' about you. You do keeps it all to yerself, always, like. Locked away. Fuckin' 'ell! Roll on, gull.'

'Well, today is different, as I do have a funny story for you. I was driving back from Birmingham, down the M5, just where you join the M50. Do you know where I mean? I'd had a very difficult meeting with the legal and regulatory team, and then a long meeting with Finance, and I admit I was a little distracted thinking about this and that, and the big tender we are working on, when I heard the siren and saw a blue flashing light in my rear-view mirror. I looked at the dashboard. Drat! I thought to myself. Nearly ninety miles an hour! I slowed down immediately but the police car kept behind me with his lights on so I pulled over into the hard shoulder and the police car pulled up behind me. Drat! I thought again. I had hoped that perhaps this policeman was on his way to some other incident and it had nothing to do with my speeding. I quickly undid my seatbelt and went to get out of the car when I noticed in my rear-view mirror that the policeman was already out of his car and walking towards me. I knew from other people's tales that this is not a good sign, if he is prepared to get out of the car then you are likely to get booked. I thought to myself 'honesty is the best policy' and I was determined to get it over with as quickly as possible. I glanced back and saw that his colleague was still sitting in the car.

"Well, well, well," he said rolling back and fore on the balls of his feet like some comedy laughing policeman. "What do we have here?" he said, casting his eye over my metallic lilac Mercedes convertible. "Do you know what speed you were doing, madam?" he asked. He is spotty and looks about 16 years old, which he obviously can't be. He has a big, condescending smirk on his face, immediately getting my back up.

"I'm very sorry officer, I think I was probably going a bit fast and possibly doing about 75 miles an hour." I knew I was doing more than that. Honesty is the best policy hadn't lasted long. "I realise that is above the speed limit. I am very sorry."

'Very sorry wouldn't be any good if there was an accident, would it?' He said in a patronising tone. He got my hackles up again, and I felt myself flush with annoyance. Just as well he couldn't see me clearly in the dark.

I tried my 'honesty is the best policy' approach again. "I accept that point, officer.' It feels strange addressing this child as Officer. 'The reason why I may have been going a little too fast is that I am in a bit of a hurry. Is there any chance you could just give me a warning and I could be on my way?"

Mistake!

After a long drawn-out pause he slowly says, "Nope!" He sucks air in-between his teeth and looks at me hard for a very long time. He makes me feel very uncomfortable and I am grateful again it is dark as at least he can't see how much I am blushing. Very, very slowly he blinks but just stands there. I don't know what I'm supposed to do or say next. Then the other officer got out of the car and was checking the rear of my vehicle. He was quite a bit older and was obviously senior in rank. He signalled to the first officer who sort of half saluted and half made a bow. The first officer returned to the car and got in to the passenger seat. And the senior guy started chatting to me and, to my surprise, was rather flirtatious. It was a real good cop, bad cop double act. I didn't have my wedding ring on, I had taken it off earlier in the day because my hands had become really swollen in the hot office. He must have noticed that I wasn't wearing a ring. So he asked me if I was single and I lied, I don't know why – saying that I am divorced. He asked for my mobile number, which I gave him, my real one. Honesty is the best policy, remember, and on the basis that his colleague had just taken all my details I thought I had better not be caught lying on top of everything else. Just as well because he took out his phone and immediately sent me a test text and my phone beeped inside my handbag on the passenger seat next to me and was clearly audible. 'Fancy going out for a drink sometime?' he asked and I nodded a yes. He smiled then and said, 'Okay then, on your way.' So, no ticket for me! Hurrah!

'But you're not going to meet him, are you?' asks Annie.

'Of course not,' I reply and they laugh again as we tuck in to more of the baked cheesecake. 'But it shows I've still got it, girls. I'm still attractive to some people, even if it was in the dark, on the M50, and to a man in a high vis jacket, but hey, at least it is someone. I can't believe that I got away with it. It's outrageous really but it saved me a fine and points on my licence. Honesty is the best policy… except when a small white lie helps!' I grin at them.

'Is all that true?' asks Myfanwy.

'Not all of it' I reply. 'Part of it is a joke that Richard told me a few weeks ago. But most of it. I did get stopped by the police'

Anyway, there are lots of reasons to be running late when you drive back from Birmingham.

SECTION THREE

30 Eton Mess

I don't know what to do. I really don't know what to do. What should I do? One thing is for sure, I certainly shouldn't have drunk that bottle of wine to myself. That hasn't helped at all. I'm totally drunk now on top of everything else I have to deal with. The house is eerily quiet. George is in bed asleep. I look at my hands, I'm actually wringing my hands. I am so full of despair. I feel totally bereft and the hollowness I feel inside is a pain like no other. Who can I trust? Who can I talk to? I need to speak to someone or I really don't know what I'm going to do and I'm scaring myself.

'Muff – it's me, Lottie! Can you come? I don't know what to do? Can you come?'

And her Newport voice replies, 'Righty-o, 'old your 'orses. I'll be there in ten,' without even asking why.

Why Myfanwy in my hour of need? Because I know now, and it's taken me a long time to realise, that she is a bloody good friend to me.

It is about 10 o'clock on a Saturday evening and my life is falling apart. I open the door to her – I'm still wearing my dressing gown, I haven't managed to get dressed today but Myfanwy seems to have arrived in her bedclothes anyway. A pink fluffy dressing gown and enormous slippers in the shape of roadrunner from the cartoons. How did she drive in them? I decide not to ask – I'm hardly in a position to judge.

'Where's George? Is 'e alright?' she asks and I slur that he is in bed. 'So, what's up then, luv? Where's Andy? Whassgoin' on, like? 'As someone died? Is it yer Mam?'

I take a deep breath and try to steady my voice and my thoughts. 'George is fine. No. No-one is dead. Oh God, I don't know how to say this. I don't know where to begin. I don't know what to do. I'm such a complete fool. And such a hypocrite.' Another deep breath, 'I'm having an affair. Or at least I was.'

'Oh my God! Lottie. You can't be! Not you! 'oo with? 'ang on. Not with that policeman bloke you did tell us about?'

'Policeman? What policeman? Oh, you mean the one on the M50. Oh God, no, not him.'

''oo then? 'ang on a minute. It's not that bloody Marie, that woman you do keep going on about? Somethin' big in finance, int she? Marie this. Marie that. I bloody knew it. All that fem'nist stuff but really you just wanted to get into 'er knickers. I said to Dai years ago that I thought you was a lezzer. Well, now I know I'm right you cun come clean. I said it, didn't I, all that time ago. One of us is bound to be gay. It's you, innit. Am I right? I bet I'm right. But, I 'ad no idea you was out. When did all this 'apppen? 'ave you always been gay and Andy was just some kinda of, whass the word? Dormant dick.'

I hear a noise. I recognise it but can't quite place it. And then I realise that it is laughter, my laughter. Even in my most desperate moment Myfanwy has made me laugh. I realise that is why I've called her in my hour of need. Because she can make me laugh.

'Muff. No. It's not Marie. And 'lezzer'? Seriously Muff, do you even live in the 21st century? And really, where do you find these expressions? Is dormant dick even a real thing? Anyway no. And I'm sorry to disappoint you but I'm not gay. But I fail to see what difference would it make if it were a woman? It'd still be an affair. I would have still have been unfaithful and broken my marriage vows, wouldn't I?'

'S'pose so,' she says sulkily, but then says in a quiet muffled voice continues, 'but a bit of girl-on-girl action, it wouldn't 'ave been a cock, would it, so it would 'ave been a bit different.' Then back to her normal volume she adds, 'so, 'oo was it or shall I 'ave another guess? Let me see…'

'No, Myfanwy… Muff. Please stop guessing. It doesn't matter who it is…was. It just matters that it is over. And I can't believe it's over. Oh God!' I slump down heavily onto the sofa.

'Of course, it matters 'oo it was. It wasn't no-one. It was someone and you might as well tell me now cos I'll work it out in the end and we will 'ave wasted a 'hool load of time. So, 'oo was it?'

'Oh, Myfanwy. It is, was, someone from work. It's, it was… oh God, this is really hard, I can't even get my tenses right. He was the MD of European Markets. He's now the EMEA and LatAM CFO.'

She looks at me, glancing from one eye to the other like some newly trained optician, and says 'What the fuck is that? Speak in proper English for once, won't you.'

'It's Richard.' I look at her awaiting her response.

'No! Not that one yer always goin' on about 'im 'n' all. I knew it. All that crap about equality for women and really 'e just wanted to get into yer knickers. Wharra complete bastard. You twat.'

Myfanwy's bottom descends towards my sofa as her mouth drops open. Her bottom cheeks brush against the brown leather but spring back as does her jaw. Upright and closed mouthed once again she says, ''e's yer boss! This is goin' be awkward,' she says as if she's solved the puzzle. 'I'd berra stick the kettle on, you need some black coffee… and so do I… and some cake. Whaddoyou gor in yer cupboard?'

Returning with a tray that has a cafetière of coffee that makes my stomach lurch on first whiff and a packet of biscuits she says, 'So 'ow the 'ell did this pile of shit 'appen?'

'I don't know. I just fell madly in love with the most amazing, fantastic, clever, exciting man I'd ever met. He's, was, is so funny. So clever. And I really thought I'd found my soul mate. And now, now…'

'Does Andy know?'

'Yes. He knows. It's been awful. I thought it was real, you know. What we felt for each other, Richard and me, I mean.'

''ow long as it been going on for, like?'

'Bizarrely, it had started that day, the day I got stopped by the police. That's why I was late. That's why I was speeding.'

'Why 'aven't you mentioned any of this before then, Lottie? I know we 'aven't seen as much of you as before but you 'aven't said a word. That was months and months and months ago when you did tell us about that policeman bloke. It must 'ave been back at, what, the beginning of the year, wasn't it?' She shakes her head as she tries to calculate the timeline. 'I didn't know you even fancied anyone, let alone 'ad an affair. You complete dick.'

'I know. I know. I know. I've been such a fool. I've ruined everything. I told Andy and he left me. That was a couple of months ago. He was so furious. I've never seen him, I've never seen anyone, that angry. And let's remember I grew up with my parents. If you want to see angry, that's the go-to. But this was something else. I did actually think, at one point, he might kill me. By the look on his face, I mean, not by anything physical, well except for throwing me in the gutter, of course.'

'Fuck! 'e threw you in the gutter? Really?'

'Well, metaphorically rather than physically. But he said he'd ruin me. Financially… and he said he'd tell everyone what I've done and that I deserve to be in the gutter, which is where I'll end up. He says I've shamed him and emasculated him. He said it is all my fault, which is, of course, right because it is.'

Myfanwy interrupts, 'But don't you see, Lottie, luv, that Andy always does this. It's always about him. How it'll affect him, what people will think of him.'

I am astounded. I'd assumed everyone would agree with Andy, that he's done nothing wrong. It's all my fault, because it is. It's all my own doing, or undoing, because it is. I am amazed, more than amazed that Muff doesn't think so, at least not completely.

'Listen, Lottie. That 'usband of yours, well, 'e's a bit of a knob, if truth be known. We all do think so. 'e's so up 'imself. And so bloody selfish and so fuckin' critical of you all the time. I don't know 'ow you puts up with it.'

'But Andy is so … handsome.' It is the only adjective I can think of in my drunken state.

'And don't 'e bloody know it.'

'And so clever'

'Clever dick.'

'And so… charming.'

'Slimy!'

And I laugh. There, she's made me laugh again. Thank God I phoned Myfanwy. 'It's worse now though,' I say.

‘’ow? I don’t understand. ’ow is it worse now?’ Myfanwy has sat next to me on the brown leather sofa. She waves a packet of dark chocolate biscuits under my nose. I decline. I can’t remember when I last ate anything, but I sip the black coffee she has poured for me. I hope my stomach will be able to hold it down.

‘Now it is all falling apart. I really don’t know what to do. What should I do? What should I do?’ I am scared by the panic I hear in my own voice.

‘Why don’t you tell me everything, Lottie, luv. I can’t make an ounce of sense of this bit. Tell me everything’ she stuffs a dunked chocolate ginger nut into her mouth.

‘I don’t know how to tell you. It is so awful. I am so ashamed of myself.’

‘Just tell me what you cun. No need to rush, we’ve got all night if you do need it. As long as you do ’ave more biscuits.’

‘It, the affair, started when we’d been working on a big bid. Richard had been so complimentary about my work and he and I thought the same way about everything. We were in the war room with the bid team. I’d done such a good job on the Y2K project that the client had specifically asked for me to be involved in the bid for a much bigger programme for them. Do you know what I mean when I say Y2K, Myfanwy? It was all that work I did last year preparing for the new millennium. Do you remember how happy I was at New Year because it all went so well? No blips.’

‘I remember you droning on about a load of boring worky stuff that didn’t make any sense when I was trying to do me Christmas shopping when we all went to Bath that time. Is that what you do mean? I thought you was talking about KY jelly.’

‘Yes,’ I say unable to suppress my disappointment that she thought my biggest project, and biggest professional success ever, was boring and she mistook it for a lubricant, even when there is such a mess here and now. ‘Yes, that’s the one. Anyway, you have to work really closely on a bid and usually, after a few long days in the office and the obligatory Indian/Italian/Chinese after work and then the pub, you are pretty much sick of the sight of each other. But not us. Not Richard and me. We got on like a house on fire. And it was so nice to have him leading the team. And he was really supportive of me especially with the rest of the team. When they rolled their eyes because I said I had to go, he was the one saying that we need to support each other and explained that I have to get home for George. No boss has ever done that for me before. Ever. Andy won't even contemplate missing squash on a Tuesday, and I have no-one else to ask, so I've had no choice but to leave early when we are working away from the Bristol office on a Tuesday.

Anyway, one night I had made arrangements for my neighbour, Joan, to have George. Do you remember Joan? She's getting on a bit to be babysitting but George is a good, quiet boy, and quite content with a maths quiz book and his Game Boy. So, what with Joan's help, and Richard's support, and the team all falling into line, it felt like the first time for a long time that I've really been able to contribute without clock watching excessively. I was so grateful. And felt so appreciated. I work hard, you know. I more than make up the time the rest of them put in – they're always taking cigarette breaks or going off for something or other. I just put my head down and get on with the work. The rest of the team on this bid – they're mostly from our grad scheme - were staying in a hotel in Birmingham because of the long hours. It was getting near to the bid submission date so we'd booked office space at the hotel and created our war room. Richard was our main link to the CFO, sorry Myfanwy, I can't help the business speak, that's Chief Financial Officer, she's the one with the reins on the money. We'd just received her projected revenues. Richard was really good about ensuring the Bid Lead reprioritised the workpackages and meetings so we could do my bits first. Then he sent the team off to get a break before the evening session and he suggested that he and I could cover off a couple of points before I needed to leave. We'd just find a quiet space in the hotel... and before I knew it I was in his hotel room with documents laid across the bed and I was lying with them. I still didn't expect anything to happen. That sounds so naïve now, doesn't it. But I didn't. I didn't know he felt the same way about me and had a major crush on me too. But least of all I didn't expect to fall madly in love with him. But I did. And I thought he'd fallen in love with me too. We were so close. We had started to do everything together in work. I knew people had started to talk but I didn't care. They were talking about me being his favourite, I don't think anyone suspected an affair. I could sense, and see, their disapproval at our closeness though. Some people even spoke to me about it. They'd say things to me like, "You and Richard are very close these days, aren't you?" I'd just smile. It was none of their business. They never said anything to him though.

I was so flattered that Richard liked me as much as I liked him. He's so clever. And funny. Did I tell you he is really funny? I can't remember what I've already said. I just couldn't stop thinking about him all the time. I was obsessing really, I suppose. I was like that at Uni. I would just get fixated with someone and then couldn't get them out of my mind until I slept with them. But at Uni it didn't matter the same way as it does now.

I can't believe you said Andy is slimy though. I thought you'd be on his side. I really think Andy is blameless in all this. Although, to be perfectly honest, when I've said at Parentcraft how good Andy is about everything, it's not strictly-speaking, 100% true. If I'm going to tell you everything I may as well be completely honest. Andy has been pretty horrible to me for a while now. Well, not so much horrible as… indifferent. It didn't seem to matter to him if I was there or not. He didn't seem bothered either way. I don't know when that started. A long time ago. Long before George started at Juniors. Gosh, I don't know when it started to be wrong for us but it feels like it has been wrong for a very long time. Actually, Myfanwy, being honest, Andy was downright nasty to me sometimes, putting me down, sneering at whatever I said, picking fault in everything I did. Or he just ignored me altogether. I don't really know how I feel about Andy now to be perfectly honest. I'm so confused. I know he is a good man. Loyal, faithful, respectable, honourable. All the things I had seen in him when we first met that made him the man I so desperately wanted to marry. He was always so in control. It was one of the things I loved about him. And he was always the centre of attention. Everyone loves Andy. He can be so charming and he is so handsome. Everyone wants to be with him.'

'They don't!' interrupts Myfanwy.

'Well, I so wanted to be with him. And all the girls at Uni did too. I couldn't believe my luck that he chose to be with me. I never thought that I would ever stop loving him and I am still amazed that I have treated him like this. But the truth is I was just drawn to Richard like a moth to the flame, and he to me. After that first time, we tried to end it innumerable times, every couple of days in fact, but we just found ourselves drawn back to each other. I can't believe this has happened to me. It honestly doesn't seem real. I have been so, so blissfully happy some days with Richard that I could literally have burst with joy. That was then. I just don't know what to think now. I don't know what to do.'

Myfanwy looks at me straight in the eye, but I notice she moves the open bottle of wine on my coffee table and tucks it away under the table. I was just thinking about another glass and must have glanced at it. She doesn't miss a trick. I thought I was coping with my drunkenness quite well – obviously not. Her expression as I talk is sometimes confused, sometimes aghast, sometimes concerned – a whole selection of emotions in equal measure as I go through my sorry tale. I can't tell what she has concluded. No doubt it is that I am a complete idiot. I am!

'Although Andy has scarcely bothered with me for a long time, years, I still thought we had a good marriage, until I met Richard. Of course, it wasn't the same mad passion but that can't last forever. I thought we were just content.' I continue, 'As long as the house was clean and tidy to his liking, then Andy was happy oh, and that there was a meal to microwave, and that I didn't interrupt any of his sports or TV, or made any plans without consulting him first to make sure it didn't clash with anything he wanted to do. Then, over time, I realised a good day was when he didn't even notice whether I was there or not. The alternative was, if I got any of these things wrong, that he would sulk with me, for days on end, not even speaking to me at all some days. That was horrible. That was cruel. I put a brave face on it for George's sake.'

'So don't you see,' Myfanwy says. ''e's not completely blameless. 'e 'as some part in the break up, or do you say breakdown, of yer marriage. 'e's no bloody innocent.'

'Oh Myfanwy, you can't justify an affair just because…'

'Why do you always want to take all the blame? Why, even when 'e has been a complete git, do you protect 'im? I don't understand? Whass yer mot-er-vation?'

'Because… because… I'm not worthy. I'm not good enough. He deserves better than this. The way I've treated him. One evening, a few months into my love affair, I was standing in the kitchen peeling potatoes, feeling blissfully happy, when Andy caught me off guard by directly asking me, "Tell me the truth, where have you really been?" I don't know why, but I decided not to lie. I said, "With someone else."

I don't know, Muff, whether film-makers are amazingly insightful, or whether human experiences have started to echo what happens in films but I felt the rush of the camera to my face, like in Jaws. Then as I looked him straight in the eye, there was a whooshing swirling noise in my head and then the thump of my own heartbeat. Can you believe this? I said to him, "I love someone else and, well you may as well know the truth, he loves me and we want to be together," and that was that. Andy knew about Richard.

I don't know what I was expecting his reaction to be. I suppose I knew it was inevitable that he would find out at some point. I don't know if I wanted to destroy our marriage. Whether I wanted, in some perverse way, to hurt him. Let's remember, Andy is not to blame here, it is all my fault. It was awful. I saw the colour drain from his face, he went a strange grey colour and then, after a tirade of foul abuse, as the colour rushed back into him, he started packing a bag immediately and went to tell George they were leaving.

George, although he is eight now, and a big boy, had tears rolling down his cheeks and do you know what he said? I still can't quite believe what happened next. George said, "Mummy, can I live with you, please?" I don't know who was the most surprised, Andy or me. I was so confused. George adores his father. And Andy adores him. It's always been about the two of them. Why on earth would he want to stay with me. Confused I said, "But why? Why would you want to?" And do you know what he said? "Because I love you, Mummy. I want to live with you, not Dad." Andy went ballistic and started shouted at me that I had poisoned George's mind. And poor

George was terribly upset. Poor boy. Thankfully, he didn't understand a lot of the things Andy was saying. He is such a dear thing. All he ever wants to do is please. He hates it when people argue. I feel so guilty for putting him through all of this. I was, I am still, so surprised that he chose me. I never thought for one moment that George would want to live with me. That he would choose me. But he did. And I felt enormously proud and honoured that he did. So George stayed with me.

So, Muff, although it was awful it had still felt like the right thing to do. I was shaken by the whole turn of events but I also felt excited so the next morning I called Richard straight away and told him my good news... the good news that I had told Andy about us and the surprising news that George wanted to stay with me, and the even more surprising fact that I felt quite elated, and proud, that George had chosen me. Then I asked Richard when he could tell his wife. He said it would be better to wait a while until Andy had calmed down a bit and accepted what had happened. Then he would tell his wife. So, that's what we did. Waited for the right moment to tell her. Well, that's what I thought we were doing, anyway.

Richard said it was better to wait to buy somewhere together until he had told his wife. That sounds reasonable, doesn't it? I wasn't being a complete fool, was I? I was so in love with him I accepted all of this happily. Then, just as we were preparing to set up our home together, his eldest daughter announced her wedding and he said that he really couldn't upset the family by leaving his wife in the middle of the wedding plans so we would just have to wait a little longer, just until after the wedding. I understood and agreed. That seems fair, doesn't it? You wouldn't want to cause any unnecessary upset, would you? It wouldn't make any difference to us. We would just have to wait a little longer to live together but everything else would be about us being together as much as possible. And we had the rest of our lives to look forward to being a couple properly. Weeks turned into months, weddings, of course, don't happen quickly, and so there were no signs of Richard's imminent leaving of his wife but that didn't matter as we were blissfully happy when we were together. We talked about when would be the right time and agreed how important it was that we got the timing right for our benefit just as much for his family. I knew it was going to be tough for him. It'd been tough for me and he's been married for a lot longer. It made sense to find the right time rather than blurting it out at the kitchen sink as I had.

Of course, I know now that there was never going to be a right time to tell her, because Richard wanted to have his cake and eat it. And for a time, that's exactly what he got. Is that fair? I don't know if that's fair. I think he wanted the same as me, at the beginning anyway. I do. I really think he wanted to be with me. That can't have all been an act for my benefit, surely? I'm not sure when it all changed for him. And I was enjoying the affair, the secrecy and the clandestine arrangements. I'm sure he was too.

A few nights ago, was it two or three, maybe four? I don't know, I've lost track. I've been off work. I phoned in sick. Can you believe that, Muff? I phoned in sick! Me. Charlotte Harrington. I've never fake-phoned in sick in my life. Never. Of course, I couldn't have worked so I was sick in a way. My eyes are so puffy I couldn't have seen my computer screen.'

'What 'appened, like? 'ow did you find out then, luv?'

'I was so happy. I was lying on my bed a few nights ago, chatting to Richard on the phone. He was at his house; I was asking him how his daughter's wedding plans were coming on, even giving bits of advice, stroking the indent in the pillow where his head had lain earlier that morning when from the distance I heard his wife calling him. He quickly said his goodbyes to me, promised to see me later in the week as we'd arranged, and blew a kiss down the phone. He thought he'd hung up. Fool. He'd put the phone down but he hadn't disconnected the call. It's his new mobile – an android. He's not used to it yet. Says he likes his Blackberry better. I should have just hung up but I could hear the distant conversation between Richard and his wife. I heard her enter the room. I heard her gently laugh, I could hear a gentle kiss, perhaps on his cheek, or perhaps on his mouth, I can't be sure, and I heard a woman's voice, her voice, his wife's voice, it was such a shock as it was the first time I had thought of her as a real human, isn't that ridiculous, I heard her ask if it was work, and the same voice then said he works too hard. I heard Richard respond using the same soft tones he uses with me, I heard him use sweet affectionate words that I thought were exclusively for me. I heard him casually say, 'love you, my darling,' in exactly the same way he does to me. I heard my whole life crumble away. And I heard a voice, a voice I know well, shouting, 'you fool, you silly, silly, foolish girl,' and I knew that voice was my own, inside my head, calling me to my senses. What a bloody fool. I loved him so much. I can't believe he has done this to me. I am totally, totally distraught, in a way I didn't think was possible. How can it hurt so much? I am such a fool and I have no-one to blame but myself. I knew, just from hearing that snippet of conversation, before I hung up, that his wife had no idea whatsoever that there was any threat to the marriage. And in truth, I heard in Richard's voice that she was right, there was no threat to their marriage – I am not a threat, I am just the other woman. I am mortified. What a bloody fool I've been.

So, Muff, what on earth do I do now?'

'I dunno, luv. But you definitely shouldn't be on yer own though. Is there anyone who cun come and sit with you, like? What about yer Mam? Could she come down?'

'Please, don't be stupid, Muff, I have enough to contend with already. I don't want my mother here. I need someone who can help me. I really don't know who to ask. I know I could try Sioned or Annie, or perhaps some of my friends from Uni, but… in truth, I'm too ashamed. Now I've told you, could you, will you, help me, please?'

'Yeah, luv, juss let me make a few phone calls, like but I cun stay yer with you, at least until I cun get you to go to sleep. So 'ow about you get into bed and I make you some cocoa?'

'That's very good of you,' I realise I am still slurring. 'I have no right to expect any help from you when I have been such a cow to you. I've never helped you.'

'Lemon pots,' she replies.

31 Crumble

I survive. Of course I do. You don't die from a broken heart. I create a parallel universe and it runs its course. I function. I return to work. I have to. I avoid any contact with Richard. I have to. I look after George. I have to. There is one thing I do that is just for me. Parentcraft. I suppose I always have done this just for me - the difference is that I know now that I want to go and I'm not going for someone else or out of loyalty or for Annie or Sioned or Myfanwy. Or even for the cakes. I am going for me. I need their friendship. I need the support of these women, especially on the days when I can't see my way out of the awful mess I've created. I also need to hear about their lives so that I can try to keep my sorry debacle of a life in some sort of perspective.

'My bloody mother,' says Annie. 'She's moving in with us.'

'What? When was all that decided?' Sioned asks.

'Last week. She is not capable of looking after herself any longer. Gareth's not pleased, obviously, but what can I do? She is my mother after all. And I'm the eldest, it falls to me. Plus Simon and Susan really don't have the time to be able to care for her the way I can. I want to show her how you are meant to take care of your family. I have to do this.'

'But is she really that bad that she needs to move in with you?'

'Yes, she's that bad. She's been diagnosed with early onset dementia. Typical of Mother. She does all the things that doctors advise people to do to avoid dementia and yet she has to get it. They say you should take regular exercise. Well, she does, she has always gone for long walks everyday with the dog, and she's too mean to pay for petrol for the car to drive anywhere anyway. She does crosswords. She plays bridge. She does all sorts of puzzles – these are all things that are meant to help. Typical that my mother is the one to get it and causes us all this upset.

She's been so difficult to deal with. She's refused to sign over power of attorney. She's young to have dementia but that's what it is. I thought a lot of her behaviour was to do with her drinking. Well, so did her doctor actually. But, as you all know, we hear the stories from the neighbours about her going into town in her nightie. She wore a tea cosy as a hat one day too. How embarrassing. She has lost a lot of weight because she forgets to eat some days. Her emotional outbursts have been getting worse and far more often. She has become quite violent too, which is obviously going to be a concern for us, having her living in the house with Ruby.

She's been phoning me to tell me about people ripping her off, you know workmen and such. Then it was the postman was stealing from her. Then it was Mrs Price was taking money from her purse. None of it was true, of course. It's so embarrassing and understandably people are outraged and upset that I could think such a thing. Which I don't… but I've had to check. She's had the police out there a couple of times and on the last occasion she told the policeman that I was the one that'd called them and I am a neurotic, paranoid bitch and that I am making it all up about the stealing as an attention-grabbing tactic and it is best to ignore me. She told them she's never accused anyone of stealing from her. The poor policemen. With all the things they have to deal with they still managed to look embarrassed at the barking old biddy. Not long ago, probably a couple of months, Gareth called in to see her and she attacked him. Literally, physically attacked him. I told you about it, didn't I? She scrammed his face with her nails, it actually drew blood in places. Gareth said that she had been very odd before she attacked him but then she went wild. She was screaming about him spying on her and something about that she knew he was selling secrets on the black market and he wouldn't get anything else from her. Then, when she spoke to me that evening she was perfectly lucid and said she just hadn't recognised him and thought he was an intruder. We just thought she was drunk.

After that she started destroying all sorts of documents for fear of them falling into the wrong hands. I've told you about Mrs Price, haven't I? Her lovely neighbour. She's getting on but dear Mrs Price has been helping to look after her, going to the house, cooking, cleaning, doing bits of shopping and she is so frail herself. That woman must be a saint. Well, the way my mother spoke to her was just unacceptable. We knew that we had to do something about it then. We couldn't let her carry on in that state. She was shouting and swearing at little Mrs Price. She hasn't been cooking for herself properly. She's been confused about her timings and what she did manage to cook has been ridiculously overcooked. "It can happen to anyone," she'd say, "I made a mistake. I'm only human. We all make mistakes." She's been drinking heavily too so that hasn't help, but I suppose it has also masked the extent of the problem. Lots of people, us included, assumed for a long time that she was just pissed again. But it wasn't every single day, that's what would confuse us, she'd have patches where she seemed to get better.

It's horrible,' Annie scrunches up her nose 'she has started wetting herself at home and in bed. We can't let her carry on like that, can we? That's when we decided that she would have to come to live with us.

After lots of discussions, well arguments really, where my mother insisted she didn't need help, we insisted she did, it was, after many trips to the doctor, and innumerable assessments by a whole host of social services (we rarely saw the same one twice) it has finally been agreed that she needs full-time care. I thought, at first, that getting that decision would be the start of social services sorting things out for her. But it's been awful. I know the NHS is hideously underfunded but, seriously! The doctor confirmed she needs full-time care and social services offered thirty minutes a day. When I expressed my shock, and wondered what my mother was meant to do for the other twenty-three-and-a-half hours, they got quite stroppy. So we had no choice but accept it. The doctor confirmed she has, as we thought, started hallucinating, seeing people and things that simply aren't there. And the thirty minutes a day was, if anything, making it worse. The staff that were sent for these thirty minutes sessions, were a mixture, some unable to speak English, poor people who were desperate for any type of work, often ill-trained… or the occasional star – who didn't stay in the job long. Not surprising when we found out what low wages and poor terms and conditions they had, as they were all employed through an agency.

For my mother, who is confused at the best of times, and paranoid at the worst, it is a nightmare. There is no consistency whatsoever. I'm going to ask at work if I can drop my working hours, and change my working pattern so that I can look after her as much as possible and hopefully compensate for the woefully inadequate care she gets from Social Services.'

I feel humbled. I couldn't even contemplate making the sacrifices Annie has, for anyone, well, except for George. I am full of awe. Today has been sobering for me. And it has certainly put my woes into perspective.

32 Biscuits

Over time, my parallel universe warps and becomes a bubble. I survive in my bubble. Self-sufficient but painfully alone. I'm not alone of course, George is here, playing on computer games in his bedroom most of the time, but I think of myself as alone. George is a good boy and, apart from having to nag him from time to time to do his homework, I can rely on him to be pretty well-behaved. He's not turned into a vile teenager, even though he has certainly hit puberty. Every day he seems to grow and his voice is now deep and his skin is oily. And he is much taller than me. It is strange to have this young man in the house rather than a boy. But I know he looks out for me and I feel grateful for his unconditional love. He's quite a good cook these days, which is just as well as I struggle to muster up the enthusiasm to cook a proper meal after working all day and just about holding it together. I've survived though and from outside I seem to have got everything back in control. George and I manage our lives well. Work is busy. Life is busy. But I am lonely. And I am proud of myself for being able to say so. Parentcraft is all the more important to me now.

We are sitting in Myfanwy's cream carpeted living room, which, if I'm not mistaken, is yet another new one. The brightly coloured walls have been replaced by subtler shades, a musty sage green with dark wood surrounds. Myfanwy has made delicate biscuits with the most intricate icing. On each one there is an image to represent us – a computer for me, a satellite dish for Sioned and a desk full of books for Annie. It seems a shame to eat them but once we started we find ourselves really tucking in. Delicate but sensational. Packed with flavour but so refined. Her baking continues to impress me. Is there nothing this woman cannot do? Through my tough times, and there have been some real lows, I've repeatedly called upon her to talk to me. She usually arrives with cake. And her kindness in baking for me has touched my heart. She knows instinctively that I need some tenderness in my silly, sorry life. 'For a big woman you have a light touch,' I tell her. The difference in our relationship means that she understands that I am teasing her, not bitching at her. She usually nudges me with her elbow or purposefully trips me up in response to one of my light-hearted jibes. We have a good-humoured friendship these days. I know I am indebted to her but my old insecurities die hard and I can't help but notice her backside seems to have got even bigger. I tell her. She replies, 'Well, that's cuz I 'ave 'ad to sit with you over the yers and eat 'uge piles of fuckin' cake with you to stop you from killin' yerself, you twat.' She has a point.

This time, Myfanwy left a message on my voicemail that simply said, 'There is somethin' I needs to discuss with you. See you at 7pm on Tuesday. My 'ouse. Don't be late.' So it wasn't until I arrived that I realised Sioned and Annie had been invited too.

'Listen up, girls,' she says as she plonks the tray with tea and more biscuits on her glass coffee table, also new, I notice. More overtime for Dai, I guess. 'Dai is going to die.' Myfanwy has a broad grin across her face.

'I don't get it?' Sioned says, biting on another delicate crumbly biscuit. 'Is this another one of your stupid jokes? Is it something to do with alphabetti spaghetti?'

'Dai, he's going to die,' says Myfanwy, the grin on her face not cracking at all.

'I still don't get it. What's the joke? Explain it to me,' Sioned says, licking some crumbs off her fingers.

'God 'as a mean sense of 'umour.' Myfanwy replies and she starts laughing, a laugh that turns into a loud, hysterical sobbing. We are all shocked, shocked so much that for a moment we don't know what to do or say. 'Yes, God 'as a very mean sense of 'umour,' she continues through her sobs. ''e is going to take my Dai away. The mean bastard.'

'What on earth do you mean, Myfanwy?'

We've been in her living room for about twenty minutes and only talked about the recipe for her biscuits so far. It must be some weird, sick joke, we wait, like fools, for the punchline. A play on words perhaps? Dai and die.

But there isn't a punchline.

'Dai 'as been diagnosed with a particularly aggressive form of bowel cancer, see. The specialists reckon 'e do 'ave somethin' like between six to twelve months to live, like. I didn't know 'ow to tell you all.'

We wait again for some sort of punchline, something that will make us all laugh and move on, the way we usually do with Myfanwy. But it isn't to be. There is no punchline. It isn't a joke. She means it. It's true, and frighteningly real.

With that my protective bubble in my parallel universe bursts. I know I can't focus on myself anymore. I am indebted to Myfanwy and now she is going to need me. All this time she has been helping me. Now I need to help her. But how? What on earth can I offer?

I can't think of anything to say that would be in any way comforting, and there is such a huge risk that I will say the wrong thing and make her feel worse. So, I am lost for words. I try 'Is there anything I can do to help? Anything practical that will help you now?'

'You could sort out me cupboards. Me alphabet 'as gone all to pot.'

I jump into action, we all do. Annie cleans out the fridge, not that there is an awful lot in it. Sioned pops the Hoover round, then unloads and reloads the dishwasher and I, after resorting her tins into alphabetic order, which is harder than you think, well I find a pile of bank statements and cheque book stubs to check – which I do meticulously. I decide I must show her how to use online banking as soon as possible. That's one thing I can really do to help. Help her sort out her finances. Money seems to be going all over the place. It is out of control. I can help her get it back in control. Yes, that is what I will do to help.

Finally, we make another cup of tea and go back in to her living room.

'Tell me what the doctor said, Muff,' I say.

'Me Dai 'ad only found out because 'is factory was making redundancies. Like a lot of 'em big factories, they told him he may be redundant one minute and then offered 'im a free 'ealth check the next. At a private hospital, 'n' all. Reckon that could be a couple of jobs saved right there, but Dai said they'd told 'im it was from a different budget heading that needed spending. Something called‘caring for our people’. Dai wasn’t going to go, but I said to ’im “you get your short arse down that ’ospital and grab everythin’ they do offer for free. So off ’e went. To Cardiff, of all places. They did all sorts of routine checks. ’e ’ad to take with ’im samples of his shit, they do call them stools, put onto a little card with a cardboard scraper, one a day for three days, ’e ’ad to do. ’e was dead embarrassed ’anding the envelope containing them to the pretty nurse but she was unflinching. She said they would be sent to the labs and that they would write to ’im in a couple of weeks with the results. She explained that sometimes people were asked to give second samples if they couldn’t get a clear reading or if they ’ad eaten a lot of red meat in the previous few days. Dai said ’e’d ’ad steak ‘for ’is tea’. So me Dai was not especially put out when they phoned and asked if ’e could do the tests again and pop them in the post. Ach-y-fi! . ’e showed the kit and special posting envelope when it arrived the next day by special delivery. I didn’t pay much attention, to be ’onest. Not much to get excited about, some bags, cards and a scraper. ’n’ I was really busy with the girls. Dai sent them off three days later.

When they ’ad received the test results ’e was asked to return to the ’ospital. I wasn’t concerned, nor nuffin, I thought ’e was probably doing the test wrong and that is why ’e did ’ave to go back, so they could show ’im ’ow to put the shit on the card properly. I didn’t even go to the ’ospital with him.

‘I thought it was ’im messing about, like, when a nurse did call from the ’ospital and asked if I could come in to pick ’ im up as they didn’t want ’ im to make ’is way home on ’is own,’ Myfanwy told us. ‘I just thought that ’e must ’ave ’ad some blood tests or something like that and was feeling a bit woozy or summin. ’e cun be a right wimp about blood ’n’ stuff. It was a bit of a nuisance, like, but I popped on me coat, and dropped the kids in to me Mam’s. I told ’er I’d only be a little while, depending on the traffic. When I went to the reception at the hospital, they were all so lovely to me, I loved it, I did. I thought to meself, ‘ooh, private ’ealthcare is lovely. I could do with some of this. All clinics should be like this,’ and then they took my arm and led me up the corridor. I was chatting away cheerily about the traffic and parking, you know the sort of rubbish

I do prattle on about and these nurses must have been thinking, 'poor cow, she doesn't know what's coming.' When I went into the consultation room I immediately knew something was wrong, very wrong. Dai was sat near the door where I came in, the doctor was perched casually on the side of the desk. I looked from one to the other. I could just tell bad news was coming.

The doctor, in a white coat, nodded towards the empty seat next to Dai. "Mrs Jones, please take a seat."

'The terrible noise of traffic was rushing in my head,' said Myfanwy, 'when I realised it wasn't no traffic, it was my own 'ead, and me 'eart pumpin' blood so fast round me body. This doc bloke says, 'I am very sorry to tell you, Mrs Jones, as I have just explained to your husband, that unfortunately the tests have proved conclusively that there is blood in his stools, although it is in relatively small quantities, and I won't know exactly what is causing it until we are able to investigate more fully. The internal examination I have just conducted on Mr Jones has identified what I believe to be a very large tumour. Now at this stage, I can't tell you if it is malignant or benign. But I don't want to take any chances and I have asked Mr Jones to stay in overnight so that I can operate tomorrow, as I have a free slot in my schedule due to a cancellation. Do you have any questions?" I looked at 'im blankly. "Do you understand what I have said, Mrs Jones?"

Myfanwy replied, 'Yeah. You've got a free slot and you're gonna to 'ave a dig up 'is arse. Is that right?'

'That about sums it up, Mrs. Jones. I know this will have come as a terrible shock to you. We have a room ready for Dai and you and he can have some privacy there, but remember, I, and my staff, are available at any time, anytime at all, if you or Dai have any questions. So, I know you have two little girls, Chardonnay and Silver, is there anybody you can call to look after them this evening so you have some time to talk.'

'Yes, me friend, Lottie. I cun rely on 'er.'

So now I understand that is why I picked up Chardonnay and Silver from Myfanwy's mother that evening. I just picked them up and dropped them off to some other relative as directed. I was so wrapped up in my own woes, and living in my own bubble, I didn't even think to ask why. Now I know. I am ashamed.

'The results of the biopsy' Myfanwy continued 'prove conclusively that me Dai 'as bowel cancer, a very aggressive form, they did say.

'I said to 'em 'but there's nothing wrong with 'im, look at him, 'e's as fit as a fiddle. Okay, maybe not as fit as a fiddle, 'e's 'ad that virus, and that stomach bug thing that made 'im feel really rough, but 'e was in work only a few days ago and now you're telling me 'e's dying. That's shit! I can't believe it. I won't believe it. I'm not being funny nor nuffin like but there must be some mistake. I'm not saying it's your fault nor nuffin, I'm not blaming you, luv, but you must, you must 'ave made a mistake. Perhaps you got Dai's results confused with someone else. That'll be it. Dai Jones is a common name, round yer.'

'I'm sorry, Mrs Jones, but there is no mistake. We take great care with our data and we are giving you the correct information. There is no mistake. Unfortunately, our investigations have shown that Dai's cancer is in Stage IV, which means it has spread to other parts of his body including his liver. For this type of cancer, and at this advanced stage, we could remove the tumours and try some chemotherapy but I am not confident this will be successful in Dai's case. I'm afraid therefore that the prognosis is not good and you should prepare yourselves for the worst. I am very, very sorry to have to tell you this. Perhaps you would like me to arrange for one of our counsellors to be made available to talk to you. To talk to both of you? Would that be helpful?'

'Yes, come on Dai Diarrhoea, let's see what this counsellor chappie do 'ave to say.'

So we walks along, arm-in-arm, the clean pastel-coloured corridor, with paintings and sculptures, 'aving just 'ad the most shocking conversation of our lives, to speak to a counsellor and see what the future does, or doesn't, 'old for us. And it's not good, my lovelies.'

I can't help but feel that it is ironic that bowel cancer is killing Dai. Myfanwy had always moaned about Dai's toilet habits. Her fascination with faeces meant that she shared with us intimate details that we really didn't want to know. 'I've spent ages scraping the skid marks off Dai's keks,' she would complain or, 'You wanna see the rusty sheriff badge imprint 'e's left on his grits.' We definitely did not want to see it. And just as I called upon Myfanwy in my hour of need, she calls upon me, and I am pleased that she does. She trusts me. And I feel like I am repaying a debt.

33 Country fayre

Inevitably the diagnosis was right. It wasn't some other Dai Jones. In the intervening months I have two roles – 1) to continue to help out with practical tasks where I can, especially the book-keeping parts of running a household and 2) sitting with her, trying to comfort her while she cries until there are no tears left. Sioned, Annie and I take it in turns to sit with her but, to be honest, I do the most. I owe her. I see Dai age in front of my eyes in the months following the announcement. It is awful. They try some chemo, to no avail. He changes rapidly from a ruddy faced healthy man to a grey shadow.

Dai's reaction to the news of his imminent death was awe inspiring. He accepted he was going to die and, after his initial silent shock, in a totally pragmatic way, he started planning for Myfanwy's, Chardonnay's and Silver's futures. At my suggestion, he saw a financial advisor, then he wrote his will, and he even went off one day and booked and paid for his funeral – he understood from his own father's death, only a year previously, that there were lots of decisions to be made and he wanted to protect Myfanwy from anything difficult when she was going to be, as he put it, 'a bit upset, like'. He wanted to make sure that even in his death he was going to be her provider. He showed such kindness to her in these acts that I was touched. He thought of everything. While he was still strong enough, he went to see family and friends and said his goodbyes. He comforted people in their grief before he had even gone. I was, I am, incredibly impressed with him – he was so much more of a man than I ever gave him credit for. And so much kinder than I realised. And so much taller when lying down – that made him laugh.

There was one revelation that took me by surprise. We are sitting in the small kitchenette we have been given access to on the ward.

'I will never forgive myself. I am just going to 'ave to live with the knowledge for the rest of me life. I asked 'im the other day, you see, while 'e was lying in the crisp hospital bed, with its crisp white sheets, and crisp nursing staff, if the cancer was agony and 'e said, 'it doesn't hurt as much as when I thought you'd fallen for one of 'em.'

'Oh, Myfanwy, how awful for you. He found out about those other men. How did he find out?'

'You really are a complete dick, aren't you Lottie.' I am very confused. 'And so fuckin' naïve. 'Ow did you get to be living in the 21st century? 'e didn't find out, as you put it, 'e knew all along. It was 'is idea, well sort of, in a way. 'ow fuckin' stupid do you think I am? You can't go fuckin' men in Caerleon without someone telling yer 'usband pretty damn sharpish. Me 'n' Dai, we 'ad a bet on 'ow long it would be until news got back to 'im. 'e did win. Less than a month before someone blabbed. 'e just pretended 'e didn't know what they were going on about, like. Then 'e would tell me 'oo told 'im what and I would tell 'im if it was true or not. It was a right laff. We enjoyed it.'

I am truly aghast. Of all the things Myfanwy has told me and shocked me with over the years, this truly has caught me off my guard. 'Oh my god, are you swingers, like those truly awful people who came to the Rocky Horror Picture Show with us?'

'Nah, luv. That wasn't Dai's thing. He didn't wanna be with anyone else.'

'So you have, what, an open marriage, do you?' I ask, failing I suspect, to hide my disgust and shock.

'What! That sounds like something from the 1970s! Or an 'ippy commune. All kaftan and no knickers. Seriously, Lottie, you are such a dope. Everything 'as to fit into a box for you, don't it? You 'as to put it into one of your categories. Well, my life ain't like that. Most lives ain't like that. We, me 'n' Dai, well ,we 'ad what we 'ad. Sex with someone else was no big deal. Not to us anyway. 'e liked it yerrin about it. I liked doin' it. I got to shag around, and I loves a good 'ard shag, I doos. And 'e got to yer all about it and 'e fuckin' loved it. Problem was, I did 'ave a bit of a thing about one of 'em though. That's where I slipped up. 'e obviously saw it or yerred about it from one of them gossips, or yerred it in my voice, like. That was wrong of me. None of it should 'ave ever 'urt my Dai. It was just about the sex, like.'

'Oh my God, Myfanwy, but it's so sordid. And isn't fidelity a vital part of marriage? How could you trust each other?'

'That's rich comin' from you, don't you think, luv? You think it is so fuckin' important but you went off and shagged someone else when you 'ad the chance, didn't you. It isn't fidelity that's important it's trust. 'e didn't go off with no-one else. 'e wasn't interested in that. 'e just liked me to go off with other blokes. 'e said he liked it that other men fancied 'is wife. There was never no threat to our marriage. We are a great team, me 'n' Dai. 'e was only upset cuz 'e did think I was falling for one of 'em like. Our marriage was strong, strong enough that I could shag 'ooever I liked but 'e didn't want me to luv no-one else but 'im. What 'e said 'urt was 'e was worried in case I 'ad loved one of 'em. That's what did 'urt 'im. So I was able to tell 'im, 'and on 'eart, that I never loved a single one of 'em. And that's true. I was starting to 'ave feelings but as soon as I realised that was the way it was going I stopped it straight away before I ended up loving some other bloke. I told 'im I just wanted a bit of cock and whoosh, gone. I explained that to Dai. I made Dai laff cuz I said I was only after cock 'n' that I loves sausage, I do. So I did tell 'im that I 'adn't loved any of 'em – just shagged 'em. Lottie… are you alright? You looks like you're going to faint or summin.'

'I'm sorry but I find all of this absolutely distressing, and shocking, and, and, and well dreadful. Just dreadful. Perhaps it was his illness that distorted his mind.'

'Seriously, Lottie, you'd prefer to think that the cancer was some'ow distorting his mind, moved from his bum to 'is 'ead, and changed 'im. Well, it's simply not true, luv. You are such a simple person ain't you! Everything has got to conform to what you do call 'societal norms' for you 'asn't it. Fall in love! Wedding! 'appily ever after! You knows it don't always work out like that. I'm not being funny nor nuffin but it didn't for you and Andy, did it, like? Of course, I can't tell no-one cuz most people would be like you. Shocked. Horrified. Think we was some kind of freaks. It's not something you'd talk about, is it! But it worked for us. Better than worked… we fuckin' loved it and we're not some sort of perverts, you know, we're normal. Normal to us anyways.'

Normal! I now see Dai in a whole new light and it has taken my thinking in a direction that I'd never had to question before. I really don't how I feel, or how I'm meant to feel, now that I know about this… taboo. Taboo? I realise she has shared a taboo with me. She knows about my secret taboo that I didn't have the maternal instinct expected of every mother. One each. We are now equals. I am free. She has liberated me from my prison of guilt.

So I accept that whatever Dai and Myfanwy's relationship is, it is none of my business and I, of all people, have no right to judge.

Weeks go by and I observe the shockingly rapid decline of Dai. From a man you couldn't tell was ill to that yellowy, waxy shadow. He quickly becomes a smaller, paler and greyer version of his former self. He looks terrible, so much older, and so very ill, until he looks like a sphynx cat, those hairless ones, he is all skin and bones. Myfanwy claims he looks like, and calls him, 'Gollum,' and he calls her 'my precious' in return. Even in these terrible times they make each other laugh… and they include me and make me laugh too. Although I dread to think what Lord of the Rings character I must be.

Myfanwy sits with him and I make time to have Chardonnay and Silver around as often as possible as they both get on so well with George. They all seem to like computers. This gives her mother some time with Dai and Myfanwy too. I know I am needed and I want to prove that their trust in me is well-founded. I want them to rely on me. I am learning, from Myfanwy, and from Dai, to be kinder.

It is a blessing when Dai finally dies. At the end, he couldn't even swallow or breathe unaided. The pain relief he needed had to be administered with increasing regularity until there was scarcely a moment when he could stay awake. He did try to smile at those rare moments though and I knew he was doing that for Muff. Brave man. The Dai we knew had already died, it was only the machines that kept him going. Finally switching them off was a release for all of them, not just Dai, but it was truly heart-breaking nonetheless.

Myfanwy had been preparing herself for it for weeks. We all knew it was the end but it was exhausting waiting for it to happen. The staff at the hospice were amazing. Such kindness. It's all part of the work they do, of course, but they showed such kindness, and humanity, all the things the newspaper would have me believe had left the UK long ago. They were truly inspirational and I, for one, will be forever grateful.

They gave her so much time with him once he was confirmed dead. They gently took out the tubes and removed the machines from the room. He immediately looked so much better. The last expulsion of breath took us by surprise even though the nurses had warned us it was going to happen, as we sat around his bed after his death with his corpse in the middle of us, looking… dead. Yet, it still seemed like he would chirp up with some wise crack at any moment. 'God, I am going to miss that fuckin' stoopid, short man so much. 'ow will I ever survive without him?' and big, strapping, strong, outrageous Myfanwy, crumpled into a sobbing heap, and cried like a little baby. And her mother takes her in her arms, like she is a baby, and then cradles and rocks her, and says 'my baby, my poor, poor baby.' And I notice how beautiful Myfanwy is lying against her mother's breast. I don't know why I hadn't really seen it before. And I, well I sit there, being strong, organising tea with the nurses, because that's what they need right now.

Myfanwy is marvellous at the funeral. There are so many people there. People from every stage of their lives. People that knew them both. People who just knew Dai. People that just know Myfanwy. She gives the eulogy at the crematorium. Having seen her during her grief of the past fortnight I am amazed at her strength. I didn't think she'd be able to speak let alone stand in front of that huge crowd. With a strong voice, she talks openly about her shock at the diagnosis, her grief, her yearning, her longing to have him back, how much she misses him every day, how she believes she had taken him for granted. She warns us all to take advantage of today as you may not have tomorrow. There are no rose-coloured spectacles but there are no confessions of her taboo either I am relieved to say. She says openly, with an honesty that is unexpected at a funeral that takes everyone back, that initially she had been more in love with the idea of being married than with Dai himself. But that she had grown to truly love him. I know, although I'm not sure I'll ever completely understand, that for Myfanwy and Dai the sex with other men had been just that, just sex – it had never threatened her love for Dai the Doubler. I've learned once again that it is not for me to judge.

'Those last few months, though, while 'e was still conscious,' she tells the mourners, 'they were full of love, thanks to all you lovely people, you little beauties. Dai knew 'e was loved. Thanks for that. And I do 'ope you all saw 'ow much I did love 'im by the way I cared for 'im, the way I nursed him. I called 'im Dai Diarrhoea, you know.' Everyone laughs, funny how black the humour is at funerals. 'It was a symptom, the diarrhoea, and the tiredness, and the bad back, but neither 'e nor me knew that. So look after yerselves, people. The bad back was the tumour, you see. Apparently 'e must have had blood in his stools for some time too. I asked 'im about it and 'e said 'e never looked! But I did… but I never saw it in 'is skid marks.' Again, people laugh. 'And then the tiredness, I put that down to 'im working all those bloody double shifts. I did love 'im though. I even wiped his arse for 'im when 'e was nearing the end. It made 'im smile. I think 'e liked it. Dirty sod.' Yet more laughter with the tears of the mourners. Her eulogy for Dai was unusual, to say the least, it was crude but heartfelt. That's Myfanwy! The mourners burst into spontaneous applause as she slowly makes her way back to her seat, next to her mother, with her two girls by her side, and she is completely enveloped by their love.

I'd never heard of the pub for the wake and had to put the address into my car's sat nav. George smiles at me as we make our way through a labyrinth of country lanes. He'd insisted he wanted to come with me to the funeral. I said he didn't have to but he insisted 'I need to be there. Chardonnay and Silver are my friends. Aunty

Muff is a lovely lady. And Dai was a lovely man and I loved him. And I love you, Mum, and I want to be there for you.' He is so sweet and strangely mature at times.

The wake is uproarious. Grief does funny things to people. Some cry, some laugh, some just look bewildered. Dai's friends from the factory all seem to be shaven-head, no necks, and steroid-induced muscles but several cry quite openly, with great big tears rolling down their heavy faces. Others try not to cry and make strange gulping and snuffling noises. Others laugh with a loudness to mask their pain. In all of this it is obvious that Dai was loved by everyone who knew him.

The wake is therapeutic for Parentcraft. We make cakes! And we lay them out like a country fayre with notes about what we'd made and the ingredients. It provides a conversation point for everyone and causes a real buzz around the desserts table, as people discuss allergies and preferences and some start awarding points to their favourites and judging the entries. Myfanwy makes cakes too – she says it helped to have something practical to do. And that's what helped us – having something practical to do. And at the end of the wake, the children were sent home with various relatives and when everyone had gone, we, from Parentcraft, along with Myfanwy and her mum tidy the plates and cups and glasses in the pub, when Myfanwy whispers in my ear. 'Stay by me, Lottie, luv. I think I'm losing it big time. I think I'm going to a dark place.' You'd never know. I feel proud that she chose me and so I stay with her until everything is done and then I drive her home. But by the time we get home her mood has lifted completely and she doesn't want me to come in with her. 'I know I've gorra get used to walkin' in and 'im not bein' there but I don't wanna start just yet. I'm gonna just pretend 'e's on a shift so it's better that you're not there or that'd be bloody odd. I'm gonna watch Coronation Street, then get the girls from our Mam's. And then I'll see if I can sleep without it all goin' through me 'ead over and over again. And then, maybe tomorrow, I might admit 'e's dead. But not today. T-rah, Lottie, luv. Thanks for the lift, like,' and she skips up the steps.

34 Teisen lap

'It certainly isn't easy,' says Annie, her tired eyes look wearily from friend to friend. 'We didn't really know what we were taking on by having my mother move in with us. It seemed like the right thing to do but it has proved to be so much harder than I ever anticipated. It's been so hard on Gareth and Ruby. It has totally disrupted their lives. She is such hard work, you see. She was hard work before the dementia but now, well it's almost impossible some days. Gareth and Ruby don't complain too much, bless them. I've dropped my hours at the office to have more time to look after her so it's had quite an impact on our finances too. And it's costing us a fortune for the day care. We're just about getting by with careful budgeting but we can't go on like this forever, and I really couldn't expect Gareth to do any more than he's already doing. At least with him out at work during the day he gets a break from her. And I must admit, I look forward to being in work in a way that I never did before, and I really look forward to that glass of red wine once I have got her in bed in the evening. Not that she ever sleeps through these days. She has really bad nightmares. She gets confused and doesn't know where she is. I do feel sorry for her sometimes especially as she has started crying for her mother at night. It's pitiful to hear and she won't be comforted. But most of the time I am just too exhausted to really show her any compassion. It takes all my energy to get her clean and changed into bedclothes.

Annie let's out a deep sigh.'Sorry to go on about it, girls' she says. 'You don't want to hear all of this, I'm sure, but I need to get it off my chest. She's driving me to distraction. I can't think straight. I have no time for me. Anyway, I'm sure you'd rather hear about cake. 'I had to go for something simple,' she says, pointing at the teisen lap she has baked. 'I haven't got the time these days. You all know how to make this already, right? You don't need me to go through the recipe, do you?'

'Aw, go on, for old time's sake. It's our tradition. It wouldn't taste the same without you describing how to make it,' Sioned says.

'Well, take 225g of plain flour, a teaspoon of baking powder and a pinch each of salt and nutmeg. Then rub in about 100g of Welsh butter, with 75g of caster sugar, a big handful of sultanas and

two small beaten eggs. Then just beat in 150ml of buttermilk. It goes in a 22cm round sponge tin for about 40 minutes in Gas mark 4. Simple!'

Simple, but delicious, we all agree.

'So, what's the long-term solution for your mother, Annie?' I ask.

'Well, to be honest, this is the long-term solution. She's not going to get any better. She'll get progressively worse. We have to watch her all the time. It is the nastiness of it all that is a real strain on the family. She is just so horrid, and aggressive. The outbursts, well, they're really hard to deal with. For all of us.'

'So, what are you going to do about it? You can't carry on like this?' I say.

'We have to, it put a strain on us all when my mother moved in with us and it's no surprise that Gareth is rather fed up with it. Who can blame him, really? She has been absolutely foul to him for years, even before the dementia,' Annie has that inscrutable look on her face again. 'Why should he have to put up with it? But we have no choice. He does it for me. And I feel so guilty as it's so unfair on Ruby too. She's a clever girl. She'll be sitting her GCSEs in no time at all, well, they all will, won't they. She'll need some stability to be able to study. It's only fair. She'll need some peace and quiet and a break from my mother from time to time. It's been hell trying to get care sorted. Honestly, I had no idea how complicated it would be. Nor how much I would have to fight for every single piece of support for her. We have a cobbled together plan of carers, day centres and I'm just trying to go through the impenetrable process to request a little respite care. I don't know why I held out so long on requesting respite care. If I'd known how long it was going to take I would have requested it as soon as she moved in. At least the current day care is okay. There are three women, all middle aged and British. I know that sounds ageist and racist but the age and cultural difference is hard for my mother to deal with. The previous carers were mostly young girls who were obviously looking for a better job - or a few Asian women who, with limited English, find there is little else on offer. All do their best but it is simply not good enough. But the three that cover the rota now seem okay – well, the fact I am here today is testament to that. Mother has been taken to a day centre.

She is really bad now. I have to do almost everything for her. She is almost completely incontinent. It's not just wee, she can't control her bowels either. I put her to the toilet before she goes to bed but I've had to put her in an adult nappy as it has been too difficult with all the constant washing of bedclothes.

'What, she do shit and piss 'erself all the time, now then, luv, do she?' says Myfanwy, once again stating the blindingly obvious. 'Your life is shit, Annie.'

'Yes, that about sums it up, Muff. Thanks! My mother gets really agitated some days. Aggressive in the way she speaks, violent sometimes too towards us but mostly in the way she speaks. She is very twitchy, fidgeting all the time whilst she is sitting in her chair. She can still get up and move around some days, but that's worse because she is very clumsy and breaks things. Or she starts moving things around like she has some grand master plan, and then she asks me in an accusatory way what she is doing. One of the carers who comes in to provide the respite daycare gives me the odd report on how she's been. It varies a lot but it is obvious she is getting progressively worse. Did I tell you she is absolutely terrified of being left alone now? She will often scream out in the night, like a child having a nightmare. I don't think I've had a full uninterrupted night's sleep for months.'

'Yes, you told us that, Annie.' It's no surprise she repeats herself sometimes. The poor woman is totally exhausted.

'Most days we don't get much sense out of Mother. She can't count properly some days, she gets confused. She will occasionally suddenly remember something from her childhood but when she speaks to me she doesn't know who I am. She doesn't remember my brother or sister either. Then sometimes she thinks Ruby is her sister and will sit and talk to her for a while. Mostly she doesn't remember anything though, not the date, or her birthday, sometimes not even her own name or anything really. She calls Gareth 'father' sometimes.

When she gets very frustrated, as I said, it can tumble over into being violent, usually towards me. She still thinks I am stealing from her. On the days I go to work I feel strangely elated, it must be the relief of having a break, but I must admit I am pretty exhausted from it all most of the time and so is Gareth. It's a wonder he hasn't left. It's a miracle he has stayed with us. I just wish I could run away with him. But he is an angel, so is Ruby, and they continue to help my mother.

Medically, Mother has had some treatment which helps a bit. But it is always difficult to get her to take her medication as she is convinced we are poisoning her. And she eats so little it is hard to sneak it in to her food. She's had counselling. And so have we. We have agreed to not try to make her remember things because it causes her so much distress and frustration and seems to trigger the abusive outbursts. So, if she doesn't remember things we just let it go. It's not that different to how we have always behaved towards each other really. Just a more extreme version. I just hope to God it's not genetic and that Ruby won't have to do the same for me. Thank God for the bottle of red at the end of the day, that's all I can say. It's like I said before, there is nothing to be done about it. This is how she will be. And she is a tough old thing. She's not going to die, barring accidents, any time soon. She could go on for years and years like this. This is how our life is going to be for the foreseeable future. I have accepted that. But it's hard for Gareth and Ruby.'

'But can't social services help more? Couldn't she go into a home?' I ask.

'She's still my mother, Charlotte. I have a responsibility to look after her. We earn too much to be entitled to much in the way of support. What I get from Social Services is absolutely the maximum. Believe me, I've asked for more, repeatedly. I get this amount of care for her but it's nothing much. Plus, in a perverse sort of way, I want to do it for her. I want to give her the sort of care and attention she never gave me. I want to show her what its meant to be like. What a mother is meant to be like. I want to mother her, I suppose. I reckon I'm not right in the head. Anyway, anyone fancy joining me in an early glass of wine?'

We all decline – too early in the day, too much else to do and we have all driven to Annie's today. Annie pours herself a large one, takes a big gulp and then cradles and caresses the half-empty glass in her hand.

35 Chocolate Pecan Fudge cake

Children seem to have brought Sioned everything she wanted in life. Despite the awful allergies in pregnancy, Sioned loved being pregnant just as she loves being a mother. She and Steve dote on their children – they stood a high risk of becoming spoilt brats by such adoring parents and both sets of grandparents, but they are turning out just fine, always very polite and somehow self-contained. Jack is very academic. He loves studying and seems to be picking up languages really well and he loves politics. I wouldn't be at all surprised if he ends up being Prime Minister. It was obvious very early on that Megan was going to be a gifted musician, taking to every musical instrument that was offered to her from a little Pingu drum set one Christmas, to her school recorder and on to almost everything she touched, guitar, violin, piano, wind, percussion – she just seems to be able to play it all. She is small, like Sioned, but is a little toughie and seems to have found her niche; she plays in the girls rugby team at school, although I suspect it is because she is so small she can run unnoticed by the girls in the other team. She is her own person. I wouldn't be surprised if she ended up being Prime Minister either.

Steve is a hard worker and his move into new media sales has proven to be very successful and lucrative for them. He is also a coach for Megan's rugby team. We sometimes wonder how they manage to fit everything in. Their days seem to have more than 24 hours in them. Sioned is the stable member of our happy band of mothers. Her life seems to be on an even keel when ours have been in turmoil.

We've made arrangements to meet at Sioned's. She sits us down in their immaculately decorated front room, with its newly exposed wooden floorboard and spotlessly clean everything and says she has an announcement. We've never known Sioned make an announcement so we knew it has to be something big so we looked at her with an awkward anticipation.

'Oh, my God, lovely, what is it?' Annie asks. 'Put us out of this agony.'

'Well, it is rather awkward and I'm rather embarrassed to say.' She looks extremely uncomfortable. 'I've been meaning to tell you all for some time but I could never find quite the right moment, in all our conversations, but' she takes a deep breath, 'Oh God, I feel such an idiot. I'm making it far worse telling you this way, but I've decided to try front-of-camera.'

We roar. Confused, she scans our laughing faces.

'Oh, don't laugh,' she says with good-humoured indignation, as we continue to roll about laughing.

'Oh, Sioned, we're not laughing at you, well not at you trying front of camera anyway. It's just I thought you were going to tell us something serious, that you and Steve are splitting up, or something like that. Or I thought you were going to say that you are having an affair.'

'Well, I thought you had cancer, or something,' says Annie.

'And I thought you did 'ave a new dildo you do want to show us,' says Myfanwy.

'Oh, I see' says Sioned joining in the giggling. 'My mum was the one who persuaded me to go for it. She said that I am too beautiful to be behind the scenes all the time. That's mums for you, though, isn't it. Unconditional love and they think you are the best at everything.'

My mother has never held that point of view. I glance across at Annie. She smiles at me and I know she must be thinking the same thing.

'I am really rather embarrassed because people seem to think it's glamorous,' Sioned continues. 'But it's really not. It's really hard work. And some of it can be quite boring and mundane.' Myfanwy does a big fake yawn. 'No, it really is quite boring sometimes, honestly. I am being retrained as my current role will almost certainly disappear in the next round of cuts. They are really sensitive about how many women have lost their jobs compared to men in the organisation so they've agreed to sponsor me and make a case study about me – especially because I have children and work full-time. They think it will be great PR for them. And I love it. Front-of-camera, I mean. I've had a go and I love it. So much more than I thought I would. Just like my mum said I would,' she says with a beaming smile on her face. 'Honestly, I love it.'

'Does this mean you're going to be a celebrity, Sioned, is that what you're telling us?'

'No, don't be silly, not a celebrity, I've got to do the training first. Then, I've got to actually pass the course. Then, I'll have to apply to get a job and it's, as you can imagine, very competitive, and there are lots of bright young things desperate to get into TV. At the end of the day it will only be local TV, even if I'm lucky. Nothing grand.'

Sioned has a spring in her step as she bounds off to the kitchen to grab the cake for the afternoon's festivities. She has made an enormous chocolate pecan fudge cake. It is a work of art. I dread to think, so decided not to think about, just how many calories will be in a slice.

'Go on then, tell us the recipe. It'll be good practice for your TV presenting,' I say.

Sioned laughs and turns to a pretend camera. 'Layers of dark, moist chocolate cake are stacked with toasted pecans and oozing maple syrup, this cake will either give you an orgasm or send you into a chocolate coma.'

'I'll 'ave the orgasm with mine, please!' says Myfanwy.

Sioned laughs and continues with her TV style recipe. *'This cake recipe is ideal for an Aga. Beat 175g of Welsh butter with 175g of caster sugar until it is light and fluffy, here's one I made earlier.' She pretends to remove an earlier version from under the worktop. 'Sift in 175g self-raising white flour, 50g of Fair Trade cocoa powder and two teaspoons of baking powder. Add 4 eggs, two teaspoons of vanilla essence and three tablespoons of water. Whisk together until it is all mixed in and an even pale colour – probably about two minutes of whisking. Divide the mixture evenly between two greased 20cm sandwich tins then bake at the base of the roasting oven for about twenty to twenty-five minutes but move them after about fifteen minutes, so that they cook evenly. With an Aga it is very much about trial and error so you may prefer to use the simmering oven. The mixture should be firm in the centre. To make the icing, mix 300g of plain, dark chocolate and 50g of unsalted Welsh butter, plus four tablespoons of milk and place in the simmering oven for about ten minutes, then beat in 225g of icing sugar and then use the simmering plate to make sure it is all mixed together smoothly. You'll need about three quarters of the mixture for the topping, so put that to one side. Add 50g of chopped pecans, four tablespoons of maple syrup. Use this as the filling and sandwich the cakes together. Then ice with a palette knife. What makes this cake really pretty is the chocolate swirls, use 200g of plain dark chocolate, just melt it at the back of the simmering oven, then spread it on a marble slab and when cool, use a knife to make beautiful curls. Then just dust with cocoa powder and add a few more toasted if you like.* I must admit, it does look rather good. Shame I can't eat it, because of the nuts.'

It is such a shame for her that her allergies mean that she cannot enjoy it with us, it is wonderful, but she asks for full descriptions of how good it tastes as her compensation. And we are pleased to report it is absolutely delicious. We all take the recipe.

36 Cinnamon swirls

It's a long time before I am able to make the next Parentcraft meeting. They get together a few times but I am so busy at work and with managing everything for George as he starts preparing for his GCSEs. His father is useless (and lets him down all the time now that he has a new girlfriend) so his occasional weekends away with Andy have all but disappeared.

Sioned has completed her front-of-camera training. She has just got her first job as a presenter. We all knew that she'd be good, but apparently she has excelled at news-reading and one-to-one interviews. So she's asked us to have a Parentcraft meeting on her first morning in her new job to distract her so she doesn't get too nervous. She called me about a week ago and asked if I'd come along. I said I'd try and she said she knew I'd be there as I'd never let her down. Wasn't that a nice thing to say? We arrange to meet her at the café by the studios so that we can all be there to wish her luck. She walks into the café in a pale grey pinstripe suit, but with the added twist that the skirt sits just above her knee and she is wearing a raspberry pink blouse and raspberry pink suede shoes. She is looking very glamorous, even for the world of TV. Although her outfit looks fantastic, it is the first time I really realise just how thin Sioned's legs have become. I remember, vaguely, saying something to her many years ago at the Rocky Horror Show but I am quite taken aback now. Her legs are so thin that they are quite shapeless. They are more like two pieces of cotton dangling from the bottom of her skirt than legs. I have been so preoccupied with dieting myself that I really hadn't seen that Sioned has been disappearing in front of my eyes.

We have breakfast in the café but Sioned just has a black coffee. We pass around the cinnamon swirls but she declines. 'It's nerves,' she says. 'I can't face anything to eat.' So, we chat and laugh the way we always do when the four of us are together. And Myfanwy makes sure she embarrasses us, the way she always does. It wouldn't be the same if we weren't mortified at least once in public. She offers to show us her thong but we manage to persuade her that we really don't need the thong test at this time in the morning.

After breakfast, we stand on the pavement outside the café waving good-bye and making Sioned laugh before we reconvene back in the café, ostensibly to have another coffee. It is Myfanwy who says, 'Fuck me sideways, when did Sioned get to be so thin? Where's she gone?'

37 Pudding Club

‘How on earth did it take me so long to notice that she has an eating disorder? I’m her mother.’

‘You can’t keep blaming yourself for not spotting the signs earlier, none of us had noticed. Not really. Certainly not how bad it has become,’ says Annie.

‘Seriously, Mrs Davies, it’s crept up on us all. I feel guilty too. I remember that I said something to her about being too thin when we went to the Rocky Horror Picture Show in Bristol. But I didn’t follow up on that because I didn’t know there was a problem. And then, when she started front-of-camera work, we all met her in that café and we commented then that she was too thin. We all agreed there was some sort of a problem back then. We just didn’t know it was serious, so we did nothing. She may not be in the clinic now if we had said something then. But we didn’t. We didn’t realise that it had got that bad. There has obviously been a recent rapid decline where it has got completely out of hand. Well, there was nothing we felt we could do. The state she is in now is nothing like then. We thought she was a bit too thin then and we thought she had a bit of a problem. This isn’t a bit of a problem. She has a major eating disorder and we are not experts in this field. How were we supposed to know what to do? So how could you have done something earlier? You are in the same boat as us.’

We have gathered together in this small waiting room which is pleasantly decorated with neutral pastel shades and light oak furniture, colours I imagine chosen to create calm as anyone here will have come for a reason that means, undoubtedly, their life is anything but calm. The three of us chat to Sioned’s mum, at the request of Sioned, who has been sectioned into St Cadoc’s with a serious eating disorder. We understand that it is anorexia and she has been admitted because her weight is too low for her to be safe at home. It’s an horrendous thought. She needs professional help. We have gathered to analyse, to try to rationalise and to console each other before we go to meet Sioned with her psychiatrist.

‘I suppose there has always been an issue with food for Sioned, hasn’t there, if we think about it. She was always so obsessive about food and wanted to know exactly what was in every cake we ever baked. And, of course, she had all those allergies and intolerances…. or did she? Was that all part of an elaborate lie to explain why she wasn't eating?' I say.

We piece together our observations over the years. The allergies, the intolerances, that she always said she had just eaten or was about to have a big meal somewhere else, the dashing off, the extensive exercise regime, the baggy training clothes and the constant tidying up of the plates so you never saw how much she was, or wasn't, eating. It all makes sense now. But only by us piecing together our collective memories. None of us had really spotted it on our own despite it happening to our dear friend right in front of our eyes. We all agree then that we are out of our depth regarding Sioned's problem.

Sioned's mum explains that she has been trying to persuade her to get help for about six months but that Sioned had vehemently resisted – until now.

A specialist from the unit at St Cadoc's joins us in the waiting room at the clinic. She says she will try to help us understand Sioned's situation. She is not allowed to, nor would she, discuss any of Sioned's personal details with us. That will have to come from Sioned herself and will be part of her healing process. Sioned has said she wants to get better and manage her relationship with food, but the specialist is concerned that this development has come too soon. She suspects that Sioned is saying all the right things so that she will be discharged quickly and not forced to eat when she doesn't want to. So when Sioned suggested enlisting our collective support, her psychiatrist thought it would be a good way to tease out some of the realities and seriousness of Sioned's condition. Sioned's mum, hugs each one of us in turn and thanks us for our loyalty and support of her daughter. 'I just want my daughter to be well again. Anything you can do to help, anything at all, I will be eternally grateful. I'm going to leave you now to talk to Sioned. I think it's important that you can talk frankly with her. I don't want to be a barrier. I'm worried enough already that this is all my fault. I must have done something very wrong when she was growing up. She was such a dear, sweet, lovely little girl and she is such a beautiful, clever woman now. Let me know if there is anything I need to do. Anything at all.'

Shortly after her mother leaves, Sioned joins us in the room. It is shocking. She is frighteningly thin and although she is wearing a baggy tracksuit, I can see she is skeletal. She looks as though she could have walked out of Belsen. Her auburn hair is clean but lifeless and she appears to have lost quite a lot of hair as you can see her scalp very clearly. Her eyes are bulging and distant. Everything about her looks scrawny and scary. This can't be happening to Sioned.

'Hi Sioned,' says the psychiatrist cheerily. 'I'm going to talk openly with you,' she says to us. 'There will be nothing that I say that I will not have already discussed with Sioned at some point. I know a lot of people worry about saying the wrong thing. Please don't worry, if the conversation starts to take a direction that is inappropriate or unhelpful then I will stop the conversation, so please feel free to be honest. As you can see she is doing very well but still has some way to go until she reaches her target weight. Sioned will not be allowed home until she reaches at least that. She has been allowed to see you today because she has managed to gain 3lbs and that is the weight gain target we agreed when she entered St Cadoc's. It is her reward.'

Anorexia is a Western disease the psychiatrist explains. You do not find people purposefully starving themselves in countries where food is a scarcity.

'The media tells us that it is much to do with modern living and the pressure to constantly look good and look thin. And I do believe that Western society, and the media in particular, is putting way too much pressure on women to look good. But the cases I see are extreme – and in 95% of the people that I see this is not necessarily the root cause. We are beginning to see some more statistical evidence of women, and it is still mostly women, but not exclusively, who suffer with anorexia, who are being referred to us who have a connection between their body-image and self-worth from media pressure. These women tend to be forty plus, like Sioned, reasonably well-off and middle class, like Sioned, but unlike Sioned, these women tend to be recently divorced or separated from a long-term partner. In this group, we do find some evidence of media and peer pressure to be young and thin. It is okay to be over forty and single in the eyes of the media as long as you don't look over forty… and are very slim. However, these women have often already undertaken drastic measures for rapid weight loss, usually some form of surgery or liposuction or a gastric band. Of course, with Sioned's job in the media this could be a contributory factor but I really don't think it is the major contributor for Sioned.' Sioned nods distractedly. She has obviously heard all of this information before.

'You see,' continues the psychiatrist. 'I don't think it is just image pressure. In fact, in most of the cases of anorexia that are referred to me, as I said, around 95%, the anorexia is a coping strategy. Something else has happened in their life. Something they can't control. But they can control their eating.' She turns and looks at Sioned. 'Does this have any resonance for you, Sioned?'

Sioned's voice is weak and strained. 'Oh yes, it probably started when I was eight.' She looks to us. 'Did you all know that I had a brother who was killed when I was eight? He was knocked over. He was only ten, bless him. We all loved him so much. We were devastated. My parents were beside themselves with grief. It was so awful for them. It's the hardest thing in the world to see your parents cry with grief. My poor mum, my poor dad. Life just fell apart for us at that moment we got the news, but we stood by each other with my little sister Catrin, the four of us – we stayed as a family. We all knew we had to be strong for each other. I don't think we could have made it if we hadn't had this unspoken pact between us. My Mum threw herself into her work, she had only just opened the salon a few months before his death so she had to. My Dad also threw himself into his work. He's such a gentle man, my dad. But I am not suggesting they didn't have time for me, or Catrin, or rejected us in any way, nothing could be further from the truth. They made even more of an effort to ensure that we were getting all the love and affection we should. There is absolutely no fault on their part.

The eating thing didn't really manifest itself until after I started working in my mum's salon on a Saturday. I had just started my A levels so I was sixteen. Like most teenagers I was carrying a bit of puppy fat. All the other women were older and were on diets all the time. So part of me wanted to fit in and so I went on a diet too. They would say things like, 'Oh, you don't need to go on a diet, that's puppy fat. That'll fall off you.' But I enjoyed being on a diet. I liked challenging myself. I liked tempting myself so I would go to the shop on the corner and buy everyone else a chocolate bar but not buy one for myself. I would feel very pleased with myself whenever I did this. One of the other girls in the salon had a right strop with me about it one day. She said, 'Sioned, do you think I don't realise what you're doing? Buying everyone else a chocolate bar so that we'll get fat and you can gloat that you are thinner than us.' I was horrified. I was just trying to treat them to something nice. Something I would love to eat but had to deny myself because I knew I was going to be one of those people that suddenly wakes up one day huge, fat and ugly. I just knew it. So I had to control it. My lovely mum has always struggled with her weight you see, so I knew I was going to be just the same.

But, I think everyone is making far too much fuss about this. Yes, I can see I have probably lost a bit too much weight. But I don't have a major problem, not really. Not like some of the girls in here. Not like everyone is making out. I eat. It's not like I am starving. I have a good diet. It's just there are lots of things I am allergic to, so I can't eat them. I get uncomfortable too if I eat a big meal, I like grazing. It just got a bit out of hand. But there is nothing wrong with me now. I'm putting on weight. I'm fine now. I just need to go home to my family, to my Steve and the kids. Then I'll be better. I just want to go home.'

The psychiatrist tells us later that this is not unusual. The deceit has become so deep that even looking at themselves in a mirror, which they hate, anorexics will still believe they have to control their eating even when they can admit they are too thin. They hate the way they look all the time. Sioned is not unusual that she had had a crisis in her life and her coping strategy had been to control something else. Also, the psychiatrist explained, that by the time they are admitted to St Cadoc's they had probably been starving themselves for years. Starving themselves and taunting themselves with the pain of hunger. She said that for years Sioned has been going to supermarkets and looking at all the delicious food just to resist buying it, or sometimes buying it and then giving it away. It must have been agony, with every bone, every pore, every brain cell, crying out for food. To starve is painful.

The psychiatrist goes on to explain that anorexics and bulimics are very different and cannot be treated in the same way. For anorexics, it is all about the control. For bulimics it is their lack of control, hence the binging and then complete purging whether by vomiting or through laxatives. She said that there were women in their early 20s in her care who had no teeth on the bottom at the front of their mouths through the acid of repeatedly vomiting.

It is hard for us to comprehend all of this and we listen, repulsed but with an awkward fascination at how Sioned's illness has probably developed.

We learn that when we first met, back at that first Parentcraft, Sioned would have clocked everybody else's size of bump. She would have registered and recorded in her mind as we confessed how much weight we had gained and she will have been putting herself in the pecking order. She would have been fighting a constant battle with her maternal instinct to nourish her baby and her desire to be thin. As soon as Jack was eating solids, she could lavish him with the very best food, the tastiest morsels and indulge him, getting him to eat all the things she would secretly like to eat herself. The same with Megan.

Her eating disorder will have made her cunning, the psychiatrist explains. Sioned is a very intelligent woman, as many anorexics are, and she has been clever at hiding the extent of her illness. The psychiatrist confirms that the allergies and intolerances, although possibly real, also gave Sioned a great excuse not to eat. The lies about just having eaten or going out later for a big meal are common. We had noticed that Sioned had started to wear baggy clothes, but not realised the extent of the problem it was hiding.

She had used other tactics too, we had noticed some, but hadn't made the connection with her illness. For one thing, she was always busy. Dashing from one thing to the next. Always something to do for one of the kids or she was rushing to pick something up for Steve, so she never had time to stop and eat with us. If we arranged to go out for a meal, she would often only be able to join us for the coffee because of some other commitment, usually with her job. It all seemed plausible at the time but now we feel like we have been tricked for a long time.

And she was always tidying up, moving the plates around after our cakes, collecting up the leftovers and throwing them in the bin which were all tactics to distract us from noticing that she hadn't eaten. I tend to think of Myfanwy as the one fanatical about tidying and cleaning but casting my mind back I suppose Sioned was often the one to clear away the dishes and stack the dishwasher. And she was fanatical about exercising. She went to numerous classes in the early years but had swapped to exercising alone in her home gym lately.

The psychiatrist goes on to tell us how they treat the condition. She explains that Sioned will have strict targets to reach, and she will be rewarded when she reaches them. There will be no exceptions and although it may seem very tough on her it is the only way to combat anorexia. For example, Sioned had hoped to reach her 3lb weight gain target a fortnight ago so she could go to a family wedding with Steve and the kids but she had not reached the target so she had not been allowed to go. They had to go without her.

We are shocked by this harshness. 'I'm not trying to question the validity of your programme, but wouldn't it have helped Sioned to be with her family, especially a wedding, and be able to show she is getting better?' I ask.

'It would for you, or for me, people who don't have an eating disorder, yes. But for Sioned, this would legitimise a view that she doesn't have to hit the target weights to get the reward. This would say to her mind-set, there is room for negotiation and actually 2lbs is okay when we have asked for 3lbs. Her mind would start to calculate cunning ways to manoeuvre and manipulate those around her to allow her to continue to starve herself. Sioned is still very, very underweight. Her periods have stopped completely, probably a few years ago if, indeed, they ever started again after having Megan. It seems that once she had decided Megan would be her last baby, and she had finished breastfeeding, that's when her anorexia started to really take hold.'

The psychiatrist continues. 'She is so thin that many of her normal bodily functions have shut down or slowed down to the lowest possible level whilst still alive. We cannot reward her for not hitting her targets. Sioned has latent pneumonia too. Unfortunately, when the anorexia is this severe, then, as patients start to improve and they put on a little bit of weight, all the latent illnesses resurface, so it is really tough for them. They start to get a little bit better with their anorexia and then they get ill from all the stuff that is on hold. This happens because they are so weak their bodies know that they will die if they get an illness so it is held in abeyance. Once they get a little bit better, their bodies think, ah well, you can cope now, take this! It's a cruel world.

I've mentioned Sioned's target weight,' the psychiatrist continues. 'That's when we will allow her to live at home. That obviously will not be the final weight she will be aiming for but that is the weight at which we are prepared to let her continue the programme from home, with the support of her family and friends. Which brings me on to why I think it is so important that I meet you all. Sioned has said that the reward she would like for hitting target, is to do some things with you, Parentcraft, I think she calls you. She's going to write a book, something she's always wanted to do. She's going to call it Take a Cake Break.'

'Oh no!' shrieks Muff. 'That means I'll be the fat one. There's always a fat one when there are four friends together in a book, like.'

'Myfanwy, do you think it is appropriate to worry about being the fat one when Sioned is fighting a battle with anorexia?' I ask.

'No, not really, no I don't,' she says thoughtfully. 'But it is true, isn't it. Sioned will get better and she'll write 'er book, 'Take a Cake Break' and I will be the fuckin' fat one in it. Bloody typical! No 'ang on a minute, Lottie, luv. It could be you. You cud be the fat one.' She gives me a thumbs up. I shake my head – she is incorrigible.

Trust Myfanwy to say something so totally inappropriate. Thank goodness she managed to make a joke out of it, and typical it was at my expense. Thank goodness for Muff. It was all very tense and now we are all laughing. The psychiatrist moves on quickly. 'She also calls you the Pudding Club.'

We all laugh again at that, it was one of the nicknames we gave the group when we first met and were heavily pregnant and waddling around. It seems so cruelly ironic now.

At the end of the meeting, after the farewell hug of a bag of bones that is Sioned, we stand around in the carpark shivering in the fresh air, as Myfanwy says, 'I'll do it. I'll give 'er whatever she needs for her Take a Cake Break, even though, and you knows me, I dun like showing off nor nuffin. I'll even tell 'er some of the rude bits. What about you lot? Are you in, like?'

'Agreed. I'm in,' says Annie.

'Agreed,' I hear myself say – although I am really not sure about appearing in a book. Take a Cake Break is a good idea, but it could ruin my professional reputation especially if it includes Myfanwy and her rude bits! I'll have to ask her to use a pseudonym for me. There is only so much Muff a girl can take!

38 Banana cake

Where is she? I do hope this doesn't mean she isn't going to turn up again. No sooner than I felt I didn't have to worry quite so much about Sioned I start to worry about Annie. And we are all worrying about Annie now. I really thought this time she was going to turn up. I rang her last week and she said she'd definitely be here tonight. She was looking forward to it. She never used to be late but over the last couple of years her behaviour has become erratic; she is often late, sometimes she doesn't arrive at all.

The three of us, Myfanwy, Sioned and me, are getting ready for our Christmas party. We've done this since we learned about Sioned's anorexia. We decided we would try to make eating out part of our social life so that we can enjoy food together, no real change there, well at least for three of us. Social eating should help to keep Sioned on track with her eating programme. Her anorexia makes her attendance erratic too though, so Myfanwy and I have had to work especially hard to keep our little group together. We have to do a lot of liaising with Steve, as he worries so much about Sioned, he needs to know where she is, and whether we have seen her eat.

Since Myfanwy bought her new house she has hosted a few of these getting-ready sessions before we go out. 'It's all part of the fun, girlies, the getting-ready.' She, at least, seems happy these days, and settled in her new home with the girls. Tonight, the three of us have been mixing cocktails from Myfanwy's new bar! Yep, the girl's got a bar in her living room. I must say my zesty, minty, lemony mojito tastes fantastic and is exactly what I need after the day I've had. My team have been working for months on a major new proposition for QXL and we were presenting to the Board in London earlier. That's always a challenge for me as Richard is now on the Board. I find it hard to be in the same room as him – not because I still have feelings for him, but because I don't. Whatever did I see in him? I caused all that upset just so I could have sex with him! It really wasn't worth it. I've no doubt that dumb decision limited my career. Gossip was rife, still is even after all these years, and apparently it was all my fault, it's always the woman's fault. I'd led him astray, him, a happily married man. And as much as my career stalled once again after all that hard work to get it back on track after the setback of maternity, so his took off. And now he is on the Board. So he is the one who is making the decision about whether my work is good enough. Thankfully, my proposition was approved today and I am left not knowing what to think. Was it approved because of our past, or despite our past, or as a double bluff to those around the table… or was it approved simply because it is a really good idea, with lots of research to back up the proposal, and lots of hard work to show how it will work in practice. I'm overthinking this! I have another mojito to stop my head whirring.

When Sioned nips to the loo, Myfanwy puts her hand on my shoulder. 'It do take two to tango, luv.'

'How did you know I was thinking about Richard?' I ask, in disbelief. I honestly think sometimes she must be a mind reader.

'I cun tell by the look on yer face. You can't keep beating yerself up about 'im all the time. Let it go, luv. Give yerself a bloody break.'

'But I still can't believe I did it. I was so critical of people who had affairs. And I had so loved Andy. How did I have an affair? And with the one person I thought was genuinely interested in women in the workplace. Of all the people to choose… I had to go and destroy the one person I thought was genuinely interested in my brain and not my body. It is such a cliché – older, powerful man; ambitious younger woman. I've always thought I was so forceful about equality for women. I am a shame to my sex.'

'Fuckin' stop it, will you. You are not responsible for the 'hool thing. 'e did 'ave an affair too, remember? You both did, remember? Equal responsibility. You've got some bloody funny ideas about equality 'n' all. You let Andy walk all over you and then you let Richard 'ave everything 'is own way. Doesn't sound very equal to me. So 'ow about you stop beating yerself up. Stop analysing everything you've ever done and feelin' guilty about it. Get over it!'

She is probably right. Sioned returns and we quickly pick up the previous conversation as I try to let go of my guilt about Richard, and Andy, and George… and everything. The conversation reverts back to Myfanwy's new house, which is absolutely amazing. What a find. It is a bit like a footballer's house in some of the decor but that's Myfanwy's taste for you. There is a lot of gold, from curtains to taps. But gold suits Myfanwy and somehow it all works as she has lavished huge amounts of love alongside money on everything. She has worked really hard to make this a proper home for Chardonnay and Silver trying, we all believe, to compensate for not having a Dad around. Nothing wrong with that though. Dai would genuinely have been so proud of her. That and the fact that she has set up her own business, WWD (Women Who Do), which is doing really well. The franchise model she established is working a treat despite the economic downturn. In fact, according to Myfanwy, it has helped.

Myfanwy came up with the name for her business, WWD, when she started to rope in other women who clean for a living, the ones she knew that were obsessive about cleanliness and doing a good job. As her posh customers would say, 'Oh, I have a woman who does my cleaning,' this became 'A woman who does'. Combined with her sexual history as a woman who also 'does' it seemed a perfect name for her fledgling business. Although I must admit, I thought she had set up an escort agency when she first told me the name. It has a lot of fancy branding now around WWD with the logo emblazoned on everything. But it always gets a laugh when she explains, 'The thing is love, I do, see. So when they says to me, do you? I says I am a woman who does. Then I either clean their house or gives 'em one.'

'Lots of 'em big, fat FM companies – that's facilities management companies, in case you didn't know, thickos – have overstretched themselves,' she tells us, swooshing a pink cocktail around in a martini glass, before popping another pink flamingo-shaped ice cube into the mix. Class! 'They refinanced when the rates were 'igh, borrowed 'ard against their property portfolios, they did, which 'ave now plummeted in value and left 'em very exposed. Although they are still profit-making their balance sheets are not a pretty sight, I reckon. I think there will be more casualties in my sector, like. 'ark at me! My sector!'

I feel very proud that she is talking about her sector. She really is a business woman now.

'How do you know all this financial stuff, Muff? You're the one that keeps saying that you're just a scrubber,' asks Sioned.

'It's not as 'ard as it looks, luv,' says Muff, nudging Sioned, with a beaming smile. 'And I'm not thick. Capex, Opex, cashflow, it's all quite easy really when you do know what it do mean. Anyone 'oo 'as ever run a 'ousehold 'as to do all these things. They just don't call 'em by those posh names, like. We do say 'big items' or 'monthly bills', or 'what I've got in the bank', don't we, at 'ome like, not Capex, Opex, cashflow but it is the same stuff, really. And all those people 'oo do say they are project managers, well I do think you should give them the task of getting the hool family on holiday. All the right stuff clean 'n' packed, passports, enough cash, yer credit cards, right airport, right time. That'd sort out 'oo can run a project or not. Or better still, get 'em to organise a kiddy's party. Sort out the food, get the entertainment, book the bouncy castle, pre-fill the party bags, remember to take the cake, a knife, the candles, don't forget the matches and all at no extra cash from 'is pay packet. Oh, and don't forget to invite the kids! That's real project management, innit. Any one of us lot cun do that. In fact, every mam I know does that without even blinking. Anyone of them mams cun run rings around them so-called Project Managers I do get introduced to at the FM companies.

Plus my moral compass is pointing in the right direction.' We laugh… a lot. The irony! 'Course I wants a business that do makes money, otherwise it wouldn't be a business, would it. But I do want everyone 'oo do work for WWD to make money too. That's what you buy in to when you buys a franchise from me. They calls it values, they doos, 'em businesses. But it's more important than that cuz everyone 'oo does the cleaning is on a proper contract. No cash in 'and. They cun all work flexible hours if they do want 'em, or set hours if that's better, or swap, sometimes fixed hours, sometimes flexible depending what's going on in their lives at the time, like, so they can work when they do want to. There ain't no such thing as full-time or part-time in WWD – there's no difference, you gets yer pay 'n' the perks no matter what. And it means I do 'ave the flexibility to ensure I don't let down my clients or any of the big contracts my franchises run. We ain't the cheapest but we are the best, and the most reliable – that's what the customers do say. I do employ quite a lot of older women, and some older men now too.

There's a lot of retired people out there, you knows, and ones that have been made redundant. Then there's all 'em working mams. Fab-lus workers but no one will employ 'em cuz of the kiddies. Bloody stupid if you do ask me. I like to bring them into the WWD family. They can register with me and then work if and when they ever want to. My franchisees love that. They have a totally flexible workforce to call on. That's what I do really, Sioned – that's what WWD is. It was Lottie who spotted it. WWD isn't really a cleaning company. It is a database of people who want to clean. I used to do it by lists but then Lottie set up this database for me. And all the people 'oo do work for WWD sort out the shifts themselves using their smartphones. I rarely 'ave to get involved at all – they just trade shifts and make sure everything is covered. It was when I knew it was really working like that, that's when I did set up the franchises. Well, that was Lottie's idea too really. So they cun use the database too. See, the thing is, when I am interviewing prospective franchisees I can tell the ones 'oo want to do the real 'ard graft, and those who want to see if they can just grab the money by employing, and exploiting, cheap labour. I always pick those that do want to do the work because I knows 'ow to make the money, and it is not through exploiting people. Then Annie explained what is involved in negotiating contracts. I only have to work out a way now to use your skills, Sioned, and I will 'ave mercilessly exploited you all. Ha ha ha!' She grins.

'So that's where I 'ave really made me money big time 'n' so quick. It's about recruiting reliable and trustworthy people that don't let you down. Like I said, that's what WWD is really – access to a recruitment process that works. I want to make sure that I do 'ave the very best people. I do all the checks, all the CRB stuff, all the immigration stuff, everything. Lottie showed me 'ow to google people and I finds out all about 'em before I even interview 'em. Fuckin' marvellous, mun. Amazing what you cun find on Facebook. Then I always take up their references. And then I take up more references. Then I goes back to 'ooever recommended them and I speak to 'em personally, like, about 'ow they do really know this person, what's good, what's bad so I cun find out if they are prepared to stick their neck out for 'em. It's amazing what people will tell you if you do ask. So I do 'ave a really good thing. I 'ave a bonus for introducing good reliable people into WWD. Most FM businesses struggle to find people at short notice but I do 'ave people on me waiting list. Queuing up to work for WWD because they knows they will be treated good, like. And then they only introduce good people cuz they want the bonus they'll get if they stay more than six months. Ooh, and I do 'ave some lovely cleaners. They gets right in there. When I set up this system that Lottie showed me 'ow, then Chardonnay and Silver did all the techie stuff, they're good at stuff like that, it's all on me website. It's called a portal. I loves this jargon, I do. So the cleaners cun sort out the shifts for themselves, once I've shown 'em 'ow, like. They don't need to come through me unless there is a problem. They cun just go on, find someone 'oo is willing to cover, and sort it out all between themselves. So many businesses say they are a people business then they treat the people like shit. We treat shit like shit and people like people. I fuckin' loves it. 'onest, I doos. Bloody brilliant, isn't it?'

Myfanwy lays much of the credit for this with me but I have merely suggested ideas. She is the one that has put it all into action. It is amazing for someone who was so reliant on her husband to provide everything. She said she didn't even touch the bank account until Dai died, other than take cash from the hole in the wall, and then it was only an agreed amount that Dai would tell her. She's right, Chardonnay and Silver are good at the techie stuff. Actually, I think they are brilliant at technology. They did a 'Programming for Girls' course at school and they are way ahead of me already. They laugh at my hierarchical approach to design of software – they are all 'drag and drop', just like George.

And you can't fault Myfanwy. She is a business woman with business sense who cares about people too. And she learns so quickly. Yes, I mentioned the database but she grasped that idea and turned it into her business model. She really has an eye for how to make money. Annie told her a bit about contract law and she was away, bidding for contracts, and winning them, in just a few months, punching way above her weight.

'I've become the provider for me family. Needs must! Dai always provided for me before and to be 'onest, I expected 'im to always provide for me. Course, 'e provided for me and the girls after he died too. I could 'ave just sat back on me big fat arse – the 'ouse was paid for from the endowment - but I realised that Dai would 'ave wanted me to do somethin' with me life, for the girls, like. It didn't take me long to get off me arse once I got the courage to start me business. I thought people would laff at me and think I was a twat. But I did it, and I discovered that I am bloody good at it. I needed the kick up the arse of losing Dai to realise that I could do things on my own. I didn't 'ave the confidence back then. It took me a long time to feel confident enough to know that I do 'ave something to offer.'

'Anyway,' says Muff. 'Lottie is the real business woman. She's the one who do know all this corporate stuff about money.'

Inwardly, I cringe. I haven't been as honest as I should and I haven't shared with Parentcraft that things at work have not been good for some time. I feel like I have let Parentcraft down somehow. They have always seen me as the successful business woman – that can cope with anything – well, anything at work anyway. I feel like they would be disappointed in me if they knew that I'd been experiencing a lot of stress as our Research and Development function just can't seem to hit the double-digit growth demanded by the C-level. I've tried to explain in work that we have a few developments that just aren't quite ready for market yet but the C-levels just don't want to hear that. Not since the take-over by the Americans. It was pitched to us as a merger. But it was definitely more acquisition than merger. And there is no doubt about it that we, QXL, were the ones that were acquired, not acquiring. Many of the C-levels took a golden handshake – a few of the old guard, like me, decided to stay. We're regretting it now. The Americans seem to think everything said with a British accent means it is from the 19th century and we are all a lot of unimaginative laggards. Despite the same language there is a huge cultural divide and we find them, the Americans, boorish, unrealistic, focused only on the next quarter with no capacity for strategy or vision. But, in fairness, they are exhausted. They work long hours like we do but don't have the sort of holidays we get so we find they are grumpy most of the time. Plus they are so bureaucratic. I had always thought Americans, home of the free, were free-spirited and all about enterprise and entrepreneurship until I worked with them and found them wrapped up in the most incredibly unnecessary governance and bureaucracy. Yet, they are up in arms when they have to comply with British legislation especially where it relates to workers' rights. We have never been a strongly unionised business at QXL but I know of more and more people who are trying to find a Union that will help them as we go through one unfair dismissal case after another. And I feel threatened too. I have to pretend I don't, for the sake of my team, but I know that my cards are marked. Especially since I met my latest new boss (I seem to get a new one every three months or so) and he came up with a really hair-brained idea and I pointed out the flaws to him politely, to which he replied, 'I don't have non-believers in my team. I suggest you rethink your career-limiting comments, young lady, and get back to me when you are on message,' in his Southern States drawl. On the plus side, at least he called me young lady, even though he can't be much more than a smudge over thirty himself.

Even apart from this upsetting exchange with my new boss, I can't help but take it all personally. The business used to listen to me as an expert. They used to take my advice. Now they seem to dismiss me as some relic from the past. I'm history. I've become all too familiar with the glass ceiling in my industry over the years but as a woman's fertility comes to an end I've noticed that it happens all the more. I wonder if, somewhere deep within our genetic make-up, this is somehow connected. Perhaps lack of fertility in our ancestors equates to lack of usefulness in the modern world. Promotions stopped long ago – it's now all about trying to defend my position. Any director who appears to be in any way supportive of women in the workplace seems to be being moved sideways quickly since the acquisition of QXL by the Yanks, in fact one of my favourites is no longer appearing on any of the new organisational charts – I make a mental note to text him and see if he is okay. And since the financial crash, I feel constantly under threat. Let's hope the economy picks up quickly as I don't know how long I will be able to cope like this. I've seen all my male colleagues that were once peers, overtake me at QXL. But it's hard to say if it is sexism as they genuinely work really hard too… and they certainly put in the hours. Presenteeism is paramount. It is not unheard of for people to stay throughout the whole night when we are working on a bid. Our grad intake is excited by the prospect. They seem to think that it is a one-off and they are some sort of saviour – prepared to go the extra mile for the company. What they don't know yet, how could they, is that there is always a crisis. A bid, a contract, a delivery, or some new competitor research that calls upon us to work ridiculous hours. No wonder that they see me as a dinosaur. They look at me with pity in their eyes when I try to protect my team from the excessive demands. I used to be praised for standing up for my team.

Worse, grads are subtly discouraged from seeking out the wisdom of older and more established colleagues. They are encouraged, subtly of course, to see us as resisters to change and their job is to coax, or force, us into making changes. Changes that we know will damage the long-term stability of the company. But everything is short-term now. And, I must admit, part of me has lost interest in the nonsense that is big business. It all seems so meaningless. The same old rubbish coming around again. I know I must appear jaded to some of my younger colleagues and who can blame them? They're right. I am.

And worse than the glass ceiling, as I've got older I have discovered the glass cliff that has meant that older business women, like me, in large corporates are punished far more harshly for mistakes, even when they are not our mistakes. Marie, lovely lady, fell on her sword for a recent bid that her team didn't win. The Americans 'heads must roll' mentality meant there had to be a fall guy… and while all the Board Members who had signed off the bid gazed absent-mindedly at the distance, or their navels, Marie took full responsibility, offered her resignation which was accepted on the spot and left, escorted by a security guard to make sure she only took her personal belongings. It was so insulting as Marie is one of the most honest people I have ever met. It sent shockwaves through QXL – that she was gone – and that she was removed in such a brutal way. I've noticed people, women, keeping their head down far more now. Sadly, the punishment seems to be meted out equally harshly by our younger female colleagues, especially those without children, especially those in HR, who want to prove their own competence by showing what big balls they have. Many of the older women, and there weren't that many to start off with, have left QXL of their own accord. Well, I say their own accord, it is hard to judge how much they are pushed. It is not always as obvious as Marie's treatment. Names are put on a redundancy list and then HR have the 'difficult' conversation. More often, these older women are encouraged to take the redundancy package. It seems there is no solidarity in the sisterhood at QXL. The younger women see older women as their rivals, the threat. I know this because now, looking back, I realise I probably treated older women in the workplace like this too, I'm ashamed to say. I've lost some really good colleagues over the years - they just can't abide the madness any longer and usually go off to do something far more worthy – for about half the pay. And I can't help but think that Myfanwy was probably right about her definition of C-level all those years ago.

Still, as I take another sip of my mojito, perhaps with today's Board approval of the new proposal all this hostility will dissipate. I just hope I haven't rushed it through too quickly to appease their insatiable demands for more profit.

We finally hear a car draw up on the gravel drive. Glancing from behind the curtains, as we are all now in our underwear, ready to put our going-out outfits on at the last possible moment, we see it is a taxi. Great, as this means that Annie has finally arrived and we all feel a great sense of delight that it will be the four of us again. The table isn't booked for another hour yet so there's still plenty of time for us to finish getting ready.

Muff opens the door and there is a right commotion. 'Whoa, whoa, oooh, girls you are going to have to come and help,' she shouts from the front door. 'Annie is wasted!'

Sioned and I rush to help, Sioned in her dressing gown and me in my underwear. The poor taxi driver doesn't know which way to look as he helps a totally inebriated Annie into the hall.

'Thanks, love. Tell Frank I do owe 'im one,' says Myfanwy tucking a generous £20 note into the driver's hand as a tip. Frank is one of her clients, she has the contract for his home cleaning, his offices and his taxi business – his taxi business is actually her most recent addition to WWD's cleaning business portfolio. She has developed and invested in a couple of mobile cleaning units that she can take to wherever the taxi is. She runs a 24/7 emergency service too for cleaning up sick in the back of cabs when the passengers don't give enough notice that they want the driver to pull over. 'There is bloody good money to be made from puke,' states Myfanwy, matter-of-factly when she told us about her new addition to her business. 'Taxis can lose a lot of money, especially on a Saturday night if they do 'ave to clean the car themselves. We can 'ave the car back on the road in twenty minutes – smelling as sweet as a rose. Well, maybe not as sweet as a rose but at least not smelling of pukey-puke.'

Annie's legs are long and beautiful but have taken on the skills of Bambi tonight. She is all over the place and is laughing hysterically as she is helped through the front door. She lurches forward and I am reminded of a YouTube video of a baby giraffe falling over as her legs buckle and her long neck swings her head around as she crumples to the ground in front of us.

'From me to you, from you to me,' she squeals with delight. 'From me to you, from you to me.' She rolls her eyes and then looks directly into the face of the poor taxi driver who is now helping to prop her up as we get her back on her feet. We all start giggling because, she's right, he does bear a striking resemblance to one of the Chuckle Brothers. She plunges her hands deep into her coat pocket. She is wearing a very stylish pewter grey raincoat, the design is based on a parka and it has lots of deep pockets and ties with toggles and a luscious fur edging around the hood. It looks very glamorous. She, however, does not. She just looks very, very drunk.

A serious look sweeps across her face. 'Ban!' she shouts. 'Ban. Ban.' It is not like Annie to shout. We are concerned about what on earth has got her so stirred up?

'What is it, lovely, what is it you trying to say?' says Myfanwy, and continues to quiz Annie. 'Baban? Is that what you are saying? Do you think we have babies here?' Myfanwy looks at us with a worried expression. 'She thinks we do 'ave the babies yer! She's more pissed than we thought. She's fuckin' lost it. I 'ope she's not going the same way as 'er mam,' Myfanwy says to us over her shoulder.

Sioned takes Annie's drunken face and looks into her eyes and clearly states, 'The babies are teenagers now Annie, cariad. There are no babans here.'

'Ban! Ban!' Annie shouts again.

'Ban what? Ban the bomb?' I say.

'Banana,' she slurs into my face.

'What's that she's saying about Captain Banana?' Myfanwy asks defensively.

'Banana!' From the depth of her pocket she produces a banana and then slurs to the driver, 'It's my tip. One of your five-a-day.'

'Thanks, Drive,' says Muff as she bundles him out of the door, he is clutching a £20 note in one hand and a banana in the other. 'Regards to Frank, like. You cun 'ave a free taxi clean next week on me, lovely – just tell the girls I said it was okay.'

On further inspection of Annie in the light of the kitchen, where we are making her strong black coffee, we find evidence of more bananas, some squashed into her coat, several protruding from her pockets, one squashed onto her bottom, where she must have sat on it in the taxi, a whole bunch in her handbag, even a couple in the hood of her coat. She slurs something about untouched fruit bowls at the office, and, we gather, it seemed like a waste to leave it behind when it is good to have bananas before going out drinking but other than that we couldn't get any sense out of her. Her drinking had obviously started much earlier in the day. That's why I am so worried about Annie. Her drinking.

She sobers up enough to sip her coffee and thankfully there are no squashed bananas on her beautiful dress. Poor Annie. She's had such a tough time. We redo her make-up, she brushes her teeth and so it is only the occasional banana-ey burp that gives her away. As long as we don't meet any gorillas in Caerleon we'll be fine.

SECTION FOUR

39 Muffins

'Welcome back.... to the final of...' there is a fake drum roll of people banging pots and pans and other objects on a table top 'Make or Bake.' I've got butterflies in my tummy. I never thought that I would be this excited about being in a studio audience. Sioned and Annie are grinning from ear to ear, too.

Caren Cross, the presenter of Make or Bake is inside the specially erected marquee at the last stage of the final show. It has been a surprise hit with the nation and viewers are now in the millions. Caren is a favourite comedian on the hard-core comic circuit, having won all sorts of awards for her stand-up, but she was still the shock choice for 'Make or Bake' as she was almost completely unknown on mainstream TV. She has been shot into the limelight and is relishing every moment.

'So, contestants,' she continues brightly, as the camera zooms out and reveals three contestants standing behind cookery benches. 'Are you excited?' Cheers and whoops erupt from behind her and the camera man nods the camera as a 'yes' whilst various members of the crew run forward and give the thumbs up, showing, lest it be not understood, that the crew are equally excited.

'So, contestants, as you know, today there are three challenges. One chosen by each of you.'

Music pumps out 'I predict a riot.' They all laugh.

'So let's crack on with this, the third and final challenge, which is going to be selected by the very popular Myfanwy Jones from Newport in South Wales. Myfanwy, how are you feeling about picking the last ever challenge on this series of Make or Bake?'

'Alright, Caren the Cake, luv.' Caren loves her new Welsh nickname. 'I'm looking forward to it, like. I am really excited today, like.'

'I've seen you in the press this week, Myfanwy. All over the tabloids. They're calling you 'Tasteless, totally tasteless, Myfanwy' aren't they? That's a reference to your own comment about your attempt at a standard white loaf in the second round of this competition, isn't it? That's when you first said 'Tasteless. Totally tasteless.' Gosh that was funny, Myfanwy. I don't think you'll ever live it down given that the judges said it was the tastiest loaf they'd ever eaten. Okay, let's go over to the random challenge selector. The team on Make or Bake have told me that there are some real crackers for this final, some are really difficult though. Let's see what you get. Go ahead Myfanwy, start the selector.'

Myfanwy, with her curly brown hair tied back, and her glamorous outfit covered in a Make or Bake pinny, rushes over to start the selector. The result appears. BAKE.

'Yes!' shouts Myfanwy with glee, and air punches repeatedly.

'Okay,' says Caren. 'That's really good for you Myfanwy to finally get a baking challenge as we know that you have been very strong on your baking all the way through, so, let's see what the actual challenge is…' Caren flicks the BAKE sign to reveal the word MUFFINS.

'Fuckin' yes,' whoops Myfanwy. 'I fuckin' loves it, I do.'

'Cut!' shouts the producer. Then he speaks to Caren in her earpiece. 'Have a word with her, will you Caren, love. Get her to calm down. We can't spend all day cutting out her ripe language. Remember nice is the new nasty.'

Caren touches Myfanwy's arm gently. 'Myfanwy, you're going to have to calm down. Please can you try, for me, to keep your language clean?'

'Is that that producer, Gabriel, moaning about me in your earpiece again, Caren, luv? I bet he doesn't say that to Gordon fuckin' Ramsay, does he? But I will try, Caren, 'onest I will, cariad.'

'Okay, let's start from where we left off,' says the producer. 'We will just have to bleep that one out. The British public are getting rather used to bleeps from Myfanwy anyway.'

Myfanwy walks back to her counter and the three contestants are given their instructions by Caren. 'The store room will be open for ten minutes. You can go in as many times as you like during the ten minutes but you must be outside when the buzzer sounds or you will be locked in. You have to grab everything you need and bring it back to your work counters – if you forget anything you will just have to make do without, I'm afraid, so make sure you think through the recipe you are going to make, and don't forget your basics like sugar and salt.'

A buzzer sounds and the three contestants run to the store room and start loading their arms with the things they will need. The camera pans out and back to Caren. 'Well, with our three contestants busy with choosing their ingredients it's time to meet our judges again. Let's have a big hand for the totally gorgeous, fashion designer to the stars and costumier for the Old Vic, Tiggy Smith... and entrepreneur and master baker, famous for the incredible O'Brien soda bread, Finn O'Brien... and finally, but by no means least, artist, sculptor, bon viveur and national treasure, Jocasta Blount... Jocasta, I love that pink turban. Really suits you. So, judges, what are your thoughts? Baking as the final challenge? Is that a good thing? Will it help some contestants more than others? Finn, let's come to you first. This is your forte, do you think it's good to get a baking challenge at this stage of the competition, and what do you think about muffins?'

Myfanwy walks behind the judges with her arms full, and shouts across, 'Everyone likes muffins.' Finn laughs as do the other judges and the audience. He turns to the camera and says, 'I agree with Myfanwy, everyone likes muffins. Of course, muffins have become really popular in the last decade or so. I am going to be really interested to see what flavours our contestants use. Traditionally muffins were eaten as a breakfast item in the US but the main focus here in the UK is as a teatime or coffee break snack. So, I would like to see individual cakes in a variety of flavours.'

Caren chats away to the other judges until another buzzer sounds. She announces that the contestants have one hour to prepare their recipe. The buzzer sounds again and Master Baker Finn takes the judges and Caren to the first cookery space. 'So, Melissa, he says, 'What are you going to prepare for us today?'

'I've decided to opt for some very traditional muffins. I will be cooking some blueberry muffins, some white chocolate chip and raspberry muffins and, in a twist on a carrot cake, some carrot and nutmeg muffins.'

Finn responds, 'Yes, all good flavours there, but they may be a little simple for the final of Make or Bake. I would have expected something a little more daring, but if Melissa can cook to the same standard she has in previous rounds then I think we are in for a treat.'

Finn moves on to contestant two. 'So, Brad, as an American now living in the UK, what are you going to be baking for us?'

'Muffins,' says Brad. He gets a good laugh from the audience.

'No, seriously,' he continues. 'Melissa has already grabbed one of my favourites, the Minnesota muffin with blueberries. But I'm going to make a New Yorker with cinnamon apple then a black treacle muffin that has a gooey black treacle centre, and finally a banana and salted caramel muffin.'

'Sounds delicious.' Finn turns to the camera, 'As you can see Brad is being a bit more adventurous with his ingredients. I particularly like the sound of the black treacle muffin with that gooey middle. That sounds very interesting indeed. Banana and salted caramel. I am very fond of salted caramel but not sure how that is going to work with banana in a muffin. I can't wait to see how that turns out'.

Now it is Myfanwy's turn. 'So finally, let's talk to the challenge selector herself, Myfanwy. What's on your menu, Myfanwy?' asks Finn.

'Ooh, fuck!' says Myfanwy.

'Cut!' says the weary producer. 'Can we try that one again, please crew?'

'So finally, let's talk to the challenge selector herself, Myfanwy. What's on your menu Myfanwy?' repeats Finn.

'Oh, gosh!' says Myfanwy, eyes sparkling with cheekiness. 'Do you know what? I didn't even think of American muffins nor nuffin when I did see muffins come up on the selector. My first thought was muff, that's my nickname you know.' She grins broadly. 'Then I just thought of muffins like English muffins so I thinks 'ow cun I put a Welsh twist on that, like, so I am going to make breakfast Welsh rarebit muffins with poached eggs.'

'Gosh, indeed' says Caren, her eyes glinting with the same cheekiness.

'But when I said gosh,' explains Muff. 'I do mean that I've got a proper problem, like. I reckon I'm going to need two hours, maybe two and a half, just to prepare the dough. I can't do this challenge in an hour. It's just not possible, like.'

'Cut!' shouts the producer again. 'Cut everything. Production team, I need you here, now! Chop, chop.' There is a short, intense meeting of the production team with the judges in the production office while the contestants hang around discussing Muff's fate. 'Do you reckon I'll be expelled, like? They don't say expelled nowadays, do they. Excluded! Do you reckon I'm gonna be excluded?' asks Myfanwy. Melissa and Brad shrug their shoulders.

Excitedly the production team returns to the studio as the Producer does a piece direct to camera. Caren introduces the audience in the studio and at home to Gabriel, the producer. With a very serious face Gabriel begins, 'We have encountered a situation in today's final of Make or Bake Challenge that we had not anticipated. When the challenge details were put together we did not imagine that anyone would select any recipe other than a sweet muffin, that is, an American muffin. One of our contestants, Myfanwy Jones, has elected to bake an English muffin. Now under the rules of the competition, the cooking time has been stated as one hour. This is obviously not sufficient time for the contestant to complete the challenge within the timeframe. However, I have discussed this issue with the judges and as we did not specify an American muffin, and because Myfanwy and the other contestants were only made aware of the timeframe after they had selected their ingredients, we have decided to allocate two and a half hours for Myfanwy. That will mean Myfanwy has two and half hours in total to complete her challenge, which we know is a tight squeeze - and one hour for Brad and Melissa. We will ask Myfanwy to start first so that all three contestants will finish at the same time. The buzzer will sound after an hour and a half. Brad and Melissa will then start the challenge giving them an hour in which to make their American style muffins. All three will then be judged at the same time when they have completed the challenge.' With that Gabriel returns to the other side of the camera and into the production office.

'Well this is going to be a really varied selection of offerings today. It is going to be very difficult for the judges to compare the sweet American offerings with the English, sorry **Welsh**, muffin that Myfanwy is making. But let's remember that the judges have only a third of the final vote, the second third is with you, today's studio audience, and the final third is with the great British voting public when this show is televised – but remember you can't vote yet.' Caren points at the camera to remind the audience at home who 'you' is.

To help with the editing of the show the audience is given the opportunity to leave the studio for a 'stretch and a comfort break.' We smile and wave to Myfanwy as we are slowly shown out with the other members of the audience. She doesn't see us though as she is head-down, concentrating and kneading.

The break is actually very much appreciated by the audience, most of all as a chance to go to the loo, plus we get to chat to some other members of the audience including Melissa's family and to Brad's dad who has flown over especially. The hour and a half flashes by and we are ushered back in to the studio for the last hour of baking. Brad and Melissa are at their workstations already, ready to go. Myfanwy is whizzing around her workstation like a whirling dervish. At times she is just a blur! A blur with big flushed cheeks.

The show cuts to some pre-recorded footage of Melissa that we watch on video screens. She is an art dealer from Brighton. She is married to a banker and has three children, Jasper aged ten, Melody, eight, and Priscilla, four. Although she runs her own business she considers herself to be a full-time mum. How does that work? They cut back to the studio and a clock which shows the countdown of the hour challenge. Melissa describes, in her posh English accent, how she is preparing her muffins. Her mixtures are already in the tray and are about to go into the oven. She is well-ahead on time and is looking very calm.

Next the footage goes to Brad. Brad is quite effeminate, slim but with a bit of a paunch that has come with age. He is a property developer and made a killing in the 1980s. He now has rental properties all over central London he announces in his montage.

Despite living in London since the early 80s he still has a strong American accent. He is originally from Nebraska but lived in New York for a while before he moved to London where he met his wife. He has two grown-up sons. It is a great surprise to everyone on the show that Brad is married with kids. It actually caused some people in the audience to gasp with surprise and then giggle with embarrassment when it was mentioned a few episodes ago. The tabloids have had a field day. He is very, very camp. Myfanwy had said to Caren, off-screen, ''ow cun he be straight? 'e's got to be gay, luv! I knows a lot about gay people, I doos. Come on, luv, 'e debated drape alignment in the curtain making round for 'eaven's sake! 'ow gay is that!'

The footage switches back to the studio and to the countdown clock. Brad is calmly injecting treacle into the centre of his first batch of muffins.

The footage moves onto to Myfanwy. Chatting to Sioned over the years means we are reasonably familiar with the way programmes are put together but even so we get a buzz from seeing ourselves on the large screen in the studio. Muff is shown in the VT with the three of us from Parentcraft laughing and joking. It was recorded quite a few weeks ago, long before we knew she would make it through to the final. We nudge each other happily from the friends and family seats in the studio. Friends and family are not allowed to vote with the rest of the audience, although there will be nothing to stop us joining in the public vote when it is broadcast next week. The voiceover says, 'Myfanwy is from Newport in South Wales'. Annie, Sioned and I cheer loudly. I smile to myself, I just cheered at being from Newport! 'She set up her cleaning business a few years ago after her husband, Dai, died tragically at an early age. Myfanwy, or Muff as she is known to her friends' (another cheer from Annie, Sioned and me) 'has built up the business as a franchise. In fact, you may soon have a WWD franchise in your own town or city.'

'Great advertising,' Myfanwy mouths to us from behind her workstation, then says to Caren. 'I'd love to 'ave 'im to work for me at WWD.' She nods towards Brad. ''e told me 'e do dust behind 'is radiators every day.'

The VT footage continues with a close-up of Myfanwy, and then angled shots, interviewing her in her home. She says, 'It was Parentcraft that got me interested in baking and then craft making, like. But I've really got me Mam to thank. She's my 'ero. And me girls, Chardonnay and Silver. And my Dai, me dead 'usband' (there had been a great deal of editorial discussion about whether they could include the words 'dead husband' in a prime-time family show – but they concluded they could because they wanted to be edgy.) ''e'd be so proud. And me Lottie, for taking me to the next level, like. She was the one 'oo suggested I did join the WI. Best thing ever.'

I feel very proud for the name check. She's right, I did introduce her to the WI. I suggested she go along to a local branch years and years ago because her baking was improving so much. After the first meeting, the Chair of the WI, Margaret, phoned me and said 'Charlotte, did you recommend Myfanwy to join our branch of WI?'

'Yes,' I said sheepishly, dreading what was coming next. Just how many people could she offend in just one meeting – all of them, I suspect.

'What a find!' Margaret said, surprising me completely. 'Well, she's a bit of a rough diamond, admittedly, but she is going to be such an asset to us. She's so young, so enthusiastic, so talented, you should see her sugar craft work. For a first attempt, it is brilliant, quite brilliant. Oh, and here's a funny thing, Charlotte, did you know her nickname is Muff! Imagine that!'

I was embarrassed but before I could apologise Margaret said, 'I used to have one of those, when I was a child.'

I was very confused. 'Did you?' I said.

'Yes,' she says 'it was very fluffy.'

It took a moment to dawn on me she meant a muff, as in a fur hand-warmer. I was so very relieved.

Myfanwy's VT ends. Caren and the judges make their way over to Myfanwy's cookery space. It is now nearly two hours into her two-and-a-half hour allotted time. 'So Myfanwy, you are currently in first place having won the first round, MAKE, with your amazing basque making skills.' The costume specialist and judge

Tiggy interjects at this point, 'May I just say that the boning work on Myfanwy's corset was truly exceptional. It really was a pleasure to see that quality of work and to think you only had five and a half hours in which to design and make it, well, that is nothing short of miraculous.' We smile remembering our previous experience with basques in Bristol.

'And,' continues Caren 'second place in the second challenge, also MAKE, the arts challenge. Again a very fine attempt, a beautiful piece of pottery, and something of which I don't think you've had much experience, but a great naïve style with rustic fashioning, just pipped by Melissa's refined jugs.' Jocasta is shaking her head in amazement. The media have nicknamed her 'Potty' and not just because of her pottery skills. She is very eccentric and has flamboyant mannerisms and wears outlandish outfits on the show. Today's pink turban is no exception. Myfanwy hoots with laughter, 'Jugs!' she squeals with delight. 'I loves refined jugs, 'n' all, like.'

'Cut!' yells the producer. The audience fall about laughing. Myfanwy has become a bit of a national treasure in her own right, and from being written off in the early rounds as too coarse and unrefined, she has blown the judges, and the nation, away with her needlework, art and baking skills. The moment her reputation was turned around was when Myfanwy was interviewed by the press and said, 'For a big girl, I do 'ave a light touch' and for some reason they rather took to her after that.

'So, Myfanwy, tell me about your recipe,' says Finn the Baking Judge, when the audience settles down. Finn has also earned himself a couple of nicknames. Judge Mental because he, too, is nuts. And Bread of Heaven for his rugged good looks and almost erotic kneading techniques. Women have been swooning across the country.

'Well, like I said, like. I only thought of an English muffin. But then I thought no, 'ell no, I can't do an English muffin they'll kill me back 'ome. They won't let me back over the bridge. So I was in and out of that storeroom gathering all the bits and pieces I do need, fast as I could.

So, firstly, I made the dough for the muffins. It's easy enough but just takes some time. And I've been making up some bits as I do go along. I started by warming 55ml of water with 225ml of full-fat milk. I used to try to do a low-calorie version of this but it don't work. You needs the fat.' She winks at him. 'When it's warm, not 'ot mind, just warm, add two level teaspoons of dried yeast and a teaspoon of caster sugar and then you do just mix it up with a fork and leave it then for about ten minutes. It do go all frothy on the top, like.

Stick the flour, when you've sifted it, there's 450g of that strong plain flour there, into a large mixing bowl with half a teaspoon of Halen Mon sea salt – the fine one mind not the lumpy one but still put it through the salt grinder anyway, just to be sure, like. Then bung in the yeast mixture and mix into a dough.

Then, Caren, I stuck it on the marble slab and gave it a good, 'ard kneading. Best way I finds to do this is to think of someone you do 'ate while you are doing it and you will feel much better after ten minutes and the dough will be very elastic. That's what I did.

Then I stuck it back in the bowl and covered it with cling film but kept an eye on it cuz it cun stick when it rises. It doubles in size in about 45 minutes, mind. I floured this work surface and rolled out the dough roughly. I then sprinkled on another half a teaspoon of Halen Mon sea salt, flaky this time mind, and some chopped chives. Rolled it out again and used the 7.5cm plain cutter to make twelve rounds.

I did stick them on a baking sheet on the baking tray. They needed another thirty-five minutes to really puff up, like.

I like to cook me muffins on the griddle using lard to stop them sticking. They take about seven minutes each side, and with this lovely big range yer you cun do 'em all in one batch providing you do keep an eye on 'em.

To make the Welsh rarebit bit, I put 225g of Welsh cheddar, 25g of melted Welsh butter, I did burn the first lot, that could have been a disaster, a tablespoon of flour to thicken it, some Welsh mustard, four tablespoons of Welsh beer. Do you get the feeling I'm Welsh? I think at least one of your researchers or runners must be Welsh – there's a lot of Welsh produce in that store room. It's like Abergavenny food festival in there.

Then I stuck in a good splash of Worcester sauce. Did you know that Worcester sauce was originally made by an Italian?'

'No, I didn't know that,' says Caren, raising her eyebrows.

'Yes, when 'e finished it, and tried it, 'e said 'ah, that's the worst-a sauce I've ever tasted.' The audience love that one – we groan as we have heard it many, many times before.

'Anyway, all I 'ave to do now in a minute is split the muffins, spread the Welsh rarebit paste over them and grill them. I'll get me 'ot water with a splash of white vinegar ready for my poached eggs and I'm good to go.'

After two and a half hours the final buzzer sounds and the three finalists finally get to present their muffins. They all look spectacular, so it will be down to the taste. The three judges rave about all the muffins. But Myfanwy's Welsh rarebit muffins bring a tear to Finn's eye.

'Those are truly delicious,' he says. 'Tasteful, totally tasteful, Myfanwy. Well done. Truly inspirational.' We all suspect that Myfanwy has got this round in the bag from his reaction, but it'll depend on the audience here, and the public vote.

Later the judges are in the production office filming their comments for the final edit. The audience have already cast their electronic vote in the three rounds but we won't know the actual vote until the results show. Brad is trailing but we know that it can all change with the public vote when the programme is broadcast.

Brad, Melissa and Myfanwy have all got a cup of tea and are perched on high stools chatting casually to Caren for some of the more relaxed shots to be edited in at a later stage. The camera then films Caren doing some nodding shots and then some smiling shots and some laughing and holding her sides. 'Always useful to have some backups,' says Sioned knowledgeably.

'So, the prize for winning Make or Bake is pretty amazing,' says Caren. 'How do you think you'll feel if you win, and what do you think it will mean to your life? Brad, let me come to you first.'

'Well, to have my own TV series would be just wonderful. Six guest experts from the world of making or baking will be fascinating. I don't think I'll win because there is such stiff competition here with Melissa and Myfanwy, but I have, as a fanciful distraction been drawing up a list of who I would like to have as my guests.'

'And Melissa, what about you?'

'It is such an amazing prize. But even more exciting than the TV series is the opportunity to have your own cookery book published. I have been collecting and inventing recipes for years, since I was a little girl, so I would love to be able to have my own book.'

'And Myfanwy, what would it mean to you? How would you feel if you won Make or Bake?'

'Well, you could fuck me sideways I'd be so surprised.'

'Cut!' came the familiar cry from Gabriel. 'Again, please, Caren.'

'And Myfanwy, what would it mean to you? How would you feel if you won Make or Bake?' repeated Caren.

'I loves the idea of me own cookbook if I win. I'd call it 'Tasteless, totally tasteless'. That'd be funny, like. And me own TV series, well, that'd be a right laff. You cun come on it if you like, Caren, as a guest. And I really like that the winner is whisked off for afternoon tea at the Ritz with a load of friends but in all 'onesty, Caren, it's not really about what it would mean to me, luv. It's what it would mean to me kids and what it would mean to my Dai, wherever 'is soul is right now. 'E would have been so proud of me, you see. I couldn't bake a thing until the kids were born. Cake meant buying one out of the shop. Over the last couple of years my business, WWD, 'as done really well through a lot of 'ard work. But to be the winner of Make or Bake would mean that I really am someone. That I achieved summin in me own right. That I am worthy of all the love and kindness me Dai did give me.'

'Cut! That's a wrap' shouts Gabriel. 'And well done to all of you – especially you, Myfanwy, on that last take. I won't have to use even a single bleep.'

'Text the bastard Pope. A fucking miracle's occurred,' says Myfanwy, 'and you, Gabriel, well you're a fuckin' angel,' as the audience shrieks with hysterical laughter.

40 Make or Bake

Make or Bake has been televised for the last ten weeks and we are now back in the studio for the live results show. It has become so popular that Sioned, Annie and me and other audience members, have been pursued and harassed by the media to tell them who won. It doesn't seem to matter how many times we tell people it will be down to the live vote tonight when the audience at home get to vote. They just won't accept that we don't know.

We've been asked by Myfanwy to bring overnight bags - as her audience guests will be going to the post-show party and then, if she wins, afternoon tea the following day at the Ritz. All the contestants have been asked to do this and there is a small room put aside in the studio for all our luggage. We see Brad's dad in there and he hugs us all flamboyantly. I know now where Brad gets it from. The show has created several spin-off shows and everything Myfanwy, Melissa and Brad have said has been unpicked, analysed and judged. Myfanwy's done really well in the shows and is very popular with the public but there has also been a lot of hate and a lot of trolling, a scandal about a Malaysian vote rigging scam, and some very horrid comments about Myfanwy and the size of her bottom by some pinched female journalists and openly misogynistic MPs. As a result, we're not expecting her to win, although she really deserves to, she has been an absolute star.

The studio looks so luxurious on TV but is quite rickety in reality. Stage hands warn us not to lean on the balconies and to take care on the steps. Duct tape is everywhere. We are led to our seats early and although not actually physically frisked it feels like we have been by the amount of people who ask us if we have put our mobile phones in the lockers. We are reminded so often that we will not be able to leave the studio to go the toilet that collectively we have become paranoid about drinking anything. I think I may keel over due to dehydration. I am though, terribly, terribly excited. I don't think I've ever been this excited.

There's a very funny warm-up guy who explains how the show will work. We're asked to whoop and cheer for our favourites. Come on, we're not American! Eventually we are at go live and

Caren Field takes to the stage to a standing ovation. She hasn't done anything yet! She looks quite nervous this evening.

She makes her way over to the talking table. It's a breakfast bar with three stools behind it and says, 'Let's meet them. The Makers. The Bakers. It's Brad from London, Melissa from Brighton and Myfanwy from Newport.' I whoop and cheer despite my Britishness!

Voting lines have been open since last week's show was broadcast and will close shortly, then the rest of the show is just filler really until the votes have been counted and verified. But it's good filler. They've planned it well. There are interviews with some of the spin-off shows. Some vox pop interviews with members of the public which prove to be eye-wateringly funny as they remember their favourite bits of the shows. Reminisces of Myfanwy get the biggest laugh. It's all great fun until things turn very serious and Caren is handed the results of the public vote. Myfanwy, Brad and Melissa all hold hands.

Caren speaks to the camera, 'All the votes have been counted and verified by our independent judges.' She turns to Myfanwy, Brad and Melissa, 'Contestants, we are live on air, please do not swear. Oh, hang on I've got Gabriel the producer in my earpiece… oh, he says, Myfanwy, PLEASE do not swear!' It takes the tension out of the air as everyone laughs.

'The winner is………

41 Afternoon tea

'It's a surprise,' says Myfanwy. 'Stop asking all these questions. You'll find out soon enough.'

It's killing me. I've no idea what is going on. Myfanwy, Sioned, Annie and I are admiring, with great delight, the silverware, those darling little silver tongs, the crockery and the cutlery. The tablecloth is the whitest cloth I've ever seen. We are right underneath an enormous floral tribute, although we could have had the choice of any table in the Palm Court. There is no-one here but us. Well no-one except, as I catch sight of them in the gleaming mirrors, us and the film crew.

'So, Myfanwy, do we have the whole place to ourselves for this? It'll be fun… but it's not going to be very atmospheric for the film crew, is it.'

''old yer 'orses, will you. Just be patient.'

The Make or Bake music starts up and in walk Chardonnay and Silver, and then Ruby, Jack and Megan… and George. He never said a word! Not even a single hint. I wonder where he stayed last night or did he come up this morning? He said he was going to stay with his father while I was here. They sit at another table. George waves at me in his nerdy, geeky way and I wave back. I'm amazed Myfanwy managed to get him away from his computer and his Uni studies. Then Myfanwy stands up and announces, 'This is what brought us together. Being mothers. And cake. But we couldn't have done it without some other people… me mam and dad.'

Isn't that sweet, she invited her parents. I wave at them as they make their way to their table.

'And the lovely Mr and Mrs Davies.' Sioned's Mum and Dad are here too. They're such lovely people. I wave at them affectionately.

'And Debbie is here too, an early member of the Pudding Club!' Another wave.

'Of course, others aren't able to be here with us today, my Dai, of course, but also Annie's Mam.' We smile sympathetically.

'But we have got Mrs Brooks.' I gasp as my mother walks in. My mother! My mother has managed to come to this when she hasn't been able to come to all the things I invite her to. What on earth possessed Myfanwy to invite her. Oh well, I'll try not to let it ruin my day, but it has obviously taken the edge of it.

'And Mr Brooks!' My father! My father is here too. This cannot be. They haven't been in the same room together since about 1978. He walks in beaming, waves to me cheerily and takes a seat at a different table from my mother – after all, the same room is a big enough battle to win. Well, hell, this is going to be awkward.

'And, not to forget Gareth and Steve.... So,' Myfanwy continues, 'The other tables, they're for Melissa and Brad's families and friends, like. I spoke to the TV company last night after the show and said it was just too mean to deny 'em afternoon tea when they 'ad their bags packed and there would be no series of 'Tasteless. Totally Tasteless' if they didn't get it sorted pretty damn sharpish. So they got it sorted pretty damn sharpish. Welcome everyone.'

What a wonderful afternoon tea. What a wonderful afternoon, filled with happy chatter. We move from table to table talking to the guests. I find myself momentarily on a table with Myfanwy again. 'How did you do it?' I whisper. 'How did you get my mother and father to be in the same room?'

'I asked nicely,' she replied. 'And I'm good at getting me own way even if it does take me an awful long time. Like you. Like gettin' you to be you. Not some stupid knobhead snob like you was when we did first meet.'

'I'm sorry about that Myfanwy. I was so up myself back then.'

'I knows you was, luv. All that laffin' at me. All that lookin' down yer nose at me. All that trying to exclude me from Parentcraft.'

I am ashamed. 'You knew I was being mean so why on earth did you bother with me?'

'I likes a challenge, I doos. I saw you look down your nose when we first shook 'ands at Parentcraft and I thought I'll 'ave you. I'll show you not to judge a book by its cover. It may take a while but I'll do it. It took me longer to do than I thought but I did! See 'ow nice you are now. All thanks to me.' She is laughing.

'I feel so ashamed of my behaviour. Is there anything I can do to make it up to you?'

'Nah, luv. You weren't so bad. I've known worse. And you're alright now, everyone do say so now.' I thought they liked me and tolerated Myfanwy. Perhaps it was the other way around. Perhaps they liked Myfanwy and tolerated me. Well, that's sobering. 'No, 'ang on, there is one thing you cun do for me,' she leans across the table and whispers to me 'go 'n' talk to yer mother. She's all by 'erself on that table.'

'So, Mummy, you came,' I can't think what else to say.

'Well done, Charlotte, you noticed. No flies on you.' Ah, nothing's changed.

'And, well, I know you're going to say that I am stating the blindingly obvious, but you're in the same room as my father.'

'Gold star.'

'What persuaded you?'

'Your friend, Myfanwy, that's what persuaded me. She talked me into it. She can be very persuasive. She's been on the phone for the last ten weeks persuading me. She is so… funny. She really does make me laugh. You're very lucky to have a friend like her.' This is rich coming from my mother, Myfanwy is exactly the sort of person she hates. 'Anyway, she said it was about time that you and I sorted out our differences before I dropped dead. Well, words to that effect anyway, only funnier. So that's what I'm here to do. Sort out our differences.'

'Oh no, let's not have a big scene, Mummy. It's really not necessary. You are who you are. I am who I am. We don't need to be best buddies. I'm managing just fine. I have my job. I have my friends. George is a very bright boy. Did I tell you he's doing very well in his studies? I don't need anything to upset me today.'

'I'm not here to upset you, Charlotte. I'm going to explain. So that you understand my side. You're so like him, you see. That's the problem. Always have been. You even look like him. You adored him from the moment you were born, it was all daddy, daddy, daddy. You wouldn't see anything but perfection in him. Well, he wasn't perfect, Charlotte. Far from it. He's a nasty, selfish, manipulative man.'

Here we go again. 'Mummy, I really don't want to hear you slagging off my father. Okay, so he went off with someone else. But you drove him to it. You scarcely spoke to him from when I was about twelve, and if, after all that he ...'

My mother interrupts, 'Charlotte, your father was having an affair when I was pregnant with you. I had Rupert to look after, I was terribly low, suicidal in fact, and his response was to go off and have an affair. He didn't even have the decency to admit it. When I confronted him he looked me straight in the eye and told me I was paranoid. That I wasn't right in the head. I had evidence. He denied it. I had people who had told me. He called them liars. I went through all the details of all the times where he wasn't where he was meant to be, he said I was fantasising. He made me believe I was losing my mind. He made me into a laughing stock in front of our family, our friends, telling them how I was a paranoid bitch. They felt sorry for him. He sent me to a psychiatrist because of my supposed obsessive, unfounded jealousy. But all the time it was all true. How cruel is that? To punish me when all the time it was true. He had lots of affairs over the years, then he would lie to my face over and over again, he got me so muddled that I believed that I was crazy. And you thought he was absolutely marvellous, just like everyone else did. Just like everyone else does. People still treat me like I'm insane. He set them off and then just stood back and let the rot set in. And yet they all think he is wonderful. Look at him now, Charlotte, charming that table and flirting with that young girl.'

I glance across at my father who does seem to have the table spell-bound. He waves to me and then says something to the table, they all glance at my mother and then snigger into their hands. I wonder what he has said. Perhaps Mummy has a point. Perhaps he's not as innocent in the breakup of their marriage that I have always thought, not driven to the arms of another because of years of a loveless marriage. Not the victim but the perpetrator. Perhaps, just perhaps, I've been a bit wrong about my mother. Perhaps, just perhaps, Myfanwy has, by persuading my parents to be in the same room, enabled me to see both sides of the story in one frame and make my own judgment. But that's not true either, what Myfanwy has really taught me is not to judge at all. They are who they are. It is not for me to judge.

Hours later I find myself on a table with George. Just George and me. He puts his new phone on the table face down. That's a sign that he is available to talk. He's fixated on his phone and he is really technically savvy – way ahead of me – and he's been downloading 'apps' and games and has been writing an essay about disruptive technologies. Like I say, he's way ahead and much cleverer than me.

'So, Charlotte,' he says, he's taken to calling me Charlotte of late. 'What about you, then? Dad's on girlfriend number three. Do you think you might start seeing someone?'

This is not the conversation I was expecting. It's been an afternoon of surprises.

'No, George. I'm content with my life as it is. I've got what I want. I have the thing that makes me happy.'

'What? Your job?'

'No, you doughnut, you. You're the thing that makes me happy. You.' I should have told him years ago. I should have told him when I finally admitted it to myself.

'Charlotte, you doughnut, I know that. I've always known that,' he says.

'Whoaaa. I nearly forgot again. Parentcraft, listen up,' I say when we are back at our table and most of the other guests have left and then, once I have attracted Myfanwy's, Annie's and Sioned's attention I say, in a very solemn voice. 'Before we all head home, I have something very important to do. Something that has been a long time coming. Sioned, here's something for you.'

I push a scrap of paper into Sioned's hand.

Sioned opens up the faded old scrap of A4. At the top of the paper I have recently added the words 'Glad you're on the mend, my dear friend, Sioned. Eat lots of this. It will give you strength and a zest for life. Sorry for the delay. At least you got it before we are all old and haggard'.

It is the recipe for parkin.

Charlotte Harrington's Granny's recipe for parkin (parkie)

- 300ml/ ½ pint of full fat milk
  - 225g/8oz golden syrup
  - 225g/8oz black treacle
  - 115g/4oz butter (preferably unsalted)
  - 50g/2oz dark brown sugar
  - 450g/1 lb of plain all-purpose flour
  - 2.5ml/ ½ teaspoon of bicarbonate of soda (baking powder)
  - 6.25ml/ 1¼ teaspoons ground ginger
  - 25g/1oz of fresh ginger pieces
  - 50g/2oz of candied ginger pieces
  - 350g/12oz medium oatmeal
  - 1 egg – beaten
  - icing sugar to dust.

1. Preheat the oven to 180°C/350°F/Gas mark 4.
2. Grease the base of a 20cm/8in square cake tin.
3. Gently heat together the milk, syrup, treacle, butter and sugar stirring it until smooth (do not boil).
4. Stir together the flour, bicarb of soda, ground ginger and oatmeal.
5. Make a well in the centre of the mixture. Pour in the beaten egg and stir.
6. Slowly pour in the warmed mixture stirring it to make a smooth batter
7. Then add the fresh ginger and candied ginger (hope this is not too gingery for you – I love it). Stir into the batter making sure the pieces of ginger are well dispersed and do not stick together in lumps.
8. Pour the batter into the cake tin and bake for about 45 minutes.
9. Cool in the cake tin for about 10 minutes before placing on a wire rack to cool completely.
10. Cut into squares and dust with icing sugar.

You can keep it in an airtight container for up to a week, and I think it takes better this way. Enjoy! Charlotte x

Appendix – the recipes.

Sioned's rich chocolate cake with almonds and orange

- Melt 225g of plain about chocolate for 20 minutes in the simmering oven
- Beat 175g of unsalted butter with 175g of caster sugar, then stir in the melted plain chocolate
- Mix in 175g of ground almonds
- Add 6 egg yolks, 75g of brown breadcrumbs, 3 teaspoons of cocoa powder, with the rind and juice of one orange.
- Whisk 6 egg whites with a pinch of salt, put about a third of it into the mixture and gently stir in.
- With the other two-thirds, fold in roughly chopped milk and white chocolate. Add a splash of milk if needed.
- Bake on the bottom of the roasting oven for about 35 minutes
- Move the middle of the simmering oven for 50 minutes.
- For the ganache, melt 150g of plain chocolate with 150ml of double cream on the simmering plate and then move it to one side to cool.
- When the cake has cooled pour the topping over the top and sides.

Annie's Welshcakes

- Take 50g of butter and 50g of lard, and mix it into 225g of self-raising flour.
- Add 75g of currants, a handful of sultanas, 75g of caster sugar.
- Add a good pinch each of cinnamon, nutmeg and some honey.
- Beat in one medium egg.
- Pat out the dough until it is flat and about 1cm thick.
- Cut the dough using a cutter or a teacup.
- Bake on the bakestone until golden on both sides.
- Sprinkle on some sugar or cinnamon.

Annie's Apple Cheesecake

- Peel, core and thinly slice dessert apples.
- Sift 275g of white self-raising flour, 1 teaspoon of baking powder, 75g of light muscovado sugar, 50g of raisins, 50g of sultanas, 50g of roughly chopped walnuts and the apple slices.

- Beat in two eggs and a little tiny bit of sunflower oil.
- Put half the mixture in the greased cake tin and crumble on 225g of Caerphilly cheese.
- Place the remainder of the cake mixture in the cake tin and leave it rough on top.
- Bake for about 1 hour and ten minutes

Myfanwy's Lemon Pots (or are they Delia's?)

- Whisk 3 large eggs with caster sugar and lemon juice, and the zest of some lemons.
- Whisk in single cream.
- Place in ramekins.
- Place the ramekins on a roasting dish filled with boiling water.
- Bake the lemon pots for about twenty minutes.
- Add whipped cream and the zest of the lemons to decorate.

Sioned's Carrot Cake

- For the topping, mix 250g mascarpone, 2 tablespoons of orange juice, 2 tablespoons of icing sugar and a little orange rind.
- For the cake, cream 225g of unsalted butter and 225g of caster sugar.
- Sift in 175g of self-raising flour, 1 teaspoon of baking powder and ½ a teaspoon of allspice.
- Add 4 eggs, rind of one large orange, one tablespoon of fresh orange juice and 50g of ground almonds.
- Beat it well then add 350g of finely grated carrot and 125g of coarsely chopped walnuts.
- Put the mixture into two cake tins, then bake for about 35 to 40 minutes in the centre of the oven.
- For the decoration, make carrot spaghetti and fry in a tiny bit of butter. Sprinkle with icing sugar.

Annie's Bara Brith

- Take dried currants, raisins, or other dried fruit providing it is chopped up small, and soak them overnight in a cup of cold, sugary, milky tea.
- Mix 450g of self-raising flour, with 1 medium egg, 4 tablespoons of soft brown sugar, and mixed spice.
- Add (optional) marmalade.
- Put in a greased loaf tin and bake for about one and a half hours until a skewer comes out cleanly.
- Serve with butter, cheese or jam.

Myfanwy's Chocolate Log

- Leave 1 kilo of dried apricots to soak overnight in about 3 litres of water.
- Add the juice from six large lemons bring to the boil, and then simmer for 30 minutes.
- Add 3 kilos of jam sugar.
- Chop a red chilli as finely as possible.
- Boil for 20 minutes. The setting point is 105ºC.
- For the chocolate log, melt 250g of butter, add 200g of dark chocolate and stir gently.
- Add 450g of the chilli apricot jam, 100g caster sugar, 4 large eggs, then fold in 250g self-raising flour and 50g ground almonds, and 100g dark chocolate cocoa.
- Place in a shallow baking tray and bake for 30 minutes at gas mark 7.
- When baked, place on a wire rack to cool.
- For the dark chocolate buttercream, melt 50g of dark chocolate in a bowl over simmering water.
- Allow to cool and beat in 100g of butter, then gradually beat in 200g of icing sugar and a drop of vanilla extract. Add milk if needed.
- Fold in the melted chocolate.
- Spread on the buttercream and roll it up. Cover with ganache, or dust with icing sugar or cocoa powder.

Myfanwy's Victoria Sponge

- Grease 2 cake tins with butter.
- Beat 4 large eggs in a mixing bowl with 8oz of caster sugar, 8oz of self-raising flour, 2 teaspoons of baking powder and 8oz of butter.
- Place half in each cake tin.
- Bake for 25 minutes at gas mark 4 – until springy to the touch and then place on a cooling rack.
- When cool, spread one cake with strawberry jam and whipped cream on the other.
- Dust with caster sugar.

Charlotte's Almond, Orange and Polenta cake

- Grease a 23cm round cake tin.
- Beat 200g of unsalted butter and 200g of golden caster sugar until they are pale and fluffy
- Add the juice and rind of a small orange, plus 3 beaten eggs and 200g of ground almonds.
- Sift in 200g of instant polenta and 1 tsp of baking powder. Beat again until smooth.
- Spread the mixture into the cake tin, and smooth with a palette knife.
- Bake at gas mark 4 for about 35 to 40 minutes, until it is golden brown.
- Cool on a wire rack.

Sioned's prune cake

- Bring about 250g of prunes to boil and then simmer them for about 7 or 8 minutes.
- Drain them and mash them but leave some bits quite chunky.
- Add 200g of butter, 200ml of water and 300g of condensed milk and bring it all to the boil, stirring all the time to stop it sticking.
- Let it cool.

- Sift 220g of flour, half wholemeal and half plain, a pinch of salt and half a teaspoon of bicarb.
- When the prunes are cool, stir in the flour then add a tablespoon of marmalade.
- Cook in the Aga on a low shelf for about two hours
- When cool, drizzle over some melted marmalade.

Annie's Chocolate and hazelnut loaf

- Melt 110g of unsalted butter.
- Stir in 85g of plain chocolate.
- Add 125g of caster sugar.
- Add 125g of plain flour, ¼ teaspoon each of baking powder and bicarb.
- Add 120ml of soured cream and beat in two eggs then stir in a teaspoon of vanilla extract.
- Finally, fold in 70g of ground hazelnuts.
- Pop the mixture into a greased loaf tin and bake at gas mark 4 for about 45 minutes.

Sioned's Baked Lemon and Blueberry Cheesecake

- Use an 18cm round cake tin with a spring release, line the base with baking paper.
- Place 150g of digestive biscuits in the food processor with 25g of melted Welsh butter and about 50g of stem ginger in syrup. Blend until evenly crumbed.
- Press the mixture onto the base of the cake tin. Bake in the roasting oven of the Aga for about 15 minutes, let it cool, then a further 15 minutes in the baking oven.
- Blend 400g of Philadelphia, the juice and rind of two small, unwaxed lemons, 125g of caster sugar, 4 tablespoons of crème fraiche and 1 egg.
- Spoon and then spread the mixture onto the warm (not hot) base. Press some blueberries about one inch from the edge of the cake tin. Bake in the roasting oven for 25 minutes, then in the simmering oven for 15 minutes. Then finally about 40 minutes in the baking oven.

- Leave it to cool for about 30 minutes then release the tin and use a palette knife to carefully remove it completely and transfer to a serving plate.
- Warm some blueberries with a dash of maple syrup until they started to ooze – drizzle over each slice.

Annie's Teisen Lap

- 225g of plain flour, a teaspoon of baking powder and a pinch each of salt and nutmeg.
- Rub in about 100g of Welsh butter, with 75g of caster sugar, a big handful of sultanas and 2 small beaten eggs.
- Beat in 150ml of buttermilk.
- Place in 22cm round sponge tin for about 40 minutes in gas mark 4.

Sioned's Chocolate Pecan Fudge Cake

- Beat 175g of welsh butter with 175g of caster sugar until it is light and fluffy
- Sift in 175g self-raising white flour, 50g of cocoa powder and two teaspoons of baking powder.
- Add 4 eggs, two teaspoons of vanilla essence and three tablespoons of water.
- Whisk together until it is all mixed in until an even pale colour.
- Divide the mixture evenly between two greased 20cm sandwich tins then bake at the base of the roasting oven for about 20 - 25 minutes but move them after about 15 minutes so that they cook evenly.
- For the icing, mix 300g of plain, dark chocolate and 50g of unsalted butter, plus 4 tablespoons of milk and place in the simmering oven for about 10 minutes.
- Beat in 225g of icing sugar and then use the simmering plate to mix together smoothly.
- Put three quarters of the mixture aside for the topping.
- Add 50g of chopped pecans, 4 tablespoons of maple syrup and use this as the filling and sandwich the cakes together.
- Then ice with a palette knife.

- Use 200g of plain dark chocolate, just melt it at the back of the simmering oven, then spread it on a marble slab and when cool, use a knife to make curls.
- Then dust with cocoa powder and add a few more toasted pecans.

Myfanwy's Welsh Rarebit Muffins

- Warm 55ml of water with 225ml of full-fat milk.
- Add 2 level teaspoons of dried yeast and 1 tsp of caster sugar, mix with a fork.
- Leave for about 10 minutes.
- Sift 450g of that strong plain flour into a large mixing bowl with half a teaspoon of salt
- Add yeast mixture and mix into a dough. Knead well.
- Cover with cling film until it doubles in size (about 45 minutes)
- Flour a work surface and rolled out the dough roughly.
- Sprinkle on another half a teaspoon salt and some chopped chives.
- Rolled out again and use a 7.5cm plain cutter to make 12 rounds.
- Leave for a further 35 minutes until puffy.
- Cook on the griddle using lard to stop them sticking. About 7 minutes each side.
- To make the Welsh rarebit, put 225g of cheddar, 25g of melted butter, a tablespoon of flour, some mustard and 4 tablespoons of beer. Add a splash of Worcester sauce.
- Split the muffins, spread the Welsh rarebit paste over them and grill them.
- Poach the eggs in boiling water with a splash of white vinegar.
- Assemble in a stack of muffin, poched egg, muffin.

Printed in Great Britain
by Amazon